Wallflower in Bloom

LOVE IN FAIRWICK FALLS

BOOK TWO

ELISE KENNEDY

CONTENT WARNINGS

See the end of the book for content warnings.

ALSO BY ELISE KENNEDY

***Love in Fairwick Falls* Novels**

Accidentally in Bloom (Rose & Gray)

Wallflower in Bloom (Violet & Jack)

Conveniently in Bloom (Lily & Nash)

Unexpectedly Bookish (Pearl & Reed)

Falling at the Barre (Olivia & Luca)

Forever in Bloom - Summer 2026 (Allison & Wells)

***Cozy Nights in Vermont* Novellas**

Fall Inn Love

Falling in Vermont

***Only One Cozy Bed* Novellas**

Pumpkin Spice & Pour-overs

Apple Cider & Subterfuge

Hot Cocoa & Mistletoe

Snowed In & Snuggle Weather

***Jingle Bell Springs* Novellas**

*For all the quiet criers
who never wanted their feelings
to be
a burden to others.*

This is your sign to let it all out.

Chapter One

VIOLET

Violet Parker white-knuckled her century-old potting table as her vision dimmed from panic.

Don't faint, don't faint.

Just get through it.

"And...finally, our n...no-plant-left-behind customer guarantee"—*You can do this*—"makes Bloom the top florist choice for the"—she sucked in a long, ragged breath—"Fairwick County Wine Festival."

She collapsed onto the potting table, finally breathing a sigh of relief. She'd nearly fainted twice from panic as she'd practiced her speech for tomorrow's big pitch.

Not her first time (the nurse had kept a fainting cot in her high school speech class), definitely not her last.

Thankfully, only plants were judging her today.

She was alone, and in her favorite place on earth: knee-deep in lush, leafy houseplants in her century-old A-frame greenhouse outside her cottage.

Her about-to-be-sold plants—*Snake* Gyllenhaal, Pedro *Paschal* the succulent, and an elephant ear plant she'd named Lord Eagleton—should have been the perfect, nonjudgmental audience.

Except she'd followed that stupid advice to imagine them naked, and, of course, she'd imagined the three *real*, sexy actors in front of her.

Holy Clover. Panic roiled in her stomach as she breathed in the comforting scent of potting soil and laid her head on her arms. *That was so, so much worse.*

She hated that she was so shy and awkward. Her stomach turned with nerves as she thought about what was at stake. Getting the contract to be the floral vendor for the Fairwick County Wine Festival would change everything for her flower and plant shop.

She'd tried on her pitch meeting clothes that morning, and they'd made her feel even worse. The pants were too tight on her thighs, but too big at her waist. *Honestly, it's like every clothing designer has never met a plus-size woman in their life.*

If I could look put together like Rose and Lily, maybe I'd be more confident.

She couldn't let her sisters down. *The shop is all we have. Well, all I have.*

Plants were her life. Her work. Her salvation.

Her only real hobby aside from her obsession with *Beyond the Manor Walls,* a sweeping historical TV romance. It was the one show that still transported her to a happier place after her dad died. She loved getting lost in the delicate

English accents, the rich costumes, the yearning romance of it all. She'd listened to every fan podcast, had the merch, and had even planned to go to a fan event. But people would have probably stared when she was in costume, so she'd chickened out.

As an inchworm wriggled onto her arm, she decided she'd had enough of wallowing in the dirt and pushed herself up.

I'll try again.

"All right, I can do this *without* wanting to faint." She gulped. "Probably."

As she took in a deep breath of the thick, humid June air, something strange caught the corner of her eye.

An adorable, chunky black and white cat stared from the end of her greenhouse, head tilted quizzically.

"Oh no," Violet cooed softly. "Are you lost?" Her heart jumped at the need to help.

The cat looked well-loved, with a healthy coat and a luxurious leather collar. A hammered gold metal name tag shone in the evening light. No one she knew in Fairwick Falls had an outdoor cat like this.

She'd look at the name tag and get it sorted out.

"I would be so sad if I lost you," Violet said softly, slowly crouching down and reaching out her hand. Her greenhouse doors were open, and she didn't want the cat to bolt out into the neighborhood.

The cat sniffed, stepping closer. "Come here, *coooome* here," Violet said, beckoning the cat toward her.

Echoes of the highest, loudest sneeze she'd ever heard reverberated from her backyard.

Did a squirrel inhale a bag of pepper?

The cat, spooked by the sound, darted out the greenhouse door.

"Shoot!" Violet scrambled up and ran after it.

Violet's fashionable sister Rose was frantically hopping from stepping stone to stepping stone across the yard in six-inch heels. "Grab Todd!" Rose yelled.

"Todd...the cat?" Violet whirled with confusion, as the cat zig-zagged through the landscaping.

Rose froze, mid-hop. "*EhhhCHEW*—yes!—*EhhhCHEW*."

Todd darted up a low-branched maple tree. Thankfully, Violet had climbed it too many times to count as a kid.

She hoisted herself onto a waist-high, sturdy branch and slowly—keeping an eye on Todd the entire time—climbed up the tall tree.

"Hey Todd. I'm Violet," she puffed. She slowly placed her sturdy work boot onto the next branch. "I really hope you have a few more lives left," she groaned as she pushed up to the next one. "Cause I might need to borrow one." She was only eight feet off the ground, but it felt like twenty.

Even still, she'd take these heights over public speaking any day.

"I'm so sorry, Rose," a man called from across the yard.

That voice. It sounded familiar.

The leaves on the maple tree were too thick to see who it was, though.

Todd had settled on a higher branch, cradling his hefty tush at the V of two branches. She was within arm's reach. "Do you like tuna? I have some tuna at home if you come with me," she said. He leaned into her as she barely grazed his chin with her reaching hand.

Todd purred under her scratches.

She pushed up on her toes. *So close. Almost in grabbing distance.*

She wrapped her arm around the steady bark, trying to move up one more branch to see if it would hold her weight. Violet wasn't taking an eye off of the cat in front of her.

Someone jogged to the bottom of the tree. "Coming up. He doesn't like people," the man called.

That voice sounds so familiar.

Violet turned to look, but her foot slipped, so she stayed put. "He's purring for me," she said in a sweet voice to Todd.

She leaned a little closer, sliding one hand up to Todd's neck, grabbed his scruff firmly, and pulled him to her so that he landed onto her chest, wrapping both her arms around him.

"Got him," Violet called, victorious.

She was crap at speaking in public and might fail during the pitch tomorrow, but she at least did one thing right today.

Todd wrapped his little tiny paw around Violet's neck.

"I know you're scared, but you're being so brave right now," she cooed to the cat who clutched her for dear life.

"Almost there," the man called up to her in a confident British accent.

British?

No one in Fairwick Falls has a British accent.

Todd must have seen his owner because he started scrambling over Violet's shoulder. Violet clutched him for dear life, losing her balance as her foot slipped on the branch.

A firm hand on Violet's waist steadied her and yanked her back against something solid.

A *warm* something solid.

"Steady on," the man said behind her, holding her closely so that she didn't fall. "Got 'im," he said as Todd leapt into his arms.

Violet turned to make sure Todd was okay, but all thoughts of Todd's safety tumbled out of her head.

The man whose hand was on her waist—whose chest was against her dirt-covered overalls—was none other than Jack Grant, the star of *Beyond the Manor Walls*.

Lord Eagleton himself.

Don't faint. Don't faint.

Don't barf.

Don't faint or *barf.*

He caught her as her foot slipped. "Afraid of heights? Me too," he said with a warm smile, his hands still firmly on her waist. "Stay right here. I'll come back for you."

His lilting English accent had Violet's stomach swooping like she was on a rollercoaster. Her mouth slacked open.

"Okay," she whispered, wondering if maybe she'd died when she'd almost fainted earlier.

He climbed down the tree halfway, enough to pass his wayward cat into Rose's outstretched arms.

"All right, that's sorted," he said with a cheerful can-do attitude as he agilely climbed back up to her. "Okay, come down to me." He reached his hand up toward her, looking like a fairytale prince, offering her a hand down from her carriage.

Violet gripped the bark of the tree hard enough to hurt just to make sure she wasn't dreaming.

Jack Grant is in the tree that I own.

How is this real life?

She gripped his hand firmly as they slowly climbed down the tree.

"All right, just one more step," he said, and jumped from the waist-high branch that Violet had climbed onto.

Violet was about to sit on the branch, not wanting to be the plus-size girl a guy couldn't handle helping off the tree. But instead, he quickly put his hands on her waist and hoisted her down in strong, confident arms.

Just as quickly, he turned to Rose to grab the large black and white cat.

Violet's brain was trying to catch up to the last two mind-boggling minutes.

She wrapped her arms where *Jack Freaking Grant's* hands had been on her waist, trying to memorize the feeling.

Gray, Rose's boyfriend, had walked up and handed Rose a box of tissues. "Vi, this is my friend who I told you was staying with Rose and me for a couple weeks."

Jack waved as he wrangled the wiggling cat. "Hi, I'm Jack."

His accent was intoxicating as it wrapped around her and into the roots of her soul.

The Heartthrob of Her Dreams stood upright as though years of proper training on being a dashing English gentleman had been ingrained into him. He looked as if he'd been polished and shined, his light brown hair swept to the side, a button-up shirt rolled up to his elbows, and designer jeans hugging his muscular frame.

She'd stared at his shirtless chest countless times in the glow of her TV screen, but it was his kind blue eyes that caught her attention now. Warmth danced in them as their eyes connected.

Was this what Miss Danbury felt like when she declared her feelings to Lord Eagleton in the season finale?

Good thing he'd never know how often she'd imagined *him* curling her toes in place of her vibrator.

Rose shoved Violet's shoulder, snapping her out of her daydream.

Oh no.

I'm fangirling.

I'm fangirling SO hard.

Jack's waving hand lingered in the air with confusion, his brows drawing together in concern.

"V-Violet," she stammered. "That's...that's what's on my tax returns."

Because it's your name, you freaking Queen of Awkwardlandia.

His large, warm hand wrapped around hers. A jolt went straight to her core and stoked the fire that already had his name on it.

"It's nice to meet you, Violet," he said softly, as if it was just a moment between them. "Thank you so much for saving Todd. It honestly means the world to me. He was so jumpy after the long flight and the ordeal at Rose and Gray's, he bolted out of the car. He's rather put out about this whole trip."

A half-smile pulled at his lips as he waited for her to say something.

But her mind went *blank.*

Say something. Literally anything.

Anything!

"Sucks about your cat," Violet blurted out.

Jack's brows lifted in surprise.

This was it.

This was the *new* low point of her life.

"Right," The Man Who Haunted Her Dreams said. "Todd is a bit old and set in his ways, and three weeks is too long to be away from him. I *am* sorry, Rose. I should have double-checked."

"Abbarently," Rose said through a stuffy nose, "I am bery allergic to cats." A red nose and watery eyes ruined Rose's usually perfect complexion and she blew her nose again.

"Three weeks. Long visit." Violet tried to be normal, but one of her shoulders shrugged repeatedly as she spoke, as if possessed.

"Yes." Jack rubbed his neck with a grimace. "Thought I'd lie low to escape some...well, some hubbub. It's why I was a bit earlier than anticipated. But I don't want to send Rose here to hospital."

'To hospital.' Omgomgomg. I cannot. I am simply dead.

Jack's smile widened with a charming glint, and Violet thought she might be having an aneurysm of happiness.

Or maybe a brain orgasm.

He shifted Todd in his arms. "Since it's so late already, could we trouble you for a place to stay tonight? I'll find another accommodation in the morning."

What.

Holy. Guacamole.

On a stick.

Deep-fried in my wildest dreams.

Violet sucked in a short breath so she wouldn't freak out. "No problem-o," she said, giving him finger guns.

She squeezed her eyes shut, trying to erase the word that just came out of her mouth. "I'd love to have you stay. Is it just you?" In every paparazzi photo she'd seen, he'd had his arm around a different girl.

"Just me and this old gent," Jack said with a bright smile, waving Todd's paw.

The hottest man she'd ever dreamed of, and a cat named Todd.

Of course this was her life.

Violet gave him a thumbs-up and looked at her feet, not able to take the overwhelming feeling of his handsomeness any more.

"Great, I'll get our bags," Jack said, walking away with Todd.

"Are you ready for the Wine Festival pitch tomorrow?" Rose said as they watched Jack walk away.

Nerves roiled in Violet's stomach. "Are you sure Lily can't cover it?"

"We need you, Vi. You know Bloom needs cash, and Lily and I know nothing about plants or grapevines. We need to wow them. You'll be *fine*." Rose smiled, almost convincingly.

Almost as if she *didn't* know Speech was the only F on Violet's otherwise straight-A transcript.

Violet watched Jack *finally* round the corner of Violet's house, out of sight. She yanked her gardening gloves from her overalls and swatted Rose. "Why didn't you *tell* me Jack Freaking Grant was coming to my house when I look like I rolled in a compost bin?"

"I believe you'll find about thirty '*oh my god we're coming over and your English Eye Candy is with us'* texts in your phone...that is *probably* inside, right?" Rose said with a raised eyebrow.

Oh. Whoops.

Violet shook out her hands, trying to stay calm. "This is just...going to be a lot to keep in. All my weirdness."

She'd always been too passionate about plants and her special interests, like Jack's TV show. She'd learned early on that it was better to not say anything rather than talk too much and have everyone make fun of you for it.

Could she keep it all in?

"Jack's a great guy," Gray said, wrapping an arm around Rose. "I've known him for almost twenty years, back when I was a photographer in LA and he was just a scrawny actor/model. Just pretend he's only an old friend of mine."

"You could have told him no. Instead of no *problem-o*," Rose said with a wry smile.

Violet jabbed at Rose's side, making her laugh. "I'm not telling the hottest man god created, the star in all my fantasies, that he cannot stay at my house with an adorably old—oh! You're back." She slammed her mouth closed.

Jack hefted a large suitcase, and a tiny hiss came from the cat carrier on his shoulder. It broke Violet's heart. "Toddrick, please be kind to our landlady for the evening."

Violet peered into the cat carrier. "Poor guy. New things are hard. I get it." Violet stuck her lower lip out. She peered up and saw Jack's beaming face looking down at her.

"You have, um...." Jack said, pointing to her hair. "May I?"

Violet stood still as he picked a large fern leaf from the chaos of her hair that had likely been there for hours.

Oh god.

He lifted it with a smile as she straightened.

She cleared her throat. "Th-thank you."

Maybe she could dig a hole and crawl in it.

How long would it take? Several hours? Several minutes if she used both hands? She'd cover herself with soil, plant some hydrangea bushes while she was at it so she didn't have to face him again.

"Hazard of the job, I guess." She managed a half-smile.

He peeked into the greenhouse. "You a gardener?"

She dusted off as much dirt as possible. "Former landscape designer. Now I grow plants for our flower shop."

"Aha." He looked around at her yard. "That's why your place looks like it's out of a picture book. I'm a sucker for traditional English gardens. Your yard looks like the manicured wildness I miss from home."

Could one burst from a happy ego? "I mostly garden for therapy now."

He nodded sagely. "Nothing so soothing as filling your hand with soil and chucking it."

She laughed. Lord, he was charming.

I'm doomed. "Should we get you and Todd settled?"

"Oh, yes. Rose." Jack turned to Rose and Gray with a pained expression. "I hope you'll let me make it up to you. I feel terrible. You know how much I adore this guy." Jack put his hand on Gray's shoulder. "I'm so proud of you, mate, and I mucked this all up."

Gray thumped Jack's chest companionably. "You worry too much. And remember what I said." He sent Jack a long look Violet didn't understand.

Jack rolled his eyes and shoved him away with a smile. "I'll see you Tuesday morning after I get Todd and I sorted."

"Violet." Rose patted her on the head, leaning in to whisper to her. "You're far too dirty for me to hug, but I love you. Just consider this payback for all the teasing you gave me about accidentally falling for Gray a few months ago."

Violet stuck her tongue out.

"Have fun, you two," Rose called, but then she shrieked as Gray swept her into his arms and walked her across the grass.

God, they were so adorable it hurt to look at them.

Jack turned to Violet with an expectant smile.

Oh god. It was like having a 10,000-watt spotlight of sexy sunshine on her.

She stared at the stepping stones in the grass instead. "Come on in. Sorry the place isn't picked up. And I'm, you know, covered in dirt."

She squeezed her eyes closed. *Literal. Torture.*

"As long as it has a place for Todd's litter box, we'll do just fine."

They walked through Violet's yard to her back porch. Fireflies winked as dusk settled over the yard.

Jack cleared his throat. "I love these things. Like little fairies meandering through the grass on their way to important business."

Ugh. Fairies meandering. Her heart couldn't take how dreamy he was. "You like lightning bugs?"

"They're enchanting and sadly not common where I grew up." He paused, waiting for her to go up the cottage stairs first. "I hope you'll allow me to pay you for housing us."

"Oh no, no, no, no, *nonono*. No." Violet slammed her

mouth shut and considered a collar and leash for it, since it liked to run so much.

She swallowed, trying to be normal. "I love hosting people."

I'm just not sure how I'll be able to sleep tonight knowing Lord Eagleton is across the hall.

Chapter Two

JACK

As they approached the cottage's back door, Jack Grant looked down at Gray's cute, curvy friend, who welcomed him and Todd with open arms.

On the way to her cottage, Gray had threatened him to be a monk-like gentleman around Violet. He'd thought his friend had been ridiculous, but it made more sense now. This woman was endearingly innocent.

Only a monster would think she'd be up for a one-night stand with a playboy like himself.

He awkwardly hefted the suitcase up the first stair.

"If you grab your bag, I'll grab Todd. Or do you prefer Toddrick?" Violet peered into the cat crate.

His lips quirked. She was cute as a button, even if she did have questionable taste in gardening clothes. Her owlish eyes blinked at him from behind large, out-of-fashion glasses that covered most of her face.

She had the most enormous eyes he'd ever seen. They'd

make a cartoon princess jealous with their innocence and sparkling humor. Her head was permanently tilted in a friendly, innocent gesture as if listening for what someone might say next.

She was nervous, and she *definitely* recognized him from the show.

God, I hope she's not a fangirl.

They paid his bills, but he needed a certain distance to keep his sanity. He could never be the Lord Eagleton of their dreams.

In reality, he was just plain Jack Grant from the West Country of England. Shite at cooking, terrible dancer, cable network celebrity.

Hopefully, she'd seen him in a supporting role in last year's Christmas movie before *Beyond the Manor Walls* had taken off.

Or, hell, maybe she'd seen the clickbait news articles about him coming out of a jail cell after being held overnight.

After he'd fucked up his life yet again with 'problematic choices,' to use his employer's terms. His agent had been hounding him since yesterday for an apology statement so the Wayridge Network, the pinnacle of romance entertainment, wouldn't fire him.

He wouldn't apologize. He couldn't on principle.

"Ready?" Violet interrupted his thoughts as she held open the door for him.

"Right, of course. Lead the way."

Maybe he'd go to bed early. He'd leave Violet to her fangirling and figure out where to spend the next six weeks so no one could find him.

Did Antarctic Cruises accept cats?

Lost in thought, Jack walked under the arched doorway of the thatched-roof cottage.

His breath caught as her living room came into view.

By some miracle, he'd stepped through a curtain of time and space into an English country cottage.

The low-ceiling cottage, easily from the 1800s, was stuffed to the brim with plants in every nook and cranny. Vines crawled along the windowsills, and lush, leafy ferns sat tucked into every corner. Chenille blankets were slung over a deep, comfy couch. Baskets of pillows were snuggled into corners, and a forgotten tea mug sat on an end table beside the sofa.

Walls of well-worn paperback books lined the room in deep, built-in white bookshelves. These were not fussy books used for decoration but the real kind that were read and loved and had cracked spines. The kind you kept because they'd become part of you—not because you equated reading with ego, but because you equated reading with happiness.

In the open kitchen, a huge old wooden farmhouse table was the focal point of the bright, robin's egg blue kitchen. Copper pots and pans draped from the ceiling above the butcher block island, and he spotted a proper tea kettle on the stove. His hand came to his mouth.

His eyes welled up at how much it made him miss his childhood home.

Maybe this Violet was exactly his kind of person.

"Is this okay?" She asked with concern.

"It's like…well, it's like home," he said, marveling at her.

She smiled back, confused, her head cocked to the side again. "Your house looks like mine?"

"No, no." He set his suitcase upright. "It reminds me of my father's cottage in England, where I grew up." Where generations of his family had lived before them. The Grant family liked stability above all else. Wars might come and go, but the cottage on Toddingham Lane was always there.

That's it. His mouth twisted with emotion briefly, but he willed it away. *I miss home.*

He hadn't realized how much he missed it until right bloody now. The last few days had been a whirlwind of poor decisions, and here he was: tucked into a quaint, safe, perfect cottage with a temporary landlady giving him respite for the night.

Violet was oblivious to his small emotional breakdown, thank god.

She lifted the carrier. "What should I do with Todd?"

"Right. If you'll show me where I'm staying, I'll let him get acquainted, yeah?"

They trudged up a narrow, half staircase and stopped in a hallway that led to several bedrooms.

"Here's your room." She opened the door to a large bedroom. "This guest room has an en suite, so I thought you'd be more comfortable here. I'm sorry though, I haven't tidied since Lily left. That's our younger sister."

"Lily, Rose, Violet. I'm sensing a theme." He smiled at her as he slid past her into the room with his luggage.

She tucked her hair behind her ear nervously. "Not many people pick that up when they meet us. You're quick, Lord Eagleton."

Oh fuck, she was *a fangirl.*

Her eyes went wide as meat pies. She gasped and slapped her hand over her mouth.

A smile burst onto his face at her reaction. "So, you're a fan?" He took Todd's crate from her, his fingers brushing hers.

"I've watched an episode or two." She nervously backed out of the room, her eyes not meeting his as she babbled. "Make yourself at home. Your bathroom's right here. I won't use this one, don't worry. Make yourself at home. I'll get you some sheets and...uh...make yourself at home." She fled the room, practically running.

He swallowed a laugh. *Maybe I should make myself at home.*

He heard a tiny meow that eternally tugged at his heart-strings.

"All right, bub." He set Todd's carrier down and closed the bedroom door. "Let's not have you meandering about the house till you're comfortable."

He opened Todd's cat carrier in the bathroom and stuck his hand in to scratch his ears. Todd tentatively peeked his head out and then went back in. "That's all right, buddy. Take your time."

He got the litter box and water dish settled and stood up to take in the space of the guest suite.

The house was quiet, accompanied by country evening crickets calling through an open screened window. The calm, rolling hills of the Pennsylvania countryside felt like he'd entered another land, far away from the bustling city where enormous cameras waited to find him.

What had he been thinking?

He couldn't lose *Beyond the Manor Walls*. Or his position on the Wayridge Network. They'd provided him with steady work for five years, and *Manor Walls* was a hit.

He fucking hated auditioning, and it would be impossible to find another acting job this stable. One where he could support his dad, his agent, himself, and the old tuxedo gent currently in the bathroom stretching his paws.

This mucked up his plans, not being able to stay with Gray. He could turn tail and return to Vancouver tomorrow, lying low and spoiling himself with food delivery while the paparazzi lurked outside his apartment.

Todd, however, would murder him if he had to withstand a five-hour flight so soon after the last one.

The echoes of crickets called to him in the indigo night.

Perhaps I could hide out here.

The guest suite was comfortably outfitted. Quilts and blankets were everywhere. Extra supplies like toothpaste, a toothbrush, and shampoo were in a guest basket in the bathroom. Violet hadn't even known he'd been coming, yet she'd been completely prepared for him.

Fascinating.

The bedroom overlooked her expansive, gorgeous back garden, and he spied a pond with a small orchard behind the greenhouse.

He pulled out his phone to check the time and saw fifteen missed texts. Two from Shay, continuing to hound him about sending a statement to the press. The rest were from random women he'd hooked up with before everything went to fucking hell.

BRITT (MODEL/ACTRESS??)

U around? Wanna try a 2 night stand?

MADI DO NOT ANSWER.

Wyd?

JESS (MONTREAL)

Had a lot of fun a few nights ago. Want to come over?

Ignore, ignore, ignore.

He couldn't do relationships. Anything more than one night, and he'd start developing feelings.

And feelings led to inevitable disappointment.

The one-night rule kept him and his dates safe, given he never knew where his life might lead as an actor.

After his mom had left him and his dad for her acting career in the States, he promised he'd never leave anyone like that. So, better to keep everyone at a distance and just have some fun.

But it was impossible to have fun when he was up to his eyeballs in stress after fucking up his life.

His stomach growled. It was 9:00 on a Sunday in a small town, so food delivery was out of the question. There had been, however, a delicious-looking plate of biscuits on the gigantic old farm table in the kitchen.

He'd brave Violet's fandom for a snack to stave off his hunger.

He wandered downstairs, and as he bounded into the kitchen, he stopped short. Violet was ferociously scrubbing the countertop as if it had cast a pox upon her family.

Her gardening overalls and the smudge of dirt adorably perched on her left cheek were gone. The old stained gardening gear had been replaced by an enormous men's Penn t-shirt and yoga pants, which highlighted shockingly shapely legs.

She whipped around as if she'd been caught stealing, her

hair still wet from a lightning-quick shower. Her unruly curly mop of auburn hair spilled out from the messy bun she'd plopped on top of her head.

He caught a glimpse of her shape as she turned, and his interest was piqued. Jack loved a curvy woman, but he'd promised Gray within an inch of his life he'd keep his hands to himself.

Gray knew Jack's weakness for lush curves that looked ripe and ready for taking. Thighs thick and sweet, like molten honey he wanted to sink into. Breasts that looked like they might be absolute nirvana if he ever got a proper look beyond the enormous, boxy shirt she wore.

But Violet's cartoon princess eyes blinked from behind thick glasses, and she looked as innocent as a startled woodland creature.

Of course, he wouldn't make a move on her in this state.

"I'm sorry the place is such a mess."

"I assure you, mine is worse." He wanted to put her at ease as he wandered into the kitchen. "You don't need to be afraid of me. It's fine you watch the show, you know. I appreciate it. But I make you nervous, so I'll find other accommodations tomorrow."

"Stay as long as you need." Violet bit her lip as her eyes darted around the kitchen, looking everywhere but at him. She looked like a deer, cornered and about to bolt.

He didn't like that she looked so scared. "Are you sure you're all right?"

"It's…I…we've got to talk about this. I'm so sorry. I'm a *huge* fan." She rubbed her hands over her face. "I'm so sorry."

"You're sorry for being a fan?"

"*So* sorry." Her expression was horror-stricken as her eyes met his.

His smile grew at how earnest she was. He adored honest people. "You should stop saying that word."

"Sorry. Sorry, I said sorry." She slammed her mouth shut. He smirked at her response. "Sorry," she blurted out one more time, unable to help herself.

They both burst out laughing.

God, she's cute. "I think I broke you, though your laugh is lovely enough to tempt me further." *Easy now.* He swallowed, chastising himself at the easy flirting that rolled off his tongue.

She giggled behind her hand, and he willed his eyes away from her breasts, which bounced with each laugh. He'd tell jokes all day long if he got to see her laugh again.

Was he a horndog? *Guilty as charged.*

"Please don't look at the saved shows on my TV." She wrung her hands and bit her soft bottom lip.

Maybe he should get her to talk, making everything less awkward. "Got all of the episodes saved, have you? Tell me, why do you love the show? God, that sounded egotistical." He waved his hands as if to clear his words away. "I mean, I love it, too. What do you connect with in the show?"

She let out a dreamy sigh, mentally transported. Her hands grasped the back of the chair across from him as she let herself get swept away. "Everything. I love the 'will they, won't they' of the romance. I love the setting. The gorgeous costumes."

"Ah, the costumes. Those damned breeches are like a second skin. They'll be the end of me. I felt half-starved earlier and thought immediately of these biscuits, which are usually strictly off limits due to my costume requirements."

"Please, please. Have some. I made them myself." She scooted the covered glass dish toward him.

He lifted the lid and nabbed an oversized, delicious-looking chocolate chip and oat biscuit.

"And there are no pecans in them," she muttered off-handedly as she turned to the cabinet.

He paused. "You know I'm allergic to pecans?"

"Crap." She muttered, her head falling. "Okay, so when I said I'm a fan, I'm not like a *creepy* fan, but I read all the posts about the network stars."

His eyebrows leapt up. His *mother* rarely remembered his allergy, let alone a complete stranger. "And you remembered I'm allergic to pecans?"

"And your favorite movie in high school was *She's All That*."

So she's obsessive but probably *harmless.*

He settled into a kitchen chair. "You know all sorts of things about me. It's time I learn a few things about you, Violet..." He paused, trying to remember Rose's last name. "Pullman? Park?"

"Parker."

"That's right. Violet Parker of Fairwick Falls, sister to Rose, who is dating Gray. What do you think's going on there? I've never seen Gray date anyone seriously."

"They are in love with a capital 'L.' It was both fun and completely annoying watching them fall for each other despite them fighting every inch of the way." She smiled at him and lifted the kettle. "Tea?"

Good. Gossiping about her sister loosens her up. "Please."

"English breakfast?"

An Anglophile after his own heart. "Mmm, bit late. Decaf?"

"Of course." She pulled out a teapot and a passable brand of loose-leaf tea. His heart melted at not having to suffer through another moldy Lipton's tea bag from an American.

"So, Violet Parker, how do you fill your days?" As a formerly out-of-work actor, he was mindful not to equate someone's worth with their job.

"I'm pretty boring. Though I am a big fan of plants."

Jack scanned the kitchen that practically burst with leafy, verdant plants, climbing from one surface to the next.

"Never would have guessed it," he teased, and her cheeks turned a cute shade of pink.

She walked over to the largest plant and picked up a cloth to dust the leaves. "They're my babies. I've had these for so long I could never sell them. This pothos has been with me since I moved in, and it's grown and grown as I've grown, and now I consider it my best friend, even talking to it sometimes and—oh my god. I'm so sorry. That sounds so weird." She shook her head, embarrassed.

He wanted to soothe every part of her that felt bad for loving something so much. "No, go on," he said.

She glanced up to meet his eyes as she smiled shyly. "Plants benefit when you talk to them, and so it's like free therapy for me"—she spritzed leaves as she spoke, talking faster and more animatedly—"and better, and richer carbon dioxide for them to grow healthy leaves and turn it into fresh air inside the cottage. A pothos removes indoor air pollutants like carbon monoxide and formaldehyde, even. A NASA study confirmed that. That's why I think everyone should own houseplants. They make you better. If you aren't caring for them, maybe you're not taking care of yourse—"

She caught herself and looked at him nervously, gauging his reaction after her accidental monologue.

Oof. It *was* going to be hard to keep his hands to himself.

He adored nerdy women.

He adored most women, but nerdy, shy women who came alive when they talked about their thing? The thing sparking their happiness, making their eyes dance with possibility?

He was a goner.

His face turned curious, still thinking about her NASA comment. "It cleans the air when you talk to it?"

A smile bloomed on her face as if he'd given her the most precious gift. "Thanks for not thinking I'm weird." She pushed her glasses up her nose as she checked the tea kettle.

He laughed to himself. She was slowly turning from cute as a button into fucking adorable. "So you like plants and hosting weary travelers."

"One of which I've watched on my TV for four years," she said over her shoulder, with a scrunched-nose grimace that screamed 'sorry' without saying it.

As she loosened up, she transformed from a panicked deer into a voluptuous milk maiden who might star in his late-night fantasies.

His phone buzzed on the table. More yelling texts from Shay. "Damn."

"Anything wrong?"

"No, it's...." He ran a hand down his face. His fucking mistake was never going to stop haunting him. "My fist had an unscheduled meeting with the face of a son-of-a-bitch who slung hateful, slur-filled words at my mate. I spent the night in jail, it was a whole thing. My agent hasn't stopped hounding me, my *mother* hasn't stopped hounding me, and mostly I want them all just to go away."

"That sounds really hard," Violet said with such warmth it made him almost cry.

It was, actually, really hard, he realized. The kettle whistled on the stove and she turned to deal with it.

An uneaten biscuit the size of his face sat in front of him.

This was a summer luxury, and he wanted to savor it. Those bloody breeches were practically painted on, and he worked hard to stay fit for them. That costume ruined every meal and invaded his consciousness for eight months of his life every year. Sometimes, he felt like no more than a piece of meat who recited lines.

Summer luxuries kept him going from season to season, like this picture-perfect biscuit in this picture-perfect kitchen with a ripe peach of a woman fixing tea as her hips swayed back and forth, dancing to a beat of her own making.

He wished she'd stop swishing her hips. He was *supposed* to be on his best behavior.

He bit into the biscuit to distract himself.

A sweet, salty, buttery explosion of love filled his senses and radiated throughout his body.

He closed his eyes, savoring the soul-shattering goodness. He moaned and didn't even feel bad about it. "Oh...my lord."

"What? Bad?" Violet turned around, worried.

"Fucking delicious." He'd marry this cookie. This cookie was his soulmate, with the right buttery sweetness and hint of salt cut through to balance it. It melted in his mouth, and warm, gooey happiness radiated from his chest. He felt actual tears spring to the corners of his eyes.

Violet looked pleased as she poured the steaming water over the tea leaves, ready to make a cuppa to go with the best goddamn baked good he'd ever eaten. "You're welcome to stay here for a few weeks."

"I couldn't put you out like that." He took a second bite and had the same orgasmic feeling. "Christ, did you put cocaine in these?" He stared at her in amazement.

Violet turned with a proud smile, holding up a tea cup. "Cream and sugar?"

With a happy, dumbstruck nod, Jack realized he was really fucking glad Rose Parker was allergic to cats.

VIOLET

Violet's heart thudded in her ears as she stared at the Fairwick County Wine Festival board.

Just breathe. You probably won't pass out. Only fifteen more minutes to go.

Rose confidently outlined what Bloom would provide for the festival if they were selected as the event's florist.

The three of them had worked overtime putting together their best pitch for the largest event in the county. Every dollar counted right now, and the Wine Festival event would bring them both much needed exposure *and* dollars.

Her stomach churned with nerves. Her feet went cold as she pictured this all going sideways once she started talking. Merely standing in front of the panel was enough to make rivulets of sweat run down her back.

It didn't help that Jennifer, her frenemy since grade school, was sitting at the head of the table sneering at Lily's designs for the grapevine-themed arrangements. They looked like a gorgeous vineyard had burst into a thousand floral pieces. Intricate roses and elderflowers were woven through thick grapevines, setting an expensive but casual vibe.

It was almost Violet's turn. She only had to say four things, then she could breathe easier.

Mention the varieties of grapevines, our commitment to sustainability, the historical significance of the flowers we chose, and how we'd keep them fresh for the four-day festival.

Just four things. She could handle four things.

Violet counted on her fingers again and again until she realized the room was silent and everyone was staring at her.

Rose gritted her teeth with a purposeful head nod at the board. "Ready, Violet?"

"Yeah, sorry." Violet tucked a rogue tuft of curls behind her ear that had escaped her low bun.

She felt so self-conscious. She'd wanted to look chic for the presentation, but all she'd found in her closet was an oversized button-up shirt and pants that had never fit right. Why couldn't she dress like Rose or Lily, effortlessly fabulous all the time?

Her heart slammed into her chest with a heavy *thud, thud, thud,* as Rose clicked to the next slide.

You're gonna say something stupid, Violet. Like when you failed speech class or when you bombed all those job interviews. Or when you bailed on your maid of honor speech at Aaron's wedding. You let everyone down.

"Whenever you're ready." Jennifer leaned across the table with an arched eyebrow.

Shit, she'd been inner monologuing.

"Right. I, um..." Her voice came out shaky and thin. "I'm here to talk about vines." Her hand trembled as she clicked the remote to advance the slide, and it clicked three times, screwing up the presentation.

"Shit," she said quickly. "I mean shoot. Sorry." A couple board members snickered.

They're laughing at me.

Oh no, she couldn't let Rose and Lily down.

She managed to get back to the right slide, and eight people stared as she cleared her throat in the silent room.

Sixteen eyes judging her, judging how she looked.

Judging what she'd say.

Her mind went completely blank.

It was a white wall of static.

She grasped for anything. Anything she knew about plants or vines or grapevines or, heck, the festival itself.

All she could think was *don't faint, don't faint, don't faint.*

Violet's hands trembled as she grasped for anything.

This was a terrible idea. She told them this was a terrible idea, but they wouldn't listen.

Bail, Violet, bail. She set down the remote, grabbed her purse, and hustled out the door.

She immediately started running down the staircase. The door opened behind her and Lily whisper-yelled down the corridor, "Get back here!"

Rose can handle it. Rose could pitch a product she'd never even heard of in the middle of a thunderstorm and have people eating out of her hand.

They didn't need her. She just messed everything up, like always.

"Violet!" Lily said, yelling down the stairwell as Violet took the last step out into the sunshine. She got back in her car, sent Lily and Rose a huge apologetic text, and asked for some space.

They had every right to come yell at her, but she just needed a day to be with her feelings for screwing up the biggest, best opportunity for Bloom.

It was a minor miracle she didn't see Jack when she got home. Through tear-streaked vision, she ran into her room and threw off her horrible business clothes.

Maybe I should burn them while I'm at it.

Throwing on her comfiest, most worn-in gardening overalls, she headed outside for therapy in the form of dirt and sunshine.

An hour later, tears still streamed down her face as she planted witch hazel under century-old oak trees. Gardening usually soothed her aching heart, but she'd messed up too badly this time.

Maybe Rose and Lily will take me off client pitches. At least they're my sisters and have to speak to me again eventually.

Bloom had a splashy re-launch in April when they had redesigned the store, but they still needed to book special events to supplement their meager income. They'd inherited a large back tax debt when their father passed unexpectedly in January, and reimagining the shop had helped them make a dent *and* give them all a new lease on life.

As long as they could keep the lights on.

Rose still had big plans, though. Events like the wine festival would bring them closer to household name recognition. Rose wanted world domination in the form of a flower and plant shop, but Violet didn't think she was cut out for the job.

She planted a witch hazel seedling and wiped her mud-covered work gloves down her old, comfy gardening overalls. It was times like these she was grateful she'd saved them from the trash more than once when Rose had lived with her.

The sun had just set, and a slight breeze blew through the trees, but the 85-degree humidity still had her wilting like a begonia in direct sunlight.

Normally after a bad day, she'd make herself a strong Long Island Iced Tea, turn the thermostat down to 60, put on thick comfy PJs, and watch *Beyond the Manor Walls* until she fell asleep on the couch.

Now? She couldn't even do that. Not when the hottest man in the world's suitcase was still in her guest room.

Violet cradled a mound of dirt to the side and lovingly dropped in a witch hazel seedling. She gently smoothed the cool soil around it, enjoying taking care of something.

She leaned back on her heels and brushed hair out of her sweaty face. Her yard looked beautiful—full of lush bushes, flowers, and climbing vines. The shade of the old oak trees cast dappled green light all around her.

Maybe I should go back to landscape design.

At least then, she couldn't hurt Bloom. Their shop was bursting at the seams with her plants. But staying out of sight and mind would be best for everybody.

A new sob wracked her body as she thought about how pitiful she was. A thirty-two-year-old woman who couldn't even stand up in front of a room full of people and talk about all the things she loved most.

"No need to cry," a gentle, British voice said a few feet

away. "I'm sure the plants can't feel pain when you manhandle them like that."

She sat bolt upright. *Oh no.* She wiped tears away from her face with her dirt-covered gloves.

Great, I probably look like a 19th-century street urchin now.

"Hey now," Jack's voice was soft as he crouched beside her. He wore a casual t-shirt and shorts today.

Thank god. He seemed a little more human in cotton blends.

"What's all this?" His hand rested on her shoulder comfortingly. She must look completely out of sorts if a stranger was comforting her.

"Oh, it's nothing," she hiccupped. She tried to smile through the tears, but a few still ran down her face.

He sat down in the grass beside her. "Violet, you are a *terrible* actress."

She let out a watery chuckle and fiddled with the witch hazel plant. "I just screwed up our big thing today, that's all."

"That's *all?* That sounds like a lot." He caught her eye, and his kind smile had her melting.

Everything sounds better in that accent. Sigh.

"It was horrible." She nodded, wanting him to understand.

"All right, quite *horrible* then. What, did you call their mother a whore, or run over their beloved pet on the way to the presentation?"

"Oh god, no." She laughed at his shockingly ridiculous suggestions. "I just walked out in the middle of it."

"Ooh." He let out a breath, and his eyes went wide in reflection. "I have been there."

She shook her head. "No, you haven't." *He's just being nice.*

His eyes grew wide, and his arms flexed as he wrapped them around his knees. "I most certainly have. You're looking at one of the only actors that hates auditioning. Loathes it. Will do anything to avoid the panic sweats that accompany it. I'd rather go to the dentist every day for a month."

"Then why are you—"

"An actor?" He finished for her. "It's the only thing I'm good at, unfortunately. Once I get the job, I adore it. But putting yourself in front of all of those people, having them judge you, not sure if you're doing the exact right thing—"

"Yes!" She pointed her finger at him. That was exactly how she felt. "Like any moment, any stray word could ruin everything. They'll see your insecurities and how you curse when you're frustrated."

"How you're not as handsome as they want a leading man to be," he added with a self-conscious shake of his head, staring at the grass.

"That can't be true," she said with a smile.

Jack's self-effacing laugh sounded like he had a thousand stories to tell her on the matter. "It is."

"But you're so—" She slammed her mouth shut.

Stupid, stupid Violet.

"I'm so what?" he said with an impish grin.

"...Famous. Everyone knows what you look like." Her eyes fell back on the plants as she gathered her things.

"Hmm." He said with a quiet, knowing warmth. "It sounds like you had a hard day."

She wiped her nose and sniffed. "And I let Rose and Lily down." *That hurt the most.*

Her lip trembled. "They've done so much for me. My house was going to be repossessed in May because our dad owed so much in back taxes and he'd co-signed my loan. They put their lives on hold to help me keep it."

"Ah. So you feel like you owe them."

She nodded, and relief washed over her to feel so understood. "But I just seem to make things worse."

A breeze rippled past them, and she sighed at the relief of it dancing over her sweaty skin. She stole a glance at Jack, whose face was turned up, staring into the branches of the oak tree, his hair rippling in the breeze.

The cut of his jaw was highlighted with brown stubble. His skin was sun-kissed and golden from the summer day. She felt a physical craving to kiss right where his jaw met his neck. Wanted to know what he tasted like right there. Then, maybe after that, she'd wrap her hands around the biceps that bulged out of his t-shirt sleeves.

Be still her heart *and* her libido.

He glanced back at her, catching her staring. "So what's the plan then? How do you like to recoup from the worst day ever?"

She couldn't tell him what she really wanted. "I'll just go to bed early."

"Oh, fuck that," he said with a snort. "Get rip-roaring drunk, or do something stupid. Eat a load of carbs, or watch the worst television you can find. Gotta do something to blow off steam."

Jack Grant's ladies man reputation was well documented, but she was sure he wasn't suggesting *that* kind of blowing off steam between the two of them.

I'm not exactly the kind of girl he'd go for. "Well, normally, I fix a cocktail."

"Hell yeah, you do," he said supportively, egging her on.

"And then I, um...." She scratched the back of her neck, forgetting her garden gloves were still on. *Shoot.* "I like to watch one of my favorite shows to decompress." *With my vibrator.*

"Which show decompresses your brains out?" He smiled at her.

"It's...um...the one you're on?" She couldn't hide her grimace.

He threw his head back and laughed. "Far be it from me to interrupt your ritual. How about this," he said, moved to his feet. "I fix the cocktails and give you a secret, off-the-record commentary on any episode you want of *Beyond the Manor Walls.*"

She gasped as her eyes went wide. "Really? You'd do that?"

"Of course. You had a rather bad go of it today. Plus, it's the least I can do, given I couldn't find a place for the next three weeks near here that would accept a geriatric cat."

A glimmer of happiness sparked through Violet. She liked Jack, not just in the 'star of her favorite series, had a gorgeous accent and was nice to look at' kind of way, but because he was a genuinely nice human. She needed more of those in her life.

"You're staying?" She bit her lip and tried to keep her hope at bay.

"Until Todd takes us on our next adventure, yes. We'll take you up on your very kind offer to stay in a perfect little cottage for the next few weeks." He reached his hands out to pull her up to stand. A simple yank had her flying up to her feet.

Whoa. Her stomach did flip-flops at realizing he could yank her around.

"You're sure I can't pay you?" He said with concern. "It sounds like money is tight, and I've been there, trust me."

"No," Violet waved him away. "Honestly, it's nice to have company. I loved living with Rose and Lily the last few months and the house is lonely without someone else now."

He nodded resolutely as if it had been handled, but his eyes caught on her cheek.

She wiped her arm there self-consciously.

"If I may." His hand came to her cheek, slowly wiping dirt off it with his thumb. "Don't want anything getting in those eyes," he murmured.

Goosebumps flooded her arms. "Safety...uh...first." She tapped her glasses as her brain blanked on how to be a normal human woman.

Oh my god, I am so weird.

"Right," he said with enthusiasm and clapped his hands together. "I'm going to start drinks, you're to get cleaned up, and we'll have a carb-laden, alcohol-filled night of all the seediest facts of *Beyond the Manor Walls.*"

"Okay," she said, smiling with quiet excitement. He turned around to walk back through her orchard and into the cottage.

This was the best, worst day ever.

Chapter Four

JACK

"For the last time, you *cannot* miss your moment, my sweet boy." Jack's mother yanked off her oversized Chanel sunglasses and glared at him through his phone screen. She leaned close, making her appear comically close.

Lord. I'm glad I'm across the country for this conversation.

"Capitalize on your name being top of mind. Run *toward* the attention, get meetings in LA. Come stay with me, my dear. I will connect you with all the best people." His mother had been a C-level movie star for a decade and desperately wanted him to follow in her footsteps.

Jack didn't want his mum's life in LA. The constant auditioning, constant hustling. Their relationship had been complex for a long time. He'd been a natural at acting, like her, but any job he'd gotten had never been enough. She'd always pushed him to go farther. He'd stopped speaking to her for four years after she'd cheated on and divorced his father, and their relationship had felt fractured ever since.

The noise of Cannon's Diner nearly drowned out his

mother's requests in his earbud. Hopefully, Gray would get here soon, and he'd have an excuse to hang up.

"Mum, for the last time, I won't position myself as a 'bad boy.' It's utterly ridiculous."

"You know I just want you to be happy." Her accent had faded over the years, but he still heard traces of the British mum she'd been.

"Look, I'll think about it," he conceded.

"That's my darling boy," she cooed.

He hated that all he wanted was for her to be proud of him. He was a grown fucking man with mummy issues. He eventually distracted her from the topic, and they said their goodbyes.

As soon as he ended the call, his screen filled with Shay's face as she called him again.

And again.

Shay would murder him, which was her right as his agent, but he didn't want to talk about it yet.

Maybe she'll give up.

But his phone came to life again on the diner table like an angry buzzsaw. He pressed the end button.

Shay would chop his balls off if he didn't devise a better plan soon.

PR GODDESS

WHERE. ARE. YOU??

I swear to Dolly Parton, I will send TMZ on a bloodhound chase to find you.

Ignoring this problem is only making it worse.

The network has rented a vacation home UP MY ASS about all of this.

JACK

My most darling dearest of agents, I'm doing exactly what you told me. Lying low.

PR GODDESS

I DIDN'T MEAN LIE LOW FROM ME!!!!

We need to fix your reputation before the network removes you from their roster.

His stomach soured at the thought of losing his job. He loved it at Wayridge, and Wayridge loved when their romantic heroes were perfect and shiny and full of swoon. Rehab? Divorces? Jail time? Never. The Network either buried news that their biggest stars weren't perfect, or fired them, citing flimsy reasons. He'd signed a morality contract promising his behavior wouldn't reflect poorly on the network, for chrissakes.

Shay was right. He needed to fix things.

But how?

He looked around the cheerful, old-timey diner for inspiration as he waited for Gray.

The diner was a busy fixture in the tiny town of Fairwick Falls. Families, couples, and old-timers all buzzed about. A couple obviously in love fed each other bites of pancake from their forks.

Oof. People in love are absolutely ridiculous.

Wait. *That's it.*

He'd just say he'd had a falling out with a girlfriend, hadn't been in his right mind, and it wouldn't happen again. They were now perfectly happy together.

Perfect, shiny, swoony. Just like the Network wants.

It wasn't the first time he'd had to apologize publicly for his behavior. What could be more romantic than a lovesick boyfriend who'd acted ridiculous after a fight with the love of his life?

JACK

Tell them I've got a girlfriend.

PR GODDESS

A WHAT.

💀

Suuuure.

You've never had one in your life.

Sure you haven't been replaced by an alien clone?

Shit. Was it his fault he'd built a protective wall around himself so no one could get hurt?

He wasn't cut out for a life where he'd disappoint someone by having to put his career first.

It was better for everyone.

He thought back to last evening, doubled over with laughter as Violet screamed at the behind-the-scenes exploits he'd spilled. He definitely wouldn't have been able to stay with a random, delightful woman if he'd had a girlfriend.

He thought of Violet's pretty face, the round curve of her ass as she leaned over to refill her tea last night. An idea dawned on him.

JACK

I've just kept it under wraps. I'm visiting her now.

She's not in the industry and hates the spotlight. But she's very wholesome, loves the show.

PR GODDESS

Pics or it didn't happen.

JACK

She hates photos, but she's got beautiful auburn curls, curves that drive me fucking feral, and emerald eyes like actual gemstones.

At least that part wasn't a lie.

The jingle of bells clanged behind him, and a chorus of hellos greeted Gray as he swaggered inside, and slid across from him in the booth.

"How's your patient?" Jack asked.

"Rose? Finally stopped sneezing after I vacuumed six times. Settle in okay with Violet? Keep your hands to yourself?" Gray glared at him and grabbed the pot of coffee on the table.

Jack threw his hands up in innocence. "Perfect gentleman, I swear. Though, I would commit murder for a taste of her cookies."

Gray paused mid-air, about to pour himself a cup, with a murderous look in his eyes.

"Her literal chocolate chip cookies, you wanker."

Gray smirked. "Todd getting along okay?"

"Still miffed for taking him on the plane, but settling in

well." Jack poured himself a top-up and dumped four creamers behind it.

"So..." Gray drummed his fingers on the ceramic cup. "What the hell happened, man?"

They hadn't had a chance to talk since Jack had arrived, and Rose had turned into a gigantic sneezing nose.

Jack swiped his hand over his mouth, thinking. "It was Nate's stag do. The Network is pissed, but I won't apologize for handling it." Jack leaned forward, anger brimming under the surface as he remembered the joy leaving his friends' eyes when a man had shouted at them. "*And* I won't apologize for going to only gay strip club I know who treats its dancers well. I was *sober*, even. I was the DD."

Gray shook his head with regret. "The DD who got thrown in jail."

"The paparazzi practically had hard-ons after taking pictures of me in handcuffs, covered in that homophobe's blood from his broken nose in front of a gay fucking strip club. My mother has never been happier."

"She's happy?" Gray's eyebrows leapt to the top of his face.

"You know her. All publicity is good publicity."

"She wants me out in LA, building a family dynasty of actors. But I like the consistency of my job now. I wake up, charge across the misty hills, and say some dashing lines in the poshest of accents. I'm back home by 5 and in bed by 10. Wake up, do it all over again."

"Sounds very domestic," Gray drawled.

An older waitress with impossibly pink nails screeched to a halt in front of their booth. "Just my luck. Aren't these the two prettiest faces I ever seen?" The waitress, who must have been at least 80 years old, had blonde poofy hair and a face of makeup that would give a drag queen a run for her money.

"Hey, Margie," Gray waved. "Two breakfast specials."

"Easy enough. You want my phone number to go with it?" She winked at Jack.

"Sadly, I'm to be on my best behavior." Jack solemnly put a hand over his heart, his eyes sparkling back at her mischief.

"That ain't gonna work for me, handsome." Margie cackled as she snapped up the menus and swished away.

Jack chuckled. He wished his diner in Vancouver came with such an entertaining delight.

Gray fiddled with his mug. "So, your mom wants you to be a movie star PR disaster like her?"

"And my dad wants me back in the UK, being a farmer and having as many grandbabies as I can convince a woman to have."

Gray snorted into his coffee. "And Shay?"

Jack looked down at his phone and saw another 12 missed texts.

"If she could reach through her phone and kill me, I'd already be chopped up in tiny pieces. She wants me to apologize. Again."

Jack took a swig of his coffee, thinking about the unending circus that was his life the last three months. "But I'm sick of apologizing for things that aren't even *wrong*. Like when a woman talked publicly about the size of my dick or the paparazzi catching me out with multiple women. I won't apologize for laying flat a homophobe who said unforgivable things about my mate on his stag night."

Gray tilted his head in agreement. "You are loyal, I'll give you that. What do *you* want, though?"

That is the million-dollar question.

"I honestly don't know." He shrugged, fiddling with a creamer on the table. "I don't want to disappoint anyone. Shay needs me to bring in the bucks to pay her bills. I support my dad and don't want to disappoint my mom. But I still won't apologize to a bigot to keep all that in motion."

"Figure out what *you* want. Does saying romantic shit right as they cut to commercial set your soul on fire?"

Jack laughed. "Set my soul on fire? No. It's stable. That's what I want. Being an actor who hasn't had to audition for five years is a luxury. Does being a flower farmer in Fairwick Falls set *your* soul on fire?"

Gray stretched out an arm across the back of the booth with a shit-eating grin. "Maybe it does."

Gray had changed so much since Jack first met him. They'd been carefree twenty-somethings gallivanting through the fashion industry. He was downright domestic now.

"You're here forever, then?"

"Damn right, I am. And if I convince that sneezing goddess I live with to stay with me forever, I'll have everything I've ever wanted."

Jack smiled, happy for one of his favorite people. "You deserve nothing less."

Margie slid heaping plates under their noses featuring an entire mountain range of bacon, eggs, and waffles.

The luxurious piles of food called to Jack like a siren. "God, I love America."

"She loves you too, hot stuff." Margie winked as she swished away.

As he ate mouthfuls of streaky bacon and scrambled eggs, Jack wondered what might set his soul on fire, and where he might be able to find it.

GRAY HAD an appointment at his farm after breakfast, so Jack wandered through the picturesque town square in the humid morning.

He did his best to stay incognito with a ball cap and sunglasses. He wasn't a big celebrity, but he needed to stay under the radar until he could get himself sorted.

He wandered past an old-time hardware store, a cottage turned into a law office, and several gift shops full of knicks and knacks. He wandered around the perimeter of the square and finally stopped in front of a tall, turn-of-the-century building with a black exterior and ornate carving on the outside.

Violet's shop. The windows were full of lush plants and bright flowers. It reminded him of a display he'd seen on his last trip to Paris. He walked into Bloom, and the welcome respite of the air con wrapped around his skin.

"Hi, be with you in a minute," Violet called out from somewhere, unseen to him.

"Take your time!" he called in a fake American accent for fun. He wandered through the trendy store that looked like it belonged in Soho, not in a small town hours outside Pittsburgh, tucked into the middle of nowhere.

A vast wall of plants crawled up the high ceiling, and the

store's finishings looked fresh and new. Tables full of local soaps and lotions spread out in stacks. The store was chock-full of thick greenery, and houseplants were tucked this way and that. He saw Violet's hand in the store at every turn.

A wall of coolers stuffed with flower arrangements caught his attention. They looked like they'd been plucked out of his dad's English country garden, and he was immediately enchanted.

He'd somehow fallen into the most colorful, magical jungle.

Violet swished around the corner. "Hi, can I—" She stopped suddenly, her eyes large. "Oh, hi."

She had on a Bloom t-shirt tucked into a long flowing skirt that, while pretty, looked about a size too large for her.

"Your store's enchanting." Any awkwardness between them had dissipated last night as they'd sat laughing at his behind-the-scenes trivia.

"Aw, thank you," Violet said, brightening. "Are you looking for something?"

"I'm looking for you."

She blinked slowly behind her glasses, her eyes widening.

"I mean—" He cleared his throat. "I realized I don't have your phone number."

"Ow, ow!" a spritely voice catcalled from the loft above.

Jack nearly jumped out of his skin, thinking he was about to have another paparazzi moment.

A pint-sized, spunky blonde with Violet's face thundered down the tight spiral staircase. "He wants your digits, Vi."

"Lily." Violet rolled her eyes. "Meet my little sister."

Jack extended a hand. "Hi, I'm—"

"Oh, I know who you are." Lily smirked. She shook his hand firmly. "I was forced to watch your show's Christmas special on repeat last year."

"Lily!" Violet threw her head back in embarrassment.

"Now that Lord Muscle-ton is here, *he* can help with your errand." Lily launched onto the counter, feet flopping as she scrolled her phone.

"You probably need to do other things." Violet shoved her glasses back up to the bridge of her nose with an apologetic look.

"I'd be happy to help the woman who so graciously agreed to house me. I've got an empty schedule this morning."

"See? He's happy to help." Lily waggled her eyebrows at her sister. "Plus, I need to get started on the Fourth of July arrangements we sold at the Bloom fundraiser. Come back in an hour. My hot yoga class finally has a few students, and I need to take off to teach."

Violet bit her lip. "Okay, but this will be quick I promise." Violet walked to the back and reappeared with a tall stack of large Tupperware containers, her eyes peeked over the top. They threatened to overtake her.

"Whoa there." He grabbed half the tubs and was shocked at their weight. "Where on earth did these come from?"

"Thanks. I was up super early this morning baking everything." Violet yawned and adjusted her crossbody bag.

It did wickedly distracting things to her breasts, and Jack forced his eyes up to her face rather than stare exactly where he wanted: right between her tits.

"Lilybug, I'll be back in thirty," Violet reminded her as they left the store.

"And don't forget to answer the five plant care DMs when you get back, Vi," Lily called.

Violet shimmied with happiness, and the Tupperware swayed in her arms. "I'm so excited we have five already. Lily asked our social media followers for plant questions so I could help them troubleshoot. I wish *that* made us money rather than pitching clients."

He'd never seen someone so excited to help other people. "Sounds like you should go after it. Maybe be a concierge service?"

Violet pondered as they crossed to the large green expanse of the town square. "Hmmm. But then I don't get to help as many people. Maybe like a video series?"

"That's a great idea. With you as the star?" He smiled down at her. She'd be bloody precious as a plant professor, so excited to help her students.

"Oh gosh. No, maybe someone else. I'd just tell them what to say." She stopped to heft the tubs she carried.

Fuck, these tubs were heavy. He needed to up his reps at the gym if baked goods made him break a sweat. "What on earth did you pack in these?"

"Shortcake. The festival starts soon," Violet said, nodding to a sign in the distance.

Strawberry Shortcake Spectacular. "A whole festival for one dessert?"

"The Methodist Ladies Auxiliary started it a few years ago, and it's gotten out of hand. It's now a tourist thing, and the whole town pitches in."

Kids were already running through the lawn of the town square as the festival was being set up. Bright white tents were propped up, and booths with games and knickknacks started to appear.

He gestured with the tubs. "Sure you didn't pitch in barbells by accident?"

She smiled over her shoulder. "Just shortcake. I made gluten-free and vegan ones so everybody could have some."

God, this woman was so kind, it hurt. He felt an instinctive need to protect her. "Violet, you're inclusive as fuck."

She shrugged dismissively, which irritated him for some reason.

"No, listen to me." He stopped, causing her to pause on the sidewalk. "The way you think about others is consistent and inspiring. It's so thoughtful to make sure everyone can participate. Nothing worse than having to tell one of them" —he nodded at the kids running through the games—"they can't have any because no one thought about them."

How many times had that happened to *him* as a kid? Too many to count.

"It's honestly no big deal." She brushed it off as if his attention embarrassed her, but he saw a shy smile as she turned her face.

A barbershop quartet started to sing old standards in the town square gazebo.

"Fairwick Falls goes all out, huh?"

"The town makes a lot of our money during the summer tourist season. People enjoy visiting small towns tucked in throughout the countryside. Oh, no." Violet blanched. Her eyes darted around, as if trying to find an escape. "I was hoping Jennifer wouldn't be here. She was on the committee that saw me screw up the pitch."

Running into somebody you'd failed in front of was never fun. "Do you want me to drop these off?"

"No," she groaned and stood up taller. "I'm a grown-up," she said, almost to herself like a pep talk. He just wanted to hug her.

Or maybe kiss her.

Some way to make it all better.

A sleek woman who had 'mean girl' written all over her was lounging in the shade, snickering with another woman as they walked up.

"Hi Jen," Violet called over.

Jen's smiled at Violet briefly, but her eyes locked on him with a knowing surprise.

Ah, damn. He'd been recognized.

"Hello, Violet," Jennifer said coolly, dismissing her. "Set those over here."

Jennifer turned to him with a megawatt smile, but he busied himself unloading the shortcake with another volunteer.

Jennifer whispered to Violet, though Jack could still hear over the conversation beside him. "You didn't tell me you have a famous friend."

"Uh...yeah. He wants to keep it under wraps." Violet pushed her glasses up and shoved at her hair with a shy smile.

"What a waste." Jennifer smiled at Violet, but her eyes were all malice.

Oh, no. Attack of the mean girl.

"What do you mean?" Violet said innocently.

"Well"—Jennifer laughed—"you know. It's not as if *you* would have a fling with him. I hear his playboy reputation is *accurate.*" Jennifer waved her fingers at him with a flirty smile.

Ugh, gross.

"Is he single?" Jennifer said in a low voice.

This was the same Jennifer who had psyched Violet out of her pitch, now insulting her after Violet had gone out of her way to help?

Not on his watch.

Time to have some fun.

He stalked over on a mission. "He is not single."

Jack kissed Violet on the cheek. Her skin was warm and velvety soft. His hand landed on her waist, and he tugged her closer to him.

"Ready, darling?"

Chapter Five

JACK

Jack squeezed Violet's side and kissed her again on her temple. The scent of lavender and jasmine lingered in his nose.

Wide, surprised eyes blinked up at him. "Uh...yeah. Yep. Ready to go."

He turned back to Jennifer. "Sorry, we can't stay. I want to get another round in bed with this one before I leave. And I didn't hear a thank you, did you, darling?" He looked down at Violet, who was still processing everything.

"For?" Jennifer glared at him.

"The metric ton of allergen-friendly shortcakes?" he added with a steely tone.

Jennifer plastered on a fake smile. "Thanks, Vi."

He and Violet walked away, getting outside the tent before they burst out laughing. His hand fell from her waist.

"She's a right tosser, isn't she?"

Violet laughed. "Tosser is right. I've known her forever, and we were best friends as kids. So, it's hard for me to say no when she asks for help." Violet looked at the tent with a smile. "I totally owe you for that."

"I'll make sure to call in my favor for something special." Jack winked at her.

A blush crept up her cheeks, and he realized that would be a fun pastime for the next few weeks, making those perfect apple cheeks turn his favorite shade of ballet pink.

"Violet! Oh, Violet!" a reedy voice called from across the street. A tiny woman in neon pink biker shorts waved at Violet, clutching an orchid. "Just the girl I was looking for, but well, well, well, who do we have here?" The pint-sized older lady peered up at him from behind enormous rhine-stone glasses.

"Oh, Mrs. Maroo, meet Gray's friend Jack."

"I shoulda known," she said, hand on her hip. "The hot ones always stick together."

A laugh escaped him. "You're too kind."

She turned back to Violet with a serious look. "I've managed to almost murder the orchid, Herbert, my new beau, got me. I need some plant mom help."

"Oh no. You're sick, aren't you?" Violet cooed as she took the wilted plant from Mrs. Maroo. "Poor little guy." She gently rooted in the soil with her finger and handled it like a baby bird fallen from its nest.

She was bloody adorable as she gently pried back its leaves so they didn't pop off the dying plant. "Why don't you come with me back to Bloom, and we'll see if I can help."

"You're a lifesaver, Vi."

"I'm going to head back home," Jack said, suddenly as he saw a couple people stare at them on the sidewalk.

"You can find your way back?" Violet looked up, taken out of her trance of saving the orchid.

"Sure thing. I'll see you later."

Time to lie low. He pulled his hat down low over his head and jogged back to Violet's house. He hadn't gotten a solid workout in recently, and his muscles had already weakened. September was coming sooner than he liked. He'd have to be back in fighting shape for those blasted breeches and shirtless scenes again.

As he jogged across the town square, a woman pointed a phone at him. *Maybe taking a photo?*

Another woman raised her phone at him. *Shit.*

He ignored it and double-timed it back home. It was nearly time for Todd's medication anyway.

He'd just happily hide out in Violet's magical cottage for the next few weeks.

Several days later, Jack's nose woke him up before his brain. The smell of bacon and some sort of baking dough tickled his nose.

A bird song floated in through the open screened window. It was still early morning, and the room had a lavender glow as the sun rose.

Staying here was the smartest fucking thing I've ever done. He felt transported back to a more joyful, less complicated time. One where costumes, contracts, and behavioral clauses didn't rule his every waking moment.

Though it had been like staying by himself, with how little he'd seen the ever-busy Violet.

He looked at the edge of the bed for Todd. He liked to keep a lookout while Jack slept and was usually curled up on the corner. He wasn't there, and the bedroom door was ajar.

There was a certain appeal to staying here instead of Vancouver. His place was too urban, with planes flying overhead and loud garbage trucks waking him up at all hours.

Thus far, he'd filled his days with books and lending a hand on Gray's flower farm. A perfect way to while away three weeks until the press died down.

He felt his blood pressure lower every day he was in Fairwick Falls.

No, he realized. *Right here in Violet's cottage.*

He stretched his arms behind his head. He'd only be here for another week and a half, so he'd have to make it count. Luxuriate in rural American small-town living. See if he could find a festival with a pie-eating contest.

The teasing scent of bacon tickled his nose for a moment too long.

Jack threw off the covers and bounded downstairs, beelining for the bacon.

He froze mid-way through the kitchen though as his eyes caught on Violet, laying on the living room couch.

Morning sunlight hit her through the window, painting her auburn hair a burnished gold. Her sleep shorts rode high on her creamy thighs, showing the curve of her ass. Her breasts spilled out the sides of a loose, rumpled tank top.

He'd never seen a more alluring picture.

Todd was curled up on Violet's stomach as she played with his front paws.

Lucky bastard.

He'd never been jealous of his cat, but he'd trade places in a heartbeat to be on top of her right now.

She kissed one of Todd's paws, then the other with pouting, full lips.

Fuck. He'd need to go upstairs and handle his cock if he didn't rip his eyes away soon.

"Morning," he growled out.

She sat up suddenly, causing Todd to scurry, and clutched a throw pillow to her chest. Curls exploded from her top knot, and a few fell on either side of her face. She pushed up her glasses that had slipped down her nose and grasped her coffee mug like a shield in front of her.

"I didn't think you'd be up this early," she said. Her voice was low and throaty in the morning, apparently.

File that *away for later.*

He leaned on the doorframe. "Todd likes you. He doesn't like many people."

Her face softened as she looked at his best furry mate rubbing himself on her legs. "Todd is the most handsomest of boys. Isn't that right, Sir Toddrick?" She scratched Todd's chin, and his purr motor started up.

Laughter chuckled out of him. "Sir Toddrick? He's been knighted?"

"He did a valiant job of finding a cricket driving me nuts this morning."

He crossed his arms, delighted by her. "Knighthood was necessary then. So, Sir Toddrick of Vancouver. Well, technically, Devon, I guess. He's been with me since I left the UK."

"Oh, Todd. You're an old gent." She leaned a hand down as Todd smashed his face into it for maximum pets and then hopped up to her lap. As he curled up, Jack envied Todd's ability to take what he wanted.

Picking a piece of bacon off the plate on the kitchen counter beside him, he dangled it over his mouth. Hot, sizzling juice ran down his fingers.

"I can fix you a plate. Can I get you coffee? Tea?" Violet said, bustling into her kitchen and pulling out a plate.

She'd unfortunately pulled a sweater over her tank top and the excellent view of her tits.

"You're not my servant, Miss Parker."

Violet burst into giggles.

"What? Never been called Miss Parker?" He poshed his tone up as much as possible, sounding like Lord Eagleton.

Violet burst out laughing. "No, I'm sorry. That's a first for me. Here let me get you some." She ladled eggs and waffles onto a plate for him.

"Oh, no waffles for me. Thank you." He slapped his stomach. "The costume requirements for the show are demanding. I have to indulge sparingly, even in the summer."

"Not even half?" Violet's sweet, hurt look in her rumpled pajamas in the morning light had his hands twitched with wanting. He'd push her wispy curls out of her face, bury his head in the curve of her neck.

Danger, man. You're in danger of doing the one thing you promised not to do.

"Oh, go on then. Half." He'd do a couple of extra miles around the neighborhood later today. She reached into the cabinet for a mug, and he saw a *Beyond the Manor Walls* mug peek out of her top shelf.

"Think I should use this mug since it has my face on it?" He reached up, angling over her to grab it. It featured a heart-shaped picture of his face with the words "The Future Mrs. Eagleton" under it.

They looked at each other and burst out laughing.

"I'm going upstairs to crawl into a hole. See ya." Violet turned around, face red with shame.

"Oh, no," he said catching her arm and grabbing the cup, using it for his coffee. "I think it's rather cute. Lord Eagleton would be lucky to have you for his lady with waffles like these," he said as he tossed a bite of buttery goodness into his mouth.

Violet busied herself, cleaning up where she'd cooked, but the air became tense between them. "Do you know what they're saying about you in the fan groups online?"

Jack snorted as he savored the waffles. "That I'm a degenerate? That the network will soon part ways with me?" He sipped coffee from the mug with his face on it. He snickered at how ridiculous his life could be sometimes. "That I'm on the 'last strike' list after last summer's scandal?"

"When you had three girlfriends?"

"I don't have girlfriends." She raised her eyebrows at him. "But yes. I am the current network bad boy at your service." He bowed and took another piece of bacon.

Three bright dings rattled Jack's phone in his pocket.

PR GODDESS

Just landed in Pittsburgh.

I will be in Fairwick Falls in 2.5 hours.

Gird your loins.

"Ah fuck. She found me."

Violet's eyebrows drew together with concern. "Who found you?"

"My agent," he said through gritted teeth as his phone dinged.

PR GODDESS

You will meet me for lunch at 11 am sharp at a place called Fox & Forrest

You WILL look dashing, be agreeable, and figure out how to fix this before you LOSE YOUR JOB, AND I DISEMBOWEL YOU WITH A SPORK.

xoxo

Jack's eyes rolled into the back of his head, and he shoved at his hair. Pushed back from the table.

He needed a run to clear his head.

What on earth was he going to say to Shay?

Would he keep up the lie he'd started with her?

Violet grabbed a waffle and headed up the stairs. He followed her up and enjoyed a guilt-free moment of her thick, curved ass swishing before him. He had an insane urge to bite it through her silk sleep shorts.

Violet turned over her shoulder and he yanked his eyes up to hers. "Is there anything I can do to help? I do owe you a favor, after all."

"Funny you should mention that." He debated with himself whether to even mention his little lie.

A fib, really.

A teensy, tiny fiblette.

But he couldn't risk losing his job. *Start off easy. Work your way up to it.* "What are you up to this morning?"

"The greenhouse. I need to catch up on a big order due in a few months. We can't keep our pothos plants in stock."

His phone buzzed three more times.

Fuck, just rip off the Band-Aid.

"How would you feel about lunch—" Her eyes perked up with a happy smile. *Ah fuck.* "—as my fake girlfriend?"

Violet blinked. And blinked.

And blinked.

You shit. You broke her. "Or...not. It's fine—"

"You want *me* to be a fake girlfriend to *you*." She wildly gestured to herself, causing every part of her midsection to sway, which had him *very* distracted. "You could get a real girlfriend. Like, immediately. Just yell out the window, and ten women would appear."

He rolled his lips with frustration. "But I don't *want* a real one. I need a trustworthy fake one to convince my agent and network I'll behave myself until the next season starts."

"Why?" she asked with exasperation.

"Because I *might* have said I already have a real girl-friend...and used your physical description." He grimaced and tried to smile at her.

Her eyes went wide behind her glasses. "Holy clover."

His phone pocket dinged three more times. "Just for five minutes. Stop by, say hi, say you have an appointment. I hate to ask but I'm being ambushed."

She tossed off her sweater with nervous energy, pacing. "You know what happens when people stare at me. I'm a loose cannon. I might faint or run away. I know I owe you a favor, but...but I don't know if I can do it." She'd paced herself into her bedroom across the hall from him.

Fuck, this is all going tits up. "It's fine. I'll figure something—"

"*And* I have a ton of work to do today." She paced back and forth in front of her snowy bed, gesturing wildly with her waffle. "I'm so behind I'm not sure if I even have *time* for lunch."

"Violet," he said slowly, finally walking into her bedroom. He grabbed her shoulders to keep her in place. "It's. *Fine.* I'll think of something else."

He wanted to pull her in for a hug but thought better of it given she was braless. He squeezed her shoulders instead. "You're not responsible for my flight of fancy." His thumbs stroked her shoulders and he savored her soft, bare skin.

Ah fuck, how was he getting hard from *shoulder* strokes? He dropped his hands and willed his cock to stand down.

"But I owe you." She peered up at him in earnest.

I am such an ass. He should've known she'd be scared of letting him down.

"That was a joke, Violet. Seeing Jennifer's face fall was payment enough. Don't think another moment about it." His smiled at her, but it didn't meet his eyes. He turned to go to his room.

"What time?" Violet said before he closed his door.

Might as well give her the chance. "Noon. A place called Fox and Forrest."

"I'll...think about it."

That's all he could hope for.

～

A few hours later, freshly dressed and ready, Jack wandered into the chic café for lunch.

He instantly spotted the simmering curvaceous statue of Shay, tapping her nails on the table in the open loft-style café. The crisp white tablecloth was offset by her blood-red manicure and the harshness of her buzzcut. It was bleach blonde this time and only drew more attention to her dark, narrowed brows that contrasted with her pale skin.

"I am so fucking pissed at you."

"Lovely to see you too, darling." He leaned across the table and kissed her on the cheek.

"Don't you 'dahling' me. Sit your ass down. So, you'll talk to me after I fly across the country, drive three hours through the middle of fucking nowhere, and find you after somebody tags you on social?"

He smiled his most charming 'but you love me' smile. "You came all this way. I can't be rude."

She let out an exasperated screech, and people turned to stare in the buzzy café. "I am going to kill you. The network threatened to end your contract."

Panic roiled in his stomach.

"You haven't made a statement. Unless you say *why* or apologize, the man you put in the hospital will sue you *and* the network. The network will make it all disappear if you promise to rectify your image. Do you know subscribers are canceling because one of the biggest stars in the network is quote a 'horrible person'?"

"Because I was at a strip club?"

"Because you were in a strip club, put a man in the hospital and then were thrown in jail."

"That wanker was fine. I only broke his nose."

"The network can kill off your character and replace you whenever they want. *How will you fix this?*" She tapped her nails on the table with each word.

Christ. He wanted to keep his spot on the top show on the network and the comfortable contract that came with it. He needed to support his dad and Shay. He was her biggest client by far.

Plus, there was the cast and crew of *Beyond the Manor Walls*. He couldn't let them down.

She crossed her arms, glaring at him. "You know they had you in mind for this year's Christmas movie. You could let Jason Masterson get the lead again. Go back to LA and start auditioning. Bust out those headshots, have 'meetings.'"

"God." He rubbed his temples. What an absolute nightmare. He fucking hated Jason Masterson, the sleaze.

And LA 'meetings.'

Shay whipped out her phone. "I'll set you up with an actress from the network. Go on some fake dates, build some network goodwill."

"I told you I have a girlfriend." His hand slammed down on the table.

"Welcome to Fox and Forrest." A perky waitress appeared beside them with a nervous expression. "Can I get you something?"

Shay glared at her. "Vodka soda. Hold the soda."

"Uh, it's 11:30."

"I need less judgment, thank you. Just a burger and fries," Shay snarled.

"Nothing for me. Sorry, she just got out of a Russian prison." Jack smiled at the waitress, who giggled as she walked away. "I will not fake date some mind-numbing actress from the network. I have a girlfriend. Tell them that."

Shay smirked, ready to call his bluff. He loved this woman like a sister, but she was such a ballbuster.

"You understand how I don't, even for one minute, believe you. It reeks of convenience."

Fuck, he wished he'd been more generic in his description. He couldn't expect Violet to lie for him. Drop everything she had going on.

Might as well confess now so we can brainstorm another option.

"This town is weird," Shay muttered, staring over his shoulder.

He followed her gaze to the front of the café.

A curvy woman in overalls with huge, curly auburn hair paced on the sidewalk in front of the café. She gestured wildly with her hands, talking herself up. Half the café was staring already.

Oh fuck. "Would you excuse me?"

Time to see if he had a fake girlfriend or not.

Chapter Six

VIOLET

*I*t's just one lunch. It's just one lunch. It's just one lunch.

Violet's heart thundered in her ears as she coaxed her breakfast to stay in her stomach.

You wanted to be braver, right?

Seize your opportunity. This isn't any different than walking around town with him.

Just a little bitty baby step to being braver.

Maybe if you can do this, you won't screw up every pitch for Bloom. Maybe someone will finally love you if you stop panicking when people stare at you.

"You came."

Jack appeared on the sidewalk in front of her, all GQ perfection.

Oh god. He looks hotter than usual.

A cornflower blue button-up with rolled-up sleeves showcased his muscular forearms. His hair was swept back, and his beard was neatly trimmed to show off his hard jawline. Muscles bulged under his shirt as he moved, and her mouth watered.

And she was wearing gardening overalls.

Crap.

"I'm sorry. I couldn't decide until the last minute and didn't think to change." She flailed her hands, trying to shake off the nerves.

He stopped in front of her and grabbed her arms. He slid warm palms down to grasp her hands.

Calm washed over her, and she looked up into his deliriously handsome face.

He wore a smile, but his eyes stared at her with concern. "You're sure?"

"It's just one lunch, right?"

"Right." His thumbs stroked her wrists, and need pulsed through her at the touch.

So intimate.

He glanced at the window. "The entire café is staring, including Shay..."

Her stomach dropped.

Oh.

Shit.

She'd paced like a crazy person in front of the biggest tinted picture window known to humanity. Of course, everyone was watching.

"...so I'm going to kiss you now. So she believes we're dating." His mouth quirked into a soft smile. He looked *happy* to do it.

Jack Grant was going to kiss her?

Her brain short-circuited, not knowing what to worry about first.

His hand moved to her face and threaded up through her

hair. His thumb stroked her cheek as his eyes connected with hers. "Okay?"

He cradled her jaw, and she felt cared for. Seen.

Safe.

Something spun up from her soul and connected with his at that moment. Into the crystal clear blue eyes she could trust.

His hands felt like heaven against her cheeks, and she let her eyes drift closed for a second as she nodded, entranced. "Should...should I touch you?"

"You can touch me," he said in a low voice. "Wherever you like."

Every stroke of his thumb against her jaw was like a bomb going off. The reverberations of it fanned deep in her core as she thought about touching him everywhere.

She settled for sliding her hands up his solid, warm chest. Liked how his heart was beating fast like hers.

"Just one lunch." He dipped his head low, murmuring above her lips. "Just one kiss."

She so desperately wanted to kiss him, but she *also* hoped the ground would open up to swallow her whole.

Her heart beating a million miles an hour, he hovered over her mouth. Their breath intermingled; his spicy, musky cologne was torturing her.

She licked her lips, imagining what he'd taste like.

His eyes dipped to her lips, mouth curled into a mischievous smile, and finally...

...finally, his mouth captured hers.

She sank into the kiss. Into him.

A sizzling need flowed down to her toes. She closed her

eyes, and his arms wrapped her close against him. He tasted like mint and something darker, undefinable.

She craved more.

He angled his head, deepening the kiss, and she melted against him, giving him more of what his mouth asked for.

Her hands fisted in his shirt, all the lusty attraction she'd felt finally having an outlet. She needed him on her. In her.

Everywhere.

He tightened his arms around her, molding their bodies together as she opened her mouth, needing more of whatever heaven-sent torture this was.

He swiped his tongue over her top lip. Electric need ran from that one touch all the way down, straight to her pussy.

Oh god. She wanted more of this.

She wanted to live right here in his arms. She heard a moan and realized it was her.

She teased his bottom lip with her tongue, exploring as his grip on her waist grew firmer. A hand dug into her hip, and he growled. Kissing her harder, he took more of what he wanted.

Their tongues touched for the briefest of moments before he stilled.

He sighed out a moan and pulled away slowly, as if it was agony to stop kissing her. His forehead rested on hers as his eyes searched hers in surprise.

What.

The hell.

Was that.

He glanced at her mouth as he pulled away. "Sorry, I uh..." He cleared his throat and dropped his hands, running a hand through his hair. "Got carried away."

Had Violet died? Had she somehow been hit by a bus on her way over to Fox & Forrest?

Maybe she was dead and currently in heaven, living a fantasy life where the man of her dreams regularly kissed her in front of god and everyone?

His eyes met hers with a soul-searching look. She saw past his fame and just saw *him*. A man who'd *devastated* her mouth.

And she desperately wanted more.

He held out his hand. "Ready?"

Ha. Right. I'll just pretend to have bones in my legs and brains in my head after you turned me to mush.

Without saying a word, she grabbed his hand as they walked into Fox & Forrest.

He opened the café door, and they were met with wolf whistles and applause. One of the long-time servers shouted, "Get it, Vi!"

Violet's face burned with embarrassment as Jack led them around the tables. He beamed back at her as an adoring boyfriend would until they stopped at a table where a stunning, intimidating woman sat.

The weight of Jack's hand in hers felt so good. She wished he'd never let her go. Maybe she could live out this fantasy for a little while longer to fool this woman in front of them.

"Shay, meet my girlfriend, Violet."

Shay raked her up and down with a critical eye. She was Violet's size and had on a perfectly fitted summer khaki blazer over a sexy leather and chain bustier-style top.

Violet envied her. And rather than blurt out the thoughts sloshing through her head—*Where did you get that top? What did the kiss mean? How soon will everyone in town know?*—she waved like a car dealership inflatable mascot instead.

"Nice to meet you. Have a seat," Shay said with a wary expression, gesturing to a chair at the table.

It was like she was being called into the principal's office, if the principal was also a dominatrix.

Violet sunk into the chair, scooting it with a loud squeak as it scraped the floor.

"It's nice to meet you. What brings you to Fairwick Falls?" Violet tried to breathe through everyone staring at the unlikely trio in the middle of the café: the fashionista, the heartthrob, and the gardener.

"I'm sure you remember, darling." Jack threw an arm around Violet's chair, and goosebumps traveled down her bare arms as his knuckles stroked her. "Shay wanted to chat with us after the jail incident."

Right. Her memory was still floating on the sidewalk after being kissed brainless.

"So, tell me, Violet." Shay drummed her long nails on the tablecloth with narrowed eyes. "You're the girlfriend to the man who doesn't have girlfriends."

Violet felt her breath go shallow in panic. She didn't want to let him down. "Yep. This guy right here. What a charmer. Couldn't resist." She plastered on a nervous smile that probably fooled no one.

"Are you...a farmer?" Shay eyed her outfit with curiosity.

"Violet's flower and plant store is next door. It's stunning; you should check it out," Jack said.

Shay glared at him.

"Violet," Shay said, still glaring at Jack. "Tell me how you met."

Crap. She was a terrible liar. She was less creative than Lily and not as confident as Rose, but she knew most things about Jack from online fan groups. She could make something work.

"The first night when he was visiting Gray, our mutual friend, I fell hard. I mean, look at him. And that accent." Violet giggled and put her hand on Jack's arm. He clasped it with his other hand and brought it to his mouth, kissing her knuckles.

"Violet's cottage," Jack interrupted, "is an absolute dream. I knew I had met someone special when I walked into a place that spoke to my heart."

Aww. He sounds so genuine. Maybe he actually likes my house?

It was easy to get wrapped up in his beaming smile. How did all of his costars avoid falling for him? "After long talks over tea and wine, we found we had a lot in common. I'm also a big fan of the show," Violet said quickly, still staring at him. "I've seen everything he's ever done."

Her pupils were probably heart-shaped at this point.

A waiter set Shay's food down beside a to-go box of Violet's regular lunch order. "Lunch is on the house today. Aaron insisted."

Aaron, her best friend and owner of the cafe, stood at the checkout counter. His arched eyebrow and '*what the fuck just happened*' facial expression told her she was in for a loooong convo later.

"Oh, that's so nice. Tell Aaron thanks." Violet flipped open the to-go box containing her favorite salad with lush bits of cheese and nuts, healthy summer tomatoes, and cold-spiced salmon.

Shay stress-ate fries with narrowed, skeptical eyes. "Seems too good to be true for this one to commit to a girlfriend after only a few days."

"Oh," Violet said quickly as she pulled out a fork, "this isn't the first time we've met. I've known Gray for years, and you've visited, what, three times?" She leaned toward Jack, tilting her head.

Ha, I'm such a good actress. Shay was totally going to buy their relationship, and then maybe, as a thank you, Jack might kiss her again.

The ghost of a smile whispered over his lips as he stared back at her. "Four, darling."

He grabbed a dressing-covered cherry tomato from her salad.

Violet panicked. "No!" She smacked the tomato out of his hands, and it rolled onto the table. "It has pecans."

Jack's wide eyes stared back at her.

"The dressing has pecans in it," Violet clarified, catching her breath.

"Oh." Jack cleared his throat. "Thank you, darling." He wrapped an arm around her shoulder and kissed her temple. "Forever keeping me safe."

Oh god, a head kiss. She lived for those.

She curled her toes. It'd been so long since she'd been on a date, had a boyfriend, or had sex with anyone who wasn't in her imagination. She was a succulent at the end of the dry season, grasping for any drop of affection to tide her over for her next dry spell.

She let herself lean into him. He had started all of this; she might as well sell it to his agent.

Shay huffed out a surprised laugh behind her blood-red

nails. "All right, I'm sold." She shrugged as if bested. "Plus, you seem quite"—Violet braced for whatever insult a fabulous woman would throw at her—"*wholesome*. This will do nicely. Excellent job, Grant. Now we just need to take pictures and post them online." She sighed contentedly as she bit into her burger.

Violet's stomach dropped. "Pictures?"

"We need to respond to all the angry subscribers calling into the Wayridge Network. We'll take photos of you on picture-perfect, wholesome Americana dates. Maybe some ice cream and shit. Say Jack was out of his mind after a big fight, that's why he went wild a few weeks ago, yada yada. Then post it on socials and release it to the press. Voila! I still get to pay my mortgage, and Jack still gets to work."

Cold panic clutched at Violet's feet. She hated having her picture taken, loathed it.

Jack rubbed her shoulders and pressed her to him. "That doesn't sound so bad." He grinned at Violet, but his face fell as he registered her panic.

She mentally sent him a *no, no, no, help* telepathic message.

"I don't really do pictures," Violet said, finally, hating to disappoint them. "I mostly wear...this." She pointed to her gardening overalls.

"Don't worry, babe." Shay reached over, grabbed Violet's hand, and patted it. "We'll do a full makeover before the shoot. You *do* want to fix Jack's problem, right?"

"I mean, I do, but..." Violet sent a shy smile to Jack. Could she stand next to the hottest man she'd ever seen in front of the entire world?

Jack squeezed her hand with furrowed brows. "We'll let

you know, Shay. I don't want Violet doing anything she's not comfortable with."

She couldn't let him down. Not now. Not after his show had helped her through her darkest times.

And that freaking kiss she'd remember on her deathbed.

Could she be brave enough? Bold enough? Willing to put herself out there and have people stare at her?

She could feel hives forming on her shins just thinking about it.

"Um, I'll think about it." Violet scooted her chair back. "I'm sorry. I've got to be across town for the Library Landscaping Committee. I'll see you at home, Jack."

He grabbed her hand as she was about to escape, yanked her back to him, and kissed her briefly. His concerned eyes connected with hers. "Bye, my darling."

Oh, right. Shoot. They were dating. People kissed when they were dating.

Curious eyes stared at Violet as she got up. She knew every single person in this cafe, and she *knew* her gossipy town.

Which meant everyone would know in about two minutes she'd kissed the most handsome man in Fairwick Falls.

~

JACK

After a brutal run that afternoon, Jack stretched in Violet's living room. Shay was staying in a BnB a few towns over and had already hounded for an answer about the photoshoot.

Fake dating Violet, which he thought would be a one-off conversation with Shay, was turning into a whole fucking thing. But...it *would* make the network happy.

And maybe make himself happy too.

He'd deal with the fallout from his mother when it happened. Her mantra had invariably been 'settling down is settling.' The phrase was drilled into him after his first relationship almost ended at the altar. He'd been nineteen and stupidly in love.

But if Jack was honest with himself, all he wanted was to settle down. Not uproot his life every five months for a new shoot in a new city.

Todd couldn't handle it, poor soul.

It had been surprisingly easy to fall into a comfortable rapport with Violet in front of Shay. And kissing her had been the highlight of his day. His week, maybe.

Shit, maybe his month.

His fingers rubbed his lips, remembering what she'd tasted like only a few hours ago.

He'd intended it to be a stage kiss, a simple meeting of the lips that meant nothing.

But kissing her was *intoxicating*.

She was soft and perfect under his hands when she leaned into him. The little moan she'd uttered made his cock thicken, and he'd broken off the kiss before he embarrassed himself.

His hands still itched to sweep over her perfect tits that had crushed into him. He'd had to remind himself they were in public so he didn't take it further, for chrissakes.

Picturing a potential ice cream fake date with Violet licking a dripping cone had his cock hardening again already.

Jesus, *how* was he going to keep his hands to himself?

He wanted her more than any recent one-night stand he could remember, but he had to keep his head on straight. A promise had already been made to Gray, and he couldn't toy with Violet like that.

She was too sweet. Too kind and pure-hearted.

Not no-strings material.

She was a lovely girl who would be a nice fake girlfriend for the summer. He needed to ensure she got something out of it, too, but this could be the answer he needed.

The network would be happy, he'd be offered the lead in the Christmas special so his mother would finally be happy, his father would be desperately happy he had a girlfriend, and he might get to kiss Violet Parker again.

Win-win-win-win.

Though her face had turned a ghostly shade when Shay had mentioned going public. He should text Violet to see if she's okay.

JACK

Thank you for saving my ass today. I'm sorry you got roped into all of this.

Talk when you get home?

Home, he thought. It did feel like home at Violet's cottage, like he'd been transported to a magical bubble where nothing bad could happen.

He perused Violet's bookshelf as he sipped his water, waiting for her reply. A series on her shelf caught his attention. It was a steamy romance series, *Heat Red*. Nearly every title on the bookshelf was a romance, he noticed.

In the first season of *Beyond the Manor Walls*, he'd started reading Regency romances during breaks to stay in character. Eventually, he found it an escape and developed a love for the genre. Though that was a secret he kept to himself.

He spotted a few erotic-looking romances with multiple men on the cover. Her copies looked well-worn, with cracked spines and dog-eared pages. He opened one to skim it.

...She sucked Jayden and Brent's cocks while Gage fucked her ass hard from behind...

He choked on the water, spitting it out in surprise. "Holy fuck."

He wiped his mouth as he skimmed the rest of the scene. One woman got *very* creative with five men and all their needs. He glanced up at the bookshelf. This book was the first in a ten-book series.

Innocent, sweet Violet has a naughty side?

Maybe she wasn't quite as wholesome as he'd initially thought.

Things were taking an interesting turn.

He checked the time. He'd meet Gray for dinner in a bit. He was to be introduced to the wonder that was a bucket of Pennsylvania's best fried chicken tonight.

His phone vibrated.

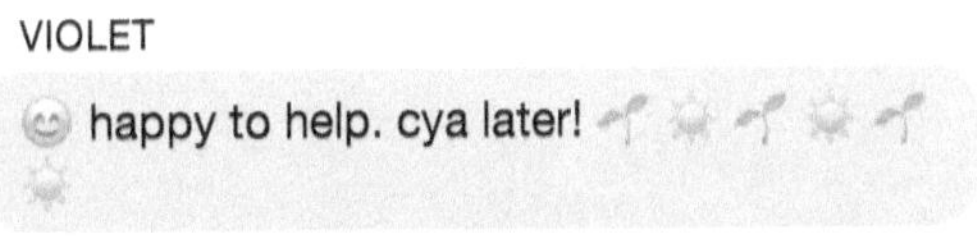

God, she was like a sunbeam embodied.

Jack returned the book and glanced at a well-worn copy of a monster menage romance.

A very naughty sunbeam, apparently.

He suddenly couldn't wait to talk with Violet later that night.

VIOLET

Violet pushed the shovel down into Ms. McClotskey's front yard as she tried to wipe The Very Hot Kiss™ from her mind.

A half-dead lavender plant sat beside her, waiting to be replanted in a sunny spot. After the Library Committee had adjourned, Violet had decided today would be the perfect moment to help her former teacher rescue the lavender plants dying in her shady side yard.

And *maybe* she was avoiding dealing with her kiss with Jack.

It was the least she could do for the first-grade teacher who'd taken pity on her when all Violet's friends had turned against her. When they'd learned how her mom had died, one of the mean girls had started a rumor it was Violet's fault. That was the first time Jennifer hadn't stepped up to defend her.

Violet hefted one more shovel of dirt, digging a hole deep enough for the lavender roots to take hold. Her mind hadn't stopped racing, no matter how much manual labor she did today.

The porch door swung open, and Ms. McClotskey walked down her front steps with a glass of iced tea. Violet was drenched with sweat in the muggy afternoon.

"See?" Violet said, smiling at the three lavender bushes now neatly lining the sunny edge of the yard. "They'll be much happier here in the full sun. Bless you," she added as she grabbed the large glass of iced tea to chug.

"This looks stunning." Ms. McClotskey was a vibrant, pretty older lady who insisted Violet call her June, but Violet just couldn't do it. "How can I repay you? This was just above and beyond."

Violet pushed her beekeeper-like UV sunhat back. "For the woman who taught me to read, I always have time to move lavender bushes."

"I was lucky to have you in my classroom. And you seem to be a lucky one, too." Ms. McClotskey's eyebrows rose with a knowing smile.

Oh, shoot. Had the gossip mill already finished spreading the word?

"About what?" Violet feigned innocence and took a long drink from the glass.

"The teachers' group chat said you kissed some hunky man in front of Fox and Forrest today." She smirked with teacher eyes that said, *I know when you're lying to me.*

"Well..." Violet scratched the back of her neck. *Crap, crap, crap. What am I supposed to say? Just kidding? It was a one-time thing?*

Ms. McClotskey's eyes softened with a motherly look.

"Oh, don't look so nervous. I think it's wonderful. You deserve a man who will spoil you silly."

"Aha!" Rose jogged toward her, out on a run in her designer workout gear, sweating buckets in the heat. "Hi, June," Rose puffed as she slowed to a walk and waved.

"Why don't I get you a glass of iced tea, Rosie?"

"No, thanks," Rose said, catching her breath. "Can't stay. Just on the hunt for this one."

"All right. Violet, I'm buying lunch next time I see you in the café."

Violet waved as Ms. McClotskey walked back inside.

Rose pulled out her phone and spoke as she typed. "Found her...I...won." She hit send, and Violet heard her phone buzz on the grass where she'd dumped her stuff. "Aaron, Lily, and I bet who could find you first after we found out."

Violet leaned over to grab her phone and whipped her head up in shock. "Why are there 427 missed messages? Is something on fire?"

"I *bet* something's on fire." Rose snickered and nudged Violet's leg with her foot. "When were you going to tell us you're making out with Jack?"

Violet quickly stuffed her phone in her pocket. "It's not real. He just needs a fake girlfriend, and I'm not even sure if I'm up for it."

"A *fake* girlfriend?" Rose repeated in confusion, stretching out her thighs as they stood in the yard. "Like, the romcoms you watch?"

Violet shrugged, not making eye contact as she finished the last plant. "You know he's in hot water with work and needs somebody to help. I like to help."

"Yeah, I bet you do." Rose snorted. "Hold on. Lily will be pissed if she misses all these innuendos." Rose hit speaker and called Lily, who picked up in one ring.

"Ugh, I never win," Lily whined through the speaker.

"She says it was all fake. That she's going to fake date Jack."

"No fucking way," came a screech through the phone.

"I'm still thinking about it," Violet countered quickly. "And this has to stay between us. It's turning into this whole thing with photos and fake publicity dates. Everyone would stare at me, and I don't know if I can do it."

Lily jumped in. "Maybe this could help you overcome your fear of being the center of attention. Today's client pitch was garbage without you. They asked all these questions about flowers, and I panicked. I *might* have said hydrangeas originally came from the 'drangea' region of France."

Rose wrapped a sweaty arm around Violet and kissed her cheek. "We need a real flower and plant expert on big pitches. And you deserve to live a life as a grown-ass woman who won't faint when talking in front of people."

Ugh. Nothing like a sisterly dose of tough love.

Violet knew they were right, but was she brave enough? It was like exercising a muscle she didn't even know existed.

"Plus, think of the sex!" Lily added.

Violet sucked in a wincing breath. "Come on, Lil. He wouldn't like me like that."

She hated reminding her two drop-dead gorgeous sisters she wasn't like them. Men didn't fall at her feet the way they did for Lily and Rose. Lily was tiny and curvy, like an angry pixie. Rose was lithe and athletic like their mother had been.

Violet felt like a lonely, alien outsider when they talked about guys and sex and pretty much everything other than their flower shop.

"Don't you think it's time you *bloom?*" Lily said through the speaker. "Get it?"

Violet rolled her eyes as Rose snorted. Aaron parked a few houses down in his driveway and walked over on a mission.

Oh, shoot. "Aaron's walking over," Violet said into the phone. He was notoriously bad at keeping secrets. He'd spilled the beans on four surprise birthday parties.

This year.

"So obviously, we can't tell him," Lily said through the speaker, reading Violet's mind.

"I mean, obviously." Rose added, "We love him, but it should stay between us unless we'd like the greater tri-state area to know."

"When exactly," Aaron's voice called out from behind Violet, in a mood, "were you going to tell me you were dating a British hottie, best friend?"

She turned to Aaron Forrest, her best friend since childhood, and had to lie directly to his face. "He wanted to keep things quiet."

"I mean, y'all basically made out on the sidewalk. It's not quiet any longer. I need all of the details." Aaron crossed his slim arms, dark tattoos swirling up and down them against his brown skin.

"It's...new." She was such a terrible liar. She'd have to get better at this. *Pretend it's real, that he does like you, and all your fantasies have finally come true.* "I didn't think he'd want people to know about us."

"Why?" Aaron's face was comically incredulous.

"Well, you know." Violet gestured at herself.

"I told you to throw away those overalls," Rose said, looking up from her phone.

"I've tried twice, and she always found them in the trash," Aaron added.

"I meant because of what I look like." Violet picked up her supplies and started taking them to her car.

Aaron shook his head as if she was crazy. "I saw the way he looked at you when you walked in. He didn't have to kiss you in front of half the town."

"Ooo," Lily called from the phone. "Tell us every detail."

This was her worst nightmare. Aaron relayed every excruciating detail, including an alleged hard-on he swore Jack had.

She wished.

"And now Vi will be famous," Lily added from the speakerphone.

"His agent wants us to do publicity shots to post online. I'm afraid the entire world will make fun of me."

Aaron grabbed her shoulders. "Violet. Do not let me down. Go enjoy that absolute *ten* of a man. I mean, did you see those biceps? And those triceps? And the shoulders. Try to enjoy the ride. Trust me, life is a lot better outside of your comfort zone." Aaron squeezed her shoulders before letting go.

"We are *miles* away from my comfort zone. His agent used the phrase 'makeover.'"

Aaron gasped. "Let me come. I'll finally live out my fantasy of tearing through your closet and replacing it with clothes that'll show off the snatched waist you hide."

Violet was a healthy size eighteen. Nothing was snatched, nor little, about any part of her. There never had been.

She liked her body. It was the world that had a problem with it.

Her strong arms and back meant she could carry huge bags of mulch, but they made clothes shopping nearly impossible. Finding shirts that fit her waist and large arms and *then* throw in her huge boobs?

Literally impossible.

She'd rarely found a pair of pants that could accommodate her meaty thighs, curvy butt, hips with extra to grab, and waist that didn't match. She hated getting dressed every morning, so she opted for oversized clothes. It was one less thing to think about.

"I'll do your make-up," Lily offered.

"This could be a *good* thing, Vi," Rose said with a hopeful smile.

Violet eventually extricated herself from the conversation and hopped in her car. She had to drive.

Had to think without considering whether to disappoint three of the most important people in her life.

A FEW HOURS LATER, after a shower and changing into her pajamas, Violet wandered through the back of her property in the dark purple light of evening.

Her great-great-grandparents had built her cottage in the 1800s, and she'd grown up running through the orchard her grandparents had planted. She loved the deep, invisible roots that tied her to each plant and stone on the small property. She belonged here in a way she'd never belonged anywhere else.

Her hands absent-mindedly skimmed the leaves of the apple and pear trees as she wandered through them. *This has been a heck of a day.* She stretched out her tired muscles and finally let her mind revisit the kiss.

Jack Grant had *kissed* her.

Not a peck, not a smooch. An honest-to-god, soul-melting kiss.

She'd go to her deathbed thinking about what he tasted like. What his hand felt like against her face, the stomach-flipping growl he emitted when they let themselves get carried away.

Goosebumps trailed down her arms and her back as she remembered what his hands had felt like. Could she stand a whole summer of hot kisses that meant nothing?

There are worse ways to be tortured.

She stopped at the bank of her pond. The bullfrogs croaked in the evening air.

Aaron's words floated back to her from earlier. *Life is a lot better outside your comfort zone.*

Kissing Jack wasn't on the same continent as her comfort zone, and that had been flipping *mind-blowing*.

All that, plus a makeover. That one word dug a pit of dread in Violet's stomach.

Though...Shay was her size, and she looked effortlessly chic, owning all of her curves.

Maybe if Shay did the makeover, it would be okay. Violet could figure out how to dress her curves like she'd dreamed of and mimic Shay's confidence.

She thought back to her dad's letter she'd received after he died. She'd read it a few months ago, and the words hadn't stopped echoing in her head. *You have great potential to help others,* he'd said, as if she hadn't already reached it.

Maybe this was how she could level up. Be a braver, bolder version she'd dreamed of being. Stop hiding and show more of who she really was.

"I'll do it," she whispered into the darkness of the pond.

Be brave, Violet. Be bold.

"I'll do it!" she roared, stamping her bare foot into the pond bank, squishing the mud under her toes.

"Do what?" a voice called behind her. She screamed and turned around, terrified in the dark.

As she registered the voice was Jack's, her feet slid backward.

Toward the pond.

Oh no, no, no.

Swinging her arms as she flailed backward in front of the hottest man she'd ever met, she considered how unfair and ridiculous her life was.

The discombobulating *smack* of the cold pond water hit her all at once, and shock flooded her system. She levered herself to the top of the cold, slimy water and gasped for breath.

"What are you doing?" she screeched, splashing water at him. She was soaked, and, ugh, something touched her leg. A blob-shaped figure crouched down at the bank of the pond.

Oh, god, her glasses. They'd fallen off.

The pond was seven feet deep, so there was no hope of getting them tonight. The world was a blur without them.

"I am so, so sorry." Jack was clearly trying not to laugh. "I didn't realize you startled so easily."

"Are you—" She shoved at her thick hair draped around her face and swiped pond scum away. "Are you laughing at me?"

"Oh no, darling, I'm laughing *with* you. You look enchanting, like a secret mermaid in there. Can you get out?"

Her stomach clenched at being called *enchanting*. It took some sting out of looking ridiculous.

Violet swam back to the steep edge where she'd fallen in. "Umm, maybe." She was glad it was dark, so he couldn't see how red her face was.

She thrashed, unwrapping a pond plant from her arm, trying to get her bearings. She found a small foothold and peered up at the white blob that must be Jack, knowing he had a gorgeous smirk on his face.

"I lost my glasses and can't see a way out. Give me a hand?"

"Sorry, Parker. Guess you'll have to get used to frogs for company," he said with a teasing lilt in his voice, but already extending a hand to pull her up. "Here, grab on."

Her foot found a solid rock to step on, and she grabbed his arm, pushing herself up with a hand on the muddy ground.

She hauled herself out of the water with the grace of a drunken sea cow, but by god, she wouldn't embarrass herself by being stuck in the muck.

She stood up, dripping from head to toe.

"Next time, warn a girl before you sneak up behind her in the dark." Rivulets of water ran off her thick long hair as she wrung water out of it. She wiggled her leg to fling off a pond plant that had wrapped itself around her.

She looked back at Jack as she wiped water off her face. "What, no smart remark?"

"Oh, sorry." He shook his head. "You...I, um." He pointed to her and then looked away.

And that's when it hit her: she'd been standing in bright moonlight for a full minute in white, now completely see-through pajamas.

With no bra on.

Chapter Eight

VIOLET

Violet quickly put her arms over her chest.

Crap on a crap-flavored stick.

She was glad she couldn't see Jack's horrified look at her lack of clothing.

Change the subject. Distract.

"Do you see my glasses?" She crouched to see if she could feel them on the ground.

"I don't see them anywhere along the bank. I *am* sorry, Violet. Can we look in the morning? I don't think we'll have much luck tonight."

She'd be nearly blind walking back through her gopher-hole-laden yard. "Uh, sure."

She took a few steps toward her house, and he grabbed her shoulders.

"Wrong way, darling."

A shiver at that simple pet name sent chills down her spine. How could she handle fake dating him?

"I'm blind as a bat without my glasses. Would you—" *Oh my god. So embarrassing.* "Uh, mind walking me back?"

"T'would be my pleasure to escort the lady." He put on his posh Lord Eagleton voice. His blurry smile looked down at her as he extended his hand.

A thrill shot through Violet's spine. Her body hummed with his accented voice that had her nipples standing erect. Awful timing, given she was currently in a see-through outfit.

He couldn't know how much she liked him.

Like, *really* liked him.

He'd never want a frumpy girl from the middle of Pennsylvania.

Time to get a move on, Violet. "Ready to lead me back?" She smiled apologetically, one arm still wrapped over her chest.

"Preferably at a distance of five feet. That pond smell is a bit dodgy." He squeezed her hand with a laugh.

"If I weren't positive I'd walk into a tree or fall into a gopher hole, I'd follow behind you."

He interlaced his fingers through hers and led her back toward the house. "I think you've suffered enough humiliation this evening, Violet."

She loved the way he said her name. Always her full name, always three syllables. *Vi-oh-lette.* Like sweet, thick syrup he took his time to enjoy. She wanted to tuck it away in her heart forever that Jack Grant knew her—little old Violet Parker.

They walked toward the house through the moonlit orchard. If the putrid smell of pond water weren't following her, it would have been the most romantic moment in Violet's life.

And just my luck: I look utterly ridiculous.

The cozy lights of her cottage drew near, and Jack helped her up the back stairs. As he opened the back door and led her in, his hand dropped from hers. Her hand flexed, already missing it.

"You got it from here?" he asked as he crossed to the fridge.

She turned to smile at him. "You worry too m—ow!" She rammed her forehead into the edge of a cabinet.

"Bloody hell, are you okay?" His hand was on her head in an instant. A thumb rubbed over the spot that hit the cabinet edge.

She cradled her aching head in her hands. "You'd think I could manage my own house, but my depth perception gets all wonky." The feeling of his thumb soothing her forehead was quite nice, though.

She'd have to switch to her arch-nemesis: contacts. The tricky little bastards.

She much preferred hiding behind large glasses. Her face looked too naked, too plain, too round, too much of everything when she didn't have them to hide behind. At least Jack had seen her at her worst already, so seeing her without glasses couldn't hurt.

She gulped, realizing she'd need to ask another embarrassing favor. It had been months since she'd last used her contacts, and it would be like finding a needle in a blurry, white haystack.

"Would you mind helping me find my contacts? They're somewhere in my room, and it'll take me hours to find them myself."

He grabbed her hand and interlaced his fingers with hers again. "Of course."

Heat rose on her face. Holding his hand shouldn't thrill her as much as it did. She'd kissed him earlier today, for goodness' sake.

He tugged her toward the staircase as the *squeak squeak squeak* of her wet feet on the kitchen floor taunted her at how ridiculous she looked. "Sorry for...well all of this," she said as they walked up the stairs, still hand in hand.

"It's hardly an imposition to rummage around a woman's drawers. And I'm sorry for everything I dragged you into today. I thought Shay would be satisfied once she saw you."

They walked into her bedroom hand-in-hand. Her other arm was still covering her boobs. "Can we talk after I depond? I think my contacts might be somewhere on my dresser."

"Of course," he replied.

She grabbed clean pajamas and headed to her en suite bathroom. "And stay out of my underwear drawer!" she teased over her shoulder.

"No promises," he joked back with a laugh.

Uh oh. How on earth would she manage her all white bathroom?

"Um, Jack." She turned around in the bathroom doorway.

She thought her cheeks might permanently blush from the last twenty minutes of her life. The blob turned toward her. *I really should think about getting LASIK.* "I have a big favor to ask."

"Bigger than the temptation of looking everywhere *but* your underwear drawer?"

She smiled, rolling her eyes at what an over-the-top flirt he was. *Like he cares about my underwear.* "Could you put the contacts by the sink? So I can find them?"

"It would truly be my pleasure, Violet Parker, to walk in on you in the shower," he said, chuckling.

Violet smacked herself on the forehead. "You know what I mean. Lean in and put them on the counter. My shower curtain's completely opaque anyway, so you won't have to see anything."

"Get to," he said quickly, in a more serious voice as he searched an open drawer.

"What?" Confused, she peered at him.

"I won't *get* to see anything," he murmured, cleaning off papers from her dresser and looking underneath them.

Violet sucked in a breath as she closed the bathroom door. She leaned back against it and blew out a long sigh, head swirling with a million thoughts, but one stood out from the rest.

He won't get to.

～

JACK

THE CLICK on Violet's bathroom door echoed like a gunshot.

Jack leaned over on the dresser and tried to catch his breath, rubbing his face. He'd had to look everywhere other than exactly where he'd wanted to when Violet was dripping wet in see-through white pajamas.

The woman who emerged from the pond was more surprising than he could have ever imagined. The bright moonlight had highlighted her picture-perfect body as her soaked clothes clung to her curves.

Where the hell had Violet been hiding all of the dips and valleys of her shape? She had a tiny waist and a mouthwateringly thick hourglass figure with full breasts and curvy wide hips he'd love to hold as he sank into her.

She had a strong back, luscious thick thighs, and carved calves.

He'd had to rip his eyes away from her dusky nipples, hard from the chill of the water.

Was this her all along? What atrocity of clothing could commit the crime of portraying her as anything less than a Grecian goddess?

Her lashes were sinfully long. He considered himself a great student of humans, but he'd missed the longest eyelashes he'd ever seen behind those damned enormous glasses. He was grateful to the disgusting pond for swallowing the hideous things. They'd been hiding Violet's most stunning feature.

Her spunk and determination had struck him as she grappled her way out of the algae-covered pond. Some women would have had a complete meltdown at that moment, but not his Violet.

His Violet? God, where did that come from? He'd barely been here two weeks and had already been sucked in under her spell.

A low musical hum interrupted his thoughts as it drifted from the shower. She sang an old jazz standard in the shower, and his heart wrenched.

She had the soul of someone who could be a perfect fit for him. If he ever decided to ignore his mother's warnings about becoming obsolete in a fickle industry and settle down.

He couldn't risk hurting someone as sweet as Violet by getting her tangled up in a real relationship with him. She was a romantic with a capital R, and probably wanted marriage, babies, the whole kit and caboodle.

His teeth ground at picturing that life with her. At someone *else* having that life with her.

"Whoa," Violet said from the bathroom and bottles clattered into the tub. "I'm okay!" she shouted.

Right. Back to the matter at hand. He scanned her room; she had a tidy, if fussy, bedroom.

The white four-poster bedpost had ornate carvings and a fuzzy gray blanket on top of the snow-white duvet that looked like heaven to sink into.

A flash appeared in his head of her auburn curls splayed on the bed under him, looking up with those big moonlit eyes.

He shook his head. At this rate, it would be March before he found her contacts.

He surveyed drawers and boxes around her bedroom. Small enough for someone to store contacts, public enough that there wouldn't be a vibrator in it.

He opened a small jewelry box on her bedside table. Probably a low risk of finding anything inappropriate in such a small container, but he suddenly *wanted* to know if she had a vibrator. What did it look like? What did she prefer?

He pushed the thoughts out of his head to focus on the task at hand.

He lifted cards, hair ties, and, thank Christ, finally, a small contact case.

"Found it!" he yelled.

"What?" Violet shouted, not hearing over the rush of the loud shower.

"I said," he pitched louder and came to the other side of the bathroom door. "I found your eyesight, Mr. Magoo."

"Oh, thank god. I tripped over the toilet earlier."

"Opening the door now, but keeping my eyes averted." He carefully nudged the bathroom door open and placed the contacts by the sink. "I'll fix us some tea."

He shut the bathroom door behind him despite everything in his body telling him to charge in, step inside her shower, and kiss her like he'd wanted to since he first got a taste.

Twenty minutes later, naughty thoughts out of his head, Jack focused on pouring the pot of tea into two teacups. Violet, covered in warm pajamas, padded down the staircase, towel-drying her long curly hair.

He handed her a cup of tea. "This has been a long day."

Her pretty green eyes widened in agreement. "The longest."

Long lashes fanned onto her pink cheeks as she closed her eyes, taking a long sip. What would they feel like against his cheeks?

"I like your..." He stopped. "Face." He coughed into his hand. "I mean, without the glasses. The contacts. They're good," he stuttered.

Bloody hell, he was like a teenager again.

She grinned behind her teacup. "Thanks. It's weird for my face to be this naked."

An awkward silence landed between them as they registered what they needed to discuss next.

"So, you don't have to—"

"I've been thinking—" They started at the same time.

"Oh, no. You go ahead."

"Sorry, sorry. You first."

Jack leaned on the counter, peering into his tea. "I thought Shay would be satisfied with my promise to lie low. But the network requires a public penance to prove it. I love my job and would love to fake date you"—he paused, shocked that the admission had snuck out—"but you went sheet white when she mentioned pictures."

Violet absent-mindedly circled the edge of her teacup with her finger and nodded. She was quiet for a minute in thought. Her finger went around and around the teacup's rim. Her long fingers delicately, somehow erotically, traced the edge slowly as she thought.

Does she know what she's doing to me when she does that? Teasing me?

And he shook his head to try to get a handle on it. Otherwise, his whole summer was going to be a walking hard-on.

"I was thinking maybe..." she started. "Maybe I would do it." A tremble sounded in her voice.

"Yeah?" he said, hope rising in his chest.

She straightened her shoulders. "I want to be brave, and it can help me step outside my comfort zone. Try my darnedest to be cool for once in my life."

He wanted to gather her into his arms at her vulnerability but busied himself with his tea instead. "Cool is overrated. People trying to be cool are terrified they aren't enough. But you, Violet, are just yourself. And it's dreadfully brave."

She huffed out a surprised laugh and rolled her eyes. "I am not brave."

"I assure you, as someone who professionally escapes into other personalities, being unapologetically yourself *is* brave. You've been brave this whole time. You just need a little help being the center of attention."

"I never thought about it like that." Violet bit her lip, and he desperately wanted to bite it too.

"We need to go on public outings to sell the relationship." He leaned on the counter. "Maybe take a few sessions of photos and post them on social media. Is that too much?" He grimaced, waiting for her to panic.

"It's not a burden to go out in public with the star of my favorite TV show." She blushed and looked away as she said it.

"*Favorite* show?" He laughed, poking her in the ribs. His finger met a firm barrier under her oversized fuzzy pajamas.

It felt like corset boning, of all things. *What the hell?*

He didn't say anything, though, not wanting to embarrass her further.

She nervously twisted a lock of hair around her finger. "I was thinking you could help me be bolder. Help me get more comfortable with people looking at me. So I can make it through a client pitch for Bloom." She sent him a wobbly smile as she sipped her tea.

"You should know it's not a hardship to look at you, Violet. But I'd be happy to help you get over your stage fright."

However, he needed to establish boundaries, or whatever was building inside him would get even harder to handle.

"What are you comfortable with? Was what I did outside the restaurant today okay?"

She sucked in a big breath and nodded enthusiastically.

He swallowed a smile. *Fucking adorable.* "Okay. So, we're okay to kiss? What about touching, like when I put my arm around you and squeezed you to me?"

She nodded, eyes trained on her slippers and cheeks burning pink. "Yep. For the record, you can do pretty much anything you want that won't get us thrown in jail."

Her eyes shot back to his briefly before looking away with a smile.

Fuck yes. He knew what he'd be thinking about tonight before he fell asleep.

Jack put out his hand to shake. "We'll fake date until I go back to filming at the end of August, and I'll help you get more comfortable talking in front of people. Deal?"

His heart was in his throat as Violet stared at his hand.

Finally, she stuck out her small, firm hand and shook his vigorously. "Deal."

A grateful whoosh of air escaped him, and he pulled up his phone. "Shay will have a cow from happiness."

JACK

Photos are fine. We can't wait to show the internet our love.

PR GODDESS

Hell yeah! I'll see if Gray can shoot it.

Tell Violet I'll be at her house in two days with clothes.

And that I plan to burn all her other clothes.

Luckily, Jack had filled Gray in about the fake dating scheme during dinner. He wasn't thrilled, and he'd made Jack promise within an inch of his life to treat Violet like an absolute fucking queen.

JACK

Spare no expense. Whatever you think she'd look great in, order it on me.

And BE NICE.

Violet is sensitive and sweet. Don't bully her.

PR GODDESS

God, you really must be dating.

Don't worry. I'll be her doting Fairy Shay-mother.

He put his phone on the counter. "Shay can't wait."

Violet was quiet and nodded in thought. Her brows were drawn together nervously. "Sorry, it's just...I should have asked before you texted her..."

His stomach dropped. Fuck, he was so close to having everything he wanted. A way to mend his reputation with the network *and* an excuse to touch Violet. But he wouldn't do anything if she was uncomfortable.

"I can text her if you've changed your mind."

"No, I—" She paused, looking up at him. "What can I do to make it believable?"

Believable? He smiled through his confusion. "Don't tell me you've never been on a date before?"

Violet looked like a cartoon baby owl staring at him

through her wide lashes. He had a crazy urge to pull her into his arms and keep her safe.

"I want people to believe you'd be...." She cleared her throat, looking anywhere but right at him. She spoke into her teacup, "...with someone like me."

She gulped her tea and set the teacup and saucer down hard, her hands shaking.

"Whoa, whoa, whoa." His hands came to her arms, wanting to steady her. Something was deeply bothering her. "What do you mean someone like you? A redhead?"

"I mean, someone...you know what I mean," she whispered, her lip trembling. "Someone like *me*—you wouldn't be seen with me. I'm not your type."

His hands fell, realizing a more meaningful, serious conversation was needed. "What do you mean 'not my type?'"

"Jack, look at me."

"Yeah, I have. I saw a *lot* of you earlier." There was that pretty pink blush back on her cheeks.

"I'm not a Hollywood model."

Ah. Fuck, he hadn't even thought about that, given his rabid attraction to her. "Violet, it's fine—"

"No, they won't—"

Her voice fell as he leaned forward over her, his hand falling on the oven hood and neatly boxing her into the kitchen corner.

"Let me be clear," he said in a low, firm voice. "I have dated women of all sizes and find them all equally sexy."

She huffed out an unbelieving laugh. "You're just saying that to make me feel better." Her brow was still wrinkled with anxiety.

Frustration furrowed his brow.

She had to know. Had to know how much he'd want someone like her.

"I can prove it," he rumbled.

Her mouth fell into a tiny 'O' shape. He shoved his hand in his pocket to keep it from tracing her full lower lip.

Her eyes held his, those large emerald gems he wanted to sink into, and her voice was barely a whisper. "How would you prove it?"

Not so innocent after all.

Fuck all his promises of good behavior. He wanted her. Wanted to show her how wrong she was.

There was a reason he'd gotten a playboy reputation.

He'd *earned* it.

He stepped into her space, leaning down to her ear. His voice was barely a whisper with serious urgency. "Because, Violet, I have a locked folder on my phone with all my deepest, darkest fantasies, and a lot of them look

Just.

Like.

You."

Chapter Nine

JACK

Tension flooded the space between them.

Violet stared back at him with a curious intensity. She bit her lip as she hesitated but finally said, "Show me."

His cock jumped at those dirty words coming out of her pillowy mouth.

A naughty little sunbeam, indeed.

"Only if you tell me what I felt underneath your pajamas." It had to be corset boning; he was sure of it.

"Me?" she said, grabbing her waist.

"Are you wearing a corset?" His curiosity got the better of him. He'd give an obscene amount of money to see her curves propped up in one.

"It...it helps me feel more confident," she stammered.

"Under your *pajamas*," he clarified, keeping a tight leash on his imagination.

"It's like...it's like my armor. It's the only thing that actually fits my body. It helps me feel sexy."

Bloody hell. Now he *had* to see it.

"Show me yours, I'll show you mine." He wiggled his phone, taunting her.

An unsure glint flashed through her eyes as she considered it. "You wouldn't want to see me."

Goddamnit.

He'd fucking show her. He navigated to the boring-looking app and entered his pin code. He handed her the phone as images loaded. "Here's the proof."

Gifs of couples, threesomes, foursomes, men and women of every size filled the screen.

"You see, Violet?" He stood over her shoulder as she registered what was onscreen.

Her wide eyes scanned the explicit photos. Women that were her size, with lush round asses and full breasts he'd wanted to drown in, taking their pleasure alone or with a partner or two.

"What do you like about them?" she whispered, mesmerized by one gif.

He tapped to enlarge it. The woman looked a lot like Violet. Milky skin, hourglass shape, heavy large tits, a sweet face.

"I love that she's enjoying it. I love how her tits swing when she fucks him. The curve of her thighs bouncing as she rides him."

His cock was a steel bar in his pants, but he didn't care. He'd beg on his knees for her to keep going.

"Show me, Violet. I want to see what's under this," he whispered, his fingers catching the fabric of her shirt. She glanced over her shoulder to where he stood behind her.

He raised an eyebrow. "Tit for tat."

She licked her lips slowly. God, she was a vixen and didn't even know it. Her plump lips formed a cupid's bow, and he wanted to bite one of them.

He might if she didn't unbutton that awful pajama top and satisfy his curiosity.

Her hand went to the top button, and each button pop was like a pump to his cock.

Finally, her breasts peeked through the opening as she shrugged her top over one shoulder.

A white mesh bustier with dark lace hugged her curves and...

Jesus fucking Christ.

Her tits.

They were propped up with the bustier, held apart in lush mounds barely covered in lace. His hands itched for them, and he felt himself drool.

"You're gorgeous," he ground out.

It was an understatement, but his brain had melted at the sight.

She bit her lip as she stared up at him, her eyes heavy with wanting. He'd promised to keep his hands to himself. This wasn't breaking that promise, right? Just staring at her heaven-sent breasts as she breathed heavily, feeling the tension thicken between them.

"You need any more proof?" he asked.

She turned back to the phone and scrolled farther down, stopping on a plus size woman riding two men, one in her ass and one in her pussy. Every inch of her bounced from the force of fucking both of them.

Violet let out a soft, breathy moan, and he realized he'd move the world for her right then.

"You like that? Maybe you're not the good girl I thought you were," he growled in her ear. His hand slid onto her hip, and he gripped her lightly, loving how she felt in his hands. He wanted to see what positions she liked so he could imagine them together when he was alone, stroking his cock and thinking only of her.

She watched the woman who looked so much like her take two cocks again and again and again. Her hand went to her breast, and she gripped it as her eyes were glued to the screen.

God yes. "I think maybe..." He pressed against her back, his mouth close to her ear, and whispered slowly, "You're a vixen. An innocent-looking, tempting little minx who is actually very"—his nose brushed the length of her ear—"very naughty."

She let out a moan as her head leaned against his. His hand cupped his cock, giving it one hard pump as she pinched her nipple through her lingerie.

She scrolled to the next gif. A woman was bent over, being taken from behind, and her tits bounced with every thrust. Violet's mouth parted, and a sigh came out. He wondered what her mouth would look like wrapped around his cock. Lord, he wanted her.

Fuck his promises. He wanted this siren under him immediately.

"You want that, darling? You want to be fucked like that?"

∼

VIOLET

A LOUD BANGING sounded at the door, and Violet jumped out of her skin, throwing Jack's phone across the kitchen.

Holy shit. Her heart was lodged somewhere in her throat.

She'd know that banging anywhere. "It's Lily." She couldn't meet Jack's eyes as she quickly buttoned her top.

He groaned and turned away from the door. "Excuse me. I need to—" He grabbed his phone from the floor, turned to the stairs, and took them two at a time.

She was going to kill Lily and then run away into the dark of night. She couldn't look Jack in the eye after what they'd just done.

How they'd let themselves get caught up in the moment.

Violet walked to the back door as she buttoned her pajamas where Lily kept pounding. She opened the door, and Lily stood holding a bottle of wine.

"Since when did you start locking your doors? I need—" Lily stopped mid-sentence.

"What?" Violet shoved at her wet hair.

"You look fluuuuusterrrrred." Lily narrowed her eyes trying to figure out why Violet looked flushed. "I didn't interrupt something, did I?" Lily peeked into the living room.

"What would you interrupt?" Violet shrugged nonchalantly.

"If you're in the middle of a sexy something, I can head back to my apartment. I was lonely and wanted an impromptu sister hang sesh."

"No, it's fine. We were"—*finishing up* felt like the wrong phrase to use—"settling down for the evening."

"We? Mhm," Lily said, brushing past her with her enormous jangling purse and bottle of wine. "Doesn't sound like nothing."

~

TWO DAYS LATER, Violet stared at the six stuffed clothing racks in her living room.

I've made a terrible mistake.

Aaron stood in the middle of her living room, vibrating with excitement. "I never thought it would happen. Violet, I'm so proud of you for being brave enough to wear a tube top." He picked up a hanger and showed her a sequin day glow yellow tube top with a mischievous smile and she shook her head violently. "Juuuust kidding. But you do deserve something nice."

Violet managed a small smile. This felt more like a punishment than a reward.

Her stomach turned as Lily wheeled in another rack. "How many clothes are you going to wear? Geez."

"She needs options, darling," Shay said, sweeping in behind her. She looked fabulous in fitted pants, a large flowing cape, and a tube top, taking up space unapologetically.

"How did you get this all here so fast?" Violet wandered through the racks of clothes.

"Jack said to spare no expense, so everything was overnighted."

Whoa. Aaron mouthed '*damn*' at her.

Damn, indeed.

"Now." Shay clapped her hands, twirling in the cottage to take it in. "We can work with this. I'm picturing *whole-*

some. I'm picturing *endearing.* 'Cottage life' meets 'plant mom' meets 'romantic at heart.'"

Sweat formed at the edge of Violet's hairline, imagining trying on all these clothes. None of them would fit, they'd all look terrible, and Jack would change his mind about their arrangement.

Violet had a long and complicated relationship with clothes, so she'd started compensating with an extensive lingerie collection. Lingerie fit her in a way jeans and khakis didn't. Corsets were made for contouring to her body, unlike her boxy floral shirts that made her look twenty years older than she was, but were the only thing she could find that fit her big arms.

Whenever she worked up the courage to try on a new dress or pants, it never looked how she wanted. She wanted to look confident, like somebody who had it all together.

Shay expertly flicked through hangers in the stuffed clothing racks. "Let's start with date looks since that's what you'll wear for photos today." She picked out ten pieces. "Where should we take these?"

"Let's go to my room." Violet pointed to the staircase but stood still, staring nervously as Shay walked up with an armful of clothes.

Aaron wrapped his arm around her shoulders and squeezed. "Come on, Cinderella. It's your turn at the fairy godmother station."

"I bet Cinderella didn't have the nervous barfs." Violet grimaced.

Todd wandered through the racks and brushed his large body against Violet's calves in a reassuring cuddle. She reached down to scratch behind his ears.

"Speaking of which, where's your Prince Charming?" Lily flopped on the couch and turned on Violet's TV.

"Helping at Gray's flower farm, I think." Violet's stomach turned again.

She'd avoided Jack like the plague since their incident the other night. If she put in long hours at Bloom, she didn't have to see him, and they wouldn't have to talk about what happened between them.

And what it meant.

Or didn't mean.

She hadn't been that brazen with *anyone* before. It had been easier to be bold, knowing he'd be gone in six weeks.

That it was all fake anyway.

Aaron grabbed her by the shoulders and marched her up the stairs. "Stop stalling."

"Ugh, you're mean," she groaned.

Aaron smiled as he smushed her cheeks in his hands. "You're going to look fabulous. Let's make your man candy drool."

The following hour was a blur of fabric being pulled over Violet's head, Shay scanning her with a thoughtful eye and then ripping it off her.

"Is this normal to go through so many options?" Violet asked as another one was tugged on. She hadn't even bothered looking in the mirror yet.

"Not all clothes are made for all people. Do you sew, Violet?" Shay pinned the loose fabric at Violet's waist so the skirt was effortlessly contoured.

This was the eternal problem; if something fit her butt or hips, she had an extra handful of material at her waist.

"No. I faint at the *thought* of needles." Violet shuddered.

"When you sew, you learn the garment on the rack should be taken as merely a suggestion. A first draft. Because every body"—she paused, meeting Violet's eyes with meaning—"and I mean *every single body* is different in this world. And they're all good."

Shay grabbed more safety pins as she spoke. "The poor manufacturer can only make one pattern, and they guesstimate what works for most people. But you, dear, are meant for better."

She tucked a flirty, off-the-shoulder top into the pencil skirt Violet wore, manhandling her.

Aaron, who sat scrolling his phone in the corner, glanced up. "Oh, damn."

"Bad?" Violet craned her neck around to look in the mirror.

"Don't move," Shay said, continuing to pin.

"Not bad. Fucking good." He snapped a picture.

Violet's face instantly grimaced, but he rolled his eyes. "It's just for Rose. She wanted proof you weren't in a sobbing heap."

"So," Violet said suddenly, thinking about what Shay said about clothes fitting. "I should get clothes handmade for me?"

"No, darling. A tailor. I get everything tailored. T-shirts, jackets, skirts, nightgowns."

"I thought that was for suits. Isn't it expensive?"

She took Violet's chin with a stern gaze. "You know what's more expensive? Hating all your clothes."

Shay gently turned her to the full-length mirror.

Wow.

A cream pencil skirt wrapped around her hips and

thighs, nipping in at her waist and skimming down her ample curves. An off-the-shoulder sea-foam green top complemented her pale skin and auburn hair. It skimmed along her shoulders and dipped in with a curve, showing her cleavage. She looked like a pin-up.

"How did you–?" And she turned around to see the skirt waist was cleverly pinned with hidden safety pins, so it was sculpted to her body.

"This will work for photos, but we'll send these to your local tailoring place. I cannot allow you to walk around in the outfit you wore to the café. No offense," she added quickly, sipping a sizable to-go coffee cup.

"Speaking of the café, gotta go," Aaron said suddenly. "Somebody fell through, and I have to cover a shift."

"But you're my emotional support best friend." Violet frowned, grabbing his hands.

"You look hot as fuck, never seen you look better. Smile big for the photos, and remember I'll have the largest slice of double fudge chocolate-chocolate cake waiting for you when you and Lord Hotpants want it."

"And dinner," Shay said, absent-mindedly scrolling her phone.

"Dinner?" Violet turned around, and her stomach gripped in panic.

"You need to be seen in public. Get paparazzi-style shots of you out in the world. When better to start than tonight?"

Aaron placed a quick kiss on Violet's cheek. "You got this," he whispered in her ear and thundered down the stairs.

"I got this." She looked at herself in the mirror and saw something like herself staring back.

She tilted her head in thought.

Had it been this simple all along?

"I think this outfit wins for today's shoot, don't you?" Shay stared admiringly in the mirror, her bold magenta lips in a proud smile.

"Shay..." Violet cleared her throat, not wanting to look at her.

She didn't want to offend Shay, but she had to know. She had to learn from somebody with her body type who looked put together.

Shay turned, sharp eyebrow arched in waiting.

"How do you have so much confidence? I hope it's okay I'm asking that. I just want to be like you and...I'm so sorry, forget I asked."

Shay let out a loud laugh, throwing her head back. "Honey, I came out this way. I've always been unapologetically me. I don't know any way else to be."

That made sense to Violet. She tried to change herself, be like all the other girls, make friends easily, care about clothes, and not escape into her pretend worlds. But she was just herself and had difficulty changing that.

Violet ran her hands down her hips. "I've tried to dress this way before, but it's never turned out like this."

"Do you like it?" Shay pointed to Violet's outfit.

It was romantic and vintage-inspired, which she liked. It felt like she was wearing a costume, and being a different version of herself was okay. Maybe a better, bolder version.

Her breasts were eye-catching, propped up in the off-the-shoulder, sweetheart neckline that plunged to reveal cleavage. Her butt looked like the letter C as the skirt molded to her thighs and hips. Her arms were mostly bare though, and they'd always been bigger. Her riotous, thick curly hair practically exploded from the messy topknot on her head.

Violet chewed her lip. "I like this, but I feel like sometimes there's just...too much of me."

Shay spun her around and grabbed Violet's hands. Her large brown eyes stared with serious intensity. "Honey, the world needs all of you. Every single inch of your body, your personality, all of it. We *need* more Violet in this world, so don't you dare hold it back from us."

Violet nodded quietly, eyes wide. *All of her.*

It was unthinkable.

"Thank you," Violet said quickly, feeling bad Shay had to go through all this trouble. "I'm—"

"If you say sorry *one more time*, young lady I will make good on my promise to burn those overalls."

Violet shut her mouth and smiled.

Shay called out as they walked down the stairs. "All right, youngest sister. She's ready."

Lily squealed as Violet came into view. "Shut the *fuck up*. Where've you been hiding all of that?" Lily circled her, looking her up and down.

Violet could hardly contain her smile, she was so pleased. Being the center of attention and feeling confident she didn't look like a weirdo was a new feeling.

Lily pulled her to the downstairs powder room. "Come on. Let's shellack some makeup on you."

Lily did some magic with a brow brush and color palettes. Violet wasn't one for makeup, but she liked the idea of putting on another shield.

They were holed up in the downstairs bathroom for better lighting, and Violet came out wanting to show Shay the final product. "I think I'm ready—oh!"She jumped as she made eye contact with Jack for the first time in two days.

His gaze fixed on her as if she had three heads.

"Fuck," he whispered. He stood stock-still as they locked eyes, and her breath caught.

The chicken he'd been taking to the microwave slowly slid off his plate and smacked onto the floor.

"Oh, shit." Realizing Todd was already gnawing on the chicken, he dropped to the floor. "No, you scoundrel. The vet said if I fed you more people food, he'd castrate me next."

Violet giggled and fussed with her curls. *Him staring was good, right?*

Finally standing up, he caught his breath and walked to her. "Darling, you look stunning." A growl in his voice reminded her of the last time they'd seen each other, watching very inappropriate things.

He leaned down to kiss her cheek, but Lily threw herself between them with a hand on Jack's impressive, sweaty chest.

"I spent too long on her face for you to mess it up. Wait until after the pictures, Romeo. Now, we need to do a quick pass over her hair."

"Why?" Jack asked, his eyes scanning Violet's enormous fluff of auburn curls.

"A blowout would look better for photos." Violet shrugged.

"I like you the way you are. It's bright and wild, like you," he said, winking at her.

Violet's stomach jumped, and she had to remember this was all an act. He was performing for Shay.

A sudden rap sounded on the door, and Gray let himself

inside. "Somebody told me there's a new model who needs some photos?" he joked as he walked in. His eyes registered her. "Holy shit, Vi."

"Careful, Roberts," Jack said, punching him playfully on the shoulder as he walked to the stairs. "She's mine."

Chapter Ten

VIOLET

Violet stood awkwardly in her greenhouse, waiting for Jack to finish getting ready. Shay decided having a sweet, hometown girl with her garden felt too wholesome to pass up, but Violet wasn't used to wearing heels in her safe haven.

Gray checked his camera and tried a few test shots. "Ready to get warmed up, Vi?"

As Violet's stomach turned, he snapped several shots to get a handle on the lighting.

"Let's get a few of you with the plants." Gray directed her to the philodendron plants in front of her.

Violet leaned over them awkwardly and started to pick out dead leaves.

"What are you doing?" Lily snorted, hand on her hip.

"I figured since I'm here, might as well be useful."

"But you're not *working* working," Lily said. "You're pretty working."

"What's *pretty* working?" Violet cocked her head to the side.

"You know, delicate."

Delicate, ugh. Violet hated that word. The antithesis of everything she was. She was strong, broad, and large. Too much, too weird.

"Let's try this," Shay said. "Tell me about the plant next to you."

Violet looked down and spotted her stalwart spider plant. They propagated so nicely; she had an army of them waiting to be sold in Bloom.

"Her name is Cordelia, and I adore her. See how spunky she looks?" She pointed to all the random little shoots poking out. "She's a spider plant and great for beginners." Violet lifted it, showing Shay the spikey, thin leaves, and went on to tell them the origin of the plant and what type of soil it liked. "I've raised her mother, Anne, for so long, and she's spawned so many spider plant babies that are now all over Fairwick Falls."

She looked up, and her eyes caught with Jack's.

He stood in the doorway, arms crossed, observing the shoot with a smile. Sunbeams shone behind him, and motes of pollen and dust in the air sparkled in the light. He looked like an actual dream come to life.

He'd trimmed his beard so it was cropped close against his face, and his sandy brown hair glinted in the sun. A dark-blue linen button-up strained against his broad chest and complemented his eyes, and his sleeves were rolled up to show his toned, thick forearms. He looked casual but polished. Khakis skimmed over his exceptionally toned ass and hung off of him perfectly. Longing pooled in her middle.

He looked like he'd been specifically designed for every single one of her fantasies.

"You look nice," she said, locking eyes with Jack. *Don't lie, Violet. Say the truth: he looks like sex on a plate you want to devour.*

"Ready to get started?" he said, clapping his hands together. "Do your worst." He threw a salute toward Gray and kissed Violet on the cheek as he came up to her.

"All right, let's get one of you holding hands and walking towards me," Gray directed, crouching down.

Seeing Gray as the photographer he used to be was so funny after knowing him as the flower farmer who'd stolen her sister's heart.

Jack leaned towards her ear and murmured, "You're doing great." Violet looked down and blushed. Maybe the pink tint of her cheeks would convince Shay and the rest of the world they were a couple.

"Thanks. You do look nice, by the way. I wasn't saying that for them," she whispered back.

"You don't strike me as the insincere type." His hand caught her chin. "I figured you were being honest." His thumb stroked her skin, and she looked everywhere but his face. Being this close to him was overwhelming.

"Let's go over to these hydrangeas since they're flower-ing," Gray interrupted, kicking them out of their bubble. He snapped more photos of Violet enjoying the fruits of her labors.

As Jack stood behind her, she leaned over to look at the hydrangea plants. *Maybe I should up their slow-release fertil-izer. The blooms are looking peaky.*

Jack leaned to whisper in her ear, interrupting her thoughts. "This pose has me thinking indecent thoughts."

Violet's eyes widened as Gray snapped a photo, and Jack's wicked smile caused a throb to start somewhere deep in her core.

"Too much?" he asked, leaning back and looking at her. His arm circled her waist and pulled her close to him.

"No," she whispered, shaking her head slowly. She'd thought of nothing else since he'd been in her kitchen, whispering wicked things into her ear.

After another twenty minutes of photos and Violet nearly begging, Shay relented and released them from the photo shoot. Lily and Gray headed back to Bloom, and Shay was only too eager to run out of town and back to Los Angeles.

As Shay's car pulled away, Violet could finally breathe. "Do you think she bought it?"

"With Shay, you never have to guess. If she didn't buy it, I'd already have five new Wayridge-approved fake girlfriends to date."

Interesting. He did this often, then.

She had to remind herself. It was all an act.

A tinge of shame flitted through her head. Maybe the other night was a misunderstanding on her part?

"Ready for dinner?"

"Are you sure we can't play hooky?" She hoped they'd be done for the day.

"Come on. It's just eating food near nosy humans with cell phones. Have to be spotted by a few people, at least."

"Should I change?" Violet looked down at herself. She was too fancy for Fairwick Falls standards.

"Don't you dare." His eyes roamed up and down her curves.

"But what if I freak out when everyone stares?" Violet tucked hair behind her ear, nervous about what someone might say.

He chucked her chin with his hand. "Okay, first lesson in being the center of attention. You, my dear lady, need an alter ego. I pretend I'm Mr. Darcy when I'm Lord Eagleton, so I don't feel so nervous being the star of the show. All those people depend on me, and I don't want to disappoint anyone. Darcy's stern countenance and noble actions mean women simper at his feet."

"My alter ego. Hmmm." They started back to the cottage to grab their things.

We need every inch. Violet stood taller.

She wracked her brain for inspiration. She needed something bold, hard to ignore, and sexy. "*Monstera Albo Variegata,*" she said with pride. "It's trendy, powerful, and so sexy."

His eyes danced with delight. "I can promise you whatever plant it is, it doesn't look half as good as you do right now."

Such a flirt. And like any classic flirt, didn't mean half the things he said. "Oh, they are *so* sexy. You know those plants that are so popular right now with the big leaves covered in white streaks? They're big and bold."

Jack nodded his head, impressed. "Sounds very sexy." He offered his arm as they walked across the cobblestones and back into the cottage. "I was thinking Vichetti's?"

"That's as fancy as Fairwick Falls gets." She grinned back at him through her nerves, eager to get today over with.

Inside, she grabbed the shell-shaped clutch Shay had picked out for her.

And then realized she needed to pee.

Badly.

Oh no.

She looked down at her skirt. It was too tight to pull up over her thighs. She should have stopped drinking liquids hours ago.

Her hands fumbled at the back of it, seeing if she could grasp the safety pins but they were trickily buried in fabric. Getting it off *and* back on the right way would be impossible.

She chewed on her lips. *So embarrassing.*

"What's wrong?" Jack asked.

It's not like they were really dating, right? She could just be herself. "I have to pee, but these pins have me trapped."

"I'm excellent at undoing ladies' skirts." He winked to make her laugh. "May I?" He leaned down to look at the back of her skirt with all the safety pins locking the waist in place.

"Sure," Violet said, trying for nonchalance. He dipped his hands inside the back to unhook the hidden pins.

This was *totally* normal, having a hot British man dig in the back of your skirt.

"Make sure to remember where they started," she said. "I want to get it exactly right. Shay worked so hard on this."

The brush of his knuckles along her lower back and waist sent a shiver down her spine, and Violet found herself holding her breath.

"Fear we might be here for the rest of the evening," he mumbled, wrestling with the pins. "I'm trying to undo them but not have them fly everywhere. Can't have my fake girl-friend arrive scratched and bloodied."

Maybe if she made herself as small as possible, it would help. She sucked in her stomach. The skirt was tight, which made it harder to get under the pins.

"What are you doing?" He stood, grasping her skirt with one hand as his other rested on her waist. The heat of his hand was all she could think about. "You can breathe," he said, voice low in her ear.

"I wanted to give you more room."

"Violet," he said in a demanding tone.

Oh no, another voice to add to the fantasy list. Violet squeezed her eyes shut, not knowing how much more she could handle of his sexiness.

"You are allowed to take up space. Go on. Let it out."

She let out the breath she *definitely* knew she'd been holding.

She relaxed her stomach muscles, and her belly pooch filled out her skirt.

"Better," he rumbled.

She wasn't even sure what to say. Yes, she felt more comfortable, but it wasn't familiar.

"All right, last little bastard is undone." He unzipped the top of her skirt and rolled down the waistband so the pins wouldn't scratch her skin.

He smoothed the fabric down, and his thumb lingered on her lower back, caressing it with a swipe that made her breath hitch again.

He *had* to notice that.

He gave her waist a friendly double tap, stepped back, and cleared his throat.

"Happy to redo them when you're ready."

How could she handle six more weeks of this?

Twenty minutes later, they parked outside the cozy Italian bistro. Vichetti's had pretty lights strung out front, and twisted vines of ivy decorated the entrance.

Jack grasped her hand and led her to the front door. Violet tried to put on a brave face, but her breath came quicker and quicker as they got close.

A panicked heartbeat thrummed inside of her. She was going to walk in, and all those people would turn and stare at her.

"What if they think I look ridiculous," she whispered, stopping ten feet from the door.

"Hey now," Jack said, registering the look on her face. He squeezed her hand. "It's going to be fine. You look gorgeous. I look barely good enough to be with you." He pulled a face to make her laugh. "Just think, what would Shay do?"

What *would* Shay do?

"She'd stroll in, acting like she owns the place."

"Rightfully so," he said. "Order the most expensive thing on the menu."

Shay's voice echoed in Violet's head. *The world deserves every inch of you.* Violet threw her shoulders back and nodded nervously to Jack.

"Let's do it."

"All right, Monstera. Let's go kill them with sexy confidence." Jack opened the door for her, and they walked into the cozy Italian restaurant.

Heads turned as they stood in the entrance.

They're staring at Jack. They're just *staring at Jack,* she told herself over and over.

Jack leaned to whisper in her ear, "Giggle as if I made a joke." Violet did a passable fake chuckle. "And remember, if people are staring, they're just wishing they could be in my place so they could put their hands on you."

Violet whipped her head around to him with surprise.

"Table for two," Jack said louder to the hostess, putting his hand on the small of Violet's back.

She gripped his hand like a lifeline as they walked to the table, his words still tumbling around and around her brain on spin cycle.

"Here's the table you requested, Mr. Grant." The perky hostess pointed to the table in the corner. It was private, but one chair was still visible to the restaurant. Jack led Violet's hand to a seat covered by a half wall and took the more visible seat.

"Was this Shay's doing?" Violet asked as they looked at the menus.

"I did recon beforehand. This was the best table for people to gawk at me without making you uncomfortable."

He perused the menu after saying the most earth-shattering thing as if it was nothing.

He'd planned. He'd thought of her.

This was a stark contrast to her last date ten months ago. Her date had been along for the ride and made her feel like she was lucky to even be asked out, like usual.

The phrase *if he wanted to, he would* echoed through her head.

Violet's heartbeat was back to normal after everyone had stared at her.

She'd *done* it.

That was a win, right? She stared at the center of the table, gathering her wits.

"Hey," Jack said, quietly reaching for her hand. "You did great, okay? We'll have a nice meal and bottle of wine; I can already see people holding their phones now." Violet peeked around the half wall and saw several people aiming their phones at Jack's profile.

"How did you...?"

He nodded toward the windows on either side of their table. "Reflection. You get used to it after a while."

Violet caught her reflection in the window. Her hair looked weird from having messed with it so much from nerves in the car. "I'm going to run to the bathroom super fast."

"We can leave if you need to," Jack said, suddenly concerned.

"No. I can do this. I'll be right back." All eyes were on her as she walked to the bathroom, her heart pounding with each step.

She walked through the restaurant with her head held high and felt a small burst of pride when she finally pushed the women's restroom door open.

"Can you believe he's here with her?" a voice said from inside a stall.

"I know," a giggly voice sounded from the other one. "She's such a mouse."

Why did that voice sound familiar? Are they talking about me?

No, don't be silly. They could be talking about anybody. Violet stood in front of the mirror to fix her hair and tried to ignore all the warning signs she felt.

"I mean, he's all over the internet. I follow at least one of his fan accounts where it's all photos of his shirt off."

Uh oh.

"She's so weird. She's way too, like, into plants." *That sounds like Jennifer.*

"Every time I see her, she asks me about one I bought from them months ago," the other one said, through a giggle.

"Plus, her ass looks like a mozzarella ball in that skirt."

Violet glanced down at her skirt as she heard both toilets flush and the doors unlock. She stood stock-still with fear, not sure what to do. Flee? Fight? A woman she didn't know walked out of the first stall, and the second one emerged.

Of course, it was Jennifer. The friend she could never count on.

And if you couldn't count on a friend, what were they? Just a person who didn't care about you.

The women went to the sinks to wash their hands, eyes downcast.

"Hi, Violet," Jennifer said with a tight smile.

The other woman perked up, pretending Violet hadn't just caught her. "Your date is so handsome. Did you win, like, a charity thing?"

Violet's heart wanted to leap out of her chest in anger. Channel Shay and slay them with a witty comeback. But her tongue was tied; she wanted to burst into tears and scream simultaneously.

She *hated* that she cried when she got mad.

Instead, she threw her bag under her arm, angry tears in her eyes, and immediately walked out of the bathroom.

She wished she had a million comebacks for all the mean girls who'd taunted her in bathrooms over the years.

She walked quickly to the table with her head down. "I'm sorry, I can't," she muttered to Jack. She escaped outside and swore she heard giggling behind her as the door closed.

She made it to the end of the sidewalk before he caught up with her.

"I'm sorry. I didn't mean to ruin it," she said, trying to catch her breath as she fought back tears.

She was just so mad. Mad at not standing up for herself. Mad at trying to be friends with terrible people.

Crap, she was ruining her makeup. Now the photos people would take of them would look terrible.

"Nothing to be sorry about. What's the matter? Do you need help with your skirt?"

"No, it's not these stupid clothes." She tugged at her skirt.

Ass like a mozzarella ball.

Jack's hands came on either side of her arms, and the heat of his hands made her want to curl against him. "We can go home, but what happened?"

"It's nothing."

How did you tell the hottest man on earth nobody believed he wanted you?

"Come here." He pulled her in for a hug. The broad expanse of his chest enveloped her, and she needed to play along. People might still be watching them.

She wrapped her arms around his waist and gripped the extra fabric of his shirt. Relief flooded her to have someone so solid and kind to hold.

"I cry when I'm mad," she said into his shirt.

"What are you mad about?" he murmured into her hair, stroking her back.

So solid, so soothing.

They were friends, right? Maybe she could talk to him. She hiccupped as she spoke. "Women in the bathroom said some things."

He pulled back, and anger flashed over his face, his eyes turning into stormy seas. "About you?"

She bit her lip and nodded, not wanting to meet his eyes. "It's fine. I should've expected it."

"It's not fine. I'll take care of it." Jack pulled away, but she clutched his hand, keeping him in place.

She didn't want to make more of a scene. "Don't. Please. Let's just go home."

Home. Their home. Where they could just be themselves.

His hand touched her cheek, stroking his thumb along it, catching a tear. "I know this was a big day. And I'm so proud of you."

She leaned into his hand, and her eyes traced the edge of his bearded jawline. Wanted to feel it scrape against her face again. Anything to distract from the last hour.

He sucked in a breath as their eyes finally connected. "People might be watching." His voice was low and intimate.

Violet didn't move her head but glanced over. Curious faces watched them in the front windows of the restaurant. "Yeah, there are a few watching."

"Come on, then. Better get in some practice kissing like we're a real couple. Let's give those mean girls a show."

He hauled her against him and smiled as his mouth met hers.

Chapter Eleven

VIOLET

It was so easy to get lost in Jack's scent as his mouth took hers. She wanted to bury her head into his neck and inhale the woodsy notes there.

Wrapping her arms tight around him, she pulled him in, wanting him closer. His hand landed on her ass, and he squeezed her hungrily.

His teeth raked along her lip, and it lit an inferno of hot need in her. Nipples pebbled with lust under her silk shirt.

He kissed greedily, pulling her to him and taking as much as she'd give him. She wanted to claw against his muscles, run her hands up and down him, through his hair, but no, they were in public.

So she consoled herself with his mouth as she breathed in his kisses like oxygen.

She ran her tongue along his bottom lip, tasting the hint of red wine he'd had. His tongue opened her mouth briefly, and she felt it go straight to her pussy.

She wanted to give him everything.

She needed more of him and pressed herself into the kiss.

Just to sell the relationship. She grabbed at the thick, taut muscles of his chest, trying to get closer and closer.

He angled his head as he gripped her tighter, the kiss turning hungrier. Primal. His teeth scraped against her lips with bruising need, and she licked his lip hungrily.

His forehead met hers as he pulled his mouth away, breathing heavily. He released her and took one more kiss, gently nipping her bottom lip as he cradled her chin. He pulled back, his wolfish smile in place.

Violet was thrumming with need. Holy hell, he knew how to kiss.

"I'm going to run in, and get our dinner to go." He pushed her hair back from her shoulders, setting her to rights. "You wait in the car, and we'll go home, yeah?"

"Okay," she whispered, trying to keep her wits about her. "Oh, wait." She tugged him back and wiped her lipstick off his lips. He placed a quick kiss on the inside of her wrist.

Gosh, he was good with this fake dating stuff.

Moments later, Jack came out of the restaurant, bags in hand, and he stopped to take a selfie with a fan, giving them a kind word before he hustled to the car.

Violet was mortified. She'd had one job: to appear in public with him as a doting girlfriend, and she'd messed it all up.

Maybe it was time to think about being a forest witch; find a cottage somewhere, cultivate mushrooms, befriend squirrels, and ensure no one had to look at her.

They rode home in silence, and Violet slowly trudged up to unlock her cottage door.

He'd figure out she wasn't the right partner for this.

He'd leave, and she'd miss him terribly. In the short time

he'd been there, she'd already settled into being his room-mate, having someone kind and warm to talk with over tea.

She just wanted to forget the day and start over in the morning. *Time to cuddle up in bed.*

Jack got out their to-go containers in the kitchen, and his eyes followed her to the staircase. "You don't want any?"

"I'm gonna go to bed."

"It's only"—he peered at the clock—"eight o'clock."

"Early day tomorrow," she lied, not meeting his eyes. Violet started up the stairs, feeling like she'd failed everyone. Rose, Lily, Jack. Heck, even Shay.

She threw herself a fantastic pity party as she took off her new clothes.

Some Cinderella she turned out to be. She'd ruined the ball and made Prince Charming look like a dummy.

"I bet no one called Cinderella's butt a piece of cheese," she muttered to Wishbone, her small aloe plant on the bath-room counter, as she brushed her teeth.

She snuggled into her comfiest pajamas and finally, in the dark, let herself silently cry all the tears she'd yet to spill. Five minutes, twenty minutes, and an hour passed, and still, the tears came. Her lip never stopped trembling after a day of having everything she'd ever wanted and letting it slip through her fingers.

She tried to sleep, but as soon as she'd settle down, a flash from earlier would pop up, and she'd start crying again.

After her third nose blow, a soft knock sounded at her door.

"Violet, are you all right?" Jack asked.

Oh, shoot. She'd learned as a kid not to make a sound when she cried. Crying upset her dad so much that she'd learned to be silent. She'd gotten rusty after living alone for so long.

"No," she said through a stopped-up nose. "I'm fine, sorry."

"What did I tell you about that word?" he said with mock irritation behind the door. "Can I come in?" His melodious accent made any question sound like the sweetest sound she'd ever heard.

"Sure." She shoved her hair and sat up, embarrassed.

Jack opened the door and tentatively poked his upper body through, holding a teacup and saucer.

"I thought you might want this." Two small cookies were tucked in beside the cup. "It's Sleepytime. Tea, I mean," he said with a shy smile.

When was the last time somebody had waited on her in the middle of the night? When Lily and Rose were here, she'd check to make sure they ate. Made sure they had everything they needed. It was an odd sensation to have someone to wait on her for once, to feel like she deserved it.

"You didn't have to do that." She wiped her eyes and pretended she hadn't cried for the last hour.

"I mean, I can chuck it out the window," he offered with a warm smile that crinkled his eyes.

She let out a watery chuckle and reached for the saucer. "Don't you dare. That's my favorite teacup."

"I noticed. May I sit?"

Could Jack Grant sit on the edge of her bed? He'd already looked through all the drawers in her bedroom; this couldn't be much weirder.

She nodded, and the bed sank under his weight next to her.

"We don't have to keep doing this, Violet. I don't want to keep torturing you."

"No." She shook her head. She didn't want to break their agreement. She still needed to grow. Get used to people staring at her so she could help Bloom. "I'm sorry for messing up the publicity stunt."

"I told you, that's the last warning you'll get about the S word." A severe, concerned look clouded his face.

He grabbed her hand. His thumb stroked hers, each stroke reminding her of the needy, wolfish kiss they'd shared earlier.

How it was all fake, but she wanted it anyway.

"But I *am* so ssss—" She paused, the word almost spilling out like a habit. "—sssausages." She managed to switch it at the last moment.

"You're sausages?" He laughed.

"Yes. Very sausages." A curl of a smile tugged at her lip. "I ruined the whole thing. And I *want* to fake date you," she let that slip, and he sent her a heated look, his eyes dipping to her lips for a split second. "But every time I try to fall asleep, I picture messing everything up all over again."

She sniffed as she sipped her tea, the smell of chamomile instantly soothing her.

"Then I need your Hoover manual."

"My what?" She tilted her head in confusion.

He arched a noble eyebrow. "Your Hoover manual, air fryer manual, any manual will do." He pulled out his phone and tapped away. "Aha, perfect. The Dust Queen 3000 user manual." He waved his phone triumphantly. "Now, lie back; get comfortable."

"What are you doing?" she said, with her teacup halted mid-air. *Had he lost his mind?*

He leaned back on his hand, phone held aloft. "I caused your misery; it's only right I un-cause it and help you get to sleep. All right. Prepare to be dazzled."

He cleared his throat and started to read. "Any person who purchases the Dust Queen 3000 comes into the *lethal* liability of the Big Ol' Sucker Corporation."

Violet burst into laughter. "It does not say that."

"It does, too." He flipped his phone quickly to her and back around with an impish grin. "Now, do be quiet. I require silence for the *most* serious of bedtime stories. The liability is assumed by the operator of the Dust Queen 3000." Jack's voice and lovely accent calmed her nerves, and she set the teacup down, feeling better.

"This is the weirdest ASMR I've ever listened to," she murmured, snuggling into her pillow.

"Quiet down in front." He leaned on his elbow, making himself comfortable along the edge of her bed.

He went on to detail the function and purpose of all 17 attachments of the Dust Queen 3000 until Violet felt the heavy drowsiness of her body slip into darkness, lulled by the gentle sway of sweeper tubes.

JACK

JACK AWOKE in the gray early light before dawn, snuggled up next to Violet under a quilt. She slept soundly, her nose an inch from his. Her hair fanned out wildly on her pillow like he'd pictured. Her mouth was plush and perfect, pursed as she dreamed.

He remembered how her mouth had tasted last night, how her curves had consumed him with wanting them outside the restaurant.

It took every ounce of willpower to keep from pulling her against him and kissing her right now. Kiss away any worries that she wasn't good enough. That she needed to change.

But once he started, he wouldn't want to stop at one kiss.

He had wanted to haul her against the nearest flat surface yesterday, and they'd been in *public*.

And she wasn't a one-night stand to him.

They'd let themselves get carried away the night she fell in the pond. Since then, he'd come in his hand more times than he could count, picturing her breasts in her corset as her nipples pebbled.

He hadn't *meant* to fall asleep in her bed. Only closed his eyes for a mere moment last night, but now here he was, warm and perfectly happy.

He could move, but where was the fun in that?

He so rarely had the opportunity to sleep next to someone. It was too hard to trust the never-ending list of women coming in and out of his life. But he trusted Violet.

Precisely why he needed to keep her at arm's length.

For her own good.

So rather than ravaging her like he wanted, he closed his eyes and reveled in the lavender scent of her linens as he fell back asleep.

Hours later, the sun was up, and Jack woke up to Violet's side of the bed neatly made.

Todd leapt up at that moment to let him know breakfast

was approximately seven minutes late and, therefore, he should be beheaded immediately.

"I hear you. I hear you," he muttered over the low meows.

God, what a day yesterday was. He'd been wiped from the unexpectedly hard manual labor on Gray's farm in the morning and then gobsmacked by a vixen who haunted his thoughts the rest of the afternoon and evening.

And, on top of it all, dealt with the emotional quagmire of her conquering her fears with him in public.

This whole thing might have been a terrible idea.

He reached for his phone, willing his morning wood away. He'd had lucid dreams about what would have happened if he hadn't been a gentleman last night. It all came crashing down when he saw Shay's text.

PR GODDESS

Luck is on your side, Grant. First photo posted today, and the internet is happily abuzz.

The first photos from their session had been posted to his social account, which Shay's people managed. A clever non-apology apology had been issued, along with photos of him and Violet looking absolutely smitten with each other.

Shit. It was out to the world. He knew exactly who he needed to call next.

He punched in the familiar number as he walked downstairs, herded by Todd toward his breakfast bowl.

"Dad, hi," he shouted. His father wouldn't admit he was losing his hearing.

"Well, 'ello there, stranger," his father exclaimed, breathless.

"Woah. Are you all right?" His father had developed health problems and had to retire early as a plumber, despite only being in his early 60s. He'd had a hard life, and Jack wanted to take care of him now so he could rest easy.

"Ach, I'm fine. You worry too much. Haulin' some gravel to the garden, and you s'prised me."

The pitter-patter of his dad's thick West Country accent felt like a hug he didn't know he needed.

"Wut are you up to this afternoon?" his dad asked.

"I'm in America, visitin' a friend." He felt his own accent grow thicker in talking to him. "Da, I wanted to tell you about a thing you might see—"

"Oi, I saw all the hubbub, but tha' fella was a right tosser. He 'ad it coming."

"Dad, I've got a girlfriend."

"A wha now?" Disbelief laced through his dad's voice. "Tha's grand! Finally settlin' down, then? Does she make you happy?"

His heart warmed for his kind father. The best man in his life. All he'd ever cared about was if Jack was happy.

"Yeah," Jack answered reflexively.

He *did* feel pretty grand. There was something comforting about Violet's presence and her home. He'd already felt like he'd lived here for months, not weeks.

Come to think of it, he couldn't remember when he'd been happier.

Jack made his way to the kitchen and saw a note on the edge of the counter in loopy handwriting.

Muffins for you in the oven. Couldn't trust naughty Sir Toddrick to stay out of them. Thanks for the bedtime story. ♥ *Vi.*

"Oh, fuck yeah," he muttered.

"Wut's tha' now?" his dad uttered.

"I'm at my girlfriend's house, and she made muffins."

"Sounds like a keeper."

Violet was a keeper for whoever was lucky enough to end up with her. She was thoughtful, dead sexy, and adorable as a woodland fairy.

"Well, tell me about 'er," his dad interjected.

"She's a friend of a friend." Jack leaned down to take the muffins out of the oven. "She's kind and gorgeous but still innocent, kind of a Marilyn Monroe vibe," he said through a mouthful of orange and cranberry muffin, still warm from the oven.

"Bet'er lock 'er down. You know I want grandbabies. Maybe three or four?"

"Dad," he warned through another mouthful of muffin. God, he needed to watch himself, or he wouldn't be able to fit in his costume. "We've only dated a little while. It's not that serious."

"Well, I'm pleased as punch for you."

Jack's phone started vibrating next to his ear. He pulled back.

Bloody hell. "Da, I've gotta go. It's Mum."

"Tell the she-demon I said hullo."

He switched to answer the video call. His mum was the polar opposite of his father. Where he was sweet and enjoyed mucking about in his English garden, she was all sharp edges and plastic surgery.

"John Nicholas Grant," she demanded into the camera.

"Hello, Mother." He grimaced, hiding the muffin off camera.

"You have a *girlfriend*?" she said the word *girlfriend* as if she meant *cyanide* instead. "I am absolutely devastated you didn't tell me first. Does your father already know?"

"Uh…"

She threw her hand in the air, her phone wobbling in exasperation. "Of course he knows. I'm invariably the last person you tell. I want what's best for you, my darling. A casting agent friend reached out about a new edgy show—you know, where everyone's a werewolf slash president or something. He agreed to let you read for it, and then what do I see from my Google alert for you? You have a *girlfriend* in the middle of *bloody* nowhere. We did not work this hard for you to get derailed."

"Shay, Wayridge, and I are thrilled," he lied. Wayridge would eventually be thrilled. "The network pays my bills, so I need to make them happy." He poured Todd's breakfast to stop the soundtrack of incessant meowing behind him.

"But Jack, darling, she's not even anyone *famous*. Not an influencer, not even a reality TV participant." She clucked her tongue with disappointment. "Now, darling, I must run. I'm late for my massage, but send in that self-tape. It's the *least* you could do after my friend considered you for a role. The sooner we get you out from underneath that network and girlfriend, the sooner the *real* work of your career can begin."

His stomach turned. He couldn't disappoint her. "I'll consider it."

They said their goodbyes and Jack rubbed a hand over his face. He was torn between what each parent wanted. In some ways, he wanted *both* things: a career to be proud of and a quiet family life.

He just needed to figure out a way to have both so that Shay wouldn't have a heart attack.

It was an impossibly tall order.

He turned the kitchen corner to find a darling little succulent-themed lunch box sitting on the table as if it had somewhere to go.

"Hold on, what's this?" He peered inside. Two matching plant-themed containers held leftovers, with a round little clementine beside them.

Something so sweet hit his heart, thinking of her packing her lunch so carefully in matching containers and then going off and forgetting it.

How was this woman so fucking adorable?

She'd gotten her little claws into him, and he could hardly think of anything else. Of what their idyllic life would be like if he just...stayed. If he ran away from his life and hid out in Fairwick Falls, where they'd read Hoover manuals and develop lovely tummies as they devoured every type of muffin.

He changed into running shoes and grabbed his keys. She'd helped him so much, it was the least he could do to take this to her. He'd walk to Bloom and then squeeze in a run around town.

Jack glanced to see if Todd was done yet and found him lounging in a spot of sunshine.

"Don't get too used to it, old man."

Todd looked over his shoulder as if to say, *I do as I bloody well like. She has excellent sunshine spots and a lap that's pleasant to sit on.*

Maybe Todd was right. The reality of leaving in over a month was pushed out of his mind as he decided to enjoy his own piece of heaven right here.

An odd feeling overcame him as he grabbed the lunch box. To know he felt more at home in somebody else's house than his own.

As if her soul had a matching lock to his key.

Chapter Twelve

Familiar voices raged at each other as Jack stepped into Bloom.

"Vi, if you don't get it this time, I'm gonna sacrifice your houseplants to the social media gods," Lily fumed.

"But I'm so bad at this. Why can't you do it?" Violet yelled back. They stood nose to nose in front of the floral wall with Bloom's neon sign. It was a two-story wall, interwoven with jungle ferns and vibrant flowers that set a trendy and modern tone for the entire store.

"If you're going to kill my girlfriend's houseplants, you'll have to go through me first." He cracked a smile.

Lily and Violet turned around to stare at him. No other customers were in the store.

"Oh, you don't have to pretend, Jack. It's just us in here." Violet's eyes lit up as she spotted her lunchbox. "You brought my lunch!"

"It's better for me to stay in character. I am a method actor, after all." He leaned down, kissing her on the cheek and handing her the lunchbox. *Right, that's the reason you can't stop touching her, you big liar.* "Thanks for the muffin this morning."

Lily burst out laughing, and they turned to look at her. "I'm so sorry," she said through giggles. "It's been a long time since I've gotten laid, and I can't keep my head out of the gutter."

Jack winked at Violet, causing her pretty blush to appear again. "Didn't want you starving after abandoning yet another meal. And why does Lily want to kill my darling girlfriend's most prized possessions?"

"I'm terrible on camera." Violet chewed her lip with nerves.

"Camera?" he said with a happy smile.

"Oh!" Lily clapped her hands. "Maybe Jack can do it."

"No." Violet waved her hands in a big X. "We are not abusing our privileges."

He shrugged happily. "I'm an actor. I love being on camera. People looking at me is my second favorite thing."

"What's your first?" Violet asked.

"Eating muffins." He winked at her.

"Oh my gosh, I adore him. Can we keep him?" Lily wrapped her arm through his companionably. "Is that allowed?"

"The American immigration office might have some opinions. What seems to be the trouble with filming?"

Violet grimaced. "We're trying to do this plant Q&A video for social media—"

"—that was your idea," Lily interjected.

Violet puffed out her lip. "You caught me in a moment of weakness because I failed us."

"Plant Mom Mondays." Lily turned to Jack. "One of our

followers has plant care questions, and Violet helps them because Violet *likes* to help." Lily shot a '*You got yourself into this mess, now deal with it*' look at Violet.

"But what am I supposed to do with my hands?" Violet asked. "My hair looks weird today, and you said this shirt looks dumb."

"I didn't say dumb. I said it's an interesting choice." Lily squinted at Violet.

"Those are the same thing, buttface." Violet shoved her with a laugh.

Jack pointed between them. "You should film this. You two are hilarious."

"Fantastic idea," Lily said quickly, lightning striking again. "But not me, you two."

"Me?" Jack looked down at the running gear he had on. "My shirt also looks like an interesting choice today."

"Oh my gosh, I'm going home to change." Violet spun around.

He caught her shoulders. "No, no, no. You look casual and lovely. Here, I've got an idea. You don't know what to do with your hands, so why not use a prop? Show *me* what to fix instead of telling the camera. I'll just be charming set decoration."

"Yes!" Lily jumped up and down with giddy excitement. "This is even better than I imagined. Go grab one of those string of pearl succulents from the display."

"Okay," Violet whined. She grabbed a small fern-like succulent with tiny round balls down the vines.

"And you're going to tell these viewers what?" Jack asked.

"How to remediate a fungal rot within the root system," Violet said as if it was nothing.

Jack nodded with feigned confidence. "Excellent. I don't know what any of those words mean."

"You're gonna do great." Lily tossed a Bloom t-shirt at him.

He removed his running shirt and threw on the t-shirt as Lily wolf-whistled at him.

Violet wouldn't meet his eyes, and her face flushed pink once he settled his shirt. *Fucking adorable.*

Jack realized the lighting would look a little harsh in the video, given the overhead lights in the store. "Lily, might I make a suggestion?"

"If it's you taking your shirt off in slow motion, I can guarantee our views will go through the roof."

"Lily," Violet threatened.

She smirked at Violet. "What? It's for the business."

Jack scanned the room. "Do you have some large sheets of paper? Preferably white."

"Uh, yeah. We have a couple of big pieces of white poster board."

"Excellent. I want you to position them here and here." He motioned to either side of the phone. "It'll bounce the natural light into our faces." His mother would kill him if he was poorly lit.

"Let me go grab them." Lily jogged to the back of the store.

"I'm so s..." Violet winced, remembering her promise. "... sarsaparilla."

He chuckled. "Saying a different word and meaning sorry doesn't count."

"It's a loophole." Violet stamped her foot with a smile. "I didn't mean to get you roped into this."

"This will be fun. I can fulfill my part of our deal by getting you more comfortable in front of people, and I get to learn about some sort of jewelry-based plant."

"String of pearls is actually a succulent with small pearl-like leaves."

"Save that for the video," Lily said, jogging back. As Lily was getting everything set up, three customers walked in.

"We're going to be filming, but feel free to stop us at any time," Violet said helpfully.

One woman leaned over to whisper to the other and pointed at him. *Shit.*

"Do you want to be our audience?" he asked, hoping to use his charm for the better.

"Audience?" Violet gasped.

"Sure. More practice for you being the center of attention. Plus, three people is small compared to online. How many people will see this, Lily?"

Lily fiddled with the settings on her phone. "I mean, hopefully, fifty thousand, but currently our organic traffic is only around ten thousand."

"Oh my god." Violet's face blanched, and she put her head between her knees.

"Don't worry about them. Talk to me, okay?" He crouched beside her and rubbed his hand on her back. "You're going to explain this to me, plain and simple. You'll help me understand, and I already think you're adorable."

She looked pale but turned to look at him with those pleading, cartoon princess eyes that knocked the wind out of him. Her knuckles were white, gripping the table leg. "Adorable?"

"*So* adorable. A baby deer would sell a hoof to be *half* as darling as you."

"Oh no. Poor baby deer," She pouted her lower lip.

His thumb came up to trace the line of it. *Just selling the relationship.* "See? Just keep your eyes on me. They'll love you."

Like I do.

Panic seized his entire body.

What.

What the fuck.

Where had that come from? *You've barely known this woman for three weeks, you maniac.*

He pushed the panic out of his head. "Ready?" He squeezed her hand and pulled her up.

As they got going, Violet started to warm up. It only took her three takes not to go blank with panic when saying *Plant Mom Mondays.*

"And I have a very special guest, Jack Grant."

"The resident plant non-expert. I'm here to ask all the dumb questions you're too afraid to." He wiggled his eyebrows and comically winked at the camera. The three ladies watching in the store tittered.

"So, Violet," he said, teeing her up. "What is a string of pearls, and can I get it for my mum's next birthday?"

She laughed, her eyes connecting with his. A jolt of lust shot through him again, like when he'd kissed her in front of the restaurant and had to coach himself to stop.

"If your mom is weird like me, then maybe."

"You don't strike me as weird, Violet." He smirked, enjoying their banter.

"Oh, but I am, Jack. I definitely give off Weird Plant Mom vibes, and they are immaculate," she said directly into the camera as a joke with Lily, but everyone in the store laughed. "One of our followers commented that her string of pearls has root rot. Let's see how to remove it so she doesn't have further damage."

Violet spoke to Jack and occasionally to Lily behind the camera as she explained efficiently and helpfully how to deal with something that sounded disgusting.

Lily made a wrap-it-up motion, and Violet signed off.

"I'm Violet, your local plant mom."

"And I'm Jack, your local plant dummy. Great job, plant mom." He threw an arm around her, squeezing her to him. He was so proud of her.

"Thanks. See you next Monday," Violet said, her eyes locked with his. It would be easy to get lost in her emerald eyes, but he pulled his focus back to the camera and gave a quick wave. Shay would be ecstatic for another opportunity to showcase their wholesome relationship.

"And we're done," Lily said, and a smattering of applause sounded throughout the store. They'd gathered a few more watchers, including Rose, who stood beaming at the counter.

"I can smell the sales." Rose walked over with a happy smile. "Bloom's phone has been ringing non-stop since your relationship went public. Maybe we'll be able to pay off Dad's tax debt even sooner."

"I'm glad. Positive reactions on my front, as well." Jack put his arm around Violet and squeezed her. "You did great today, darling. Or should I call you sausage? Or muffin?"

"Darling is fine," Violet said, nervously tucking her hair behind her ears.

"Oh my gosh, we are such fans," one of the customers exclaimed. "Could I get a selfie?"

"It would be my pleasure." He squeezed Violet before he broke away.

He already missed not having her in his arms, but he needed to protect her from himself.

Before his heart got further entangled.

VIOLET

"AND JACK IS OFFICIALLY A PLANT DADDY!" Lily called over the noise of the party as she read off comments from their followers.

The sun was setting over the rolling hills of Gray's flower farm, and barbecue guests milled around the large patio.

"Plant *daddy*?" Jack chuckled, taken aback.

Thank you, internet, for the perfect name, Violet thought as she refilled the ice in the drink cooler. Jack *was* a plant daddy, all elegance, rounded muscles, and warmth that could turn hot at any moment.

The Plant Mom video went viral a week ago, and online sales had poured in. They'd already sold a truckload of *Weird Plant Mom Vibes* t-shirts on their website, and Bloom's phone rang non-stop for potential partnerships.

All three of them had cried when Rose hit send on the last payment for their dad's back taxes. They decided to celebrate like he would have: inviting the whole town to a barbecue at Gray and Rose's house.

There was a weightlessness in the air as laughter flitted through the yard. Like a yoke had been lifted off of Violet's shoulders.

It felt like *anything* was possible.

Violet stood a little taller. *And I helped make that happen.*

The comments under the video were mostly kind. A lot had mentioned how she and Jack couldn't take their eyes off each other. She'd watched it countless times, wishing it was real.

Hoping it was real.

He'd kept to himself and spent more time with Gray since the video went viral. It felt like he was avoiding being alone with her, and she'd only seen him a few times in the last week. That morning, he'd looked tortured when he said goodbye, but his eyes had drifted to her lips, she was sure of it.

Maybe she'd done something wrong?

It was hard for her brain to process being flirty in front of others and then remember that they weren't really together later.

But here they were in front of a large crowd, being couple-y again. Rose insisted Violet come in her trendiest summer outfit so they could take more fake dating photos for all of their social accounts, and Jack's hands had lingered on her bare shoulders all evening.

Shay had convinced her to try a flirty off-the-shoulder cropped top and high-waisted linen pants that flowed like water over her legs. Violet loved how they cinched in at her waist, curved around her hips and gave her legs plenty of room. The warmth of his large hand felt delicious against her bare skin, and she was grateful she'd been brave enough to try the crop top.

People meandered on the deck overlooking Gray's farm, carrying plates of coleslaw and hot dogs.

Violet did what she normally did at parties and busied herself. She cleaned up plates and put covers over casseroles to save them from bugs. It was easier if she cared for everyone else. She was out of the spotlight but wasn't left out.

"My girlfriend has abandoned me for potato salad droppings." Jack put his hand on her lower back.

"Come on. I insist you not play hostess when it's not your house." He tugged her hand toward the outdoor dining table that had been beautifully decorated.

"But I was helping." Her eyes still lingered on an uncovered plate of cake she'd brought.

He squeezed her hand with a warm smile. "You're allowed to enjoy yourself, my darling. Plus, it's time for our photo shoot. Meant to tell you Shay is over the fucking moon with all the press coverage. You are her new favorite human."

"More than you?"

"Definitely more than me." He laughed, eyes bright. "It's you, Dolly Parton, every single Spice Girl, then me."

"All right, plant parents. Showtime!" Lily balanced a large glass of white wine in one hand and her phone in the other.

"Oh, I should go check my makeup." Violet stood up, but Jack gripped her hand.

"Nonsense." He tugged her down to sit.

"But my lipstick's fallen off from eating."

"Where we're going, we don't need lipstick." He winked at her and gave her a chaste kiss. "You ready, Lily?"

Lily started setting up her shot, fussing with the table decor in front of them.

They decided to forego Gray's fancy camera for a more low-key, casual photos for social media. Just a normal couple caught by their friends in a *totally-not-staged-at-all* private moment.

Violet stretched her arms as they waited for Lily.

"Sore?" Jack asked. He'd spent most of the day inside, working on an audition for a new show.

Violet rolled her neck. "Yeah, I got up super early to make up for all the lost time in the greenhouse."

"You can't make the plants grow faster." His hand traced a lazy circle on her back, and it started a throbbing somewhere deep inside her.

She was having a hard time concentrating. "N-no, I can't," she stuttered. "But we have a lot of online orders to process."

"All right, look at me." Lily took a photo, looking at the light. "Oh, shoot. Hold on." She went back to rearranging the table in front of them. He extended his arm behind Violet's chair. The warmth of his skin glowed against her back.

"Why don't I help you tomorrow?" Jack offered.

"Oh, you couldn't do that." She shoved her hair, hating the idea of inconveniencing him.

His fingers playfully pushed the hair out of her eyes, his thumb lingering on her cheek. "Sure I can. I helped my dad every summer growing up. He had impossibly high standards in his vegetable garden. His courgettes, er, zucchinis you'd call them here, have placed first at the county fair for the last twenty years."

"No way." A delighted laugh bubbled out of her, picturing him in the garden.

He threw a hand over his heart. "I wouldn't lie about something as serious as the Devon County Fair. Has a whole wall of ribbons. He's quite proud."

"I cannot handle the adorableness." She giggled with him, imagining an older version of Jack holding up a prized zucchini.

"All done." Lily stashed her phone in her pocket. "I'll edit these tonight and upload tomorrow. Do you want me to send some to Shay?"

"What?" Violet was taken out of her dreamy Jack-filled bubble and looked at Lily. "I thought you were going to take photos?"

"I did. You guys were being fucking adorable, and photos were taken. Check mark. Done. The end. I'm gonna go eat some pie."

"Oh, not the buttercream. It has eggs," Violet called as Lily walked away.

Lily threw a thumbs up over her head.

"You made multiple types of pie?" Jack asked.

"She's vegan, so I wanted to make sure she's included."

"God." His jaw ticked as he stared at her mouth, and his hand claimed her jaw and brought her face towards him.

His mouth met hers briefly but lingered over her as his nose nuzzled her. She adored the scent that was manly and cedar-y and just...him.

She nuzzled him back. *For the cameras, for everybody else.* But she stole one more tiny kiss just for herself.

"I'm sorry we haven't spent much time together the last few days. I wanted to ask..." He paused and thought, biting his lip in concentration.

His eyes connected with hers, and she felt something shift. As if he was hiding something.

He stood up. "Actually, I want a drink. Can I grab you anything? And no, it's not an imposition," he said sternly, already cutting off her preemptive argument.

"White wine," she said with a shy smile.

"Good." He nodded with a proud smile and walked inside.

She looked around at the empty patio and realized they'd been the only ones out there.

No cameras. No one else.

What the heck did that mean?

Chapter Thirteen

JACK

Jack washed his hands in Gray's powder room and chuckled. He and Violet were doing a bang-up job passing themselves off as a real couple at this party.

The thought of Violet's soft shoulders and full breasts in her flirty outfit made his cock twitch as he dried his hands. *It's no hardship being her fake boyfriend, that's for damn sure.*

He wrenched open the door and jumped in surprise as he nearly ran into two people.

Hand on his chest, he stopped nose-to-nose with a scowling Gray and Gray's enormous friend, Nash. "Bloody hell, Roberts. You scared me."

"That was my goal." Gray turned Jack around by the shoulders and pushed him back into the bathroom. The two tall men walked in behind him.

Jack looked over his shoulder with a smirk. "The fuck are you doing? Need me to hold your hand while you take a piss?"

Gray rolled his eyes over his shoulder at Nash. "See? Such

a smart-ass. He knows, by the way." Gray threw a thumb at the enormous man behind him. "The whole fake dating thing. I told him so he understood why I might need to toss you on your ass."

Nash looked like a wall of muscle who'd earned an MBA, but somehow not in a douchey way. He stuck out a hand. "It's a weird place to meet somebody, but nice to meet you finally. I've heard stories."

Utterly confused, Jack shook his hand with a half-smile. "Cheers. You the muscle of this ambush?"

Nash crossed his large arms. The motherfucker was 6'5" if he was an inch. "I am when it's to protect our girl, Vi."

Gray leaned on the sink with his arms crossed, his anger simmering at Jack. "You said you'd keep your hands off of her. You were all over her outside."

He *had* to keep touching her so no one at the party would be suspicious. Right?

Jack glanced to the doorway as partygoers walked past. He lowered his voice. "We need to be believable. I'm *supposed* to touch her."

Gray's eyes narrowed. "Not like that, you fuckin' don't."

He didn't realize Gray had such a soft spot for her. "Why do you care so much? She's a grown woman."

"Violet is the nicest person I know and she rarely dates. *You* have a new flavor every week. I love you, man," Gray said, rubbing a hand down his jaw, "but come on. You're not exactly known for keeping a woman's feelings front and center."

"Hey," Jack said sharply, taking umbrage. "Women know the deal. I don't string them along. It's all consensual, just like this is. Violet understands it's all fake."

Though the word *fake* was getting harder and harder to say.

Nash widened his stance, settling in. "I've known her since we were in diapers. She hasn't dated much, and when she did...well, she didn't look as happy as she did out there with you. We're...worried she might get her heart broken. By you." Nash took a step forward and Jack stepped back instinctively. "What exactly are your intentions?"

Christ, this was not what he signed up for.

They should protect me *from* her. He hadn't had a good night's sleep since he'd slept in her bed.

"I respect Violet," Jack said, throwing his arms wide. "She's an adult and smart and knows what she's doing. How many more times can I say it's consensual?"

"Yeah, but you won't hurt her, right?" Nash said, taking a step closer, his voice more menacing. "I need to hear you say you won't hurt her."

"Jack! There you are." The spritely voice of Lily sounded behind Nash as she peeked her head from around his arms. "Move, you big oaf." She shoved Nash as she walked around him.

"Why are you guys all in the bathroom? Oh my gosh, did you all get your period? Now our cycles will be synced," Lily said with a smirk.

"We were just warning Jack not to break Violet's heart," Gray offered, still glaring at him.

"Hmm." Lily turned, her eyes suddenly full of bloodlust. "Wait, I like this game."

Shit. Violet was sweet and angelic, but her sisters were downright terrifying.

Lily angled an eyebrow. "You did look awfully chummy

out there." She turned to Gray. "Did you tell him she doesn't date much?"

Nash stepped closer to Lily. "We told him—"

"I wasn't asking you," she said testily up at Nash.

Jack slid a glance at Gray, who shrugged, unsure what was up between the two of them.

"How long are you going to be mad at me?" Nash asked her.

"I said I'm not talking to you," Lily said quickly, turning back to Jack. "So what 'promises,' exactly, are you going to make to Violet? And how will you keep her safe and happy and protected?"

"I know I have a reputation, but Violet is different."

"Damn right, she is." Lily crossed her arms with a proud smirk.

"And I'd never do anything to hurt her," Jack added.

Nash leaned his arm against the wall. "But if you do—"

"You'll wish you stayed in fucking Canada," Gray interrupted with a menacing tone.

He looked at the wall of mismatched people in front of him: Lily, tiny and bloodthirsty; Gray, menacing and hulking with tattoos up and down his arms; and Nash, the all-American guy who looked only too happy to break a couple of legs if needed.

"I see we're having a conference." A sultry voice sounded from the doorway, and all three parted for the most terrifying creature of all: a threatening older sister.

Rose sauntered in. Never breaking eye contact with Jack, she closed the door and locked it.

Oh fuck.

"I noticed things were looking very *cozy* out there," Rose said quietly, walking slowly toward him.

This bloody powder room was starting to feel like a sardine tin. Could he climb out the window behind him? It was a two-story fall, but it had to be better than being cornered by Rose and her three henchmen.

He gulped. "I'm just trying to make her happy."

"Hmm." Rose's mouth was curved in a smile, though her eyes threatened murder. "I'd hate for you to lead her on. To play with those deep, earnest feelings of hers."

She tapped her fingers on her crossed arms, her blood-red nails feeling like a threat.

"I would never do that. Gray knows I prize loyalty above all else," Jack said.

He hated that they didn't think about Violet as an intelligent, competent woman who could make her own decisions. "I have full faith in Violet and her ability to kick me to the curb when she's done with me."

A slight satisfaction glimmered through Rose's eyes. "Good, because"—she took a step closer to him, her cat-like eyes narrowing—"if you hurt my *peach* of a sister—the softest, sweetest, kindest person we know—I will destroy everything you've ever loved, and then I will reach down your throat, pull out your intestines, and punch you in the balls with them. 'Kay?" Rose looked a little *too* happy describing the torture.

He gulped.

"Okay," he said quietly, his stomach turning. Without another word, she turned around, unlocked the bathroom door, and walked out.

He blew out a breath. "Jesus fucking Christ."

"She's great, isn't she?" Gray said, smiling. "God, I love her." He chuckled and walked out the bathroom door after punching Jack on the shoulder.

Jack got out of the bathroom as fast as humanly possible. That'd be the last time he'd let himself get cornered by this crew.

~

THE NEXT AFTERNOON, Violet appeared in her greenhouse with enormous bags of mulch on either shoulder.

"Oh my god, let me help you with that." Jack rushed to her. He'd insisted on helping her catch up.

While staying on his best behavior after being roughed up by her protectors last night, obviously.

She shook her head. "It's fine. I do this all the time."

"That's got to be at least 40 pounds each." He knew guys at the gym who couldn't do that.

She threw them down and shrugged. "Comes with the territory. Also means I don't have to pay for a gym. Win-win."

So that's how she'd gotten her solid arms and sculpted back he'd admired yesterday.

"Well, I can grab the next two," he said, hoping he could carry them as well as her.

"You don't have to do that." She shrugged, looking guilty, as if his help would be too much.

He'd practically had to force her to let him help. "Violet, I swear if you tell me to go inside again—"

"Sausages!" she called over from the back of the green-house, and his lips twitched with humor.

He brought several bags of mulch and dirt into the greenhouse. No wonder Violet had been sore yesterday. He'd fire his trainer and be a gardener instead when he went back to filming.

"How's your audition going?" She picked out dead leaves from the plants, ready to go into Bloom.

"Ah, the self-tape. It was fine. I haven't done one in a long time, so most of my takes were absolute shite. This character is far removed from Lord Eagleton." He started picking out leaves too. His father had taught him that, as far as gardening was concerned, don't wait to be asked. See what needed to be done and do it until told otherwise. "The character I'm auditioning for oozes possessiveness. Supremely alpha male."

"Oooh," Violet cooed, shimmying her shoulders. She was wearing overalls, but given the intense afternoon heat, she only wore a sports bra with a low scoop neck under it, revealing the vast expanse of her breasts.

He found it difficult to concentrate on the leaves at hand. He licked his lips, pushing indecent thoughts out of his head.

"Oof, let's go outside. It's too stuffy in here." She grabbed tools from the box in the back of her greenhouse, including a knee pad and some work gloves. She started weeding the rows of philodendrons and fiddle leaf fig trees she'd planted in the half-acre between her pond and greenhouse.

"Did you ever find your glasses?" he asked, thinking back to the night he first *really* saw her.

"They're lost to the pond forever. My old pair is super scratched, and I keep meaning to order replacements, but I've been so busy."

"You don't like contacts?" He pulled weeds out of the rows of dirt.

"My face feels so naked without glasses. I like being able to hide these cheeks." She pointed to the two crab apple-sized circles that had been regularly tinged with pink blushes the last few weeks.

He'd dreamt of what kissing her on each one would feel like.

Lick them, bite them, *anything*. It's like she was taunting him.

"Your cheeks are perfection."

Violet wrestled with the weeds in front of her. "This plant would be perfection if it wasn't trying to be choked right now." She tugged hard with both hands, and a large root finally emerged, throwing dirt over her.

Dirt clods landed in her cleavage and all down her over-alls. "Oh, shoot. I'm such a klutz." She took off her gloves and unhooked her overall front to dump out the dirt.

"Let me get you a rag." He stood up to go to the green-house, but then she did the damnedest thing: she reached inside her considerable cleavage to clear out the dirt.

Maybe he'd fantasized about her for too long. Maybe he needed to get laid.

But as he walked away, he couldn't take his eyes off her manhandling her tits.

He imagined what it would be like if he was the one reaching in to help. What her breasts would feel like as they overflowed out of his hands. The sweet fullness he'd kill to feel on his face, on his cock. Anywhere she'd let him touch her.

He couldn't take his eyes off her as he walked across the yard.

Suddenly, a sharp pain blasted through his head, and he went flying down to the ground. Had a rogue cricket bat clobbered him out of the blue? As everything went dark, he registered the tree limb above his face in a blur.

He woke up a few seconds later with Violet hunched over him, her overalls unhooked and draped down her front.

She looked so pretty, but her face was full of worry. "Oh my god, are you okay? What happened?"

"I, um." He had difficulty looking away from her enormous, delectable tits over his face.

He'd knocked himself out cold, walking into a goddamn tree, admiring them. "I think I need to go to the, um...." He grasped for the name. "The place. The place with the people in the coats."

"The what?" Violet gently put her hand on his head.

"Ow!" He sucked in a breath at the sting. "The place with the people. With the things around their necks." He mimed the thing that was just out of his reach. *What was it called? Where they helped you get better?*

"Oh my gosh. Of course, you need to go to the ER. Here, can you stand?"

"Yes, I'm not an invalid," he said, pushing himself up too quickly and then thinking better of it as the ground shifted under him.

He grasped onto her and hoped his hands had landed in the appropriate places. His other hand found the tree branch above him, which hung precariously low. "It's all your fault," he grumbled.

"Who, me?" she asked, putting her arm around him as they walked to her truck.

He clutched his pounding head. "No, that bloody apple tree."

Chapter Fourteen

VIOLET

Later that night, after a thorough exam and dose of extra strength Tylenol, Violet led Jack up the stairs of her cottage.

The doctor had cleared Jack to sleep for a few hours, but he couldn't sleep alone without someone checking on him.

"I'm cutting that tree branch down first thing tomorrow," Violet said. She felt terrible that he got hurt while helping her.

He groaned as she pulled him up the staircase, her arm around his waist.

Violet set him down on his bed. "I'll come back in a few hours and check on you."

He flopped back on the bed. "I don't know what the big deal is." He curled into a ball, his face in a grimace.

"You have a huge concussion." Violet yanked off his shoes and started to take his belt off but thought better of it.

He rubbed his head and mumbled into the pillow. "If you're going to wake me every two hours, you better have a scandalous fact ready. Otherwise, I'll toss this pillow at your head."

Violet smiled. This head injury-drunk version of him was a new side she hadn't expected. She crouched down beside the bed to meet his hazy eyes. "Need anything else?" She pushed hair out of his face.

"That'll be all." His mouth met hers in a slow, melting kiss that simmered down to her toes. Her eyes were open, trying to understand what was happening.

His nose nuzzled hers, tracing the length of it as he placed a slow kiss on the side of her mouth. "Wait." He pulled back, looking confused.

She was stunned into silence, her heart beating somewhere outside her body.

He scratched his head. "We don't need to pretend now, right?"

"No." Violet bit her lip to keep from smiling at his scrunched face and tousled hair.

"Well." He flopped down in bed and closed his eyes, "I wanted to do it anyway."

Her mouth hanging open in surprise, Violet shut his door behind her.

Don't get your hopes up. It's just the concussion. And you know he's the biggest flirt.

But...still.

Maybe there's a kernel of truth somewhere deep down.

She smiled to herself, dancing in the hallway.

He wanted it anyway.

After two hours of trying to think about anything other than the man who wanted to kiss her in her guest room, she came back to check on it.

He didn't stir when she came in the room.

"Jack," she whispered, gently pushing him awake. "You need to wake up."

He snuffled and snorted. "I was having the most brilliant dream." He put his hands over his eyes, rubbing them. "I was in a fairy cottage, and the sexiest little fairy came in."

He opened his eyes. "Oh, it's you. The sexy fairy."

Violet burst out laughing, trying to ignore how that comment lit her up from the inside.

She smoothed her hand over his hair before she straightened. He was so unfairly adorable, all sleep-addled and cozy. "Okay, well. You're alive, so you can go back to sleep I guess."

"Don't go." He grabbed her hand as she pulled away. His voice was low and scratchy with sleep. "Todd misses you. He doesn't like it when you're gone."

Violet looked over to Todd's cat bed in the window. He hadn't even bothered to stir when she came in.

Warmth in Jack's eyes made her want to melt as she looked at him in the waning evening light.

She smiled, squeezing his hand. "*Todd* misses me, huh?" Be still her mushy heart.

"Very much. He says it's lonely and sad when you're not here." Jack pulled her down so she sat on the bed next to him. "Todd isn't usually quite so needy. But when he has a head injury, it's hard not to be." He rubbed his hand over his temples.

Poor guy. Maybe she could help. This whole thing was her fault.

"Still have a headache?" She rubbed his temples, hoping to ease the pain.

"Oh lord," he groaned in ecstasy.

A shiver went down her spine at his guttural moan of pleasure.

"Please keep going until we both die of old age." He opened one eye to glare at her. "And where's my scintillating fact?"

Dang. She hoped he'd forget. "Umm...I love cinnamon sugar donuts."

"Bullshit," he said quickly. "Funner than that."

She snorted.

She thought back to *Todd* wanting her to stay and what Jack had said after he'd kissed her.

I wanted to do it anyway.

She bit her lip, hedging her bets. "You're my first fake boyfriend."

"You're rubbish at this game." He grabbed her hand at his temple and rolled over, taking her arm with him, and tucking it around his waist.

She took the hint and crawled into bed beside him, the big spoon to his little. Her arm draped over his chest, and their hands interlaced on the other side as her fingers entwined with his.

Heat radiated from his body, and she had to physically restrain herself from nuzzling her face into his back.

"Try again," he murmured.

"I've never been the big spoon before?" she offered.

He snorted. "Someday, you can be the little one when I feel better."

"I didn't have this on my want-to-try list."

"Want-to-try list?" Jack turned to look over his shoulder and made blurry eye contact with her in the dark room.

Violet stilled, realizing what she'd said without thinking.

"What's a want-to-try list?" He asked.

Shoot.

"You know." She bit her lip from nerves. "For the things you've never done in bed and—oh god. I can't believe I'm telling you this." She buried her face in the mattress.

He moved onto his back. "Now, *this* is a fun fact worth getting up for," he said slowly, a smile in his voice. His thumb stroked her hand. "I need to see this want-to-try list."

"Absolutely not," she said firmly, her face still in the mattress. She'd die of embarrassment first. Just get him to go back to sleep. "You need to rest."

He yawned as if on cue. "Ugh, only because I can't keep my eyes open. To be continued." He turned back on his side and tucked her arm under his tightly, and she scooted closer to nuzzle his back.

She let herself wallow in his dreamy, male scent intermixed with her fabric softener. It was an intoxicating perfume, but she reminded herself it wasn't permanent.

This was a fun happenstance to keep him safe because he didn't feel good. Just cuddling.

She set a two-hour timer on her phone and willed her body to fall asleep, even as every nerve ending screamed this was the craziest dream come true.

A foghorn alarm blared in her ears two hours later, waking her. She shut it off as Jack groaned.

"You okay?" she said, rubbing her eyes.

His hands cradled his forehead. "I need another dosage of Paracetamol."

"We call it Tylenol here, and you know it." Violet smirked as she poked his side.

He chuckled. "But you still love to hear me say it, don't you?"

"Maybe." She rolled her eyes. She shouldn't have admitted to being such an Anglophile last week over their nightly pot of decaf tea.

She wandered into the guest bathroom and found the large bottle of extra-strength Tylenol. She filled a glass of water and handed both to him, even putting the pills in a small paper cup.

"You are an excellent bedside nurse." He sat up and threw back the pills. "Now, I have been mauled by a throbbing headache for the last 30 minutes. The only thing that's kept me from not downing a bottle of gin or jumping out that window"—he rubbed his head—"is knowing what's on your want-to-try list. Couldn't fall asleep after you told me."

Violet's face burned with embarrassment.

This was a lose-lose scenario. She couldn't say anything too vanilla because then she'd be desperately uncool, and she couldn't say anything too crazy because he'd run for the hills.

"I don't know." She stood at the bedroom door.

"Come sit." He pointed to the empty side of the bed.

"But I was going to let you rest."

"You can't leave me. I am injured." He coughed.

Her lips quirked. "I thought it was your head."

He put a hand to his heart and pulled a forlorn expression. "Heads don't make sounds. Remember, *your* tree injured me. Spilling all your sexual fantasies on this list is the *least* you can do."

Violet let out a bark of laughter. He got comfortable

under the covers and pulled back the coverlet for her, inviting her in.

It's only one night. Just until he feels better.

Violet slid under the covers and avoided his eyes. "I can barely talk about sex, let alone tell you about *fantasies.*"

He turned to her, nuzzled into his pillow. He closed his eyes. "I was a theatre major at university." His voice was low and intimate in the small space between them. "I have heard, seen, or done everything. You cannot shock me."

Hadn't she wanted to be brave and bold only a few days ago? Where had that gone?

Violet wasn't a virgin, exactly. She had experience, but not a lot, and not recently. Certainly not as much as a publicized playboy like him.

She didn't usually enjoy sex with another person. Thoughts of what she looked like and being the perfect girlfriend always swirled in her head. It was hard to let loose and focus on herself, the pleasure of it all. She'd only rounded a few bases and hit a home run to say she'd done it.

Her want-to-try list was long and scandalous by comparison.

She looked back at him, and his eyes were closed, but his thumb stroked her hand.

"We are waiting," he mumbled, half-asleep.

Be brave. He was well on his way to sleep anyway. "You might have been a theatre major in college, but I've been a romance reader since high school."

He pulled her closer, wrapping an arm around her so she nuzzled into the nook of his chest. Every single nerve ending was awake, and goosebumps trailed down her arms.

This was exactly what she'd dreamed of. What she'd craved.

"And?" he whispered groggily.

Be bold. "Which means my want-to-try list is more of a want-to-try notebook. If I've read it, it's...it's probably on the list," she admitted, her heart racing.

A beat of silence hung between them, and she thought maybe he'd fallen asleep.

"Fucking hell," he slowly groaned. "As soon as the ice pick stops hitting my brain, we're going through that notebook. Line by fucking line."

He nuzzled her head and let out a big sigh, settling down for the night. Violet was frozen solid, trying to process what he'd just said.

A minute later, she heard his gentle snores and let herself wiggle with the excitement and absolute nerve-wracking realization that maybe...just maybe...he meant it.

JACK

AFTER SEVERAL DAYS OF REST, the pounding in Jack's head finally faded away.

He'd scarcely seen Violet between her volunteer work, Bloom, and her garden. He and Todd had lain low, snacking on all the bits and bobs she'd left him in the kitchen.

He still hadn't admitted he was so distracted by the mere *possibility* of her breasts that he'd knocked himself out cold.

He thought back to their last conversation. He was *sure* he hadn't hallucinated her incredibly sexy want-to-try list.

He'd fantasized non-stop for the last 72 hours, imagining what was on it. Imagining them completing it together.

This was dangerous. It was getting harder to keep her in the wholesome fake girlfriend box.

The things he imagined on that list were the furthest *thing* from wholesome.

He finally felt well enough to wrestle with the second self-tape he'd yet to submit. The mafia show producers had a new script they'd wanted him to try. He remembered why he loathed auditioning: he was rubbish at it.

Jack meandered downstairs, needing a break before trying again.

Violet was in the living room in her overstuffed chair, comically propped up with an industrial-sized can of coffee underneath one arm, another pillow at her back, and what looked like a giant stuffed teddy bear under her other arm.

He felt that jolt of happiness at seeing her face for the first time in two days.

"Oh, hello! I didn't know you were home," she said brightly, looking up from her laptop.

Her sunny smile hit him right in the stomach. She was so fucking genuine. So kind.

And based on her pinched eyebrows, looked to be in some sort of pain. "Is everything okay?"

"Oh, yeah. My back was spasming," she said nonchalantly as if it was normal.

He peered over her screen and saw the words 'Apple Festival Email Campaign.' "Perhaps because you're working too much."

"Oh no, it's fine." She shrugged, returning to her typing. "This happens all the time."

She worked nonstop in her garden, at Bloom, and he'd heard her talk about three different volunteer committees. "Your body is literally telling you to slow down, Violet. You deserve rest."

"But I told Jennifer I would have this to her today." She shoved at her hair in frustration.

As if her time wasn't the most precious thing in the world. As if *she* wasn't the most precious thing and should be protected at all costs.

"The she-demon can be disappointed. Here, let me help you."

"The heartthrob of a romance TV show is going to organize the end-of-summer Apple Festival?" She shot a sarcastic eyebrow up at him.

He much preferred this side of her versus the woman who hadn't been able to look at him a few weeks ago.

"Of course not. I don't know the first thing about apples," he joked. "Never eaten one on principle."

She threw her head back and giggled. There was that same tinkling, fairy-like sound that had haunted his first concussion dream.

And oh, how he'd dreamt.

"Let me help you with your back." He lifted the laptop from her hands and pulled her up to stand as she groaned.

"I might suggest using a cart instead of hauling 40 pounds of dirt on your shoulders."

"I'm fine. Honestly," she said, even as she stumbled forward.

"You are most certainly *not* fine. You conscripted that teddy bear into your servitude."

She rolled her eyes with a smile. "He's used to it."

His mouth quirked as he guided her to the couch. "Now lie down."

She grumbled but lay face down on the couch. "I should book time with Nick, Aaron's husband. He was a massage therapist and sometimes still does it for friends."

He perched next to her hip on the deep couch and placed his hands on her back. "But then I wouldn't get to do this."

"You wouldn't *have* to do this," she murmured into the pillow.

He grew more irritated with each second. She rarely accepted help; she wouldn't believe what he said. "Violet, I choose my words very carefully." His voice was stern, and she looked over her shoulder to see him. "I am not in the habit of lying. Aside from this whole fake dating thing. It never occurs to me to lie to people I care about."

"You care about me?" she said slowly, her eyes meeting his.

His heart couldn't take it. She was absolutely too sweet. "Of *course* I care about you. You take care of everyone. I need you to take care of yourself too."

"I'm sorry," she said reflexively, her eyes downcast.

"Well, now you've done it," he said, tongue in cheek with a comically arched eyebrow. "You said the forbidden word."

She laughed and shook her head as she lay back down. "I think I can handle whatever punishment I get for that."

The scent of her shampoo teased his nose, beckoning him for more.

"Your punishment..." As he leaned over her, staring at the plump curve of her ass, his hold on his restraint broke. "...is to tell me your list of things you want to try."

She went very still.

"You...you remember that?"

He smoothed a hand over both shoulder blades. "Of course. I was concussed, not blackout drunk. Now, where does it hurt?"

"Um..." She paused. "In my shoulders."

His thumbs dug into tense, knotted muscles. "Right here?"

"Holy shit," she moaned from the depth of her soul.

His cock instantly went hard. He wouldn't be able to stand for two weeks if she kept moaning under him like that.

He kept rubbing her muscles anyway, digging into her shoulder blades to make her feel better. "This pressure okay?"

"Yes," she sighed out the word, drawing it out in pleasure.

Fuck me; this is a brainless idea. But he had to keep going.

Needed to hear her moan at *least* one more time.

The work shirt she had on was rough under his fingers. He'd noticed Violet's skin was sensitive. Even the barest scrape would leave a mark.

"Is the fabric hurting your skin?"

"Um, it's not too bad," she said hesitantly.

"You could take it off," he offered. *Please say yes.*

She looked over her shoulder, her voice barely a whisper. "I don't have a tank top underneath."

Jackpot. "A bra is no different than a swimsuit top, right?"

They were both adults, and she was currently in pain. He was just helping, right?

She rolled her tongue over her lip, thinking for a second, and sat up. He wanted a taste of that tongue again. Would kill to see her tits.

She turned her back to him as she unbuttoned her shirt.

The back of her work shirt slid down her shoulders and revealed the lacy straps of another bra that would haunt his thoughts. The shirt lay down around her elbows, and he moved his hands along her shoulder blades, feeling her warm, velvet-soft skin.

Her back was to him, and as her head lolled to the side, he had a picture-perfect view of the breasts he'd fantasized about since the last time he saw them.

The curve of them pressed against the coral-colored lacy bra, nearly spilling out at the edge. Her breasts slowly moved with each press of his thumbs into her shoulders. Just like he'd pictured every night stroking his cock since the apple tree incident.

He licked his lips, needing them in his mouth on a molecular level.

Fuck my promises.

I'll happily get knocked on my ass by Gray for a taste of her.

His lips grazed her nape as his thumbs worked in the muscles of her back. She leaned back against him and gasped as he found a knot in her shoulder blades. What he'd give to hear that gasp again.

And again.

"I have a confession," he murmured, kissing her neck with a whisper-soft touch. Her cloud of lavender and jasmine was bewitching him.

"Mmm?" Her eyes were closed, enjoying the massage. She leaned into him, arching her back, and he'd remember this view until the day he died. Heaven-sent full breasts spilling out over lacy cups, beckoning to him.

"I've fantasized about you, about this, since I saw you

last." He placed a kiss along her shoulder blades and felt her still.

Those big emerald eyes locked with his in surprise. "This? With me?"

He nudged one bra strap down onto the roundness of her arm. "This. Especially with you."

Nuzzling her neck, he slid the other strap down. She relaxed under his hands, sighing into him, and goosebumps covered her skin under his touch.

"But you don't"—she whimpered as he kissed a spot on her neck—"date people."

"So we keep this no strings. I'm an *expert* at no strings." His tongue darted out for a taste of her, soothing a spot he'd nipped with his teeth as he made his way along her shoulder. "We still sleep in separate rooms, still pretend to date for the cameras, but work through your list."

That fucking list. He had to know what was on it.

She bit her lip, thinking as he turned her to face him.

He leaned an arm over her, boxing her into the arm of the couch. He ran his lips over her earlobe and heard her suck in a breath. She tasted like lavender and need. One of her hands grabbed the edge of his t-shirt, tugging him closer.

Yes.

"Have you ever prioritized your pleasure, Violet? Just had fun with someone you trust?" He kissed his way down her neck, and she sighed against him, her head leaning on his.

His mouth moved to the tops of her breasts, pressing hot, slow kisses to them. Hands tangled in his hair as she held him close. This was it. He'd hit the lottery.

His hands framed her waist as he fanned kisses across her breasts.

His hand found her nipple over her bra and tweaked it.

She cried out in pleasure. "I don't usually enjoy being"—another swipe on her nipple with his thumb had her gasping—"with someone else. Too intimidating."

"But you like this? With me?"

"Yes," she sighed, nails digging into his hair, urging him on. "Especially with you. Easier with no strings."

He licked the deep crevice between her breasts and thought he might come in his pants right here.

He pulled away and leaned over her. "So we'll have no-strings fun until I go back home. On one condition."

Her eyes were wide and dark with wanting, and her hands fisted in his shirt. He kissed the side of her mouth, leaving a small lick with his tongue, desperate to taste her.

She breathed heavily under him. "Which is?"

He went back to the heaven that was her neck. "You must tell me your top three fantasies on your want-to-try list," he sucked on her earlobe and murmured, "so we can do them."

She shuddered underneath him. *Yes.* He wanted to watch her come so badly.

His hand moved to the button of her jeans, and he leaned back, wanting to see her as he unbuttoned them. "Let's see how bad you are, Violet."

Her eyes locked with his as he slowly slid down her zipper, the metallic sound like a pump to his cock.

Her lace panties matched her bra, and he ran a finger along the top of them. "Your stomach makes me feral. Like a greek goddess, all soft curves." He wanted to see all of her move underneath him. On top of him. Anywhere.

"Not too much?" She gasped as he dipped his fingers under the fabric.

He ground his teeth, looking at the curve of her belly against his hand. "Not by a long shot."

She bit her lip, watching his hand slide into her panties.

"Fuck," he ground out, leaning his head on her shoulder as need buckled him. His hand cupped her tight as his mouth hovered over hers. "These are soaked through, Violet. So fucking hot."

Her mouth finally found his, breaking the dam of need between them. His tongue met hers as they devoured each other, and his finger circled her throbbing, soaked clit. He felt like his soul was being lifted from his body at the sweet sensation of her under his fingers.

She threw her head back, panting, enjoying his torturous circles.

"You want me to suck your nipples, don't you, minx?" He would give every penny he owned to take her into his mouth. Feel her. Taste her.

"Yes." She reached behind her to take off her bra.

Good girl.

"Christ," he moaned as she pulled the fabric away. Her heavy tits stood proudly, the mouth-watering hard nipples he'd dreamed of called his name.

He could die a happy man tonight.

He circled her dripping clit. "Look at how hard your nipples are, Violet. You want to be sucked so badly, don't you?"

"Yes," she gasped. She gripped his head and moved it to her breast.

His tongue licked one nipple, but he paused, a wicked grin on his face, knowing this was *just* the beginning.

"Then tell me, Violet. What are we going to check off?"

JACK

Violet's hands flew to her face as Jack slid his finger inside her pussy and crooked it. She arched her back, tits in the air and cried out with a needy sob.

Fucking hell, she was hot. He sucked a hard nipple into his mouth, moaning.

Don't come. Not yet. He pressed his face into her tits and sucked hard as she moaned, raking her nails up through his hair for more.

"Tell me, Violet," he teased as he moved to the other one. "I want three of your naughtiest fantasies. C'mon. Scandalize me."

She bit her lip, lust in her eyes. He wanted her to trust him with this. Trust him to make her feel so good.

He slid another finger inside of her. God, what would she taste like? Decadent, he'd bet.

"Sex," she panted, "in public."

Holy fuck, she's perfectly wicked.

Just like me.

He rewarded her with a slow circle around her clit, her hips thrusting against him.

Interesting. She hated people looking at her, yet she wanted to be taken where someone might see her. He had an inkling of what she might be into.

"You want to get caught doing something so bad?"

She moaned and nodded, her pussy gripping his fingers. Her dripping down his hand was all he could think about.

"Being fucked in public where someone might catch you. You *are* very bad. But good news"—he sucked hard on her nipple, in heaven—"so am I."

He wanted to live here. Die here. Violet's tits were the end and the beginning of his need.

"So bad," she sighed, and her nails ran through his hair as he sucked her nipple, savoring it.

"And number two," he said, licking his way to the other breast. He sucked hard on her other nipple, feeling it pebble under his tongue.

Her hands held his arms tight, squeezing his biceps. "It's embarrassing," she admitted breathlessly. She bit her bottom lip and he *needed* it.

He kissed her, sucking her plush lip into his mouth. Everything about this woman was so soft. So perfect. So fuckable.

He thought of his cock thrusting between her lips and groaned. God, he hoped she had that on her list.

He broke away, his voice low and hoarse with desire. "Violet, the things I want to do to you are unspeakable. Tell me."

Her hips pulsed again under him as he stroked her. "I...I want to sit on someone's face."

He pinched her clit, and she cried out.

"Good fucking girl," he ground out.

He'd be first in line. She could ride him until he died of hunger. They'd set a world record. He tugged on his cock, needing relief from just thinking about it.

"And the last one?" He circled her clit again, faster, needing more from her.

She cried out as she built to orgasm, throwing her head back and grabbing both breasts. They spilled out over the top of her hands.

She rocked against his hand, her tits jiggling with every bounce. He'd build a fucking monument to them, they were so perfect.

"It's so bad," she whispered.

Mmmm fuck yes. "Good, be my little minx and be so fucking bad for me." He paused his hand in her dripping panties. "You won't be allowed to come until I know just how bad you are."

"I..." she started, and he circled her clit as a reward. She drew a line between her breasts. "I want you, here and then..." She gasped as he flicked her clit.

His hips thrust involuntarily at the thought of fucking her tits, and loved making her gasp out her fantasies. "You want what, minx? My mouth? My cock?"

Her pussy gripped his fingers as his words. God, she'd be so tight for him.

"Your...cock, and..." She panted.

He leaned forward, whispering in her ear, heart thudding in his chest. "And then what, Violet?"

In a quiet, breathy voice, she whispered, "You come on my face."

"Fuck," he groaned as lust made his hips thrust at the idea of coming all over her pretty face. He rubbed her clit as fast as he could. She deserved the best fucking orgasm for that mental picture. He wanted to claim her with his spend, painting it on her body and marking her as his.

She screamed, throwing her head back and pulsing her hips against him, bucking wildly. Yes, fuck. He loved watching her take what she wanted. What she deserved.

Violet writhed, grabbing all of the pleasure of her orgasm, and pulled him to her as she reached for his cock. "I want you," she panted. "Want this."

Look at his little vixen, taking what she wanted.

He stood, a challenge in his eyes. "Then take it out."

She bit her lip, cheeks rosy from her orgasm. She practically glowed. Her fingers fumbled at the band of his athletic shorts, pulling his boxer briefs down with it. His cock sprung free, and she sucked in a breath, staring at it.

"You see how hard you make me?" he ground out. He palmed his cock, giving himself the hard pumps he'd been craving.

Her wide eyes, heavy with wanting, took him in, and she nodded in surprise. That perfect mouth in a little O for him.

"What will you do with this cock now that it's yours, Violet? Do we get to check off that very naughty item on your list?" He dragged a thumb across her bottom lip.

He leaned over her, and her curious hand caressed his cock, making it twitch.

She licked her lips but hesitated. "You don't mind?"

So sweet, his Violet. His sly smile captured her mouth, soothing away worries as his tongue glided over hers. He pulled back and held her gaze. "I'd sell my eternal soul, without question, to come all over your pretty face while you finger your pussy."

His fingers toyed with her nipple. And her eyes rolled in the back of her head.

"Where do you want my cock, vixen? In your hands? Your mouth? Right here?" He traced a line between her breasts. God, he hoped she said the last one.

She nodded, her hand over her face in embarrassment.

"I need your words, Violet." His hand came to her cheek, wanting to soothe her.

Then fuck her.

"Please," she whispered, grabbing her breasts, "right here."

He leaned down to nuzzle her neck, sensing she might be overwhelmed but still into it. "I'm going to put this cock between the two most perfect tits I've ever seen and fuck them."

She panted as he tweaked her nipple again and nodded. "It's so bad."

He licked her breasts, getting her ready for him. If there was an afterlife, he hoped his would be right between Violet's tits. He nuzzled in, letting himself linger on her soft skin for a moment.

He stood up and pulled her to the edge of the couch. "You're my perfect little minx, aren't you?"

She nodded with such a happy, sexy smile that his heart cracked in two. He'd give her exactly what she wanted. Everything he could give her.

He tipped her chin up to him. "Which is why you're going to put your hand into your panties and make yourself come again for me."

She surprised him by putting her hand down her panties but then taking it out and spreading her wetness on his cock.

He pulsed unexpectedly in her hand. "Fuck me," he cursed. He gathered his breath, and a slow, teasing smile played on her lips.

Maybe she *was* a minx in disguise. A siren sent to destroy his self-control and bewitch his cock.

As he held her perfect huge tits together and sunk his cock between them, slick with her wetness, he thought there'd never been a better idea in the *fucking universe* than fake dating Violet Parker.

Her hand was in her panties, rubbing as she looked up at him, lip caught in her teeth. He wouldn't be able to last much longer.

"God, you are perfection." He pumped his cock in the slick valley between her breasts as he kneaded them, thumbs flicking her nipples. It was an impossibly delicious sight as he held them. Moving in and out, pumping against her. "I've dreamed of doing this every night since I saw you dripping in that pond."

Her eyes closed, and she sobbed, nearing climax as the head of his cock popped in and out between her tits.

"Rub that wet, needy pussy for me, Violet. Show me how you come when you're so bad."

She arched her back, wanting more, and he pumped harder, his leaking tip making a slick runway for his cock.

"Come on my face, Jack," she whispered, her eyes pleading as her hand rubbed her clit. "Please."

That one sweet word did him in. A curl in the base of his spine clawed at him, and he palmed his cock as he leaned over her on the couch, shooting cum in hot wet spurts over her face as she came against her hand, crying out. He thrust into his hand again and again, needing every last bit of his spend on her. They panted and stilled. Her face curled into a smile as it dripped off of her.

The heat of the moment now waning, his hand cupped her precious cheek, and he waited with bated breath for her reaction. "Good?" He wanted to hold her and make her feel so special. So cherished.

She fluttered those ridiculously long eyelashes open, and her tongue darted out to capture a drop of cum along her lip with a cat-like smile. "Perfect."

And he realized 'perfect' was the exact word he'd forever use to describe Violet Parker.

THE NEXT DAY, Jack propped open the door to Bloom as Violet carried in the Venus flytrap they'd use for their next Plant Parent video.

They'd managed to keep the morning fairly awkward-ness-free. When he'd surprised her with pancakes and bacon, one would have thought he'd gifted her the largest diamond he could find.

It irritated him that she seemed unaccustomed to being taken care of.

Sure, her sisters were protective, but protecting some-body and *caring* for them weren't the same.

She'd looked so soft and huggable that morning that he'd tried to take another dip in the want-to-try list, but she'd insisted they didn't have time. He was forced to stare at her beauty as they prepared the table for their next segment.

Violet looked like a summer dream in a pastel flowing dress. It nipped in at her waist with a sweetheart neckline and flowing sleeves. She'd been only too happy to shout, "And it has pockets!" when he'd complimented her this morning, firmly solidifying her place as a treasure to be protected at all costs. Her curls were piled on her head, and she wore a mint-green headband with curls framing her face. She breezed past him, sending him a shy smile.

Visions of what they'd done last night danced in his head.

"What else can I help with, darling?" He liked playing up their relationship because it felt like such a vacation. On the one hand, he was playing a part. On the other hand, what he felt for her was real.

He wanted to make her happy. This connection they had felt otherworldly, like they were cut from the same tea-and-biscuits, cozy-cottage-dream cloth. He hadn't had that in so long. Decades.

Oh god, wait.

Had he *already* fallen for this alluring vision in front of him?

He needed to get a handle on this. Thinking he loved her the other day had just been a slip. Like he loved pancakes, and his friends, and the woman he'd started a casual no-strings sex situation with. He loved them all equally in the exact same way.

Violet turned around, her face beaming. "This Venus flytrap and I are ready to dazzle the internet. You ready?"

Rose stood at the side, tapping away on her phone. "Don't forget. We need to film a second one today. For our new sponsor, who we *all love*." She arched her eyebrow with a meaningful glance at all of them.

"Wait, who's our sponsor?" Violet asked.

"Gardener's growth serum."

"That's not the kind I like." Violet scowled at her sister. She hadn't yet shown her temper, but Jack felt he was likely in for a show.

"Vi, we take the ad sponsorships we can get because they help keep our lights on," Rose said with a chiding tone.

He didn't love her sisters bossing her around. Many things could be said about him: he was a playboy, a flirt, and indecisive, but he was loyal as fuck.

"If she said it's not her favorite, we shouldn't do it," Jack said, drawing his arm around Violet's waist.

Rose scowled at him, unimpressed. "It's not that simple. I said we'd do something for them because they paid us *money*."

"You should have checked with me first." Violet crossed her arms.

Damn right. He was so proud of her and squeezed her side in support.

"Vi," Rose fumed and shoved at her hair.

"I can't put my name on something I don't believe in. I won't help people if I tell them to use a crappy product." Tears threatened Violet's eyes.

His stomach clenched, not wanting her to cry.

Rose looked like she was at her wit's end. "Vi, just do it this one time. I swear I'll ask you in the future."

"I have an idea," Jack said, hoping to be helpful. "How about if I promote it? Violet won't be associated, and I, the local plant dummy, can say, 'Use it and tell me what you think.' It still makes the viewers start a conversation about the brand, right?"

Rose slid her eyes from Jack's hand on Violet's waist with a measured glare. "That would work," she said slowly as if she were saying *fuck you.*

"Work for you, plant mom?" he said, protectively squeezing her shoulder to him.

"Uh... yeah, I guess," she said, dumbfounded.

"Great! Everyone wins."

They decided to shoot that first as Violet got her stuff ready, and Jack felt grateful for all the years of improv classes his mum had made him take.

He spewed out something he hoped was charming and funny about a product he knew nothing about. Shay would throttle him for product endorsements without payment, but this would be a one-time thing. This was only to help his Violet.

His Violet. There was that phrase again. What was coming over him?

Rose watched it back on Lily's phone. "Amazing. Ship it." She went back to typing furiously, head in her phone.

"All right." Jack clapped his hands together after setting the product down. "On to the next. You ready?"

"Hold on, final makeup check!" Lily said, rushing over to powder Vi's nose.

"I think she looks stunning."

"Barrrrf," Lily teased, rolling her eyes at him while primping Violet. Satisfied Violet's lips were sufficiently pouty, she went back behind the camera. "All right, I'm also going to field you some viewer questions."

He grabbed Violet's hand. "I'll be right here."

Violet nodded, blowing out a breath. "On today's show," Violet started with an unsure, shaky voice.

"It's not a show, Vi," Lily reminded her over the running video.

"Oh, right," Violet said, shaking her head. "Sorry."

He cleared his throat and bumped her hip with his.

She rolled her eyes and chuckled.

There, that's better.

"On"—her voice shook—"today's... Plant Parent..." Each word was more challenging than the last.

"Hold on," Lily said, stopping the video on her phone. "Vi, what's the matter?"

"So many people are going to watch this. Before, I thought it would be, like, ten people from Fairwick Falls who would see it. Now it's going to be the whole internet."

"Pretend all of them are naked while watching it," Lily offered.

"Oh my god!" Violet's hands flew to her face in a comical grimace. "That's so much worse!"

Jack burst out laughing at how adorable she was.

"Darling," he said, turning her shoulders to him. "Come on." He gently pulled her hands from her face. "We'll get warmed up. Why don't I do the first intro, and you take it from there? I'm the lovable dummy learning alongside you; it doesn't mean I can't intro. Would that help?"

"Yeah. I think so. What do you think, Lily?"

"Ugh, whatever works. I've gotta make fifty more baby shower centerpieces today. I have carnations practically coming out of my ass," Lily said as she took a long pull from an enormous iced coffee.

He turned to Violet, her emerald eyes hitting him in the

gut with their earnestness. "Remember, we're partners." He leaned in to whisper in her ear. "I won't let you fall."

"My own personal safety net." She beamed up at him.

That's more like it.

They went again.

"Hi, I'm Jack, and this is…"

"Violet," she piped in.

"And we're here today to take another Plant Parent question. What do we have today, plant mom?"

She picked up the piece of paper. "Gidget47 writes, 'I have a Venus fly trap.'"

"Ooh, naughty." He waggled his eyebrows at her and the camera.

She elbowed him, and he bumped her hip, biting back laughter. "Those crafty li'l buggers who eat flies and worms and housecats?"

Violet's eyes lit up with humor. "*Not* cats. They evolved in swamps and ate bugs to get enough nutrients."

He turned to the camera to liven things up. "Ah, like when I came to America and started eating fast food burritos since mushy peas were nowhere to be found."

Violet's eyes had a sparkle to them as she spoke with passion. She was lively and unselfconscious. "Jack, back to the plant. Gidget47 says her Venus flytrap has dropped its traps."

"*Very* naughty," Jack joked, his eyebrows furrowed in mock discipline at Violet.

She flitted the paper up into her face. "Stop being so flirty," she whispered behind the paper.

"We're allowed, darling." He kissed her soundly, and her eyes shone with happiness.

"All right, well. Venus flytraps are tricky." Violet straightened herself up and got down to business. "Since it's summer, the plant isn't dormant where that might be normal. So make sure it's in indirect sunlight and has humid air around it. And it also needs moist but *not* soggy soil. See what I mean? Such a diva." Violet turned to him with an honest expression.

"Should I buy you a Venus flytrap for our three-month anniversary?" Jack said, putting his arm around her. That would match the timeline they'd told the rest of the world.

"Though I love a challenge, they're super hard to take care of, and I don't have time for that kind of commitment."

He put his hand to his heart. "Oof, I'm not worth the commitment."

"Well, you're always worth it," she said, poking him in the chest. "But"—she turned back to the camera—"I wouldn't recommend people get one unless they're experienced plant parents. These are the divas of the plant world, hard to keep alive, hard to grow, and, you know, prone to eating things. Thanks for watching today's Plant Parent Corner—"

"Wait, we have one more reader question about you guys," Lily said, reading from her phone. "About how you met," she said, smirking.

Violet's eyes went panicky.

"Let me tell it." Jack put his arm around Violet's waist. "My friend lives in Fairwick Falls, and in coming back to visit him, I met my Violet. It's a small town, and her beauty sticks out like a rose in a sidewalk crack."

She blushed and shook her head but said nothing.

"Once I worked up the courage to talk to her, I had the

good sense to offer to buy her any plant she wanted if she'd go out with me."

Violet shrugged. "Plants are the way to my heart."

"Your muffins are the way to mine." They shared a heated look as he thought of what they'd done the night before. What they'd do tonight if he were lucky.

Lily cleared her throat to bring them back.

"Right. And once we were together, I fell in love with her laugh, smile, and how she cares for everybody more than they deserve. Definitely more than I deserve. She's thoughtful and kind and gorgeous." His hand had come to her chin and threaded through the side of her hair. He remembered himself; the camera was still on. "And I couldn't be happier. Your turn," he said, jostling her.

She huffed out a laugh. "What he said."

Her eyes hadn't left him, and he knew he wasn't acting. Had she magically become a great actor, too, or if was this starting to slide into something more natural and permanent?

"Wrap it up, Romeo," Lily called.

Shit. Right.

"That's all from your local plant dummy—"

"Don't you mean plant daddy?" Violet said with a teasing smirk.

He pointed at Violet. "And local plant mom." They threw a wave at the camera.

Chapter Sixteen

VIOLET

"And cut!" Lily yelled. "Nice job."

Violet let out a big breath, feeling like three gigantic weights were taken off her shoulders.

She'd dreaded the second Plant Mom video because it might not live up to the first one.

But with Jack's help, she'd gotten lost in trying to help someone care for the demanding little Venus flytrap. Jack had been right there, being her safety net, ensuring she wouldn't falter too much.

"Oh, fuck," Jack muttered as he looked down at his phone.

"Is everything okay? Do you need to go?" She felt terrible—she'd already taken so much of his time.

"No, no. It's fine. It's Shay." He turned his phone to her.

PR GODDESS

Where are all the photos of you two on dates???

I demand pics of pure, wholesome fun. Wayridge still isn't returning my calls.

I require small-town festivals. Dogs, babies. Something!

You need to be America's goddamn sweethearts.

"Any clue on how to be America's goddamn sweethearts?" He smirked, leaning on the table in front of Violet.

Violet wracked her brain. "There's an ice cream festival today in Elliottsville. It's about forty minutes away. We can get some shots there."

"Ice cream with my favorite girl? That's all you had to say."

She allowed herself to lean up and kiss him on the cheek. She desperately wanted to ask *What were they? What did this all mean?* But she decided to be grateful for the no-strings fun and becoming more confident in front of people.

An hour later, they were stepping out into the crunchy, dry summer heat of the confusingly named 'Saturday Sundae' ice cream festival.

Each table around the Elliottsville square had crazier flavors than the last. Espresso and lemon ice cream from the coffee shop, pickle ice cream sponsored by the local grocer, beer ice cream from the microbrewery, and even flavors named after classic books in front of the bookstore.

They tasted samples from nearly every vendor. Violet had felt self-conscious and thought she'd get only one, but Jack had insisted they stuff themselves.

Violet tugged on his hand toward the bookshop. "Let's

stop at the book table. I want to try Sense and Sensibility and Snickerdoodles."

Jack looked down at the menu. "I might try the erotica flavor, Hot and Bothered."

"Cayenne pepper ice cream?" She pulled a face at him. "Are you out of your mind?"

"When else will I get to have Cayenne ice cream?"

"You can't have my Snickerdoodle if yours tastes terrible. Look, mine has a 'Dashwood' of cinnamon and nutmeg." She elbowed him at the pun, and he beamed down at her.

The breeze ruffled his hair, and she pressed a kiss to his cheek. She wanted to enjoy each moment they'd have together. She hadn't had this much fun in so long.

Well, not since the night before, when they'd done unspeakable things together.

"Oh my gosh, it's them! I'm so sorry to bother you. Can we take a photo?" Two young women dressed for a fabulous weekend in matching 'Saturday Sundae' t-shirts stopped them in the street.

"Want me to take your photo?" Violet said, pointing to Jack and the two of them. It was her thing. She loved taking photos of other people on special occasions. She liked being part of their moment, especially because she was behind the camera.

"Oh no, I meant with you," the woman said. "You're the plant mom girl, right?"

They know who I am? "You want *my* picture?" Violet asked in confusion.

"I'm officially obsessed with your store. I've already ordered one of the shirts." The girl's sunny smile hit Violet with a shock of happiness.

"Wow," Violet said, dazed by the realization. "I mean, sure, happy to grab a photo." She was too surprised to be nervous.

One of the girls was plus-sized like her, and it wasn't lost on Violet that she'd ordered the t-shirt. She tried to shove down all her emotions roiling around while she struck a quick pose.

"Thanks so much!" the girl said as they walked away and waved.

She dug into her Sense and Sensibility and Snickerdoodle with a tiny tasting spoon, processing everything.

She hadn't wanted to freak out even a little.

"How does it feel to be famous?" Jack took his first bite of Hot and Bothered.

She savored the ice cream as she processed. "Good. Weird. A tiny part of me still thinks they were maybe making fun of me, but I didn't faint, so that's progress."

"Fucking hell," Jack said. His eyes bulged out of his head, and he stuck his tongue out like he was breathing fire. "How can ice cream set my mouth on fire?"

"Too hot for you, huh? Here." She laughed and shoved her ice cream at him.

"No, no," he said, taking a bill out of his pocket, throwing a twenty at the table, grabbing the nearest ice-cold bottle of water, and chugging it. "That was quite hot, and I am terribly bothered."

"It's disappointing to know you can't handle your erotica," she said, licking melted ice cream from her hand. She wrapped an arm around his waist, remembering she had an excuse to act all couple-y.

"Hmm, just you wait," he said, squeezing her waist back.

They spent the next 30 minutes going through the festival and getting various pictures together. Violet's favorites were where he would lean down to kiss her and insist they take a few more to try different angles.

She had to keep her head on straight, or she'd completely lose track of the 'no strings' part of their arrangement.

After the seventh or eighth take in front of an ice cream truck, she decided either she was a terrible photographer, or he was interested in more than photos.

Jack looked at his watch with surprise as they walked to the car, his arm wrapped around her waist. "Oh man, I didn't realize what time it was."

Violet panicked, trying to remember if they were supposed to be somewhere. "What time is it?"

He looked down at her with a wicked grin and whispered in her ear.

"It's face-sitting o'clock."

VIOLET THREW the front door open, Jack's mouth never leaving hers as they stumbled over the threshold. He kicked the door closed as his hands dove into her hair.

"Thought of this all fucking day. Especially"—he moved to lick her neck—"when you had ice cream dripping down your chin."

Violet's pussy clenched, thinking of what they'd done last night. How free she'd been with him. She felt safe with him, and she wanted him to wreck her.

Sex her into oblivion while he still could.

She'd squirmed on the car ride home as he'd described what he'd do to her in excruciating detail.

She'd heard he was a playboy, a flirt, but she hadn't expected he'd be so freaking *good* at it.

His hand traveled under her skirt as his teeth raked her bottom lip. She clenched her pussy, already dreaming about what it would feel like to have his tongue right there.

He walked her backward into the dining room. "How about right here?" He asked between kisses.

She panicked. Her front windows didn't have curtains. "Not private enough. And I should shower. I'm sweaty," she panted. She wanted to be flawless for him.

His mouth caught hers with a growl as his hand dove into her panties.

God, that feels so good. She craved him, and her hips moved against him, needing friction.

She was so wet already from his thirty-minute narration, and he took his hand back out and slowly sucked his fingers. "But I like the taste of you just like this."

Holy hell, this man.

I'll be a walking puddle if he doesn't stop.

"Give me ten minutes," she begged, edging toward the stairs.

"You get ten minutes, little vixen," he relented, stepping back and panting. "Not a minute more."

After the fastest shower of her life and lotion thrown on her skin, Violet tied her favorite corset with white lace and little flowers. Her breasts looked amazing in it, and she'd even found white thigh-highs that connected with the garters at the bottom. She'd paired it with a matching white lace bikini.

She looked at herself in the mirror. She was about to have one of her fantasies come true, and this outfit was for *her*, not for Jack.

She wanted to feel sexy and confident, and with a shock, she realized she'd done it. She'd piled her curls on her head to avoid getting them wet, and the result looked like she'd already been wrestling with someone in bed.

She looked *wanton*.

And she *liked* it.

She threw her shoulders back, and her lips curled into a seductive smile. *Take up every inch.*

Monstera Albo Variegata was now here, and she was about to bang her dream man. With a wink at herself in the mirror, she opened the door to her bedroom and saw Jack standing beside her bed, holding a worn paperback.

He sucked in a breath and slowly fell to his knees on her rug. "Holy..." His eyes roamed her body. "...God." His hands reached out for her.

Monstera decided she was pleased. She sauntered to him.

"Violet, you look..." His hands ran along the backs of her thighs. "I don't deserve you," he muttered, kissing her thighs.

What would *Monstera* say?

Violet lifted his chin so he'd look at her. "Then earn it."

She licked her lips, and he stood, capturing her mouth.

His tongue danced with hers. She loved his taste, how his beard scratched her cheeks in the best way. What would it feel like between her thighs? She clenched, thinking about what they were going to do.

A vision flashed in her brain of how she'd tried this once

with an ex and how he'd laughed at her. She faltered. Maybe this was a bad idea?

"Are you sure you want to try this?" Her alter ego fell in tatters by the wayside.

"I'm dying to get my tongue on you," he growled, his fingers tracing the underside of her corset.

Her eyes searched his. "But what if I hurt you?"

"If I die, I die." He winked as he bent down to nuzzle her neck. "It's my preferred way to go. But first, I had an idea. A warm-up of sorts."

He reached beside him and held her copy of *Bred by a Royal Duke*, a smutty Regency erotica she'd spent a *lot* of alone time with.

"I see you've enjoyed this one." He pointed to the cracked spine and worn cover.

She bit her lip and nodded, a little embarrassed. "It's surprisingly good."

"I know. It's one of my favorites."

Her eyes flew to his. His sexy smirk was replaced by a shy smile. "And now you know one of my secrets. Now turn to page 187—"

My favorite scene.

"—and lie down so I can finally taste your pussy properly."

She lay on the bed, propped up on her arms with the book in hand, still confused.

He climbed onto the bed between her legs and spread her wide. A shock of need shot straight to her core.

He traced his fingers along the edge of her stockings and kissed her thighs where her garters skimmed them.

"You're going to read that scene again and again until

you come all over my face. Come until you can't take it anymore." His voice was low and needy, with an edge of demand.

Her pussy throbbed, and she just wanted his mouth, his hands, everywhere.

She didn't want Jack Grant, the TV star. She wanted the man she trusted, who would make her feel sexy, cherished, and so damn good.

He kissed her inner thigh, crawling between her legs. "God, I love your scent. It's haunted me all day."

He pressed his face against her panties, nuzzling between her thighs, and groaned. "I'll replace these, I swear." He ripped her panties in two, and his tongue was on her clit through the remnants. She cried out at the wet, writhing pleasure. She'd only done this once before, and she'd felt guilty for asking.

But Jack wanted it. Badly.

His tongue was insistent, expert, as he traced along each edge of her pussy, making her legs tremble.

His hands grabbed her ass, digging his fingers in to give him stability as he ate her with abandon.

She'd never forget the picture as long as she lived: his sandy, windswept hair buried between her thighs, thigh-high stockings on either side of his ears.

The hottest thing she'd ever seen.

He lifted his head and peered up at her. "I don't hear any reading, minx."

Oh crap, right.

His tongue laved lazily around her pussy. She had to bite her cheek to concentrate.

"The Duke laid me at the end of his four-poster bed," Violet

whispered, *"and slowly spread my legs apart so I was exposed to him. I'd never seen my new husband naked, but I knew his cock was engorged."*

Jack spread her legs and bit her clit. She arched back, overwhelmed by the sensation. "More," she cried.

Jack huffed out a happy laugh. "You are a greedy little minx." His tongue started a lazy exploration of each ridge and peak of her pussy, in no hurry.

Violet settled back in her book. *"I swore I'd never be his, not even on our royal wedding night. He only wanted to breed me, nothing more. But seeing his ravenous eyes and the need he barely kept at bay, I admitted I wanted him.*

The Duke growled low in my ear. 'I will make you mine, wife. You will be my mate in every sense of the word.' My nipples pebbled as he pulled me toward the edge of the bed, my head almost hanging off. 'Your scent is intoxicating.' He dove his head into my—"

Violet paused.

Jack smirked up at her. "Go on."

Violet blushed and returned to her book. *"His head dove into m-my...cunt."*

Jack slid his fingers into her pussy, already so wet. She clenched around him on the precipice of her orgasm.

"The Duke's tongue destroyed me. His cock looked so tempting, thick in his trousers above my face. I needed him inside me. I pulled his trousers down, and his enormous cock sprang free. I grasped it above my head and licked it, desperate to make him mine in return."

Jack went back to licking her clit and started humming. Violet's back arched without warning, and she grasped his head, shoving it down harder. "Yes, Jack," she cried.

Jack spread her legs even wider and spread her pussy lips so she could see him suck the tiny nub at her center, pulsing with need for him. "You taste so good, Violet. The best pussy on the bloody planet."

Her inner walls clenched, wanting to claim him like in her book.

"More," he demanded, his head gesturing to the book.

Violet wanted this to last forever. Maybe she'd never come so they could spend eternity with his head between her thighs.

"*The Duke pumped into my mouth as he sucked on my clit. 'My wife loves this cock, doesn't she?'*

'Yes,' I sobbed. I'd always been a good girl. Too good. But now I was being bred by a Duke and loving it. He pulled away from me and moved my hips around to the edge of the bed. Then he flipped me over and pulled my hips up so I was spread and waiting for him."

Jack dipped his fingers in her, and his hand came up to pinch her nipple, now escaped out of her corset. "Fuck yes," he growled. "More, Violet."

"*He slowly thrust inside me, fucking me into the mattress as his finger slipped inside*—Oh god, Jack—*inside...my tight*—"

Violet cried out, Jack's intense sucking on her clit taking her over the edge. She threw the book down and grabbed Jack's head, needing more of him. Blinding pleasure curled her toes as need wrapped and squeezed around her. She pulsed against his mouth, his hands keeping her in place so she could writhe under him. Violet screamed, letting herself experience all of what he gave her.

She came back to herself, pressing her hands against her face. *Holy shit.*

Jack Grant had gone down on her while she read her favorite book.

She had to make him feel good now. Needed to make him so happy.

He kissed her inner thigh and pushed back. "We're not done yet, love," he murmured, grabbing her hands to pull her off the bed.

Love. That's a dangerous pet name.

He tugged her to the edge of the bed. His hand cradled her head as he kissed her. She tasted herself on him unabashedly. *So hot.*

He reached for the bottom of her corset and tugged it down, freeing her breasts. "I need to see them, minx. I need to see them when you sit on my face. Bouncing over me."

It's still my turn? "More?"

"I told you you're going to come again and again until you can't take it. I say what I mean. Don't you want more?"

She bit her lip and felt her pussy throb, still craving and needing attention. *More, more, more,* it pulsed in response. She nodded.

He lay down on the rug beside her bed and tugged her hand down to him. She knelt down, straddling his head, still feeling nervous despite him having spent the better part of fifteen minutes in her pussy.

"More," he demanded and tugged her hips down to his face. "Take what you want."

Violet panted, hovering over his face, and he stared at her with desire. She looked behind her and saw his pants were unbuttoned to free his hard cock, already leaking at the tip. "But what about you?"

She wanted to be fair. To be generous like he was.

"This *is* for me, Violet. You'll see. Now *sit*, minx." His hands came to her thighs, spread them wide, and pulled her down hard to sit on his chest.

She knelt, her ass on his chest and stared down at the impossible sight of his face disappearing into her pussy.

She leaned against the bed, dipped her hips against him, and his tongue came to greet her.

God, that felt so good, taking what she wanted and knowing he'd be there to give it to her.

Not too much. Not too big.

Wanted and desired with a man practically begging her to sit on his face.

Her hand ran through his hair, tugging on it as she moved over him. His arms were tight around her thighs, devouring her as though she were his last meal.

She was so sensitive from her climax a few minutes ago. "I don't know if I can handle it," she said, sobbing from the contact but still wanting more.

"You can take it," he said, leaning up to nip at her clit. "Fuck my face, Violet. And keep reading."

She moved her hips along Jack's face slowly, each pulse so intense.

She grabbed her breast as she took what she wanted. *"The Duke tweaked my nipple. 'I think you can handle a little more, wife.' He came back with a polished jade cock from his dresser and a small decanter of oil."*

Jack swatted her ass, gripping it, and she pulsed her hips against his face. She bounced for him so he could watch her breasts.

He moaned. "Again, minx."

She ground against his face quickly so he could watch

the sway of her breasts. He tightened his grip on her legs, bringing her pussy down harder, and sucked hard.

"*He thrust his cock into me again, covering my exposed cheeks in the warm oil. His finger explored my tight hole. 'You like being taken by me, wife? Being filled in every hole?'*

'More,' I moaned. I felt so naughty, enjoying being bred. He covered the jade cock with oil and slowly pushed it into the tight opening of my ass.

'You'll drip with my seed,' he growled, 'and beg me to fill every hole like this.'"

Violet felt the ropes of desire pulling her toward climax again. She slicked her pussy on Jack's face as she rode him, bouncing. His hand drifted to the spread of her ass and grazed along the valley between her cheeks.

"Is that on your list, minx?" Jack murmured under her.

"Yes," she hissed, feeling so naughty.

"Please, Violet, let me. I want to be the first to take you here."

"Oh *fuck*, yes." She grabbed the bed covers beside her head as she collapsed in pleasure, spread out at his mercy. Jack moved his hand to her pussy, getting his fingers wet. He teased the bud of her ass while his tongue moved over her clit, and Violet clenched her walls, wanting to be filled.

"We're so bad," she whispered as she thrust against his face. He slowly teased the rim of her ass before gently pressing in with his slick finger. She felt exposed and needy, a new craving pulling at her for more of this wicked heaven.

She panted through her cries, rocking against Jack's face harder and harder. She took what she wanted, how she wanted, and being fucked in exactly the right way that felt so perfectly wrong.

"So goddamn perfect," he ground out as she fucked his face, and she climaxed against him, hot impossible pleasure twisted her muscles.

Jack moaned as she screamed, pleasure shooting through her every nerve ending, craving *more more more* until there wasn't another drop to give.

She panted against the bed, sweaty and out of breath.

Finally stilled, she looked back to see he'd come without even touching himself.

His hands had been on her the whole time.

"Holy. Mother. Of god." His breath came in wracking heaves.

She pushed back, giving him space to breathe.

"That was…" She leaned on the bed. "Unbelievable." He still had his finger in her ass, and something about it made her feel so wanton. So sexual, and filthy, and his.

They both caught their breath, and her hand came to his face, covered in her wetness. He looked happy and satiated.

"Good?" she asked.

He blew out a happy laugh and kissed her thigh slowly, nuzzling her. "It's always the quiet ones who are best in bed."

Chapter Seventeen

JACK

"I thought you hadn't played this game," Gray yelled.

He and Jack wrestled with game controllers, staring at the large TV screen in Gray's game room.

"Maybe you're just horrid at it, Roberts." Jack jammed his thumbs at the controller, sneaking up on Gray's character.

The game buzzer sounded. "Ah, fuck," Gray muttered. He tossed his controller to the side. "Want some food?"

"Only if it's a salad. I've been eating too well at Violet's house."

A vision of Violet riding his face the previous week came back to him. He needed to immediately switch gears if he didn't want to get an instant hard-on next to Gray.

Violet had been under the weather from a cold for the last week after their explosive night together. He'd happily waited on her hand and foot, but the list had to wait until she felt better.

He'd been only too happy to have her tucked in his arms most days, falling asleep as he read to her.

"How's it going with the whole situation?" Gray levered

himself up from the couch. Duke, Gray's small mutt, hopped up into the warm place vacated by Gray and insisted on pets from Jack.

Jack got lost in thought, thinking about tucking Violet in last night, her sleepy, happy grin.

How it had been torture to sleep in his own bed. How he'd wanted her desperately that morning, but she'd already left for Bloom to catch up from being out.

"You have the dopiest-ass grin I've ever seen on your face. You know that, right?" Gray eyed him.

"Because your dog loves me," Jack said, scratching Duke behind the ears, causing his tail to blur with happiness.

"Bullshit. You said you'd keep your hands off of her," Gray warned, a steel glint in his voice.

They'd been friends for a long time but had their share of arguments. He'd called Gray out on his shit when he'd started drinking too much, when he was beginning to destroy his life.

When Gray had gotten sober, he'd thanked Jack for not abandoning him when everything went to hell, for sticking by him and fighting for him. So disagreeing was worth it if it protected the ones you loved.

"Have you slept with her?" Gray said bluntly.

Jack rubbed his hand down his face. Jesus. He couldn't lie. "There have been"—he paused—"activities."

"Fuck, man. I told you. She's innocent. She has a heart of solid fucking gold, and gold crushes easily."

"You underestimate her," Jack said, thinking of the gorgeous, stunning woman who writhed in his arms last week and stood up for herself when she disagreed. "She's not some little fragile cupcake princess. She's a grown woman who sets boundaries and consent. We both agreed to no strings attached."

Gray leaned forward. "I've seen how you go through women, and I don't want to see her get hurt. Her dad was one of my best friends, and I told him I'd watch out for her. I also don't want to get castrated by Rose because I introduced the fox into Violet's hen house."

"That I can see as a genuine fear. Rose is *fucking* terrifying."

"Hey." Gray said sharply, with a hint of a smile. "That's my soon-to-be future fiancée,"

Jack sat back, happy to see a smile on his friends face. "I didn't say she wasn't gorgeous and made for you."

The back door opened, and Duke let out a long *awoo.*

"Hey, man." Nash nodded his head at Jack in the universal bro greeting.

Gray had requested an all-day gaming session with the greasiest food Fairwick Falls offered for his birthday. Nash plopped down two enormous pizzas.

"Still want that salad?" Gray restocked the mini fridge in the game room with soda. They'd planned an all-day-long game tournament.

"Eh, I can eat a salad tomorrow," Jack said, holding up a hand as Gray tossed him a cold diet soda.

"How's our Violet?" Nash said, glancing at Jack.

Jack supported Gray's sobriety but thought these conversations went better over a beer. Diet soda didn't pair well with, *yes, I'm trying to fuck your childhood friend every which way I can.*

"I'm fortunate Violet has even deigned to fake date me."

Nash nodded approvingly. "Damn right. She's always

been a sweetheart, though a little too soft-hearted. She gets roped into everything in town."

These were supposedly two men who knew her the best, and yet, how could they get her so wrong? It's like no one had ever *seen* her.

They'd only seen helpful Violet, unobtrusive Violet, not everything she was at her core.

Thoughtful. Smart. A sex kitten who would be the end of his sanity if he didn't fuck her properly soon.

"How's the audition for that thing?" Gray grabbed a slice of gooey, cheesy pizza and held it above his face as it dripped down.

"Shite, but done. I sent it in last week. He's a lot grittier than I usually play. And even if I got the part, my mother still wouldn't be happy."

"Oh, I know all about that," Nash said, somehow eating the drippy cheese pizza with absolute precision. Not a drip or grease stain in sight.

"You've got one, too?"

"Does yours have 'connections' to the 'good wife candidates?'" Nash asked, using his free hand for air quotations.

"Lord, you do have one." Jack nabbed a string of cheese, and he took a bite. "My mother wants me to go back to LA to level up my career."

"I have the 'settle down and have babies' flavor, but same breed, you know?"

"To mothers," Gray said, raising a toast with his soda. Jack and Nash held theirs up. "May their therapy work or may ours."

"I would literally pay my mother to go to therapy," Nash said after chugging his drink. "Hell, I might even settle down, marry, and have babies if she'd go. It would do us all a world of good."

From what Gray had told him, Nash had moved back a few years ago from New York and was the head of the Fairwick Falls Bank. He and Gray had bonded over being the only two unmarried guys under 50, but that would probably end soon with how moony-eyed Gray was.

"What does your mom think of Rose?" Jack asked.

"She's happy I'm happy."

"Lucky," Nash muttered.

Gray shrugged. "Our parents got to live their lives. Now we get to live ours, so they can fucking deal with our choices."

Jack mulled over the utterly foreign thought in his head: doing something that may disappoint the people he cared about most just because it made him happy.

Maybe it was time to take fate into his own hands.

JACK THREW his car into park outside Violet's cottage and sat in the cocoon of cicadas and evening birdsong.

As he'd played four rounds of the game with Gray and Nash, a thought kept itching at the back of his head. The life Nash's mother wanted for him sounded like the *best* thing he'd ever heard.

He'd sworn off relationships because, deep down, he knew it was exactly what he wanted. If he let himself get too close, he'd abandon all his dreams, all the things he'd worked for.

All he wanted was the idyllic, bucolic life he'd had

growing up. A family with no expectations other than love. Having regular kids at a regular school and a wife he was excited to come home to after doing something productive.

What would it be like to trade mothers with Gray? Having a mum who just wanted him to be happy would be nice for a change.

A delivery truck pulled up and dropped off a small package as he sat in the car. *Fuck yes.*

He walked to grab the present he'd found for Violet.

The single light was on in her greenhouse, and he wandered through the decorative hedges toward her. It had been scorching hot that afternoon, so she must be catching up now that it was only oppressively hot rather than deadly.

Violet worked with her hair tied up, only wearing a sports bra and khaki linen shorts. She worked by the light of a battery-powered lamp, propagating more plants.

She looked utterly unbothered, in her element, and he craved her with an animal-like need. He let himself dream for a split second what it would be like to have her as his wife, a mother to his child.

He could imagine coming home to her after a long day of filming, cuddling up with her on a couch. Drinking properly made tea and sinking his teeth into a biscuit.

Into her.

But she was inextricably linked with Fairwick Falls. Practically with the soil underneath his feet. He'd be back in Vancouver within a month. Hopefully, she could handle being the star of the Plant Mom videos by herself.

He thought back to how she had initially struggled with them and a realization hit him like a thunderbolt: she was a *terrible* actress.

Just absolutely the worst.

How had that escaped him until now?

She was fake dating him, yet she was a natural when they were out together. No one ever second-guessed it.

She leaned over to coo at a new plant she'd just settled in its holder, and as he enjoyed the view of her round, heart-shaped ass facing him, reality hit him like a ton of fucking bricks.

Oh fuck, he wasn't acting either. He wanted her.

Badly.

All of her—her heart, her body, her mind. He gulped.

He'd duped *himself* into a relationship. What kind of absolute moron could he be?

It might be time to talk about how *not* fake this entire thing was between them.

"Burning the midnight oil?"

Violet shrieked as he came around the doorway of the greenhouse.

"I'm sorry." He chuckled. "I honestly didn't mean to scare you."

She clasped a hand over her heart. "I'm buying you a bell." She bent over, trying to catch her breath.

The low dip of her sports bra left little to the imagination. Her soft stomach dipped in at her waist, and the linen shorts clung to the curve of her backside. His hands itched for her. "You've had enough work time today. I can help you catch up tomorrow."

"I need a few more hours, and then I should be caught up." She ran her hands through her hair and tugged on her ponytail, causing her curves to sway.

He practically growled. "I'll happily help all day, every

day, as long as I get time with you now, minx. I've craved you with each atom of my being for the last seven days."

Her eyes sparkled at him, even as she glanced at the plants next to her. "But—"

He reached over and turned off the lamp. The bright moonlight came through the old greenhouse windows, dappling her cheeks like a lavender brush stroke.

"Enough," he said.

Enough of all of this.

Enough pretending, enough of dancing around what he wanted and not taking it because he thought it wasn't for him. Because he was afraid of what a relationship might do to his career.

He'd tell her tomorrow this no-strings arrangement had failed.

He'd developed strings.

Feelings.

Needs for her.

Wanted to see her first thing when they got up and see her face before he fell asleep. Wanted to know what crazy new Fairwick Falls volunteer scheme she'd been roped into so he could help her handle it all.

His hands found their rightful place on her waist, and she slid her arms around him as he brought his mouth down to hers. He pressed a long, slow kiss to her plush lips. He wanted to protect her from everything.

Even himself.

Because he was falling for her, and he couldn't stop himself from wanting every bit of her.

It had only taken his brain a month to catch up to what his heart had known the first moment he saw her.

He'd climbed up through that oak tree, enchanted by her chattering to Todd and as soon as she'd turned to face him, he'd lost his breath. A single word had ludicrously flashed in his head, tugging at his gut as she'd stared up at him with those pretty green eyes.

Mine.

"I wanted to do that all day," he murmured. "I missed you this morning."

She laid her head on his chest, nuzzling her face in. "I missed you since last night."

He grasped the inside band of her shorts, popped the top button with his thumb, and leaned forward in her ear.

"You've got a present." He rattled the small box next to him. He tugged her shorts closer to him, his mouth hovering over her lips.

She pulled back with a happy smile. "What's my present?"

His finger fiddled with the elastic of her panties. He wanted to see her out here. Wanted to picture her writhing, coming in the place he'd forever associate with her.

Her greenhouse was tucked back behind her cottage, surrounded by thick trees and the darkness of night. It'd be private enough.

"The Duke's book last week inspired me." His hand cupped her breast as she leaned into him, her nipple already hard in her sports bra. He pinched it, and she sucked in a breath.

He kissed the curve of her shoulder and slowly rolled down her zipper.

"But I'm all sweaty," she said breathlessly.

"Mmm, even better. I love your taste." He licked a salty path up her neck to suck on her earlobe.

She kissed his cheek. "Presents," she whispered, reminding him with a smile.

He handed the box to her, and his stomach danced. He hoped she'd like it.

With his hands still toying with the top of her lace panties, she opened the shipping box and brought out two small objects.

"You got me...lube?" She looked up at him with a surprised laugh, holding up the small bottle.

"Unwrap the other one," he said with warmth, wrapping his arms around her from behind.

She opened the small bag and pulled out a small silicone plug with plant leaves on the end. She sucked in a breath, and her eyes grew wide.

"It sounded like this might be on your list," he murmured into her ear.

She nodded excitedly. "Can a butt plug be adorable?" She turned her smiling eyes to him.

He chuckled as his hands started to slide under her panties. "Everything you do is fucking adorable. It's small to start. Eventually, we can work our way up to what the Duke does."

He turned her around to face him and took the plug. The small cone at the end of it would be just right for teasing her.

He rubbed it over her nipple. "After a week of cold-induced celibacy, I'm half-crazed with need for you. Tell me, minx. What are we checking off tonight?"

Her eyes rolled in the back of her head as he rubbed the plug back and forth over her hardened nipple. "Too many..."

He moved the plug over her panties, dragging it over the fabric to find her clit.

"Umm...too many to try. But it depends," she said, with a sigh.

He rubbed it against her clit, and her hips bucked ever so slightly. *Good girl.* "Depends on?"

Her eyes opened, a smile curving her lips. "If you want to finish in my mouth or in me."

Holy fucking hell.

She always did this. Was always three steps ahead in seducing him. The combination of that dirty mouth and her curved, angelic face with those plush lips meant he was a goner.

Whatever type of woman Violet Parker was, that was his type.

"I've never done either. If you want to try that," she whispered as he circled the plug's end around her clit.

If he wanted to finish in her?

It was all he'd fucking thought about. If she only knew how similar he was to the Duke in last week's story.

"I know you have your list, but I was wondering..." Fuck, he'd never told anyone this before. "I've never been able to trust my one-night stands. Couldn't share this side of myself. And—" He paused. *Shit. Too late, can't back out now.* "I didn't want to scare you, but your books..."

Her eyes were heavy with lust and concern. She licked her lips, staring at his mouth. "You have a list too?"

He bit his tongue, trying to be brave like her. "Like the book you read last week. I...I have a breeding kink." His eyes met hers, gauging her reaction.

She sucked in a breath and bit her lip; her hand had

found the tip of his cock along the zipper of his jeans. Her hands grasped at the button of his pants. His cock had hardened ages ago, but he had to make sure she understood.

He leaned forward and nuzzled her cheek, his hands dipping under her panties. "I'd love to role-play that with you, Violet. My cock filling you up with my cum," he clarified, "but only if you want to, and I know you're on birth control. I was tested before I left, and I'm clear."

"I'm on birth control," she whispered through her pleasure.

His finger never left her pussy, and he circled her clit, causing her to moan. *Mine*, he thought, petting it.

"What do you love about it?" she asked, her eyes closed in pleasure.

Fuck. Of course she'd want to know something so perfectly wicked yet kind.

He couldn't take it anymore and pulled the sports bra over her tits. He turned her around and pressed her into the workbench. The greenhouse glass let in the moonlit night, and he salivated over her shoulder at the view.

He grasped her breasts and pressed her close to him, enjoying the heavy weight of them in his hands. "I love the thrill of it. The fantasy of taking what I want and leaving it all in you. Of fucking you hard and making you mine. Do you want to try that with me, Violet?"

He pinched her nipples, pulling out her tits so he could see them.

"Yes," she groaned. "I love reading breeding kinks because I love doing something bad. Being used and wanted."

He sucked a spot on her neck as his hand dove into her

panties again. The need to claim her was a desperate physical craving inside him. He circled her clit faster. He wanted her dripping and begging for him. "God, I want you so fucking much, minx. I want to come in that tight little pussy and fill you up. Make you mine. Breed you."

"Now," she demanded, her hands in his hair as he nipped her earlobe.

He dug his fingers into her hips, squeezing all the softness there. He'd never wanted to fuck someone so badly.

He grabbed the plug. "I'd love to use this with you." He'd dreamed of seeing her get fucked from each side after she'd read her book. "Do you want to be fucked in two holes tonight, darling?"

She nodded slowly, eyes excited.

"Bend over then, and show me how well you take it."

He bent her over the workbench and pulled her shorts and panties down so they were still on her thighs. "Spread your legs, love."

She was bent over the low table, naked except for the shorts that had hastily been pulled down. They looked so sexy there. Like he'd walked in and taken her, was only there to mate with her.

There was something so filthy about having her naked where anyone could walk in. Where they'd see who she really was. A sexy, greedy girl who he adored.

He loved how her breasts lay against the table, heavy in perfect pools. Her belly was soft and round, and he wanted to squeeze it, cherish it.

He held the small bottle of lube and ran some along his finger, then leaned over her, covering her naked back with his body.

"You want to be bad, don't you, minx? Want to be fucked in any hole I can come in," he whispered in her ear.

"Need you. I want it all," she murmured.

He circled his finger around the tight rim of her ass as his other hand went back to her clit.

Violet moaned as he slowly dipped his lubed finger into her ass, exploring the tight circle of nerve endings.

"More," she sobbed.

"Someday, you'll take my cock right here."

She sucked in a breath. "Yes. Just like that." He moved his finger in further. She let out a moan, and her hand went to her breast. God, he'd come right here if he kept thinking about what it would be like to take her here, feeling her so tight for him.

"You're doing so good. Such a good little minx for me." He lubed the plug.

Any gif, any video on his phone would never compete with her bent over and naked, pushing against him as he nudged the anal plug into her. He watched it sink in slowly past the rim as she cried out his name.

"So full. So good." She bit her lip, and his cock twitched. Her eyes locked with his. "Again."

"That's my girl." He slowly pulled out the plug with one hand while his other continued to tease her clit. She bucked against his hand as he slowly slid it back in past her rim.

"Need you in me," she ground out. Her legs had started to shake from pleasure. "I want to make you feel so good."

"Love, I've nearly come from the sight of you bent over and dripping. You're doing so good. Touch that wet clit for me."

He unbuckled his pants and palmed his cock. It was

already leaking at the tip. She'd been torturing him for fucking ages with her delicious, sweaty body. He kept his pants on, loving how it felt to only undo them a bit. To make it feel like this was wrong and dirty, and he was taking her as fast as he could.

He guided himself to her entrance. The sweet little palm fronds of the plug were visible, and the minute he eased the tip into her tight pussy, he knew he wouldn't last long. The sight of her was too much.

He pushed into her a little more. "Fuck *me*, you're so tight," he cursed. It was like he'd slid home into perfection. Into bliss that was his to claim.

"Yes." She pushed back into him. He slid his cock into her slowly, inch by hard, thick inch.

"Fuck, love. You're so tight," he gasped.

She clenched him harder, and he saw actual stars. He grasped for the table, catching himself before his knees buckled.

Her muscles tensed around his cock, rippling with an orgasm.

"Look at you." He fucked her slowly, gripping her hips as he thrust harder. "Look how well you take this cock. My tight little minx loves being bred, doesn't she? Can't wait to take my load."

She whimpered as he thrust hard into her again. He needed to fuck her, to rut, release into her.

"Yes. Only yours," she whispered.

Oh fuck he pictured her pregnant, her round tits and belly heavy with his baby. Bred and dripping and happy.

He wrapped an arm under her breasts, pulling her back to his chest. He whispered in her ear, voice low and insistent. "You're going to take this cock until your pussy is dripping."

"Please," she gasped as he thrust up harder, his belt jangling. She sighed as he squeezed her tit. "Breed me. Use me."

His other hand squeezed her hip, stuttering in his thrust at how fucking much he wanted that. He was safe with her. Could admit his fantasy out loud.

"You'd love it if I fucked you until you were pregnant, wouldn't you?" he growled in her ear, thrusting up harder, pressing her against the table so her belly pooled against it.

She moaned loudly and he clamped a hand over her mouth. The greenhouse doors were still open.

"Love it if I filled you night after night, until these tits got bigger. This belly"—he slid his hand from her mouth and grasped the curve of perfection under her belly button—"filled out. Pregnant and bred with my baby. Used, claimed."

"Need it," she moaned. She pulled his head down to kiss her. He claimed her mouth, tongue licking inside of her, needing to be in her in every possible way. He toyed with her butt plug, teasing it in and out as he thrust in her.

"So full." She rubbed her clit faster and faster, as he pumped into her, wild with need. Needing to fill her up.

"You can take it." Jack reached down to flick her clit as he slid out. He slammed back in, and her screams of pleasure were muffled by his hand around her mouth. He fucked her harder, and her tits mesmerized him as they bounced. He reached down to grab one, needing it. Needing her.

"You're gonna come for me, aren't you, love? Take every drop?"

She nodded, moaning with those pouty plush lips. He got

one last look at her furiously fingering herself as she bounced against him. His balls tightened, and he couldn't wait to fill her.

Mine, mine, mine. Breed her, claim her. Keep her forever.

He climaxed with a shout, emptying everything into her as she came around his cock. His brain blanked as her pussy rippled around him, milking his cock again and again and again.

He rutted mindlessly, wringing every drop out of his body until finally, *finally* he slowed.

They collapsed on the table and caught their breath, he was still inside her, not wanting to leave. She lay her head on the table with a happy sigh.

He covered her body with his as he wrapped his arms around her, pressing a slow kiss on the velvet skin of her shoulder. Their breath echoed in the quiet greenhouse.

"Jack?"

His cock twitched inside her. Just hearing her voice made him want her more. "Yes, love," he murmured into her neck.

She let out a contented sigh once more. "I'm really glad you read romance novels."

He chuckled against her skin, but *something* inside him clicked into place as he inhaled the jasmine scent of her hair, squeezed her tighter against him. Thought about how this woman was kindest, the sexiest, the most adorable.

Something that had been missing ever since he could remember.

Something that felt...quite permanent.

Chapter Eighteen

VIOLET

"And that's all from us at Plant Parents of Bloom."

Violet felt like she was *vibrating* she felt so good. She'd managed to do most of the talking in this week's video.

She'd only relied on Jack a few times to ask well-placed curious questions and make her laugh to get out of her head. They even had a few people watching in the store, and it didn't bother her. She hadn't frozen or felt like fainting once.

Not even once!

Was this what it felt like to be invincible?

"And...we're done. Thanks all for watching." Lily hit her phone to stop recording and smiled at the small crowd watching in the store, and they politely clapped.

"You did great, darling." Jack kissed her deeply, and that blossom of need and happiness unfurled in her core again, like it always did.

She'd tried to be nonchalant about everything when they'd eaten breakfast this morning and came into Bloom together.

Still, it felt like something was shifting between them. She'd loved exploring her pleasure with no strings, no expectations, no need to be the faultless girlfriend.

But as they'd fixed breakfast, him handing her a spatula, her giving him coffee, she realized they'd fallen into a rhythm she'd desperately miss.

Something that felt like more than a fake relationship and no strings.

He was no longer Jack Grant, the heartthrob of an English countryside soapy romance. Instead, he was Jack Grant, the sexy man who muttered to himself while he did dishes, who was surprisingly commanding in the bedroom and had a deliciously naughty side he didn't trust to show anyone else but her.

After their greenhouse sex last night, he'd walked her to her bedroom. They'd spent ten minutes just kissing before saying goodnight. She'd desperately wanted to sleep next to him. To cuddle up and block out the lonely world.

He'd even started to tell her something before thinking better of it and saying they'd talk later.

Probably for the best because she'd been practically dead on her feet after her first day back *and* being thoroughly taken in her greenhouse.

She found her hand interlaced with his as he talked to Lily about something in the store and asked a question about the video.

"You did so great, Vi." Lily beamed at her.

Her heart melted into mush. "It felt great," she admitted.

"I'll be sorry to go back to my real job after this." Jack squeezed her hand. "It's far more fun to stare at your pretty face than charge across a misty field at 4 am."

"Wouldn't it be fun if Wayridge had a show like this?" Violet mused. "I could help so many people."

Lily clapped her hands. "Ohmygosh. *Beyond the Plant Parent's Walls.*" She and Violet giggled at the ridiculous pairing of historical costumes and houseplants.

Someone walked to the register, and Lily went to help them. "Gotta go make some bank."

Jack turned to Violet, his brows drawn together in a nervous expression. "I know you need to get back to the greenhouse, but could we take a walk outside? I wanted to... talk."

Her stomach dropped. In her limited experience, 'talking' usually spelled disaster.

But he'd been so kind and sweet today. Maybe it was about last night?

"Uh, sure. Let me get my stuff."

As she gathered her bags, Jack pulled out his phone with a surprised look. "Hi, Dad."

Violet loved that he and his father had a great relationship.

It still hurt to think about the loss of her dad. She'd tried to take care of him but failed. He'd had a heart attack when he was sleeping, but maybe if she'd tried harder, fixed him more vegetables, maybe something would have changed.

She'd cried buckets when he passed and worked through most of her big feelings when Rose and Lily lived with her. It had since settled into an ache she wasn't sure would go away.

Maybe she even hoped it wouldn't go away because then she'd never forget him.

"You're here?" Jack said, turning to Violet with panicked

eyes as he tried to piece together what was happening. "In the States? In Fairwick Falls?"

Violet gasped. "He's here?" she whispered.

"Five minutes away from the square in Fairwick Falls. What a pleasant surprise," Jack said slowly as he mouthed *'what the fuck'* to her.

Violet started to panic. Jack's father was here. What did that mean? Would he stay with them? Would he figure out they weren't *really* dating?

"Yes, of course. It's the black front building with the flowers in front. I'll meet you outside." He hung up. "I am *so* sorry." He ran his hands over his face and up through his hair.

Violet's hands framed his cheeks. "It's totally fine. We'll figure this out, okay?"

"It's just that it meant a lot to him that I was dating someone, and happy and...thank you for grounding me." Jack kissed the inside of her wrist.

A zing of desire curled up her arm from that kiss. "He should stay with us," she offered. *Ease his worries, be helpful, and maybe he'll want you as much as you want him.*

"But my stuff's not in your room. It'll be obvious to him that this is all—" Jack glanced to the front window as a car pulled up in front of Bloom. "Fuck, he's outside."

"We'll think of something, okay?"

"Okay." He blew out a breath, gave her a kiss on the cheek, and walked out.

Lily snorted as she walked up, sipping her iced coffee. She leaned over and whispered, "And the plot thickens."

"A nice sister would help me brainstorm," Violet whispered back.

Lily stuck her tongue out. "I prefer to be a mean sister who hopes you'll admit your swoony fake relationship isn't fake at *fucking* all. Consider it payback for me still being single."

"It's his dad. He'll know this is all fake," Violet whined. Lily shushed her as a customer walked by. They moved to the edge of the store.

Lily rolled her eyes as if Violet was overreacting to the most unlikely scenario. "You guys are already a couple anyway. You're all moony-eyed when no one's watching. You like him, he likes you, you're bumping uglies—"

Violet thwacked her shoulder as her face flushed. "Stop it."

"Germinating your seeds, pollinating those stamens," Lily said, grasping for plant metaphors. "Churning his clotted cream," Lily continued as she walked to the cash register to check out Ms. McClotskey, who held a flower arrangement. "Slaggin' him a bit o' your crumpet," she said in a terrible Cockney accent.

"Lily," Violet said sternly as the front door swung open and the bells clanked.

Jack walked in, and an adorable shorter, slope-shouldered man followed him in. He wore a short-sleeve button-up shirt with an honest-to-god bowtie and a newsboy cap with glasses. Violet had an odd sensation of wanting to put him in her pocket.

"Dad, this is my girlfriend, Violet."

Violet put on her sparkliest smile and tried to remember to be brave and bold and channel what her heroes would do. "Hello!" she said with a warm smile. "It's so nice to meet you."

"Gerald Grant," he said in a country British accent that sounded more like *Geruld Grun.*

Squee. He was cute as a button. "I'm excited you're here."

"It's so nice to meet you, miss," he said, shaking her hand warmly with both of his. "I'm pleased as punch my Jack has foun' somebody so charmin'. And your store." He looked around in wonder. "Marvelous, absolutely lush. I feel like I've been flown to Heaven, not America."

"That's so nice." Violet's heart expanded, hoping she was making a good impression. She wasn't an awkward wallflower anymore. She was somebody who could make Jack proud.

They talked about his last-minute flight deal from the UK.

"I insisted he stay with us, love." Jack eyed her with a knowing glance.

"Oh, I'm so thrilled."

"I couldn't trouble ya," his dad said. "I foun' an excellent BnB 'bout an hour away. I can't put you out."

"Don't you want to see Todd?" Violet offered. She could sense a fellow old soul and knew he'd love Todd as much as she did.

He clutched his heart. "Oh, I do love that boy. You know I gave him to Jack as a kitten." Gerald's eyes connected over Violet's shoulder and lit up. "Well, hullo again."

Violet turned to see Lily and Ms. McClotskey walking toward them.

"You found it." Ms. McClotskey had a pretty blush on her cheeks as her eyes locked with Gerald's.

"She was my savin' grace since my GPS wasn't workin'. Gave me directions when I was hopelessly lost on the other side of town. I only got lost once more before findin' my way here." Gerald laughed with Ms. McClotskey, seemingly in their own world.

Ms. McClotskey shook her head as if realizing how she'd been staring. "I'm glad you made it safely. Enjoy your visit. Our Violet here is the absolute sweetest." She put an arm around Violet and squeezed. "I've got to be going."

Gerald stared after her. "Thank you again." He waved with a wistful smile. His eyes followed her out of the store.

"I absolutely insist you stay with us," Violet said, trying to get Gerald's attention. "I love hosting."

Gerald snapped out of his trance. Jack and Violet's eyes connected, humor in them.

"It's true." Lily threw an arm around her shoulder as she waved to another exiting customer. "She put up with my sorry ass for four months before I finally escaped her clutches. I'd still be there if I didn't move out in the dead of night."

"This is my sister, Lily," Violet said, mentally rolling her eyes. She couldn't wait until Lily fell for someone so she could get her back.

"Pleased to meet you," Lily said, grabbing Gerald in a hug. Gerald was surprised but patted her back gingerly.

He was a precious man who seemed nervous to take up any space. Violet wanted to keep him close to her instantly.

"Love," Jack interrupted and touched her elbow. God, she loved that nickname. She wanted to just melt. "While you get to know each other, I'll go home and get Dad's room ready." Violet knew that was code for *get my crap out of my room and put it in yours.*

"Extra sheets are in the linen closet for the second guest bedroom," she said.

He gave her a solid kiss before he left, and she felt those flutters again.

The *maybe this isn't so fake after all* flutters.

"Jack tells me you're a gardener," Violet said, trying to find a point of connection. She and Gerald wandered through her store, and he asked insightful plant questions the entire time.

Once she'd given him a tour of the space, he took in the storeroom with awe. "Jack said you redid the space?"

"Yes, with both my sisters."

"Ah, so you're here to stay, then." Gerald gave her a measured look.

"I love my hometown," Violet said. "I can't imagine living anywhere else. I went away for college and was happy to come back to where everything felt predictable."

Violet checked the clock in the store. It had been twenty minutes since Jack had left, and they could start making their way home. "Ready to see where we live?"

Oof, that '*we*' was an unexpected jolt for her.

Don't get attached, Violet. You promised no strings.

They walked outside to Gerald's rental car. "I had a brief memory lapse of which side of the road was which when I first got in the car, but it's been fun revisiting the States after so many years."

Eek. She should have offered to drive.

"Have you been in the States much?" She hopped in the passenger seat and hoped for the best.

He checked his mirrors and slowly pulled out into the street. "When my ex-wife and I were together, we lived in

California briefly, but it wasn't for me. I prefer the country life in my village where the Grants have been for hundreds of years."

Violet knew she'd found a kindred spirit when she first saw him.

"You know, Jack's never had a girlfriend since he's been out of school," Gerald said out of nowhere.

Uh oh. He thought this was a serious relationship. "Is that why you came to visit?"

"Just wanted to see how he was doin', and how you were treatin' him and he was treatin' you. He wouldn't do something like this unless it was serious."

It's definitely been serious. Serious for the career Jack needed to keep. Serious for her to figure out how to stand in front of people and not faint dead away.

She wasn't sure what to say, so she gave him directions to turn left up ahead. "So, he's never had any other girlfriends?"

"Our Jack is loyal to a fault, and I think he's scarred from his mum. Wouldn't want to leave a family like she left us." He tapped the steering wheel. "But here, look at me talkin' about this. You both seem happy as clams."

"Take a left up here on Wilson," she said, pointing to the stop sign. "And I'm the cottage right here."

"Isn't this a picture? This is all yours?" His eyes grew wide with excitement. "Grand. Just grand."

"It was originally owned by my great-great-grandparents, then my grandparents, and I bought it about ten years ago with my dad's help."

He pulled into the gravel cottage drive and parked. "Is he still aroun' here, your father? I'd luv to meet 'im."

Her stomach dropped. *Oh, no, don't cry in front of this cute little man.* "He, uh, passed about seven months ago."

"Oh. My darlin'," he said, patting her hand. "I am sorry, dearie. I didn't know."

Unexpected emotion clutched at Violet's throat. She usually tried to keep it at bay so she didn't bother anybody else.

"It's fine. It was sudden, but"—Violet sniffed, wiping her eyes that had started streaming tears—"I didn't get to say goodbye, you know?"

She hardly knew this man, and here she was, telling him how she hadn't processed the loss of her dead father. Not exactly prime hostess material. "I'm so sorry for blubbering."

"Oh darlin'. No need to be sorry. It's not a bad thing to be caught missin' someone you luv." He offered her a hankie from his pocket. "But if I may, as a Da meself, there is no such thing as goodbye, you know? The love your da had for you, it's still here, isn't it?" He pointed to the house.

The idea gripped Violet's heart as she considered her dad was still here, in some way. She wiped her eyes with the hankie and nodded.

Gerald laughed to himself, seeing Jack walk out of the cottage. "Me? I'll love Jack until the sun burns out. And probably after that. I guess I hoped...well that he'd never say goodbye to me. That I'd always be there, somehow, with him." He patted her hand and opened the door as Jack approached them. "You'll understand someday."

Violet wiped her eyes, thinking about how her dad might still love her somewhere in the universe. That maybe she'd never had to say goodbye to begin with.

It was a balm on a deep cut she hadn't realized had still been hurting. That maybe she wasn't so alone after all.

She opened the car door and a rogue breeze shoved open the door wide and cooled her cheeks, hot from her tears. She closed her eyes, savoring it and the sound of rustling oak leaves above her. The sound of home.

Violet wiped her eyes as Jack jogged toward them with a bright smile.

"Are those Café au Lait Dahlias you've got there?" Gerald pointed to the enormous, newly blooming peach dahlias in her yard.

"Yes, I planted those this spring. They're Lily's favorite. They're a beast to deal with, but they make her so happy."

"It looks like Kew bloomin' Gardens," he said, taking in all her landscaping. He clapped Jack on the shoulder with a smile. "You undersold her, my boy."

"Oh, I—it's just a hobby now," she babbled, even as pride washed over her. They wandered through the blooming hydrangeas and up to the back door.

"Are you okay?" Jack asked with concern. "You've been crying?"

She wrapped an arm around his waist and squeezed him. "I just really like your dad," she said with a wistful smile.

"This looks like an English country cottage." Gerald beamed. "Now I know why you're so at home here. A beautiful woman, beautiful plants. What more could you need?"

"You haven't had her chocolate chip cookies yet. That's the real clincher." Jack squeezed her as they walked in.

She tried to hold onto the feeling blossoming inside her. The sense of being seen for who you were and still loved for it.

Celebrated for it, even.

Todd trailed down the steps as they came into the kitchen.

"There's my handsome boy," Gerald cooed. There were several minutes of snuggling and leg weaving on Todd's behalf.

"Why don't we get that welcome when we get home?" Jack asked.

Todd let out a simple meow and went back to weaving through Gerald's legs as he leaned down and scratched Todd's head.

"You've made quite a home for yourself, young fella," Gerald said, straightening and clapping a hand on Jack's shoulder. "Now, when exactly am I going to get those grandbabies?"

"Da," Jack warned. "I'm sorry, love. He's one of *those* kinds of parents." He turned to Violet with a comical grimace.

Violet blushed, thinking of what they'd done the night before. She wouldn't mind making grandbabies with Jack Grant one bit.

She might even be first in line to volunteer.

"Do you want kids?" Gerald asked with a hopeful face suddenly, turning to Violet.

"Da, you can't ask people that," Jack said, now stern.

"Just lookin' out for the future strappin' line o' Grants."

"I would love kids," Violet said with a smile. "But there's no rush."

She wanted to give Jack an out and not get his father's hopes up.

A twinge twisted in her heart at the thought of kids with

Jack. She wanted a family but didn't want to do it alone and assumed it'd never happen for her. Finding a partner who would fit so neatly into her life seemed impossible.

She noticed Gerald looked tired. "Can I get you something to drink or start dinner?"

Gerald scratched his head, having a hard time keeping his eyes open. "Just need to get some shut-eye. I've been up a full day."

"Let's get you settled, then."

"You sure I'm not puttin' you out?" Gerald asked, grabbing his carry-on.

"Absolutely not." Violet would have loved to open a bed and breakfast in another lifetime. She wanted to make Gerald's stay as comfortable and convincing as possible.

Caring for others helped her feel more solid, more loved. She'd make sure everyone felt like they belonged since it had been so hard to feel like she ever belonged anywhere at all.

Chapter Nineteen

VIOLET

After settling Gerald in his room, Violet puttered around the house that evening to keep her mind distracted. She could *feel* the ticking clock toward bedtime.

Where she and Jack would sleep in the same bed.

Don't be ridiculous, Violet.

She shook her head at herself as she scrubbed the kitchen. It's not like this was even the first time. They'd accidentally slept in the same bed a few times, but not since lines had become blurry.

Jack was picking up the living room but had stopped to scratch Todd's chin, cooing at him. His hair was disheveled, and he was in a simple t-shirt and shorts, but the fabric on him strained at all her favorite places. The picture of him perfectly at home was too much for her to ignore.

Oh god, she was in love with him.

Didn't it take *months* to fall in love with someone? But no—it had only taken her four measly weeks to fall head over heels for the intoxicating combination that was Jack Grant.

The kind man who helped without complaint, cared without fuss, gave without expectation.

She loved his soul as if it were an extension of herself. The magic ingredient that brightened her life and made it come into focus.

The most impossible, unattainable man who never did relationships. Of *course* that's who she'd fall in love with.

They'd gotten into a rhythm she'd miss when he left. She'd poured a glass of water for him without thinking and handed it to him. He put his hand around her waist and squeezed as he passed her to get to the cabinet. His hand lingered, and she adored that he was always touching her. He did it likely without thinking, but it was still a preview of living life with the person she loved.

"You did a great job today. You seem more confident in front of everyone." His eyes beamed with pride.

"It helped to have a safety net beside me." She *had* felt more confident this time.

She'd been so in the moment, she'd forgotten people were watching while they filmed. If she could concentrate on helping people, the worries about what they thought of her and what she looked like all disappeared.

"Hopefully, the next few will cement your confidence, and you can keep going when I'm gone," he said.

She gulped water and forced a smile. "It won't be the same, but I'll try to make you proud."

"You already make me proud," he said, a slow smile spreading on his lips. "Ready for bed?"

"I'll meet you up there."

She needed a minute to remember what this felt like,

winding down for the night with her guy. It felt like the first bloom of spring, hopeful.

And when she had Jack, she had hope.

She trudged upstairs, and he brushed his teeth in her en suite bathroom.

Piles of his stuff were haphazardly tossed onto her chair. She opened one of her dresser drawers and made room, neatly folding his t-shirts and tucking them in snugly next to hers. She liked seeing them side by side, and ran her hand to smooth his t-shirt there.

"I'm sorry my dad ambushed us," he said from the bathroom.

"Relax, Jack. One more night sleeping next to you won't change me forever," she lied.

Like how kissing you, having your tongue lick my pussy until I screamed, didn't change me. Finding the other part of my soul, unfortunately housed in someone so unattainable to me, hasn't changed every atom in my body.

"Your dad said you talked about me. You told him I was a plant goddess." She met his eyes in the mirror as she walked into the bathroom.

"Because I did. And you are," Jack said as he rubbed in expensive face lotion.

She fiddled with her toothbrush and met his eyes in the mirror. "You don't think it's weird I'm obsessed with it?"

"Violet, I like you as you are. Get it through that thick head of hair of yours." He kissed her cheek and tugged on her ponytail as he walked past.

As I am, she considered. A shiver of happiness went through her.

He sat on the bed and faced the bathroom while she got

ready. "I'm sorry about the nosy comments my dad made." He took off his watch and set it on the bedside table.

"Oh, it's fine. Dads will be dads."

"You don't talk about yours much," he said quietly.

"Still too raw. Too new," she said, starting to wash her face.

"But the part about wanting kids, were you...trying to make my dad happy?" His tone was tenuous, choosing his words carefully.

"I want kids, but I don't think it will ever happen for me." It was her automatic response when someone asked her. Because saying *too late to get my hopes up* made people uncomfortable.

Jack huffed out a laugh. "That's the most ridiculous thing I've ever heard. You'd be a brilliant mum."

A thrill ran through her at his words as she slid into bed beside him. She couldn't let herself fantasize about kids with him. About being a 'mum.' Or she'd never recover. "I don't want to have kids unless I have a partner who's committed to raising them with me. Plus, I know it's old-fashioned, but I want to be married first. Have somebody promise to love all of me."

"He'd be a fortunate man, and you'd be a most excellent mother," Jack said quietly.

As long as he was playing with fire, she might as well play too.

"Have you ever thought about kids?" Violet asked nonchalantly, trailing her finger along the edge of the sheet.

He propped one arm up under his head and faced her. "I'd love kids. If I'm honest with myself, all I've ever wanted was a family."

Her ovaries practically reached out to grab him.

She cocked her head. "But your reputation. You don't even have girlfriends." It didn't make sense.

"Yes, a *playboy*. Who almost got married at 19." He smirked back at her. "My mother explained I'd throw my future away if I saddled myself with a relationship that young. I still don't know if she was right. But I've kept women at arm's length since I tend to fall hard. After I became famous, it was easier to let all the one-night stands have their fantasy of me. Protect myself and not show them who I really am."

"And who you really are...wants a family?" She smiled at the surprise.

His eyes lit up as he dreamed. "Wife and kids, the whole adventuring family going to beaches, zoos, amusement parks. The three or four or five musketeers."

"You'd be a good dad," she admitted, thinking of how he was with Todd. How he'd cared for her when she couldn't see straight from her runny nose and coughing.

His finger hooked around hers. "Yeah?"

"You're thoughtful, loyal, helpful. You jump in and help without being asked, which is every woman's wet dream."

"That's the bare minimum, love." His knuckles ran along her arm as goosebumps appeared.

She'd never get used to that nickname.

"It's rarer than you think, the helping." The few times she'd hung out with her ex's friends, she'd spent most of the time in the kitchen fixing snacks. "It's hard to remember that sometimes. I feel like people might love me more if I do it all."

"They might appreciate you, but you're lovable regardless." His hand left hers and cupped her cheek, tilting her chin to look at him. He placed a gentle, slow kiss on her lips, and she let herself sink into it.

It felt real, and earnest, and dangerous.

"You said at Bloom you wanted to talk about something?" Her eyes searched his.

He hesitated and looked at the clock. "It can wait until tomorrow. We should sleep since I'm sure my father will be up at dawn."

His hand threaded into her hair, and she tilted back to see him. She craved his touch. Would have paid good money for it. For the glimpses she got of it every day.

"Could we cuddle first?" She felt her cheeks pink up. It was desperately hard to ask for what she wanted.

He gathered her into his arms. "I'll cuddle you to the moon and back any time you like."

She nestled into his nook, that perfectly-made spot where his shoulder connected with his considerable chest, and her nose grazed his throat. The pulse of his heartbeat thrummed in front of her, and she thanked her lucky stars she got to be this close to him. To cuddle and sleep together even if he'd never love her back in the same way.

"Tell me about your childhood in England," she asked, wanting to be lulled to sleep in his arms by his melodious voice one more time.

Huge green and white Monstera leaves surrounded Violet as she wandered through an endless warehouse full of plants.

Clouds of mist rolled under her feet, and as she looked down at her hands, she suddenly saw a seat belt.

Violet buckled it into the seat she was now in and looked around; a gray minivan surrounded her. She was in the driver's seat, and beside her in the empty passenger seat sat the "Future Mrs. Eagleton" mug with Jack's face on it. It was full of cold, milky tea sloshing on the seat as she drove.

She looked in the minivan's rearview mirror and saw three empty rows. No children, but—no, the seats weren't empty.

Turning around, she saw the rows were full of dead plants. Broken terracotta pots and soil were tossed along the seats.

The radio turned on as she barreled down the highway, and a chorus chanting, "*No one wants you. No one wants you. No one wants you,*" sounded through the speakers. She fumbled for the radio, but the words got louder and louder as her heart thudded.

She was losing control of the minivan while a deafening chorus of "No one wants you! No one wants you!" reverberated in her bones.

"NO ONE—"

Violet sat up in her bed, panting.

Just a nightmare.

Tears fell onto her cheeks before she even realized she was crying.

Jack was fast asleep beside her, so she quietly slipped out of bed. She crept across the room, avoiding the squeaky floorboard, and walked into her small walk-in closet stuffed with all her new clothes—and all the old ones, too.

This was her comfort closet, where she'd cry when she was little and staying with her grandparents.

She was only seven when her mom had passed, and this quickly became her favorite place to cry silent tears. Hiding in the solitary comfort where she wouldn't bother her grandparents with all her feelings, with all the tears somehow endlessly inside of her.

She slid down the wall as tears fell down her face, and she muffled the sobs wracking her chest. Trying to be quiet.

So, so quiet.

No one wants you echoed in her head.

The nightmare was scary, but the reality was scarier.

The likelihood of finding somebody who wanted to stay in Fairwick Falls was infinitesimal, impossible. No family, no partner.

She'd be alone forever, always watching from the sidelines, always crying in the closet.

A loud sob escaped her mouth, and she slammed her hand over it.

Sheets rustled, and the bed frame creaked. *Oh no.*

She stopped breathing, afraid she'd woken him up. Creeping footsteps came to the closet.

"Violet?" Jack asked, his voice raw and sleepy. He poked his head through the closet door. "Why are you in here?"

She couldn't answer through the sobs. Just shook her head. *He doesn't want you. Just being nice.*

He crouched down and wiped a stream of tears from her face with his thumb. "Oh no, my love. What's wrong?"

She tried to think of a lie to shield herself, but she was too tired.

"No one"—she gasped for breath—"wants me."

"What's this all about?" He sat beside her on a pile of clothes.

"Bad dream," she hiccuped. "And I won't have anybody. You'll go. I'll be alone because"—a sob wracked her body—"no one wants me."

He gathered her up in his arms. She couldn't stop the tears from coming. At least if she was crying in her comfort closet, it was nice to lean on a solid chest.

His hand smoothed her hair, and the weight of his hand felt like torturous perfection.

"Fuck all, this is my fault. I should have been brave sooner," he muttered, rubbing her arms. He kissed the top of her head, and she let herself feel a drop of happiness in the sea of tears.

"What if—" He paused and pulled back so she'd look at him. "What if *I* wanted you?"

She shook her head vigorously. Why couldn't he understand? "Not like that. I want somebody to want my *soul*. I want them to *see* me and still want all of it."

She was at her wit's end. How could he possibly understand? How could anyone that handsome understand no one wanted all of her? All her quirks and needs and oddities. They never did.

"Violet." He lifted her chin to meet his eyes. "I've seen your soul. I saw it the minute I walked into this cottage. You are romantic and caring and kind and stubborn and...a packrat." He gestured to the surrounding closet. She let out a watery laugh.

He pulled her onto his lap and cuddled her against him.

The beating of his heart was a fast drumbeat in her ear against his chest. Violet sniffled, trying to piece this all together.

She couldn't let herself hope this could be true. It would hurt too much if she misread the situation.

His lips brushed against her hair as she heard his heart speed up.

"I know we said no strings," he whispered in a nervous voice, "but I failed miserably. *Weeks* ago. I fear my strings have been hopelessly twined with yours."

Weeks ago?

Was she still dreaming?

"But you're leaving," she said in a watery voice. "Your life is there. I'm here. Forever. It couldn't work."

He smiled slowly, impishly as if he'd caught her with her hand in the cookie jar. "So, I take it...you feel the same way?"

Her eyes widened, surprised it wasn't plainly written on her face.

She stroked his stubbled cheek, having a hard time finding words for all the feelings inside. "I feel everything for you," she whispered, not looking him in the eye. "I can't wait to talk to you at the end of the day, I miss you when you're not around. You've become my favorite person, and this has become my favorite place," she said, putting her hand on his heart. "Right where all my strings are tangled, too."

She finally looked up to meet his eyes, and they held the same look of delicious, romantic torture she felt. "But how?"

He kissed her cheek slowly. "We have four weeks left," he offered. "We could ignore this undeniable connection or make the most of it."

Four weeks. Four weeks to live out her dream of dating, *really* dating, the man she loved.

"Dating. For real." She sniffled. She needed to be crystal clear. So sure they were on the same page.

He squeezed her to him. "It stopped being fake for me the moment I really saw you: the brave, kind, gorgeous woman who confronts her deepest fears to help others. Because my soul feels alive when I'm with you. Because I *want* all of you."

A new burst of tears wracked through her as she leaned into his chest, not wanting to believe this was real.

"Violet Parker," he said into her ear as she nuzzled in the crook of his neck. "Will you be my *not* fake girlfriend?" The smile in his voice had her smiling through her tears.

"I need you to"—she hiccuped—"say that again."

"Be with me. *Actually* date me." He pulled back and looked into her eyes, the mischief dancing in them that she adored.

"Again," she whispered, not taking her eyes off his mouth.

"I want all of you, my greedy little minx," he muttered as his mouth came to hers.

Her heart beat like a kettledrum. She needed to feel every inch of him to make sure this was real. He *wanted* her.

She pulled him down on top of her and stretched out on the closet floor. Wanted to feel the weight of him against her.

His tongue met hers as their kisses grew hungrier, more needy. She wanted him inside her, wanted him everywhere. Her hands skimmed across his muscular back. She tugged his shirt off, needing to feel his skin, the crush of his chest hair against her.

He buried his head in the curve of her neck as he kissed his way down to her breasts. She had the distinct feeling of being worshiped as he so carefully placed each kiss. "I'm sorry this isn't on the list," he murmured against her skin.

She arched into him. "Forget the list."

She pulled back and took off her tank top, her breasts free for him to grab. Needed to feel him against her.

No more pretense, no more armor. Just her body against all six feet of him.

He sucked her nipple into his mouth as he shoved down her silky shorts.

She fumbled with his shorts, needing him naked *yesterday*. "I need you inside me," she whispered urgently.

A growl sounded in his throat as his hands wrapped around her waist like a vise. "God, I've thought of nothing else all day," he said, his voice low.

He clicked the closet door closed with a shove of his foot. He shoved his pants down, his impressive cock finally free, and she palmed it. It was thick and hard like steel, and he hissed as she handled him.

"No more of that, or we'll be done too soon, love." He ranged over her, crawling between her legs as they lay on the floor, grasping for each other.

She loved the heat of his skin against hers. She wanted to tangle their limbs together, twisting together so they'd never be able to leave one another. He placed hot kisses on her neck, down her breastbone.

A small nightlight in the closet highlighted the curves of his muscles as he arched over her.

"Spread your legs for me, my love."

She opened for him, not embarrassed any longer.

"God, your pussy is gorgeous." His hands traced it reverently. "Every time you're near me, I think about this. About filling it up." He slid a finger, then another, into her as he placed a soft kiss on the curve of her stomach.

She arched her back so he'd suck her like she wanted. His mouth came back to her nipple as he pinched the other. "Yes," she whispered with her hands in his hair, pulling him toward her still. "Claim me."

He tightened his hold, clamping the palm of his hand down on her clit, gripping her. Her hips moved against his hand, needing more. He pulled away from her breasts and met her eyes, hovering over her face with a look of pure yearning. "You are perfection. My every dream," he said as he ground his palm against her, and pleasure shot through her.

The embrace of his scent surrounded her, and she never wanted to leave. She brought him down to her, needing to feel his weight to convince herself this was real.

He showered her with sultry, long kisses, his lips landing on her cheeks, her eyelids, her nose, and finally claiming her mouth. His thumb teased her clit in the most torturous way as his mouth sweetly took hers.

He was somehow fucking her *and* making love at the same time, she realized. Exactly what she'd always craved. Connection *and* sex.

The feeling of his muscles rippling against her hands as his mouth lingered on hers was too good. Too perfect.

He wrapped his arms tight around her, burying his head in her neck. "You're like the sun. Hot and perfect and bright," he murmured softly as his hard cock settled between her thighs and slid against her pussy.

Need consumed her. It was all she could think about—

being taken again. Being wanted by this man for who she was. She ran her hands through his hair. Her pussy throbbed with each touch. "Need you," she panted.

He lifted his face, and a wicked grin shone back. "What do you need, love?"

"Your cock. Deep." She kissed his hulking shoulders as he lifted up, his hand cupping her jaw. His eyes locked with hers as his cock pressed against her entrance.

Their eyes searched each other as he slowly pushed in, his gaze dipping to where she bit her lower lip.

He placed a soft, slow kiss on the side of her mouth as the excruciatingly slow heaven-sent torture continued. She clenched around him, needing it. Needing him to complete her.

Strings have been hopelessly twined with yours....

They took each other in as if they both realized this magic could last forever, and Violet felt the gravity of making love. Being the lock to the key of a man so perfect for her it hurt.

Her hand brought his mouth down to capture his lips. She wanted to savor this moment, make it last past four weeks and into forever.

She clenched her walls around him, loving the feeling of being filled.

"Fuck, love," he moaned hoarsely against her lips, laughing at himself. "I feel like a teenager. Scarcely able to last two minutes."

Pride flooded her, loving the effect she had on him. "Good thing we have four weeks to keep trying."

He smirked and thrust inside her. "Saucy minx. We'll see

how long *you* last," he whispered. His hand came to her clit and circled it delicately, teasing her.

Her hips bucked against him, and he growled as he kissed her briefly. Violet grabbed her breasts and pinched her nipples. His girth was so wide she felt stretched and full.

His eyes went lusty at the sight. She loved she could do that to him. "Spread your legs, and let me take you deeper. Need to see you take every single drop," he growled softly.

Fuck, she loved being taken. She spread her legs wide in the small closet, and desire clouded his eyes.

He grasped her hands, interlacing them with his own over her head, and pumped hard inside her, bouncing her tits. His eyes locked with hers, and something shifted as they ground against each other.

His mouth recaptured hers. His body was flush with hers, forever intertwined.

"Violet, my love," he breathed, his head resting on hers.

A connection spiraled from her heart to his, shifting them off a cliff neither expected.

"I know." She arched toward him and wrapped herself around him, never wanting to lose contact with his body. "I know," she whispered.

He pumped inside, moving them. She buried her head into the curve of his neck, needing him as close as possible. She bit down on the soft skin and hard muscle, wanting to claim his heart as hers.

His hand held her jaw as he angled up, his blue eyes seeming navy in the dim light. Like an ocean she wanted to sail into. Be at home in. She moved her hips in time with his, never wanting this to end.

As their eyes locked, he pumped harder and harder, his

hand going back to her clit, circling with a light, teasing reverence that had her tightening and tightening. "I want you, Violet," he ground out. "Just like this. Just you."

She came in waves, rippling around his cock, and had the distinct feeling their hearts were wrapped around each other, tangled beyond repair.

Chapter Twenty

JACK

The following morning, Jack strode through the kitchen at the ass-crack of dawn, searching for Violet.

He'd hoped to find her snuggled beside him that morning, but he'd woken up alone. He'd hopped up immediately to find her. Couldn't risk even the chance of her getting scared of what could be between them for the next four weeks.

It had been a long fucking time since he'd had a girlfriend, and he wanted to make the most out of every minute.

"Dad? Violet?"

He'd bet his life on where to find them. He wandered outside, and sure enough, they were bent over her fiddle leaf fig tree sprouts. His dad made a joke, and Violet threw her head back with raucous laughter.

He sighed out a breath of relief.

"Good morning, sleepy head," she said with a sparkling smile. Her cute dimples winked at him, and his dad looked happy as a clam, mucking about in her garden.

Violet fit perfectly with his father. She fit perfectly in his *real* life.

His dad stood up with a broad smile on his face. "Did ya see what she's grown over here? This woman's a veritable pile of green thumbs."

He tossed an arm around his dad's shoulders. "Sleep okay?"

"Ach, sure. Been up since three. Todd and I had a long chin wag this mornin', catchin' up with all his goings on."

Jack might have gotten his looks and acting talent from his mum, but his personality was all Gerald Grant. The kind of man he most wanted to be when he grew up. Someone helpful and kind who made others feel important. "Don't believe a word Todd tells you."

Violet took her phone out of her back pocket and raised her eyebrows. "I think you're in trouble," she said in a sing-song voice as she answered a call. "Hi, Shay."

"How did she get your number?"

"We text," she said, her hand over the phone.

"No, he hasn't fallen off the face of the earth. Want to talk to him?" Violet tapped the phone. "You're on speaker."

Jack gave her a quick kiss as he took the phone from her and braced himself for the onslaught of Shay. "What have I done wrong now, Miss Brown?"

"Hello, darling. Nothing wrong, you're an angel," she said in one fell-swoop. "In fact, you're such an angel, I have a surprise for you."

"You got me more money?"

"Even better. Wayridge has officially forgiven you, and they'd like you at the Heart and Roses Film Festival."

"No," Violet said, putting her hand over her mouth. "Everyone on the network will be there."

Holy shit, they'd done it. The film festival was a fan event, but only the top Wayridge stars were invited. They'd stroll the red carpet and discuss upcoming projects. Then, media and fans would screen the fall lineup and reveal the upcoming Christmas movie.

It was important to be invited, but Jack's stomach turned at the idea of going.

"I told them you'd be there," Shay said.

"Shay," Jack warned. He detested these things. The pressure to be as dashing as Lord Eagleton was immense, and he hated running into his network arch-nemesis, Jason. He'd hit on Jack's last three dates to the festival, trying to get a rise out of him. "You know I'm bad at these things."

"Of course you're not. You're deliciously charming," she said, smoothing all her charm onto him. "You just don't *want* to go."

"I'm enjoying life right now." He winked at Violet.

"Let me rephrase. You *have* to go," a steely tone in Shay's voice shot through the speaker.

"Oh, pleasepleasepleaseplease," Violet begged. She pouted that plush, biteable lower lip at him, and he kissed her briefly, unable to help himself.

"Listen to your brilliant and gorgeous girlfriend," Shay said. "A huge fan response could mean big things at the network. The last Plant Parent video was recently featured on a news syndicate, so everyone and their grandmother have seen it. The internet has officially forgiven you thanks to the girlfriend wanting to accompany you."

"You'd be okay walking the red carpet with me?" he

asked Violet. He didn't want her crying again on his account. She'd paid her dues as his fake girlfriend, and he wanted every moment of their four-week relationship to be marvelous. Wanted to keep her tucked away, safe from the world where he could savor her.

The color drained from her face. "I thought I'd be with the fans. No one wants to see *me* on a red carpet."

"Violet, what the fuck did I tell you?" Shay demanded.

Violet jumped and blinked quickly. Damn, there were those tears again. He considered hurling the phone across the garden and tugging Violet back to their bedroom to keep her safe.

Her eyes caught his with an unsure glance. "The world deserves every inch of me?"

"And that world includes Canada," Shay said with finality.

He hit mute on the phone. "We don't have to go. But I'll do it if you want to." He'd do anything for her. Anything to see the light sparkle in her eyes again. Anything for his *girlfriend*. The word turned round and round in his head, like a carousel fueled with joy.

"Hellooo," Shay called from the phone. "Did you mute yourself, motherfucker?"

A spark of confidence lit in Violet's eyes, and she clutched her hands together. "I want to do it."

Fuck yes. He was so bloody proud of his girl. His eyes held hers as he spoke into the unmuted phone with a broad smile. "Consider us booked, Shay."

"Hell yea. Vi, the event's only a few days away, so I'll have a selection of dresses prepared and waiting in your suite, and then you can choose one. Sound good?"

She twisted her hand in her shirt. "Um, sure."

"Excellent. Jack, you know the drill. I'll have someone swing by your place and grab your tux."

"You're the best, Shay."

She sighed into the speaker with satisfaction. "I am, aren't I? Ciao!"

He turned to his father, feeling terrible. "I'm so sorry to leave right as you got here, Dad."

"Oh, it's no bother. I'll be here when you return. Will you be gone long?"

"Just a few days. Violet and I have an appearance when we get back."

A local home and garden festival had asked if he and Violet would do a meet and greet in a few weeks. He was so proud she'd said yes without hesitation.

Violet let out a small gasp. "Oh no. My plants. The peace lilies I'm prepping for an event need to stay damp for the next week."

"Don't you worry, lass. I'm rather handy in the garden. Now"—his dad straightened up—"you tell me exactly what to do while you're gone."

Violet shook her head with an apologetic smile. "It's too much, I don't want to trouble you on your trip. I can ask Gray to handle it."

"Nonsense, young lady. You've made my son 'appier than I've seen 'im in ages. The least I can do is care for all your plant babies."

"You call them plant babies, too?" Her eyes went wide with delight.

Oh, my heart. This was too much for Jack. Too much

goodness, too much perfection. Too much of everything that would slip through his fingers.

"Well, of course. You grew them from nothin'. You feed n' care for them; they all have their li'l personalities, like having a strappin' young lad."

Violet's eyes twinkled. "My father didn't love the flower business. But it still helps me feel near him when I'm out here."

"Hmm." Gerald nodded sagely. "I know the feelin'. My nan taught me the secret to courgettes. That's why I luv 'em. Kept 'em fed durin' the war. Now tell me about your waterin' schedule."

Jack realized with a smile he might not even be needed here. Maybe Violet had found her new best friend, who was, oddly enough, a 62-year-old farmer from Devon.

AFTER A WHIRLWIND few days of packing and calming a nervous/excited Violet, Jack was happy to be back in his adopted hometown of Vancouver for the film festival. Only two days longer, and then he could go back home.

Violet's home, he corrected himself.

He gulped. He'd made that mistake a few times now over the last few days.

His actual home was a condo 45 minutes across town, but he didn't want to deprive Violet of the five-star accommodation Wayridge provided. She'd stared at the hot tub on the hotel website as if it was her newborn baby. So, he'd insisted on packing her in her sexy retro-style swimsuit and a plush hotel robe to the spa for a massage and a soak. The next 24 hours would be stressful enough, and she'd been working non-stop since Bloom had exploded.

He paced in their hotel room. After weeks of not hearing back from the mafia show producers, they'd responded that they needed *another* reading with a third script. They happened to be in Vancouver, and he hoped to squeeze in a meeting before he left, so he'd need to finish this bloody thing.

He hit the delete button on his last take for the 67th time. He expected it to give him a middle finger the next time he pressed record.

Maybe he wasn't meant to play non-romance roles. Maybe his acting ability was limited to scowling in posh 18th-century drawing rooms, not able to portray the real drama of an American mafioso that required *talent*.

The door to the hotel room creaked open, and a blissed-out, pink-cheeked Violet sauntered through the door. Each step was heavy as if her purple flip-flops were made of lead.

"I would like to formally declare my hand in marriage to this hotel chain." She flopped onto the king-size, fluffy bed, spread out starfish-style.

Fucking adorable. This was how she preferred to sleep, he'd learned. Ironic, given that she took up as little of people's space as possible when awake. She'd even apologized to the arm of the empty seat next to her for having to put it up to be more comfortable on the flight.

He leaned down to kiss her hair as he moved a hand over it. She was so incredibly precious. "Never thought I'd be jealous of an international hotel chain."

She beamed up at him with glowing, pink cheeks. Her skin

was dewy after the combination of massage and hot tub. She looked relaxed and happy, at ease with herself for once. There was no one for her to take care of, no chore to do or plant to worry about. He made a mental note to whisk her away for another weekend before he came back to Vancouver permanently.

Permanently. It stung with a bitter taste in his mouth.

Violet propped her head up on her arm. "Get a take you like yet?"

"Ugh, I have a million takes, and I hate all of them," he said, running a hand through his hair.

"Can I get you some food? Water?"

"A gun," he uttered, his hand smashing his face to feel some tension release.

"Aw, I'm sure it's not that bad."

"My American accent is tenuous at best. Add on a gritty mafia boss? Rubbish. All one thousand takes."

She walked toward him and raised her arms for a hug. "You need a break."

She pressed her robed body against his, wrapping him in a tight hug. He cuddled into the welcome embrace and felt a coil of tension within him release.

He'd been at this for hours trying to get it right, which wasn't exactly in the spirit of a self-tape. Maybe this was his sign from the universe that he should just learn to disappoint his mother. He barely wanted the role anyway.

Violet's hug was firm like she meant business. He breathed in the scent of her hair, the lavender and blossoms he now associated with sleeping like the dead. Something about sleeping next to her allowed him to finally relax. He pulled back and gave her a quick kiss on her cheek. Nuzzling into the heaven that was her skin had become his favorite coping mechanism lately.

"Thanks. I think I needed that."

Her hand came to his beard, and her thumb brushed his cheek. He leaned into her hand, feeling that deep, core jolt of happiness when his body connected with hers. The white robe clung to her curves, and her hair had been neatly swept up. Those big emerald eyes took him in, and he wanted to drown in them. Jesus, he wanted this woman. Craved her.

"Tell me about the scene." She smiled guilelessly up at him.

He swallowed his feelings and tried to focus. "Uh, a mafia boss's wife has been captured. He vows revenge for them hurting the only woman he's ever loved."

"Ooh, dark and gritty." She shivered.

"A far cry from Lord Eagleton, unfortunately. Maybe too far a cry." His hand tugged at his hair as he looked at the script for the millionth time.

"I believe in you. You're nothing like Lord Eagleton anyway."

He snorted, eyes peering up at her. "I'm not hopelessly charming?"

"You are not a cold, obtuse, 18th-century peer. You are hot and funny and goofy *and* charming."

"Hot, huh?" he said, his thumb running underneath her robe and nipped at the edge of her swimsuit, and she giggled.

"Keep your eyes on task, Mr. Grant. Maybe I can help."

He stroked his chin. Maybe that was his problem. He usually worked with a scene partner. "Stand behind my phone so you're in my eye line. I'll imagine you've been captured."

"Ooh, I've got an idea." She grabbed a scarf, tied it over her mouth like a captive, and placed her hands behind her back.

Seeing her trussed up had his blood pumping. He should have tried this trick hours ago. He hit the record button on his phone.

Closing his eyes, he channeled his inner rage at someone capturing Violet, torturing her, and locking her away.

He would fucking *murder* them.

Anger coursed through him, and he opened his eyes, glaring at Violet next to the camera.

"You've made your last enemy," he growled in a thick Brooklyn accent, staring beyond the camera. "You would take someone so precious, so innocent, the beating heart outside my fuckin' body and drag her through the mud of our business? This was low, Mick, even for you."

He took a breath, imagining beating a man senselessly for hurting her.

A sinister smile twisted his face as he gained steam. "I will *delight* in breaking every bone in your body as *your* wife watches, screaming and begging me to stop. And on the day you're lowered into the ground, I will dance with my wife on your muddy grave. I will make love to her, make her scream *my* name because I'm still alive."

He stepped closer to the camera. Anger simmered in every fiber of his body and he spoke slowly. A growl sighed out of him, a threatening promise. "I'll find every last person you ever loved and destroy them. For taking my wife, my everything? You. Will. Have. Nothing."

He ground his teeth, breathing through his rage, imagining what he'd do if anybody ever hurt Violet.

Coming back to himself, he blinked and hit stop on the recording.

Violet's wide eyes were molten as he walked to her, ripped the scarf away, and took her mouth, needing to hold her. Needing to feel like nothing bad would ever happen to her. She wrapped her arms around him, and he pressed her head to his chest. His heart thundered as if he'd run ten miles.

God, he didn't want to lose her. Didn't want any of this to end.

How could he protect her from across the country? All-consuming thoughts raced in his head of how to keep her without staying in Fairwick Falls. How to keep his precious girl safe and happy. He'd do whatever it took.

And then the realization he'd been avoiding for the past weeks hit him like seven Mack trucks all at once. He screwed his eyes closed, the wave of it washing over him was too powerful.

Bloody fucking hell.

I'm in love with her.

Chapter Twenty-one

VIOLET

The next day, Violet stepped out of the steamy hotel bathroom and started doing mental math on how long everything would take to get ready. She'd taken an extra-long shower to mentally prepare for the most nerve-wracking day of her life: the Hearts and Roses Film Festival.

"Going down to the gym for a while," Jack said, putting in an earbud. "But I'm having a package delivered here in a few minutes. Would you mind grabbing it from the door?"

"Sure." She bit her lip through her nervous grin. She couldn't let him know how scary this all was. She'd even been the one to beg him to make the appearance, so she couldn't let him down now.

"Hey." His hand slid under her robe along her stomach, and he placed a kiss on her neck. "I can stay and help you work off some anxiety."

Welp. Guess he can see right through me anyway.

"Go," she giggled. "I need to get ready." It would take her hours to shellack on her makeup and wrestle with the straightener. She wanted to make him so proud after everything he'd done for her.

He gave her a quick kiss and walked out the door.

Violet splayed out on the bed, contemplating her life choices as her brain ping-ponged from terrified to thrilled. How did she go from a wallflower in Fairwick Falls to walking the red carpet at a film festival? Five weeks ago, this would have been her worst nightmare. She'd have just fainted dead away at the *suggestion* of going.

Thinking about seeing her favorite stars made butterflies tumble through her stomach with excitement.

But what if a fan said something? Or someone posted something online about her? The internet might rear its ugly comment head.

She started talking herself out of the whole thing when a knock sounded at the door.

She rolled out of bed to get Jack's package, opened the door, and came face-to-face with Shay and Aaron.

"Oh my god, oh my god, oh my god!" Violet jumped up and down, her brain short-circuiting. "You're here!"

They both burst out laughing. "We're here!"

She wrapped her arms around Aaron and squeezed tight.

"Girl, I just saw you two days ago." He chuckled even as he squeezed her back.

"I know, but you're here, and it's scary." She caught Shay in a vise-like hug.

"We wanted to make sure you got everything you needed, including confidence," Shay said, winking and sauntering into the hotel suite. "How did the dresses work out?"

"I'm trying to choose. They feel amazing; it's like they were made for me."

"I had them pre-tailored based on your measurements," Shay said with a nonchalant shrug but looked pretty proud of herself. "A makeup artist is en route."

"I was just getting ready to start straightening my hair."

"No," Aaron said slowly, taking her in, glancing from the dresses back to her. "Rock your natural curls."

"We should go extra volume," Shay said. "Blow dry it upside down, put in extra volumizer, really play it up."

Violet looked at her hair in the mirror. She currently looked like a drowned rat, with her sopping wet hair hanging on her shoulders. "I'm going to need a *lot* of fairy Shay-mother magic to pull this off."

"Good thing I packed a lot," she said with a wicked grin and a wiggle of her hips. Shay started playing with Violet's hair. "Come on. It'll look fucking hot. We'll set a few in the front with big rollers and let your natural volume do the rest of the work."

There was a sharp knock on the door. Violet ran to grab it, hoping it was Jack back from a workout. Instead, it was a bottle of champagne on ice with three glasses and a note.

Have fun my love. I'll be out for a few hours. ♡ Jack.

Violet's heart melted. Was this her life? Did she really deserve all of this?

She made a mental snapshot of the feeling of fullness and warmth in her heart right then. It felt exactly like all the love she had for Jack.

After hours of buzzed giggling and hair and makeup, Jack opened the hotel suite's door. "Hey, hey!"

She was still in her robe, but she turned around. "Makeup done, hair done."

"You look gorgeous." He kissed her temple.

"We have to leave soon." Violet nervously glanced at the time.

He started slipping out of his shoes. "A shower will take me two minutes."

"Don't forget to parade around in your towel first," Aaron yelled from the suite's living room area. Jack threw his head back with laughter as he walked to the shower.

"How come it's taking me *all day* to get ready?" Violet looked in the mirror.

"The patriarchy, dear," Shay said, hands on her shoulders. "The patriarchy." Aaron and Violet both nodded their heads in agreement.

They'd narrowed it down to the top two dresses. One was a basic black gown Shay almost vetoed, but it fit like a glove.

"I will *pay* you not to wear that black dress," Shay said, sipping her third glass of champagne. Her heels had been toed off an hour ago.

"But it hides my tummy."

"What's wrong with a tummy? Just another curve to rock," Aaron said. "Seize your moment, Cinderella. Own it in that purple gorgeousness."

Violet eyed the dazzling purple gown next to the black one.

Shay pointed to it. "This looks like it was made for you, hugging your delicious curves."

"But—" Violet said.

"But?" Shay sent her an arched eyebrow, daring contradiction.

All the insecurities Violet thought she'd laid to rest clawed their way back to the surface. "People might look at me."

Aaron threw his head back in frustration. "Of course people will look at you. You're a drop-dead gorgeous redhead standing next to one of the biggest stars on the network. They're going to stare at you regardless. Do you want to look like a fucking queen, or do you want to look like part of the crew?"

"Like a fucking queen?" she asked with a grimace.

"Winner winner, chicken dinner," Shay toasted her and downed the rest of her champagne.

A few minutes later, they had secured and snugged her into her most comfortable corset. Aaron zipped her into the silky purple dress.

The lining of the dress felt like water against her skin. She took in the moment with the sweetheart neckline showing off her ample cleavage. The dreamy, sweeping off-the-shoulder sleeves lay on her arms, making her feel more comfortable with her muscular arms and her slight farmer's tan from working outside.

"Shay, I can't thank you enough," she said, blinking over her shoulder. Not fully able to believe this was real life. "What will you do tonight?"

"We'll be watching the fancast and ordering a mountain of room service, charging it to one Mr. Jack Grant." Shay giggled with Aaron.

"Did somebody say my name?" Jack said, coming around

the corner. He looked down at his wrist as he walked in. "I need help with these cufflinks."

He was an absolute smoke show in a fitted black tux, crisp white shirt, and simple bowtie. It showed the broad expanse of his chest but tapered down into a crisp fitted waist. It was like staring at a kind, smiling secret spy.

He glanced up, and his mouth fell open looking at Violet. "Holy fuck." His eyes roamed the length of her body and stopped for a solid three seconds on her breasts.

"My face is up here, dear." She laughed. The term of endearment had slipped out, but she liked it.

Dear. He *was* so dear to her.

He jerked his head upward and smirked. "I want to buy you that dress in every color and have you wear it for the rest of your life." He walked around her, taking her in.

"I've never seen you look more handsome, even at last year's event." She took in his long, muscular build in the classic tux. His hair was swept to the side, reminding her of every expensive bridal ad she'd ever seen.

"Am I allowed one kiss?"

"Not on her face!" Aaron said. The makeup artist had worked wonders and set everything with a setting spray to last several hours.

"I think you'll both need to leave the room in that case," he joked with a simmering smile and kissed her bare shoulder instead. "You look breathtaking, love. Ready?"

Violet turned back around, her eyes panicked, looking for Aaron.

"You got this, sweetie," he said, handing over her purse. "Be the queen little Violet and little Aaron needed to see crushing it on the runway, okay?" Goosebumps covered her arms at the thought. "Do it for them."

"Okay," she whispered. Her throat suddenly constricted, and her eyes blinked away tears.

She'd do it for herself, for the little girl inside her who never saw a gorgeous, confident, plus-size woman in the arms of her dream man. She'd do it for all the girls who still needed to see it.

"Back straight. Take up space," Shay said, giving her a quick, light hug, careful not to mess anything up. "We need every inch," she whispered in her ear. "Every. Inch."

Violet willed her eyes to stop tearing up, picked up her skirt, and walked through the door into the biggest, scariest night of her life.

As she exited the limo on wobbly, nervous legs, she regretted past Violet's bravado. The throng of the Hearts and Roses Film Festival backstage energy hummed around her, and she coached herself to breathe.

Don't. Freak. Out.

Jack gripped her hand and winked as they stood at the talent entrance. He'd spent the five-minute ride reassuring her how gorgeous she looked and how much she would kill the short walk across the red carpet.

They walked through the waiting area, dodging and weaving between frenzied crew members and talent. Glamorous, gorgeous men and women prepped to walk the red carpet, checking their makeup and guzzling water in the summer heat.

Violet recognized every third face, either a starlet or a supporting cast member from her favorite shows and holiday movies. She marveled at how short everyone was in real life. Jack kept waving at friends and fellow cast members.

"There's a man chocka block with handsome looks," a chipper voice said behind them in a New Zealand accent. A familiar tiny blonde woman approached Jack and wrapped herself around him.

"Holy crap," Violet whispered, throwing a hand over her mouth. It was Missy Barnbrick, Jack's love interest from *Beyond the Manor Walls*.

She was *such* a fan.

Jack happily introduced them.

"Oh, hello." Missy turned her blinding smile on Violet. "I adore your videos."

"*My* videos?" Violet said, shocked.

"I watch everything this one does." Missy squeezed Jack's side. "Your store is a stunner. I ordered one of the mugs." She beamed a thousand-watt smile back at Violet as if they were already friends.

Violet blurted out a loud laugh. "Wow," she said, unable to form coherent thoughts. *Missy Barnbrick knows who I am.*

"I've got to find Robert so we can get through this and go home to the kids. You know I hate this stuff. Catch up when you're back before we shoot?" Missy squeezed Jack's hand with a look of old friendship.

"You know it."

"Have fun!" Missy gave Violet a cartoon princess wave. Violet managed to wave back like a child meeting one of her fairy princess heroes.

"Wow," Violet whispered, turning back to Jack.

"She's the best." He threw a thumb over his shoulder.

"She's so nice. And she knows who I am!" Violet danced in place.

Jack laughed with her, putting his arm around her waist. "I told you you're famous."

They got in line to walk the red carpet, and Violet's nerves were on high alert.

"They finally let you out of prison!" a booming voice said behind Jack.

They both turned around, and Violet saw the man she'd seen on every holiday special for the last five years: Jason Masterson.

A forced grin grew on Jack's face. "Jason." Jack curtly nodded and turned to go.

"Surprised they let you out on bail tonight." Jason laughed at his own bad joke. He turned his wolf-like eyes on Violet. "Aren't you going to introduce me, Grant?"

Face-to-face with Jason, she realized how good of an actor he really was. Something about him gave her the ick in real life.

Jack put a hand around her waist protectively. "Gotta do the carpet thing."

"Hold on," Jason said, playfully pushing Jack's shoulder to the side. "I've never met one of Jack's *real* girlfriends." He sent Violet a wink. "Come on, give us a twirl."

"We don't have time," Jack said, but a crew member caught his elbow, distracting him with a question.

"Come on. You look so gorgeous, Miss...?"

"P-Parker," Violet stammered.

His eyes raked up and down her body, and she didn't

enjoy any part of it. It felt like he was measuring her, finding her weaknesses. Jason took the opportunity to lean in, his hand lingering on her hip.

"If he disappoints you," he whispered, "you let me know. I can double whatever he's paying you."

Suddenly, his presence was ripped away, and Jack was between them.

"You're done." Jack pushed Jason's shoulder back, and Violet sighed in relief. Jason smirked and laughed it off as people turned around.

"Come on. Let's go." Jack pulled her toward the red carpet. Anger simmered through his physique, back hunched and jaw tightened. "You okay?"

"I'm fine," she whispered. *Just keep it together, Violet.*

His eyebrows narrowed in frustration as they stopped outside the red carpet entrance. "You sure? We can go home."

"Home?" She stopped suddenly, pulled out of her worries. "No. I'm not going to let him ruin this for you."

A murderous look passed over his face. "Did he say anything? Do anything?"

"His hand lingered too long. It's fine," she said, shaking her shoulders to get rid of the icky feeling.

"Hey." He pulled her to the side behind a curtain. "We don't have to do this."

"But you have to—"

"I don't *have* to do anything. I'll go home right now. Your happiness is all that matters to me." His thumbs stroked her hands as he clutched them.

She looked up into his handsome, sweet face full of worry. She was here with *him*. The dreamy, kind man of her actual fantasies who somehow lived up to the hype in her head.

"No," she said suddenly, standing taller. She remembered watching the red carpet coverage of the festival 15-some-odd years ago, never dreaming she'd see somebody like her with him. "I need to do this."

It was easier to be brave—to be yourself—if it helped somebody else be themselves.

Jack nodded, kissing her hair as he led them to the entrance. "You've got this. I'm so proud of you."

A realization hit as she stepped one foot onto the carpet.

I'm proud of myself, too.

Chapter Twenty-Two

VIOLET

As they stepped onto the carpet, Violet had an out-of-body experience. Her soul floated beside her, watching her walk the red carpet with her dream man.

Camera crews and photographers crowded in rows along the red carpet. Hundreds of fans lined up behind the lights and cameras. A thunderclap of screams went up as Jack raised a hand in greeting, his broad, happy smile in place.

Violet snapped out of her trance and remembered to throw her shoulders back. She took up space and smiled as big as she could. Her eyes were trained on Jack; she was the girlfriend, not taking up the spotlight.

"Jack! Jack!" photographers called. He turned and waved, his hand always in hers or on her waist. He gave different camera crews their shot. "Plant mom! Plant mom!" a couple of photographers yelled. "Over here!"

"Holy clover." She spun to Jack in shock. "They said my name!"

"Here." He positioned their bodies so she was in front.

Shay had prepped her for this, and she tried to remember her instructions. *'Look bored but smug. Like you have a secret.'* She tried to look bored and pouty, but a laugh of happiness burst through.

*I'm doing the impossible, and it's kind of...*fun.

She couldn't stop her grin from radiating and heard the shutter of photos being snapped. She and Jack posed a few different ways, with him murmuring silly nothings in her ear (*"I'm so sausages for making you come to this." "I wish you had the plant butt plug in right now." "I hope Jennifer is watching at home and sees how hot you look."*) to keep her laughing.

They finally walked to the end of the carpet near the theater entrance, but two red-carpet interviewers flagged them down for the fan live stream.

Violet thought she'd stay off camera, but Jack interlaced his fingers through hers and pulled her with him.

"I don't know," she whispered, her stomach ping-ponging with nerves.

"You'll be great." He squeezed her hand. He wrapped his arm around her, and a stunning blonde woman holding a microphone came up next to Jack.

"Jack Grant, Lord Eagleton himself. We've loved watching your silly side this summer. Oh my gosh, hi!" The host peeked around Jack to see Violet behind him. "Come on. We need both of you." She pressed her ear, getting something from a producer off-camera. "Yes. So many of our viewers now know you as the famed Plant Parents."

Jack squeezed Violet's waist protectively. "We've had a lot of fun working together."

Violet nodded, unsure what to say without sounding like a giant weirdo.

"Now, what I'm desperate to know," the bubbly host said to Violet, "is if Jack Grant was a plant, what would he be?" She stuck the microphone in Violet's face.

She silently thanked the universe for a fun and easy question where she could be herself.

"Oh, that's easy," Violet said with a smile. "He's a fiddle leaf fig tree. He's tall, good-looking, and *kind* of a diva."

The co-host threw her head back and laughed. "Any response?" She held the mic to Jack.

"She's the expert, and I am, indeed, quite a diva." He laughed, squeezing Violet.

They extricated themselves from the camera as the co-host found another person to interview.

"You were fucking brilliant," he whispered in her ear.

Violet giggled, unable to hold in her excitement. "Thanks, though you're not *really* a diva."

"Violet," he opened a heavy theater door for her. "I pay far too much for facial products. I'm aware of my diva-ness."

They crossed into the cool, quiet theater lobby.

It felt like pulling into the station after riding a roller coaster. It wasn't half as bad as she thought it would be, but she had *no* plans to get back in line.

"I did it," she whispered to herself.

"You were excellent. Did you hear them calling your name?"

"They called me plant mom." She laughed as they found their seats in the theater.

Jack stood unexpectedly. "Are you okay on your own for a minute? The head of the studio just signaled me over." He pointed to a short bald man standing on the edge, talking to a circle of other old, tall, white men.

"Sure. I'll can people-watch."

"Okay. Call me if you need anything."

"Jack, you'll be 50 feet away."

He planted a kiss on her cheek and walked over to the head of the studio.

Violet was happy to observe her favorite celebrities in their natural habitat. This felt more like a zoo than a premiere for her. The girl who was a wide-eyed ingénue in the holiday specials looked absolutely peeved at her date. The male supporting lead from *Beyond the Manor Walls* sat beside a handsome man, and they made heart eyes at each other. And as she was getting lost in her own story about their relationship, she felt a tap on her shoulder. She turned to see Jason sitting down in Jack's seat.

Shit.

"Has that no-good rapscallion abandoned you already?" Jason's forced smile caused her stomach to turn. His face was unappealing up close, and the stench of his breath made her turn away.

She smiled tightly, feeling uneasy. "He's chatting with the network. I am such a big fan," Violet said, wanting to distract him from talking more about Jack.

"Ah, you are?" He leaned forward and put his arm on the back of her seat, angling his body so they sat face-to-face. "I thought I might have pegged you for one of Jack's groupies." His hand grazed her bare shoulders.

"Oh, I'm not a groupie," she said, smiling as she pulled away from the back of the chair. "I'm his girlfriend."

Where was Jack? She wasn't used to telling men to go away.

"Groupie, girlfriend, all the same," Jason said, a sinister smile on his lips. "My offer still stands. I bet a beta like Jack doesn't know how to handle a woman like you." A thumb caressed her shoulders, and he leaned in.

Violet went still, not sure what to do.

"What's it costing him to fuck you? Ah—" Jason was lifted out of his seat with a hand clasped in his shirtfront.

"Get your fucking hand off her, or I will *happily* go back to jail tonight." Jack's cold fury above her had Jason stuttering.

"Jack, no." Violet stood and grabbed his hand. He was going to ruin his reputation again. And worse, do it in front of everyone at the network.

"What did you say to her?" Jack spat through clenched teeth at Jason's smug face.

People were starting to stare. Violet stood and pulled on Jack's hand fisted in Jason's coat. "It's fine. Jack, please. For me, just let go."

Jack blinked, his eyes catching hers, and he released his death grip on Jason's shirt-front.

Jason sneered, adjusting his shirt, and tapped Jack on the shoulder like they were two friends sharing a joke.

"Enjoy watching me on screen for the next hour and a half, *buddy*," Jason said with spite in the last word as he walked away.

"How did the conversation go?" she asked, trying to distract Jack from the alpha male showdown.

Jack's eyes followed Jason down to the front row with a thunderous look. "Are you okay? What did he say to you?"

Don't make a big deal of it. "He had a hard time accepting I was your girlfriend."

Jack sat down next to her and clasped her hand in his. "That's not all of it. Tell me."

Violet bit her tongue, but dang it, this man knew her. Really knew her. "He insinuated...he'd pay me to sleep with him."

"I'm going to fucking murder him." Jack stood up as the lights dimmed.

"No." She snagged his arm. "Just stay with me. I don't want to be alone." She couldn't let his temper ruin how far he'd come.

His eyes locked with hers as the flicker of the large screen lit up the room, and he slowly sank back into his seat. He kissed her temple, drawing her close as the premiere started. "Anything for you, darling."

Despite all the drama, she was so proud to be with him at such a public event. Everywhere she looked in the crowd, there were beautiful, public faces. The upper tiers of the enormous theater were filled in with raucous fans, and they cheered when Jack's face popped onscreen briefly as Wayridge ran the hit shows promo before the premiere began.

The screen lit up with a twenty-foot version of Jason's face as the premiere began. Jack grimaced uncharacteristically through the hour syrupy love story kicking off the fall romance season.

As the credits rolled and the cast went on stage to take their bows, Jack tugged her hand through the row and hurried out the back entrance. An angry glint still clouded his eyes.

"Are you feeling okay?" Violet asked.

"No." His tone was sharp as steel, and his eyes were dead set ahead.

His grip on her hand was a vise.

"Where are we going?" She jogged to keep up as they walked to the elevators in the theater lobby.

"You'll see." The elevator opened, and they stepped inside. His grip tightened on her hand.

"Is everything okay? Something seems..." There was a security guard in the elevator. She left the rest unsaid until they could be alone.

Jack simmered as they rode to the fourth floor. As they got out, they walked past the large circular glass balcony overlooking the theater's lobby. Violet could see down several floors through the atrium opening, where people started trickling out of the theater.

He pulled her into a deep hallway past offices lining the glass balcony. They stepped behind several large ficus trees at the end and into an alcove to the side. The crowd gathering in the lobby below was still partially visible. People in gowns and tuxedos wandered out, chatting between the premiere and the after-party.

"What are you doing?" she asked as she turned to face him. The nook in the hallway was the size of a phone booth.

Jack turned, eyes dark as he stared at her lips. "That bastard touched you. Instead of smashing his face into a cement wall, I'm doing this."

His mouth captured hers with all the passion of unspoken promises. There was possession and claiming in his kiss. She felt her core ignite into molten lust at how his hands grasped her possessively. His fingers dug into her ass, sliding across the silky material and grabbing each hip, pulling her closer to him.

Yes, yes, yes. She wanted to be taken. She needed him.

"We're ticking off that third item," he growled, his hands bunching up the back of her skirt as his mouth sucked on her neck.

Her pussy throbbed at his words. "Here?"

"You wanted to be fucked in public." He turned her around so her back was flush against him.

He grabbed her bare ass between them, and the heat of it felt like a brand. Claiming her as his.

Twenty feet of hallway led to the glass balcony in front of them. She could see the tops of heads in the lobby, buzzing from the premiere.

"Old theater saying: if you can see them, they can see you." His other hand came to her breast and squeezed it hard as she panted. Desire curled around her. She wanted to spread herself for him.

"And I'm going to fuck you where they can see," he whispered. His possessive tone had her practically dripping with need.

Her heartbeat kicked up at the thought of being so bad. "But what if we get caught?"

He tweaked her nipples through her dress as his teeth scraped the nape of her neck. "They can fire me. But I *will* have you, Violet. Don't you want to be fucked where someone might catch us?"

So bad. "Yes," she panted, not daring to believe this was real. She wanted to be filled, taken.

"Then spread your legs. Be my greedy little minx."

She was soaked just thinking about it. She grasped his

hair behind her as he lifted her skirt higher, kicked her foot out so she spread her legs. The cool air kissed her ass and pussy, barely covered by a thin thong.

His voice was low and gravelly as he stood behind her. "I've thought about nothing else for the last three hours. Wanted to fuck you so badly in the limo. Wanted to lift that pretty skirt and bury my face in your pussy." *Yes.*

His fingers stroked the wet fabric of her thong over her clit, unhurried. He whispered in her ear. "How many people down there do you think want to fuck you like this?"

She felt so exposed and naughty. Her pussy throbbed, and she bucked her hips as he teased her clit. "I-I don't know."

His nose grazed along her ear. "I counted seven staring at your tits," he growled, his fingers teasing her entrance.

Her pussy throbbed at that news. He sounded *jealous*. He moved her panties to the side, found her clit, and circled it to continue his teasing. "I bet there are double who want to bend you over and eat you out. But only I get to taste you, Violet."

He bent down, and suddenly, his tongue was inside of her. It was hot and dirty and so, *so* good. She clenched around his tongue, and he spread her ass and thighs wide to bury his face in her.

She clamped her mouth shut so she wouldn't scream his name like she wanted to. Her eyes were focused on the bobbing heads in view at the event below. How anyone could walk around the corner and see her being tongue fucked.

The wet, writhing pleasure of his tongue entering her, licking her, as he teased her clit was almost too much.

His tongue was ripped away, and she heard the zipper of his pants and the clink of his belt. "Who's taking this pussy tonight where they can spot us?"

Everyone was currently too busy talking to notice them, but they'd be spotted if someone looked up.

"Jack," she sighed out his name, loving the feel of it, loving the feel of him.

He slid the tip of his cock into her entrance. Her body was on fire with how much she needed him. She clenched around him and pushed back, needing to be filled. Wanting to be claimed.

"I'm fucking you because you're mine, minx." He thrust into her on the last word, and she felt like she was being split in two. Her hand came back to her mouth, not trusting herself not to scream when she came. Her eyes watered with the friction and the fullness.

"Show them the tits they don't get to touch."

She grabbed her neckline and pulled it down far enough to pinch her nipple. She felt brazen and so naughty where anyone could catch them. Jack fucking her was better than she could have ever dreamed.

He leaned over her, his cock still thrusting inside her. "You're mine, Violet," he whispered in a ragged growl. "Only I fill this tight pussy with my cum." He thrust into her again and again, his hand reaching around to find her clit. "And you're going to walk the rest of tonight with it running down your legs so you remember"—he thrust in again, hard—"that you're mine."

"Yes," she whispered as she clenched around him. "Yours, only yours. Fill me up."

She groaned, and his hand clamped over her mouth, and *fuck*, it turned her on so much.

He thrust in a rhythm, claiming her. His voice pounded into her with a chant of "Mine, mine, mine."

As he rubbed her clit faster, she came, moaning his name into his hand, thinking *'mine, mine, mine'* with him.

JACK

The next afternoon, Jack stared at the eerily youthful face of Edward Bellingham, the aging CEO of Wayridge. He'd requested that Jack come in for a 'casual chat' at last night's premiere.

"Jack." Edward extended his hand as Jack entered his office. It was early Sunday afternoon, and the building was quiet.

"Enjoy the party last night?" Edward asked, reclining in his chair with his fingers steepled.

"My girlfriend and I both had a fantastic time."

"Yes, lovely girl," Edward said, nodding. "Glad you found a calming influence in your life."

He loathed these meetings. Entertainment types talked in subtext. '*A calming influence*' actually meant, '*You've stopped embarrassing us, but she's boring.*'

Jack nodded with a grin, thinking how Violet had come around his cock in the theater hallway.

Calm, ha.

"This viral series you started with her—"

"It's her series. I'm merely helping," Jack clarified. He didn't want to take any credit from Violet and her sisters.

"It's turned a corner for you. Your virality score has soared." Edward turned his laptop, queued up with a dashboard.

"My virality?" Jack leaned closer.

"We monitor all our stars, tracking their social media impact, headlines, who's trending. You've blown everybody else out of the water. Finance says we could double our holiday revenue if you star in the Christmas special."

"Wow." He rubbed his lips, still processing. "That sounds great."

Jack selfishly glanced through the chart for Jason Masterson. He was pleased to see it was third behind Missy and himself.

"The special would be shot on location in England. We can arrange for it to be in the West Country," Edward said with a fatherly smile. "Filming will start in a month. We'll make sure the *Beyond the Manor Walls* schedule works around it. You'll be a busy man for the next six months."

Busy and far away from Fairwick Falls.

Earlier that morning, Jack had met the producers of the mafia show, and they'd finally offered him the role. He needed to talk to Shay immediately to manage these competing demands.

"I'll need to talk to my agent," Jack said quickly before letting himself say yes to anything.

"Of course. Just wanted to tell you in person your future is bright with the network if you keep your nose clean."

A self-effacing smile appeared on Jack's face, thinking of

how Violet had stopped him from being thrown in jail again last night. "My girlfriend's to thank for that, sir."

Edward's calculated smile didn't meet his eyes. "You might consider how well it serves your virality score to have a girlfriend…or more."

Jack's stomach turned. God, he hated this business. "But Missy's right beneath me and has a family."

"Our viewers appreciate family-oriented female leads. You'll notice all these fellows here; they're all married." He pointed to the bottom of the chart. "Our audience likes to imagine falling for the male main leads. It won't necessarily kill your career if you marry Vivian—"

"Violet," Jack corrected.

"Sure. But think about where you're going and if she's the right girl to be there with you."

Jack clenched his jaw, narrowly keeping his temper at bay. "What do you mean?"

"Will she add to your score or hurt it?" Edward shrugged and stood up, and Jack was only too eager to leave the conversation behind.

As he walked back to the hotel, he talked with Shay. She threatened to kiss him senseless for getting two big offers within 24 hours.

She left the decision up to him since both jobs would earn the same money. Either way, he could keep taking care of his dad, Shay would be okay, and his mum would be proud.

The mafia show could catapult his career to the next level, opening doors for movies and high-budget TV shows in LA.

His stomach churned at the thought.

He shuddered at the idea of being within driving distance of his mother. He'd already ignored several calls from her today, knowing she'd want to gloat.

She'd insist on him coming to all the biggest parties, meeting all the 'best' people. He'd never have a day to rest and relax, read his books, sip some tea, or stare at pretty green things.

Jack walked along the neighborhood streets, wrestling with his thoughts. Wasn't this what he'd been working for all along? The idea of picking up his life and starting over in LA caused every nerve ending to scream *no*.

Things were about to take off in his career, so why did he want to pump the brakes more than ever?

I just want to go home.

The cottage nestled in Fairwick Falls, not the high-rise one-bedroom on the opposite side of town. That apartment had never felt like home; home had always been elsewhere, usually in England, but never anywhere where he worked.

Could he live a life where his job was in one place, but his heart was in another?

An hour later, Jack swiped his card to the hotel room. He expected to see Violet still lounging in bed after their raucous night. After a few cocktails, she'd been a chatterbox, and they'd stayed at the party late into the night meeting all her favorite stars. *His* favorite moment was when she met Nate of the infamous jailed stag night and hugged him within an inch of his life for inadvertently introducing them.

Instead, when he walked through the door, he found her sipping coffee, freshly showered, and their bags all packed.

"I said you could sleep in," he said as he hugged her. She did too much for him.

Her sunny grin beamed back. She looked fresh and delicious in an artfully slouching t-shirt and stylishly cut-off shorts that made him want to sink his head between her thighs. Maybe he should take her back to bed before they left for their flight back to Pittsburgh.

She kissed his cheek. "The time difference messed up my sleep. Plus, I wanted everything all ready when you got back. How did it go?" she said, her eyes cautious.

They hadn't known when he left that morning whether his meeting would be good or bad news. "They want me to headline the Christmas show. And I got offered the mafia gig."

She squealed. "That's huge!" She threw her arms around him.

It felt foreign to have somebody so utterly proud of him without pretense, without wanting something else from him.

"That's a big deal." Her round, precious cheeks were wide with her smile. Her dimples were in full effect, and he was dazzled by the full force of her happiness.

"All thanks to you." His fingers caressed her cheek, trying to memorize the velvet softness of her skin.

His heart already started breaking for future Jack, who'd be so far away from this stunning, selfless woman. It seemed he hadn't done nearly enough for her in return.

"I'm so proud of you," she said, squeezing him around the waist. "I'm looking forward to putting on my Christmas sweater, snuggling up, and"—her face fell a fraction—"watching you on TV." She tried to smile as her eyelashes fluttered.

He didn't even bother to ask why her eyes went watery.

He could feel it, too. They'd only have three more weeks together after this. Sand trickled through an invisible hourglass over their heads.

"Come to the premiere," he offered. Just because he was leaving soon didn't mean they couldn't see each other after that. "We'll work something out. You can see all the glitz and glamor when it premieres in December."

She let go of him and busied herself with her coffee. "Maybe. You might be...busy, then." Her eyes fell as she sipped her coffee.

Did she mean busy with someone else?

"Or you might be," he countered slowly. He thought about how he'd taken her in the hallway last night. '*Mine. Mine. Mine. Mine.*' still echoed through his head; imagining some other man touching her set his blood to boil.

He needed to take her home to Fairwick Falls, to enjoy her for as long as he could keep her.

He laughed to himself, realizing that a tiny town in a foreign country had become his home...all because that's where Violet was. *His home.*

MANY HOURS LATER, Jack drove through the town square of Fairwick Falls, relieved to be back. He liked Vancouver, but it was just a faceless city. Fairwick Falls had a heartbeat you could see and grasp onto with both hands.

An old-timey band performed as he drove past, and kids ran through the lawn as their parents enjoyed the summer concert. A familiar song drifted through the open car windows.

Sometimes it felt like he'd been plopped into one of the small towns in the Wayridge Christmas movies. Maybe he loved it so much because everything would always be okay in Fairwick Falls.

As they pulled onto Violet's street, she snuffled herself awake. She'd dozed all the way home from Pittsburgh.

"I can't wait to see how the plants are doing. Maybe I'll have new shoots," she said groggily. He pulled into the cottage driveway.

Violet let out a mewl as she stretched out in her seat. "Thanks for driving."

God, she's precious. He didn't want to leave her for two seconds, let alone forever. He had to make the most of every single moment.

He leaned over, thumb on Violet's chin, as he brought her to him for a brief kiss. He'd miss her taste. The warm musky scent laced with lavender that instantly calmed him. She pulled back and stared into his eyes.

He was such a coward for not telling her how he felt. That *holy fuck, I love her* realization was kept to himself, but only just barely. Better move before it spilled out of his mouth, making life even more complicated. They got their bags out of the car and walked to the cottage.

His dad sat on Violet's back patio next to the pretty older woman he'd greeted in Bloom. A bottle of wine and a candle flickered between them, and he noticed his father holding the woman's hand.

His head spun, processing the view of his dad.

"Welcome back!" His dad toasted with his wine glass.

"Violet, we saw the fancast yesterday and you looked radiant," said the woman beside his father.

"Ms. McClotskey, this is Jack. My boyfriend."

"Jack, I am such a fan. And please, call me June," June said with a pretty smile. His father's hand was still wrapped in hers.

"It's nice to meet you," Jack said with a measured glance.

Violet tossed her bags down. "I'm going to check on the plant babies."

June hopped up. "Oh, me too. I want all of the celeb gossip." She and Violet walked back to the greenhouse in the dusky light.

"Have something to share?" Jack said, sitting down beside his father.

"I already know how the birds and the bees work, son." His dad took a swig of wine.

"Christ." Jack swiped his hand along his face, trying to wipe away this never-ending day. "I didn't know you"—he waved his hand in June's direction—"dated."

"I like June." His dad beamed. "Really like her. We've seen each other every day since I landed."

What the fuck? He'd been so caught up in getting ready for the event he'd missed his dad having a whirlwind relationship under his nose.

When the Grant men fell, they fell fast and hard, apparently.

His father smirked into his wine. "Might stay a bit longer than I planned to see if it's an *as long as we both shall live* kind of thing."

Fuck. Did he think Jack was going to stay in Fairwick Falls forever? "I adore Violet, but I don't want you making any forever plans based on me."

"This has nothing to do with you, my boy." His father

had a shy, happy grin. "I knew when I saw June's smile as 'er hair glinted in the sun, givin' me directions to Bloom that first day, that somethin' was there. Somethin' I wanted to hold on to."

Jack nodded. He thought back to the first night in Violet's kitchen, hell the first moment in her oak tree.

He was happy for his father. "You deserve only the best. Don't let her tell you otherwise," he said, winking as his father chuckled.

"And do you know?" his dad asked, nodding towards the greenhouse. "If this lovely lady with the sweetest disposition and unearthly ability with plants is *the* one?"

Jack scratched the back of his head nervously. "I got the big Christmas gig and have to film in England this fall. Violet and I are keeping things...loose," he said, biting his lips nervously.

"I'm proud of you either way," his father said. "But you only live life once. I'd give my entire veg patch to have met June even a year earlier. A *month* earlier. Who knows how much time I have left? How much any of us have left? Nothin', not a single penny, is worth a broken heart. Not fame, nor money, nor prized courgettes."

His dad stood up and tapped him on the shoulder with his fist. "Now, let's see what nonsense our ladies are up to."

His father strode off with a wine glass, bizarrely at home in a country not his own, in a *house* not his own, but firm in the knowledge he'd found a lovely woman to spend time with, for however much time they all had left.

Why the bloody fucking hell couldn't he be like his dad?

Chapter Twenty-four

VIOLET

"Thanks so much for coming in." Violet handed a bag full of chocolates, candles, and a small air plant to a customer.

Bloom's business had been doing well the last few weeks. They'd covered for her while she'd been out for a few days, and had finally found a balance in the chaos of their viral success.

Violet rubbed her back. She'd put in early hours at the greenhouse that morning to try to catch up from being gone.

Rose flipped through their online orders as she leaned over the register, scrolling through a long list. "All set for Plant-a-Rama?"

Violet's stomach jumped at thinking about making another public appearance. She'd eagerly agreed when Rose had caught her in a moment of confidence.

"I guess. Jack will be there, which will help, but it's so many people."

"No more than on the red carpet a few days ago."

The premiere earlier that week now felt like a dream to her. "Sure, but all attention will be on us for *twenty* minutes."

"Thirty, actually." Rose grimaced. "It's fantastic local exposure for the store. Plus, it'll position you as a personality."

"I don't want to be a personality," Violet said, pouting. "Lily's the outrageous one. Why can't she be the personality for the store?"

"I am not *outrageous*," Lily said, sliding down the spiral staircase from her loft apartment. "Just opinionated."

"And loud," Rose called over her shoulder.

"I'm little. I have to pipe up—"

"—To be heard," Rose and Violet said together, as if they hadn't heard *that* their entire lives.

"You have the bridal bouquet design for the Lopezes?" Rose asked.

Lily had done a fantastic job with the oldest sister's wedding a few months ago, and it had connected them with the entire family, who now wanted bridal bouquets and centerpieces.

"Yes, taskmaster." Lily waved sketch papers in the air.

"Oh, that's gorgeous, Lily," Violet said, taking the sketch in hand.

"She wants it to scream Christmas wonderland," Lily said proudly. The snowflake-themed bridal bouquet had spunky dusty miller ferns like frosted icicles, silver brunia like tiny snowballs, eucalyptus accents with silvery leaves, and white roses. "I've outdone even myself. Speaking of bridal bouquets, how are the proposal plans for Gray going?" Lily leaned over the counter.

"The what?" Violet turned in shock.

"I'm considering it." Rose shrugged with a secretive smile.

"Oh my gosh, tell me everything," Violet said, hunkering down.

"Still thinking about it. I'm not sharing anything yet," Rose said, flicking them away as she stared at her computer.

"How did you know," Violet said slowly, hoping for nonchalance, "Gray was the one?"

They slowly turned their heads, eyes narrowed at her.

Damn sisters. It's like they have a spy camera in my brain.

"Why do you ask?" Rose said with a cunning smile.

"Jack and I decided to make our relationship..." Violet avoided their eyes as she traced her hand on the counter. "...*not* fake."

"Pay up." Rose opened her palm to Lily.

"God*damn*it. I always lose these things." Lily rolled her eyes and pulled out her phone.

Rose leaned against the counter. "Gray and Nash lost, too. Remind me to collect their twenty bucks."

"How did you know?" Violet was shocked. *She* hadn't even known until a week ago before the event.

"It was so obvious," Lily said, snorting. "Even if I did pick the wrong date."

Violet let out a long sigh. It was incredible *and* horrible being known down to your DNA. "You didn't answer my question. How did you know Gray was the one?"

Rose shrugged. "Simple. He's seen me at my worst, and he loved me anyway. I think he maybe loved me *because* of my worst."

"You mean when you'd yell at him and then kiss him a

whole bunch?" Lily laughed as she rearranged the chocolates in one of their displays.

"No, when I was petulant and mean and so desperately sad. He saw all the good, despite all the flaws. It's worth hanging onto someone who loves you despite knowing how you may disappoint them."

The door to Bloom rattled.

"Welcome!" the three of them said automatically, and Jennifer walked through with one of Jennifer's close friends.

The familiar chant of *no one wants you, no one wants you* sounded in Violet's head. Like a flash, she remembered the buried memory. In first grade, all the kids had chanted at her on the playground after the rumor had started about her.

That's where it had come from that night, in my nightmare.

She studied Jennifer with this new friend. She was so different with her, giggling and smiling. Violet was always the first to reach out to Jennifer, always the first to offer to help. Never the other way around.

Jennifer slid her sunglasses onto her head. "Hi, Violet," she said as Violet placed houseplants on a display. "Congratulations on all of the buzz you're getting."

Well, that was nice.

"Thanks," Violet said, smiling back. *Maybe all the issues were in my head.* "I had a lot of fun. Hopefully, got some buzz for the store."

"You know, you're so *brave* for going in front of the cameras," Jennifer said, touching her arm as if giving her thoughtful advice.

"Brave for what?" Violet cocked her head.

"You know, going in front of all the cameras and looking

like..." She paused. "You know," she said quickly, smiling, not quite meeting Violet's eyes.

Was she trying to say it was because Violet was plus-size?

Her friend piped up. "I mean, you called Jack Grant a fig bush. That's *so* awkward." She and Jennifer laughed in the way Violet remembered. The laugh that said *we're not laughing* with *you.*

"Let me just run up to the front to get this," the friend grabbed a plant. As she neared the front, Rose unplugged the cash register.

"Oops," Rose said, dead-pan. "Guess you'll just have to get the fuck out of our store." Rose's cold eyes moved from the friend to Jennifer.

Their jaws dropped.

"You all just think you're better than everyone else now," Jennifer said with a sour face. They swirled around and walked out of the store.

Lily walked over and hugged Violet. "You know they just call her Jennifer because 'stick up her ass' isn't allowed on a birth certificate, right?"

Violet shook her head. "I don't even know what just happened."

"We got a case of the *mean girls*." Rose shrugged. "Good thing I have a lifelong case of the *bitchy older sister's*." She smirked and plugged the cash register back in. "You can't let her talk to you like that, Vi."

"You know me. I have a hard time with confrontation."

"You're hot shit now," Lily said as she looked through the arrangements in the cooler and pulled out a wilted one. "Use all your newfound confidence to tell her to go to hell."

Telling Jennifer to go to hell, Violet mulled over in her head. *Maybe someday.*

OVER A WEEK HAD PASSED since they'd returned from the premiere, and Violet and Jack hadn't talked about the clock ticking down around them.

It was the unspoken elephant that traveled with them everywhere; to their bed as they made love, to the greenhouse, out and about, to any videos they made together.

This is fun. I like you. You're so sweet. You're gorgeous.

We're over in two weeks.

In the car coming back from an evening with Rose and Gray, Violet turned it all over in her head.

"Rose asked if we wanted to grab dinner with them next week. What do you think?" She turned through the town and back to the cottage.

"I'm not sure," Jack said offhandedly.

"You've got other big plans in Fairwick Falls next Friday night?" she said with a smile.

He chewed on a nail and stared out the window as she drove. Ever since Gray and Rose had discussed a vacation they'd planned for next year with Gray's son, Alex, Jack had gone distant.

This was a new one; usually, he was gregarious, the one trying to cheer her up. She pulled up to the cottage, and they got out.

He still hadn't answered her.

As they set their things down in the kitchen, his response finally came. "I was waiting to tell you," he said suddenly.

A pit of dread dropped in her stomach.

"I've, uh," he hemmed and hawed, chewing on that nail again. She hadn't ever seen him this nervous.

"What's wrong?" She wanted to make it all better. Soothe it all away and ask what was for breakfast the next morning.

"They moved my *Beyond the Manor Walls* shoot date up two weeks to accommodate the Christmas filming schedule."

Her heart plummeted to the ground and broke into jagged, sharp chunks. "You're leaving now?" she asked, not wanting to understand.

"I've known for a few days and didn't know how to tell you." He shoved his hands through his hair.

She could feel the gap between them widening as they stood in the kitchen. He was already floating away from her, from the life they could have together. Tears instantly flooded her eyes as her voice broke. "But we had two more weeks."

He rolled his lips together and shook his head. "I need to leave tomorrow evening at the latest."

She blinked rapidly, trying to process having everything she'd ever wanted ripped away from her.

"Violet." He reached for her.

"It's fine, it's fine." She took a step back. She had to protect herself. They'd known this was going to happen.

She shook out her hands.

Just don't be clingy. Don't put too much pressure on him. You don't want him to never talk to you again.

His hands grabbed hers. "Violet, look at me."

She willed her eyes to meet his. She wanted to blurt out, *I love you, stay please stay*, but she couldn't. She couldn't embarrass herself like that.

"Come with me," he said suddenly.

Her heart beat somewhere outside of her body at the possibility.

But no. It was impossible. "To Vancouver? I can't leave; my family's here." She thought of the lonely graves she'd visited a few months ago where her parents were. Of her sisters who'd uprooted their lives to be with her in Fairwick Falls.

His thumbs stroked her hands, even as his own shook. "We can come back and visit. My dad's moving here, I think. We'll come back all the time."

"I can't leave. My family is here. Permanently. In the ground." It slipped out before she could help it. She softened. "My family won't leave me."

Jack's eyebrows drew together with hurt in his eyes. "You think I will?"

She shrugged, feeling sorry for herself. "You're leaving me right now, aren't you?"

"I'm asking you to—" He cut himself off, pulling his hands away. "You're stuck in the past. You have this old narrative that no one wants you, but people are falling all over themselves to have you. I want you to come with me. I *want* you."

"In Vancouver," she clarified.

"Wherever my work is."

He needed flexibility to maintain his career; she knew that. Film wherever. Be wherever. "I can't do that. I have commitments here. Greenhouses aren't built for remote work."

"So, if I do what I want"—he poked himself in the chest —"that's it? We're done?"

Her heart was breaking, and she could see his breaking too. A single tear rolled down the edge of his cheek, and he wiped it away quickly.

She wanted to be the good guy. She was *always* the good guy.

"I've been so happy here with you. You make me so happy because I—" He bit his lip and shook his head. Todd pounced onto the counter. "Because Todd and I have both been happy," Jack said finally with a sad smile.

Violet knew what she had to do. She couldn't get in the way. If she sacrificed for him and did the hard thing, she'd be a little more lovable; be the nice girl who didn't ask for too much.

Wouldn't be rejected if she rejected him first.

"I think I'm officially breaking up with you," she said as her lip trembled.

"Love—" he said, grasping for her.

"No," she interrupted, holding her hand up. "You know I don't want this. You know I wanted two more weeks. I want a whole lot more, but I deserve the life I want. Kids and a family, and plants, and my cottage. Everything. You helped me see I deserve it."

He nodded, a proud but sad look on his face. "You do deserve it. I want that life, too."

"Then choose me," she said, letting a sob escape, her facade slipping.

"It's not that simple," he countered, heat in his eyes. "I have people I support. My dad, Shay. Maybe...maybe long distance could work."

She shook her head, her eyes willing him to see her. "How would you attend a Little League game from across the country? How would I hug you after a long day when there are 12 states between us? What if I craved pickle ice cream in the middle of the night when I'm pregnant and there's a toddler already in bed? I'm supposed to do it all myself?"

"No." He sucked in a deep breath, holding her gaze.

He didn't play it off as if she was crazy for thinking about their future, about having a family together. His gaze scored through her, and she knew at that moment he'd imagined the same. He looked down at his hands, and a tear fell off his eyelashes.

She ached to hug him to make him feel better.

"My, um—" he paused, clearing his throat. "My flight's tomorrow evening. Todd and I will leave in the morning. I think my dad is moving in with June. So I'm sure he'll be out of your hair soon."

Violet walked over to Todd, and he rubbed his face against her hand, purring loudly.

"Oh, Todd." Her voice broke. "Who will I talk to early in the morning?"

"Violet." Jack's ragged voice was low and desperate, and he tugged her toward him for a hug. She couldn't say no to one last hug. She let herself wallow, trying to memorize the scent, the ridges of his chest, and cried quiet tears.

Always so, so quiet.

"I don't want this, but I accept your decision," he said, his head resting on hers.

She sniffled, nodding her head. She'd had one spectacular summer. An unimaginable dream she was lucky to have even one day of, let alone six weeks.

"I think you should sleep in the guest room," she said quietly, even as her lizard brain planned to trap him in her closet and keep him forever.

"Maybe someday there will be a right place, right time."

She turned silently and walked back up the staircase, starting the first night of the rest of her lonely life.

THE MIST WAS STARTING to burn off in the early morning. Small wisps of it had infiltrated the greenhouse.

Violet ran her hand along the leaves of the Boston Ferns, ready to be sold at Bloom. At the beginning of the summer, these had been merely tiny shoots, but now they were full, healthy plants.

Had she grown in the same way they had? Was she different now, too?

She'd hardly slept that night, crying in the closet for most of it. Now it only reminded her of Jack.

The man she loved.

And she'd cried even harder.

After several hours, she gave up on sleep and went out to her sanctuary, but ghosts of their time together surrounded her still.

Jack appeared at the greenhouse door, freshly showered with bags under his eyes, and rapped with his knuckle. The silence was strained between them.

"I'll, uh." He pulled a hand down his face. "Looks like I'll be back in a month. I don't know if you heard, but my dad is getting married," he said, throwing a thumb over his shoulder.

She nodded. She'd seen Ms. McClotskey's happy updates on social media the night before. Their romance had been a whirlwind, but it wasn't surprising with how smitten they'd been.

Violet would be a liar if she said she hadn't suspected her feelings for Jack after only a few days too.

When you knew, you sometimes just knew.

He stood an arm's length away from her, hands in his pockets, looking tortured. "Violet, you understand I don't want to do this, right? I don't want to go, but I've got to. And if I didn't know you better, I'd beg you to come with me."

"I would, but I can't," she whispered.

He nodded slowly. The blue of his eyes looked more like a stormy sea as he fought back tears.

"I have a present for you." He brought in a decorative pot with a small starter plant.

Violet gasped. *Monstera Albo Variegata.*

The large healthy leaves were dark green and had signature open holes. Several leaves looked like someone had spilled a bucket of white paint along them. It was exquisite.

"These are expensive," she breathed. She knew several plant enthusiasts who would give their firstborn child for a healthy variegated Monstera starter.

"I wanted to thank you and for you to have something happy to remember our summer by."

Our summer.

He handed it to her, his fingers brushing hers, and her breath hitched. Her fingers delicately traced the edges of the leaves, careful not to look up into his face as he stared down at her.

"It reminded me of you," he said quietly. He hadn't

stepped back, and she felt like a sun-starved leaf, unable to move away from the pull of him.

"Because of my alter ego?"

His voice was low. "Because it's striking and bold and hard to find. Its beauty calms your soul. It makes you imagine a future with it."

His hands found their way to her cheeks and brushed a tear from one side. "It's one-of-a-kind, one anyone would be lucky to have in their life, and one I wish I deserved. I wish I could do anything other than act, Violet. Otherwise, I'd find any excuse to be here."

His hands combed through her loose hair, falling around her shoulders. It was delicious torture, but every second he was here hurt even more.

"Don't," she whispered as her lip wobbled. "You're making it worse."

He tilted her chin up so she'd look him in the eye. "It's important you know." His lip trembled as his eyes went misty. "I'm torturing myself while I do this." His lips landed on her cheek, lingering, the scrape of his stubble and his nose trailing along her cheekbone.

"If I figure out how to bribe the cast and crew of *Beyond the Manor Walls* to film in Fairwick Falls, you'll be the first person I call." He squeezed her arm as he stepped back. "Until then, I'll see you in a month."

Violet nodded, unable to get a word out because she was too afraid of how she'd beg him to stay.

Chapter Twenty-five

JACK

"All right, that's break!" the assistant director shouted. "You both doing okay?" She looked over to Jack and Missy, wrapped in each other's arms.

They were in the middle of the promo shoots for the next season of *Beyond the Manor Walls*, and he was sweating buckets.

"Yep." He released Missy and tugged at his collar because it would be impolite to say *I'm being strangled by this fucking neckcloth.*

His costume was choking the life out of him. He'd put on a few pounds that summer and the unexpectedly fast call back for promo shoots meant he was unprepared for this bloody costume.

He'd been back in his normal routine, but the whole operation no longer felt familiar. It felt sad, like he'd outgrown the fair.

Everything around him—the familiar set, the familiar morning routine—felt like it was holding him back, like his future was taking off without him.

Missy tugged her bonnet off. "Lord, it's hot, yeah?"

"Yeah, I can't say I've missed the neckcloth." He smiled, though it didn't meet his eyes. "You were great in the last take." He was so lucky to have a scene partner like Missy.

"It's been nice dusting off our prissy miss governess again. Maybe she'll finally get laid this season." She chuckled with him.

This was the part he loved about the work—the chit-chat with fellow actors. Just getting in a good chinwag in-between playing pretend. Missy stretched her arms and took a swig from a water bottle tucked behind a prop. "How's Violet?"

"Uh, I wouldn't know," he said with a frown.

"Oh no," she said slowly as if her heart was breaking with his. "Don't tell me you chopped off the only thing good in your life."

He shrugged, and he appreciated she really knew him. He'd fielded a million angry texts from Gray, threatening his manhood for hurting Violet. And honestly, he probably deserved it. He'd promised not to hurt her, and that was precisely what he'd done.

"I'm here. She has a plant business. Remote work and frequent travel isn't an option for her." He tried to muster a smile, but his mouth didn't quite make it.

"Bummer. I liked her. Sorry, bud." Missy rubbed his arm. "But life happens. Sometimes you've gotta change your priorities."

She shrugged and lifted her skirts to catch the breeze of a nearby fan. "When I met Robert, the timing was terrible. I'd just been signed to do a global theater tour. When I got pregnant with Lyla, I'd already booked a swimwear modeling job four months later." She laughed as she thought back to it all.

"String of bad luck?" he offered.

"More like a string of clarifying situations," she said with a thoughtful nod. "I had to choose what was more important: a job or finding my person. It all worked out. I ditched the swimwear gig and instead ended up mooning over you for five years. I snuck in a couple of off-Broadway runs here and there. Work is meant to fit around life, Jack."

At that moment, he desperately wished for an older sister, but he guessed Missy had kind of become that—a mentor of sorts. She'd been more successful in this business for longer than he had.

"What would you think about this being the last season?" he said tentatively. He didn't want to put an entire cast and crew out of a job just to chase down someone who *might* want to love him. To be with him.

Until death did they part.

Fuck, he didn't even know if he could properly *be* in a relationship, seeing as how he'd never done it. Could he throw everything away in front of him for the *potential* of something special with Violet?

Their contracts renewed each season, and he and Missy could say they were done. The writers hadn't finished the arcs for this season yet, and if they were going to decide this was it...now was the time.

Missy's eyes widened. "So she's the one, eh?"

"Mama, mama!" a little voice piped up through the crowd of the crew milling about.

"There's my poppet," Jack said, bending down. Missy's rambunctious four-year-old daughter, Lyla, tumbled through the crew and cables, quickly followed by Missy's husband with a sleeping infant strapped to his chest.

"Unca Jack!" Lyla ran toward him, but Missy stepped in front.

"Hand check," Missy demanded.

His costume had been marred by sticky jam hands more than once. Lyla dutifully flipped her hands front-to-back to prove they were clean, then threw herself into Jack's arms.

"Well, hullo dearest." He swung her up high to hear the giggles that melted his heart. He loved being Uncle Jack. They'd had a hell of a time hiding Missy's pregnancy with Lyla in the first season. His honorary niece had been coming to set nearly every week since then. He settled her on his hip.

"Rob." Jack fist-bumped Missy's husband.

"Catch the match?" Rob asked.

"No, been prepping for this," he said, looking around the scene. He'd desperately wanted to slack off work and just watch the football match. Anything to take his mind off the steam engine barreling his life away from Violet.

"Jack thinks this might be the last season," Missy said, cutting to the chase.

Rob's eyebrows lifted with hope. He clamped his hands around Lyla's ears. "Hell yeah." He dropped his hands. "As a fan, I'd also love for all the Lord Eagleton edging to stop and for the governess to finally be happy." He placed a kiss on Missy's head. "It'd be nice to see more of this one."

Missy wrapped an arm around her husband. "We've been talking about me working less, seeing the kids more. What about the Christmas special? Would you still do it?"

Jack shrugged. "It makes my mother happy, but I don't

know. I'm sure she'd just move the goalposts again." He looked up to see Missy and her husband in their own little world as Missy sweetly kissed the baby's head . Lyla's head had fallen onto his shoulder, playing with one of the buttons on his coat.

He physically ached for this kind of life and wanted to stop being an outsider.

God, how was he so stupid? He had everything he'd ever wanted laid out right in front of him, and he'd let this *work* determine whether or not he got it.

Yells from a loud, British voice echoed across the sound stage. All of them turned, and Jack's stomach dropped.

"Oh, fuck."

"Mama, Unca Jack said—"

"I'll put five dollars in the swear jar." He kissed her head as he set her down and walked across the stage to deal with the devil herself.

His mother.

He dashed across the soundstage to find his mother yelling at a production assistant to let her through.

His apologetic smile didn't meet his eyes. "Hi, Mum. Sorry, everyone. Forgot to add her to the visitors list today." *Liar.*

She swiveled on him. She'd worn an expensive suit as if she was on her way to an industry meeting.

Not simply crashing his promo shoot.

"So, you *are* alive." Her arched eyebrow sent a shiver down his spine.

Okay, maybe he hadn't returned her phone calls since he'd said no to the mafia show. His heart was broken. What was he supposed to do? Console her, too?

"Why don't we step out of the way," he offered, gesturing to the craft services table.

"Did you know you're second billed?"

He smiled at the crew she'd pissed off and made a mental note to pick up lattes for them for the next week. "It's lovely to see you too, Mother."

"Some *child* is billed above you. In the Christmas special. Kayla what's-her-face."

"She has a big following on social media," he said, lowering his voice. "The network thinks she'll bring in new viewers."

His mother huffed. "You need to keep building your empire. Second billed is second best." Her eyes looked hungry as if every second was slipping by him, and he was a fool not to climb his way up the slippery, never-ending sand dune of fame.

He thought back to his conversation with Gray and Nash. *I wonder how often their moms barged into their workplaces, belittling their achievements.*

"I thought you'd be pleased I'm headlining it this year." He tried to rub away the ache in his chest. It was the feeling he'd get when he wanted to talk to Violet, desperate for her touch.

He'd forced himself not to text or call her, though he had thought about it a million times in the week they'd been apart.

"I'll be pleased when your career finally takes off. You need to want it more, Jack." She checked her makeup in the mirror on the back of her phone.

His mother would never be happy. She was an unending well of ambition. He could be top-billed, and she'd ask, '*Why wasn't it on a bigger network?*'. It could be on a bigger network, and she'd ask, '*Why wasn't the budget bigger?*', '*Why wasn't she in it too?*'

"Are you happy with your career?" he asked, genuinely curious to know the answer.

She rolled her eyes as she put on more lipstick. "Of course not, my darling. You can never be too happy. Then you'll stay stuck in one place just like your father. Complacent in a pile of English mud."

He wanted the life his dad gave him: sturdy, dependable, and memorable. Jack would come home every day, and his dad would be there, eager to hear about his day. They'd made memories at school plays, picnics, and county fairs, him carting all of the prize vegetables up for his dad.

The weeks he'd visited his mom in LA had been glamorous but empty. They'd felt too sporadic and too unexpected. He never knew what he'd get: a fabulous time or a mother in the depths of despair because an audition didn't go her way.

Everything came into focus. He felt hunger, but not for his career. Felt it in his bones, for his life.

He glanced at Missy and her family, giggling between takes.

What a bloody fucking idiot he was. He'd been playing a game with his mother he couldn't possibly win. The game of *will you love me if I make you happy?*

He should have chosen what he wanted this whole time: a life with his Violet.

"I need you to be happy for me for once. Because I've fallen in love." The words were foreign but felt so bloody right coming out of his mouth.

She gasped. "Not with *that* woman."

"Yes, with that incredible, beautiful, kind woman who I intend to win back if she'll have me."

The bell rang on set, signaling the end of break and a plan formed in his head at the sound.

He stood up straighter. Had it really been this easy this whole time?

He'd been successful at Wayridge and had a bigger following than ever. They'd be foolish not to be game for what he'd propose. And if not? Then he'd risk it all for his Violet.

He shepherded his mother toward the exit. "Now, you have two choices: see us at our wedding, or lose contact with any grandchildren."

He deposited her outside the door and kissed her cheek. "She's pregnant?" she yelped. His mother's face was incredulous as the door closed on her.

Jack strode back to the stage with a determined smile and muttered under his breath, "She will be."

Chapter Twenty-six

VIOLET

The lonely notes of *Someone Like You* drifted through Lily's studio apartment as Violet lay on her couch eating Lily's Oreos. Dog reunion videos played on repeat until Violet swiped to the next one.

Oh no. This one was even sadder. An elderly man being reunited with an elderly dog. A new batch of tears welled in Violet's eyes.

Rose walked over with a hot cup of tea. "You need to hydrate." She settled beside her so Violet could put her head in her lap.

"They just love each other so much. They had to come back and find each other," Violet said through a wobbly lip.

"Sounds like somebody else I know." Rose laid a hand on Violet's hair. "I don't like seeing you like this. This is worse than…"

Than how you were after Dad died, she finished the thought for Rose in her head.

"I know," Violet whispered.

"We're all worried about you," Rose said, squeezing Violet. "You've practically moved into Lily's studio."

Violet's clothes, tea mugs, books, and blankets were tossed around the large open studio apartment.

Her cottage felt so empty and sad. It was full of memories of people who had left her. Her grandparents, her mom and dad, then Rose and Lily, and now, finally and most painfully, Jack.

She'd broken down in tears when she found a jar of Todd's treats this morning.

It had felt like *their* home, even though she'd been lying to herself the whole time.

She thought she was lovable, but she just hadn't been enough to keep any of them.

A quick knock sounded at Lily's apartment door. "You decent?" Gray's voice called.

"We've got pancakes," Nash offered.

"Come in!" Rose yelled.

The two gorgeous men walked in holding to-go containers from Pop's diner.

I wish I had a gorgeous man. A new wave of tears sprung out.

"Margie sent your favorite." Nash lifted a bag. "She offered to rename it an '*English (heartthrobs can suck it) Break-fast*' in your honor, but we said we'd check first."

Violet couldn't keep in a watery laugh. She was embarrassed, looking completely disheveled, but happily accepted the heaping to-go box of pancakes and eggs. She sniffled through a stuffed-up nose. "Thanks."

Gray handed Violet a large to-go coffee. "Breakups are a bitch."

"How would you know?" Rose said, standing up and wrapping her arms around Gray's waist. "We've never broken up."

"Hey, there were a few nerve-wracking hours." He kissed her soundly.

"Ugh, go away." Violet sniffed. "You're too in love."

Gray sent her a sympathetic smile. "Let us know if you need anything, Vi. I checked on the plants in your garden, and everything seems fine."

Her heart warmed, thinking of how much her honorary family had grown in the last year. It had only been her and her dad in Fairwick Falls for so many years. Once Rose had moved back and fallen for Gray, he'd been part of the family from then on out.

"I think I should be mad at you," she said, digging into the pancakes. "You brought him here."

"I specifically told him to stay away from you, Vi. I mean, you're basically my little sis—" Gray stopped himself and cleared his throat, looking like he'd said too much.

"She's your what?" Rose said, squeezing his waist with a lovesick smile. "You're adorable, Roberts."

"Ugh, go away," Violet yelled through her mouthful of pancakes. "You're making it worse."

Stomping footsteps sounded up the stairs that could only be the chaos incarnate of her little sister.

"Violet, turn your weepy white girl music down. We can hear it in the store," she said, popping up the stairs into her apartment.

"Who's watching Bloom?" Rose asked.

"Eh, Mrs. Maroo is holding down the fort. It's slow this morning, anyway. Everyone's getting ready for the Founder's

Day parade." Lily's eyes caught on Nash standing in her apartment, and her cheeks turned instantly pink.

Nash stared at Lily with an intensity Violet hadn't seen before.

He handed Lily a to-go coffee cup. "Hey, Lilypad—er, Lily. I brought you an oat milk latte."

She snatched it away, her eyes narrowing. "Thank you," she said flatly to him.

"We should go," Nash said with a resigned sigh, tapping Gray on the shoulder. "Time for you to lose another one-on-one game."

"Gray," Lily said, making it a point to ignore Nash. "Would you tell Mrs. Maroo I'll be down in five?"

"Sure thing, *Lilypad*," Gray said, mocking Nash's nickname for Lily.

Lily rolled her eyes. The room was silent until the door clicked shut behind Gray and Nash.

"What the hell, Lily?" Rose said. "What is your deal with Nash?"

"There's no deal." Lily shrugged, sipping the coffee. "Ugh, and he got it right, too. So annoying." Lily paced in front of them.

Rose and Violet glanced at each other with curious looks. Lily had crushed *hard* on Nash when they were kids. But this was turning into something else entirely.

"You were so prickly with each other at the barbecue, and now you practically jump down his throat?" Violet asked.

"He's the one who kissed *me*. I wasn't the one jumping down *his* throat."

"What?" Violet and Rose both yelled in shock.

Lily's eyes went wide, realizing her mistake. "Uh, I hear Mrs. Maroo—"

"Stop right there," Rose commanded, and Lily froze.

This was worth getting up for. Violet pushed herself up and put her leftovers in Lily's fridge. "I am heartsick and lonely. I deserve hot gossip."

Lily puffed hair out of her eyes in annoyance. "It was a one-time thing. It's not going to happen again. It was a mistake. He said so. I agreed," Lily grumbled as if she wished the most painful death upon him. "Plus, I'm not here forever, and you know he is."

Lily had agreed to stay for a year after Bloom opened to get it off the ground, but their free-spirited sister couldn't be tied down for too long.

"It's not even worth talking about." Lily shrugged, but Violet saw a flash of emotion she tamped down.

"I haven't seen you this worked up over a guy in a long time," Violet said, wrapping Lily in a hug.

"Maybe it was my master plan to get you out of your funk," Lily said, winking at her.

Violet stretched. "Ugh, I guess it's time I'm done wallowing. It's been a week. It's just lonely at home."

"I know you miss him," Lily said, bumping her shoulder against hers, "but you're cramping my style."

Violet smirked as she gathered her things. "Maybe I should trap you and Nash in the cooler since it worked so well for Rose and Gray."

Rose's jaw fell open. "*You* trapped us?"

The first glimmer of happiness in a week sparkled through Violet as she slyly smiled. "What can I say? I love

love. And *maybe* my foot nudged the doorstop as I walked past, locking you in."

Rose gathered her in a fierce hug full of laughs and tickles. God, she was happy her sisters were here.

It was probably time to emerge from her cave of Big Sad Feels. She snatched the rest of the Oreos. "I'm taking these with me."

"Ugh, fine, but only because I love you," Lily said, leaning up to peck her cheek.

"How are you feeling about the Plant-a-Rama talk since you'll be solo?" Rose turned to Violet.

Violet's stomach turned. "What if no one shows? What if *everyone* shows?" she said suddenly.

"You're not the same girl you were, Violet. You're not the junior in high school, you're not the first grader, and you're not even who you were in *May*. You're literally the face of our store, and you're doing great." Rose ran a hand down Violet's hair. "You are so strong, especially for other people, and you'll kill it by yourself."

She wrapped Rose in a hug and felt so grateful for the older sister who never abandoned her.

"Just think of all the people you'll help," Lily said as she bounded down the stairs to Bloom.

Violet turned the thought around in her head. The more people who were there, the more she could help.

Rose straightened as she grabbed her keys to head downstairs. "Now," Rose said with a sneaky smile as she walked downto Bloom. "How long do you think it will take until Lily and Nash kiss again?"

Ten minutes later, with an open bag of Oreos in hand,

Violet walked out of the back door of Bloom looking like a cave-dwelling snack gremlin.

Unfortunately, she walked right into the Founder's Day information booth pathway, and Jennifer caught her eye.

Jennifer waved her over. "Violet, you haven't returned my calls or my texts."

"Yeah, I've been busy," Violet said, wiping her eyes.

"We definitely need your help for the end-of-summer pool party. Can I count on you to head up the snack committee?"

"Um," Violet said slowly.

"We'll just need a couple dozen cupcakes in the next few days, and for you to secure sponsorship from a couple of businesses around town, no big deal," Jennifer said, smirking.

And suddenly, like a montage, Jennifer's face smirking at her for the last ten years all solidified into one thought: *she doesn't like me.*

A friend is someone who likes *you. And I don't need to bend over backward for someone who doesn't like me.*

"I *have* changed. Rose was right," Violet said out loud to Jennifer's confused face.

"Uh, okay?" Jennifer looked at her as if she was crazy.

Violet straightened her spine. *Every inch.* "And the word you will hear from now on is 'no.' I am now a *former* people pleaser, fully in recovery, who is willing and happy to tell you to go to hell."

The word *no* felt strange but so, *so* good.

Jennifer's shock elongated her already overly long face. "You are—"

"I don't care what you think I am," Violet said, moving

past her to go home, already done with the conversation. "Because I'm brave," she said to herself, "and bold and taking up every inch."

THE NEXT DAY, Violet nervously tugged at her shirt as they walked through the Plant-a-Rama Home and Garden Show. She'd opted for a mint-green Bloom shirt with her 'Let's Be Weird Together' phrase that had gone semi-viral from the last episode.

Aaron had insisted on rolling her shirt up so it grazed the top of her high-waisted, wide-leg linen pants. He'd gathered her t-shirt tight to her body, pinned so it fit snugly, showing off her waist, and rolled up the t-shirt sleeves. They'd styled it with dangly earrings and fresh-faced makeup.

"Now, don't forget," Rose said. "Plug the store and tell them to check out our website for 10% off."

Lily smacked Rose's arm. "You're gonna freak her out even more. She has too many things to remember already."

"It's fine. I'll be fine," Violet said to them as they looked at a map of the exhibition. "It's only going to be a few people who have questions about plants, right?"

They peeked inside their scheduled room.

It was packed with hundreds of people staring at a lone microphone on the large stage.

"Holy clover, I'm gonna barf." Violet leaned over as a wave of panic-nausea rolled over her.

"Nope, you're not." Rose turned her around and dragged her back up. "You got this."

"Oh my gosh, Vi." Lily elbowed her as she peeked through the doors. "Look at the third row."

Three young women sat in a row, excitedly chatting. They all wore shirts with her silly Plant Parent phrases on them. Two were plus-size and dressed in happy, pastel colors like she often wore when filming.

"You have fangirls, Vi," Lily whispered in awe.

Fangirls. Not possible. She shook her head, unable to process it. "I was just doing what I love," she murmured.

"Maybe it helped them feel seen," Lily offered.

Violet's eyes caught on the next row, and the sight broke her. A mom and little girl were both wearing Weird Plant Mom Vibes shirts. The little girl looked like a carbon copy of Violet at that age; nourished, round cheeks, a round little tummy, and a happy, shy smile. Her glasses were even color-coordinated with her pigtail holders.

What she would have given to have somebody in a bigger body to look up to when she was young. To make her feel not so alone and weird.

But sometimes, to see what you want in the world, you have to be it first.

She thought about how that girl might feel during recess. How she might be self-conscious like Violet was, nervous to play with other kids who might tease her.

I can do this.

She could go out there and be the most *herself* she'd ever been, especially if she cleared a path for others to be themselves, too.

Because if everyone was the most themselves, maybe the world would be a little happier, a little brighter.

What was the worst that could happen if she bombed?

They'd take away her plants? Her sisters? The memories of the most miraculous summer with the man she loved?

Violet threw back her shoulders, murmuring, *"Every inch,"* and marched out onto the stage.

A thousand hands clapped together as she walked to the mic.

They're just 500 people I could help. As her smile widened, their smiles brightened back.

She pulled the microphone from the stand and let out a laugh, unable to contain her joy.

"Hi," she said as the applause died down. "Sorry, I'm kinda nervous." She tugged at her shirt. Several "woos" sounded back in encouragement.

A smile blossomed on her face as she realized these weren't mean girls here to laugh at her. These people were here because they loved the same things she did. Several even had plants in their lap as if they'd brought them for show and tell.

"I'm Violet Parker, one of the plant parents of Bloom." The applause sounded again, and she bit her lip, swallowing another laugh. *I've got this.* "And I'm so excited to help some fellow plant parents today. If you line up, I can take a few questions."

A woman scurried to the microphone with a dying calathea plant cradled in her hands. The large plant should have had deep green and lime leaves, but instead looked like it'd been tossed in an air fryer.

"Oh no," Violet cooed with a smile. The audience giggled with her. "She's so sad. Can I see?" Violet reached down to grab the plant. The woman explained where she'd been keeping it: in a hot, bright sunroom.

"Oh, poor baby." Violet turned it and examined the soil and the branches. "First, what's her name?"

The woman had an embarrassed grin. "*His* name is Plant Daddy. I was inspired." The audience laughed, and Violet had to nod as if her heart wasn't breaking because Jack wasn't there with her.

Violet coached her to stave off further damage by putting the plant in a nice, humid place with a spritzing schedule. "Bye, Plant Daddy," Violet said, cooing to it as she handed the calathea back.

From there, she answered countless questions, joking back and forth with the crowd.

Maybe she'd found her people.

Her people who loved the same things she did, the things that spoke to the secret part of her heart.

Maybe by finally showing her true self, she'd found the people waiting for her this whole time.

A burly man finished his question about his Monstera seedling, and the girl in pigtails emerged at the microphone with her mom.

"Hi," Violet said sweetly.

The little girl got shy and whispered something to her mom. The mom took the mic. "She wants to know how you're so brave?" The mom shrugged, smiling.

Oh. Her heart.

This wasn't the pitying question Jennifer had asked weeks ago. About how she could dare to exist in spaces not usually occupied by shy, plus-size people.

This was the young version of Violet asking for a map to navigate the choppy waters ahead.

"You mean talking in front of people?" Violet said, clarifying. The little girl nodded her head, embarrassed but excited.

Emotion clutched at Violet's throat. She blinked the feelings away for a second.

"I do it scared."

The little girl tilted her head in confusion.

More detail on the map, Violet. "I think about all the people I could help, which helps me be brave even though I'm scared. When I was brave, I met new friends, went to fun places, and got to wear a *very* fancy dress. So, just know if you have to be brave, there might be good things on the other side."

Violet felt so lonely doing this without Jack. It wasn't half as fun without him egging her on, joking, and helping her share even more of what she loved.

Rose gave her the 'wrap it up' motion. They were out of time.

But something nagged at her.

She couldn't talk about being brave and not actually take the big leap she feared: putting it all out there. Asking for what she wanted instead of doing what made life easier for others.

"I have a confession," Violet said into the microphone, her mouth having run away with her sanity. "Recently, I wasn't very brave. I didn't stand up for myself because I wasn't willing to risk being told no. To feel rejected. I took the safe route instead of asking for what I wanted." She looked around and saw people filming with their phones.

Crap. You gotta keep going.

"And what I wanted was just...him. Plus, I hear they have houseplants in Vancouver." A chuckle sounded in the crowd.

"I took the easy way out and didn't risk anything, but I know I should have been more courageous. Because love and plants are worth being brave for."

She was sad to see the hour end as her confession was met with applause. She genuinely enjoyed helping people and even had a small line form to talk to her afterward.

When the little girl asked for a photo, Violet held back all her emotions but one tear and smiled so happily for the camera.

With the help of Rose, she eventually left an hour and a half after her speaking wrapped up, tired but happy.

They walked out through the convention center.

"I knew you could do it," Rose said, squeezing her side.

"Violet Parker." Lily pretended to hold a microphone. "You just crushed your first solo public event. What are you going to do next?" Lily held the pretend microphone to Violet.

"I'm going to Vancouver."

"What?" Rose and Lily yelled in unison, stopping in the parking lot.

"At least to tell him how I feel. I never even told him I loved him." This was the time. Be bold, and other people could be bold, too.

Even if nothing changed between them, even if they'd only be friends who dated for the summer, she had to tell him how she felt.

How falling for him had let her become her best self.

"Damn, Vi," Rose said. She wrapped her arm around her neck and pulled her in for a kiss on her head. "That is the bravest, scariest thing anybody could do."

"Don't talk her down from it." Lily danced with excitement as they walked towards their car. "She needs to admit her very obvious feelings to him."

Violet piped up as she slid into Rose's car with a smile. "Now, maybe somebody *else* can finally admit *their* feelings for a very tall bank president."

"Oh my god, you guys are the worst. I'm gonna walk home," Lily grumbled as she climbed into the car.

As Rose pulled out toward Fairwick Falls, Violet felt braver than she'd ever thought possible.

Chapter Twenty-seven

VIOLET

That night, all the lights were off in Fairwick Falls as the sleepy town had tucked itself in bed.

Unable to sleep, Violet looked over her pond in the dark moonless night and pondered how much everything had changed in the last six weeks.

How much *she'd* changed.

She'd done something impossible today.

I spoke in front of hundreds of people and didn't think about fainting once.

She'd waited 33 years to start living her life, but it felt like it had finally begun.

On the way home from the event, she'd bought her plane ticket to Vancouver, and she'd leave in the morning.

Maybe I should text him now.

But no, what would she even say via text? *Hi, I love you. I'm so sausages for waiting to say it?*

A rustle through the orchard trees took her out of her thoughts.

"I don't accept it."

She spun quickly, yelping, and her feet slipped toward the pond.

Oh no, not again.

But as she teetered, a firm hand caught her by the waist and yanked her back.

Jack wrapped his arms tight around her, and she slammed into him shocked but happy.

"I've gotta stop standing here," she said, breathlessly looking down at the pond bank. "How—what? Are you—?" Was he a mirage of thick, hard muscles in front of her? She moved her hands across his chest, but he grabbed one and clasped it to him.

"You can imagine my surprise when I hopped off the plane three hours ago, turned on my phone, and found I was tagged on every social media post known to man with the tag #plantdaddywanted." His hand came to her cheek, and his brows drew together with wanting and humor.

"You were already here? But we decided—"

"I don't accept it," he interrupted. "I'm choosing you. I want you, and I don't accept you breaking up with me to make *my* life easier. Now if you don't want a life with me, I'll leave. But if you do..." His breath came in shallow pants as if he was asking for the moon.

Rather than just her heart.

"I love you," she blurted out.

She might be living her dream life, but she'd *always* be Queen of Awkwardlandia.

A surprised smile ghosted over his lips.

No time to back down now. She closed her eyes and barreled on. "I'm in love with you. And not just because you're gorgeous but because you're kind and funny, and you care so deeply about people. I feel...safe with you. Like I'm finally myself. You don't have to say it back, but I just wanted you to know you're loved just the way you are, without all the glitz and glamor." She gasped for breath.

She willed her eyes to meet his.

A smile blossomed on his face, and relief washed over it.

"My darling love," he whispered, his arms settling on her waist. "You have been patient through all of my irritating indecision, never failing to support me and to show me who you are: someone who is kind and good, who cares for others, even though I wish she cared for herself more."

Violet sniffled as her heart pounded.

His lips grazed her cheek. "And I would not bring my good tea and every book I own to Fairwick Falls if I did not love you with my entire soul, being, and body. I've had a glimpse of my future, and I want it all. With you and you alone."

Violet tried to memorize this earth-shattering feeling as she stared at the handsome face she wanted to see in ten, twenty, fifty years. *He loves me.* "But your career. I can't let you sacrifice—"

"The only sacrifice would be if I didn't live my life with you. A life of late mornings, and festivals, and endless hours kissing in a greenhouse? I want that with you. I quit Wayridge."

Her heart slammed in her chest. "You quit?"

His eyes danced. "Okay, *technically,* I quit. I told them this would be the last season of *Beyond the Manor Walls* and to reduce my screen time by half."

He grabbed her hand and pulled her toward the orchard. "I tried to quit outright and leave the show immediately, but they sweetened the deal by offering me the option to produce a new show. I was thinking…" He squeezed her hand, and they stopped at a picnic blanket he'd laid down, sprinkled with hydrangea flower petals. "…maybe a home and garden show where a hapless host and a gorgeous, curly-haired expert help people with their gardens."

A thrill ran through Violet, and she bounced on her toes. He wanted to do *her* idea. "My idea? We'd do a show together?"

He pulled her into him, and she felt dizzy with happiness. "Only if you want to. I told them we'd need ultimate flexibility to accommodate ballet lessons, Little League…" His nose ran the length of hers as his voice went soft.

"Trips to the zoo?" She whispered.

His thumb came to her chin and that simple touch resonated as her eyes met his. Feeling like he'd claimed her. "With the three or four or five musketeers."

His voice was low as his mouth hovered over hers. "You are the last thing I expected and everything I've never deserved. I finally realized I'd been waiting my entire life for a bloody *adorable* plant mom." His eyes fell to her lips, and as he lowered his mouth, she sank into him, slowly melting as their lips met.

His tongue licked her lip, curling her toward him like he'd hooked a finger and pulled her in. Her hands fisted in his shirt, needing to feel how real this was.

His arms corded around her, crushing her into the nook of his chest. She completely melted into the feeling of him surrounding her.

Yes. This was her forever.

This was worth risking everything for, she thought as he slanted his mouth against hers.

He sucked and pulled harder. Their breath caught as though they'd wound together, forming a strand that couldn't be broken. An insistent throb started deep inside her as his hand moved to her ass, pressing her against him.

"I love you, Violet Parker. I love this spot," he said, kissing her neck as goosebumps showered down her skin. "I love that you angle your head just like this when listening to me babble on about Todd."

His hands moved to her waist, and her core turned molten with wanting. "I love that you're strong and work harder than anyone I know, but that you have delicate places, like here." He kissed each side of her collarbone. He kissed her neck, his hands unbuttoning her pants. "And I love that you're mine, and I intend to keep you for however long you'll have me."

"Wait!"

He froze, panic in his eyes.

She looked around for a cat carrier, his words finally clicking into place. "Where's Todd?"

"Christ, woman." His hand came to his heart with a sigh of relief. "I thought you were going to toss me to the curb. He's happy as a clam with my dad and June. He never left."

"You left him here?" But he loved Todd. Todd was his soulmate.

"Part of me knew I could never leave you." He cradled her jaw, and tingles shivered down her spine. "You're my home. And I'll never leave it again."

"I love you more than I can bear." Pure beams of happiness radiated through her as she pulled him down, needing his mouth. He pulled her tight against him, and she wrapped her arms around his neck, never wanting to let him go.

His mouth caught hers, open-mouthed and wanting. Need pooled inside of her as she sucked in the taste of him. The safety of his spicy scent surrounding her. His arms pulled her tight, and she could feel his biceps squeezing against her.

Pure. Bliss.

She wanted to take everything about him and carry it with her forever. This feeling of being his.

He kissed her cheek slowly. "I can't wait to build a life right here with you." His beard tickled her skin as he lazily fanned kisses over her face.

Her hands moved under his shirt, needing to feel the cords of muscles underneath. Needed to scrape her nails against his back and feel him shudder. "With muffins?" she said with a smile.

He huffed out a laugh as he slowly, reverently kissed each eyelid. "And tea. And books. And babies toddling through the garden chasing fireflies."

Jesus, this man. He *knew* her.

She needed him with a fire she rarely let herself show. An inferno ignited at his words, and desire took over as she pulled his mouth to hers.

There would be a lifetime of soft kisses later.

Right now, she wanted him so badly.

He groaned as she pressed into him, and he gripped her hips, his fingers digging in. She grabbed his ass, rocking him against her.

"Thank the gods for cloudy, moonless nights. Please say

being taken in the garden is on your list," he panted. His hand grasped her breast, squeezing it, claiming it.

"It is now." She tugged his shirt off and feasted her eyes on his broad chest. She kissed the muscles she'd missed so much and placed a hot kiss over the soft beating heart she loved.

"Good, because I owe these apple trees a debt of gratitude. If I hadn't been bewitched by your tits and run into them, I would have never found out about your terribly naughty list."

She laughed at the real reason for his concussion as he tugged her Bloom t-shirt over her head.

Her laughter died as she registered his face.

He looked like his brain had melted out of his ears.

Oh right.

She forgot she'd worn her favorite plant-inspired lingerie as inspiration for the event today.

The soft, moss-green mesh bralette featured vine and leaf filigree edging that cupped around the curve of her heavy breasts. They curled and swirled around her, ending at the peak of her nipples. The bottom mesh formed a cage around her upper ribs, and vine-like ribbons snaked along the edge and upward, crisscrossing to create bra straps.

He fingered the delicate lace edging along the cup, biting his lip with wanting. "You are beautiful." His eyes met hers as he found her nipple and rubbed it between his fingers over the mesh of her bra. "So fucking gorgeous. Just like this. This is the real you, Violet."

She clenched as desire snaked through her, winding its vines around her.

He lowered himself to his knees on the blanket so her

breasts were at eye level. "You're soft, and romantic, and sexy"—he kissed her soft stomach—"and just a bit kinky. Perfect." His eyes locked with hers as he sucked her nipple through the mesh bra.

Her clit throbbed as the hot, wet heat pulled against the delicious friction of the mesh. She dove her hands into his hair, needing more. The torture was too good. His tongue moved against her, swirling around the peak of her nipple. Sucking, laving her with his tongue again and again.

As his hands pulled down the zipper of her linen pants, she remembered it had been laundry day, and she'd pulled her naughtiest pair of panties from the back of her underwear drawer.

A cat-like smile curled her lips as he pushed her pants past her hips down to the ground.

He was in for a surprise.

His eyes locked on the pink lace crotchless panties in front of his face. "Holy..."

The lips of her pussy were framed as the lace fanned out around her midsection, wrapping around her legs. His large hands moved to her thighs. His thumbs plucked the strings holding the panties in place around her legs. "Like a bloody present made just for me. Decadent."

"I ordered these when you were here."

His head fell against her stomach, and his fingers traced along the lips of her pussy, teasing her. "Such a naughty minx. You walked around all day with this pussy just ready for me to take." He slipped a finger along the inside, rubbing against the building wet heat of her clit. He circled around and around, peering up at her as she grabbed a nipple.

She held his shoulders as her knees started to buckle, and her thick hair swung down curtaining around them.

He looked up at her with adoration. "You *are* a siren. Lush and ready to lead me to acts of pure"—he kissed her belly— "debauchery." He leaned on his heels and lifted her leg onto his shoulder, burying his face in her pussy.

She clutched a low branch to steady herself as he sucked her clit, his arms gripping her thighs in a vise as his head dove into her.

She was being invaded, feasted on as he pushed his face into her again and again. She wasn't sure how long she'd last before she came.

He nipped at her clit, and she pulsed against his face, her fingers tangled in his hair. Craving more friction, feeling so empty. Shocks of need pulsed through her as his mouth took and took and took. She squeezed her thighs together, needing him closer. Needing him inside her.

"Need your cock," she panted.

He stilled, looking up at her. Pulling back, lowering her leg to the ground.

"Say it again," he ground out, unbuckling his belt and pants like a promise she'd need to fulfill.

She cupped his face, and he kissed her wrist, lingering there. "I need you," she said.

She pushed his shoulders, and he lay down on the blanket.

She tugged his pants off, wanting to see him. Tight dark boxer briefs gripped his muscular thighs and hid nothing about his steely, thick cock.

She straddled him, and the fire in his eyes took her

breath away. She ground her bare wet pussy against the cotton of his briefs. "I need you inside me."

His hand wrapped around her neck, bringing her down onto him hard. "You're dripping for me, aren't you, love?"

His hand grabbed her hip and rocked her back and forth along his cock.

"Yes," she sobbed.

"Tell me what it feels like to need this cock." His fingers pinched her nipple, and she whimpered.

She rubbed her breasts against him, needing the friction on her nipples. "Like I'm empty. I'm gripping for you. I need to be filled. And only by you."

"That's fucking right with *my* cock." He sucked on her earlobe, and a shudder ran through her.

He shoved his briefs down and positioned himself at her entrance, notching himself inside her, teasing her. "Again, minx." His voice was low and raw.

She leaned down to whisper in his ear, moaning. "I crave your cock. Fill me up." She slowly—so, so slowly—slid down onto him, gripping her inner muscles as she went.

He pulsed his hip in spasms. "Fuck," he cried. "Fuck, you feel too good."

She landed on his cock, settling her hips and spreading her thighs. Her hands ran the length of his stomach. He was sexier than the first time she'd seen him. His muscles had a healthy, thick roundness over them. She wanted to bite them, lick them, devour them.

His hands grasped her meaty thigh and belly as if he were staking a claim.

She loved it.

Her breasts pressed together as she leaned over him, still in the mesh bralette, and the straps fell on either side of her arms.

"Goddess divine." He spasmed. She clenched around his cock, now fully seated. His eyes rolled back in his head. "You're my dream come true. A woodland nymph with the best tits."

She rocked against him, taking her pleasure. Her breasts began to spill out of her bra as she straddled him.

His hands interlaced with hers, giving her purchase as she rolled her hips against him. "Take what you want. Use me," he panted.

She threw back her head, taking up space in the inky night. Her breasts spilled out as she rocked against him. She felt wild, taking what she wanted as she rode him hard.

She *was* wild.

Wanton.

Her breath came faster as she moaned, unafraid. Her hips pistoned faster, bringing her aching clit against him as Jack rocked her up and down his cock.

She leaned over him, needing his mouth on hers. He rolled her over, still inside her, and somehow took her deeper. He pulsed his cock inside her. "I've dreamt of filling this pussy up. Cum gushing out of you while you say you love me."

Jack leaned back, kneeling, and pulled out of her.

"More," she whined. She ached with need.

His thumb brushed her mouth and dipped inside, pulling her mouth open. "There's my greedy little love."

Yes. Fuck.

He hoisted her onto his kneeling lap, her ankles coming to either side of his head. She felt so exposed and vulnerable. His cock slammed into her pussy.

"Holy fuck," she cried. He hit the spot inside her pussy that curled her body with need, demanding more.

He angled her, with her hips above her head, and her breasts bounced with his every thrust, pressing against her chin.

A feral smile grew on Jack's face as he thrust inside her, his grip on her calves keeping her legs in place to make her even tighter for him. "You're helpless here, minx." He brought his thumb, wet from her mouth, and teased her clit with it. Her hips pulsed, wanting more.

"More, Jack." Her fingers clawed the ground, fisting in the blanket as she ground against his hand.

He pulsed his cock in and out, driven like a madman as he fucked her. "Say you're mine." A flick of his fingers across her clit teased her more.

"Only yours," she moaned. "Forever."

A groan sounded from him as he gripped her legs, thrusting into her like a rutting mad man. "This pussy is mine," he growled. He circled her clit again and again as she felt the climax overtake her, spiraling desire and need around her. "You. Are. Mine."

She bounced with the force of his final thrusts, feeling hot spurts as he came inside her.

She let out a moaning cry in the night as she came. An unmistakable sound of how *bad* she was as he destroyed her clit. White stars burst behind her eyelids as sizzling sensations wrapped their vines around her nerve endings, and she lost herself in taking every drop of pleasure.

They stilled, her aftershocks pulsing around him. He placed a kiss on her calf and lowered her legs, leaning over her, still catching his breath. He was still inside her, and she never wanted him to leave.

"Welcome home." She smiled. He covered her, his arms propped up on either side of her head. His hands cupped either side of her face as he kissed her gently.

"I love you, my Violet."

His Violet.

He rolled to the side and pulled her into his chest.

"I love you more," she said, kissing the wall of muscle under her cheek.

"We're going to need three more rounds tonight." He huffed, still catching his breath. He pulled her in for a quick kiss. "I've been tortured the last week, and my soul and cock need mending."

She snorted as she snuggled into his nook, her new favorite place on Earth.

He lazily traced his fingers along her arms, and she thought of what their next week, month, forever might be.

Violet considered the idea of being on a cable channel. "What if I'm not up for the show?" she said, biting her lip.

She'd spoken to a whole room of people today, but it was a lot scarier being broadcast to millions of cable subscribers.

He snuggled her closer, kissing her head. "Then I'll be away from home a couple weeks each year doing guest spots. College tuition will be even more expensive in twenty years."

Whoa.

"And the Christmas movie this year?" she asked tentatively.

His hands danced along her stomach. "I hoped I could

convince my girlfriend to join me at my childhood cottage in the English countryside for the duration of the shoot." His hand cupped her cheek. "But if she said no, I'll pass on the movie."

Her breath caught. Fall in the English countryside with Jack. An actual dream come true.

She couldn't, though. She'd let everyone down who depended on her here. "That sounds like a dream, but—"

He squeezed her. "The plant babies will be fine. Gerald Grant has already reported for Grand Plant Parent duty. Gray said he'd help with anything else you needed."

"But the store—"

"—I told Rose I'd do a million ad spots so you can hire part-time help. After caring for everyone else for thirty years, you deserve a four-week vacation in England, surrounded by tea, biscuits, and books with no one to worry about but yourself." He leaned back to look at her. The kind face of a man who loved her and cared for her.

Who *wanted* all of her.

Look at you, Violet. Look at you being loved by people who help you. By a man who cares for you and thinks you're precious, lovely, and kind.

Violet marveled at herself as she permitted herself to dream of a life she never thought she could have. "And this will be home, but we can still go on adventures? Like to premieres?"

"Anywhere you want to go." He looked tickled as she tested out what this new life outside her bubble might be.

She sighed and settled down into his arms, surrounded by the sound of cicadas and rustle of the apple tree leaves as the breeze blew through them.

She considered the future before her. This would be a new balance. But she had deep roots to keep her grounded and new lovely, long vines to explore the world with her love.

Maybe, just maybe, I deserved it all along.

Epilogue

THREE MONTHS LATER

VIOLET

"Lily, talk us through your sketches for Mrs. Maroo-Cannon's sunroom," Violet said with a bright smile.

Violet leaned against the worktable in Bloom and tried to ignore the enormous black film cameras and bright lights a few feet away.

Jack had his arm around her as they intently watched Lily talk through her designs for the pilot episode of *Plant Parent SOS*.

Lily pointed to her sketch as a camera got a close-up. "Since she wants a water feature, I've made a section here so any additional runoff will go into the Birds of Paradise, as these plants love a little extra water."

"Smart," Jack piped in.

Violet took the sketch from Lily and continued. "We'll have planter boxes along the edge of the room filled with peace lilies, ZZ plants for foliage, and colorful spiky bromeliads. They'll come with interchangeable inserts for easy maintenance."

The bells on Bloom's door rattled as someone opened it. Mrs. Maroo-Cannon shuffled in with a cardboard box so large, it almost overtook her.

"I brought the penises you wanted!" she called behind the large box.

A moment of stunned silence rang as the camera guys' eyebrows shot up. Jack smiled at Violet. "Exactly what kind of garden are you planning for her?"

Violet's hand smacked her forehead. "Can we cut?"

Everyone burst into laughter.

"Let's take ten, everyone!" Jack yelled at the crew. They'd hired a skeleton TV crew to shoot the pilot. Then Jack would take the edited version back to Wayridge to see if they'd fund an entire season.

Violet walked to grab the box from Mrs. Maroo. "You didn't need to come until later. This was too heavy for you to carry in this bad weather." The November day was gray with wintery sleet.

Mrs. Maroo-Cannon shook out her arms. "Sorry, dear. Didn't mean to ruin your filming, but I knew you'd need the bachelorette stuff for tomorrow."

Violet plopped down a heavy box on the table and saw the neon penis-shaped straws, tiaras with glitter penises on them, penis balloons, and light-up penis necklaces.

"Since I'm a *remarried* woman again, I don't need them anymore," the older lady said, waving her new wedding ring in the air.

"Your bachelorette party was a rager," Lily said, poking

through the box and pulling out a light-up necklace that said *Same Penis Forever, Let's Celebrate!*

"Rose will hate wearing these," Violet laughed as Lily gave her a high five.

"Loathe. I can't wait to get pics of her in this one." Lily snorted, holding up a tiara and bridal veil covered in sparkly penises.

Gray and Nash walked in from the back entrance.

"You about ready to go, Jack?" Gray called.

It was only one month until Gray and Rose's wedding, and the guys were heading to Montreal for Gray's bachelor party after they finished filming.

Mrs. Maroo-Cannon cocked her hip and stared at the three gorgeous men in front of her. "What trouble will you boys get up to in Montreal?"

"Seeing as I'll have my five-year-old best man with us"—Gray smirked—"staying up past our bedtime and eating far too many snacks."

Violet's heart clutched at the thought that Gray included his five-year-old son, Alex, who spent part of the year with his mom in Montreal.

"What time should we be at the Honky Tonk in Elliottsville tomorrow?" Mrs. Maroo said, turning to Violet.

"Shh," Lily said. "Rose still thinks her bachelorette is just a spa day."

"It's going to be lit," Mrs. Maroo-Cannon said, wiggling her booty.

Lily and Violet snickered. Rose would never ask for a neon, 90s-themed bachelorette party, but she would get a kick out of it. After treating her to a spa day, they'd karaoke all night long and ply her with shots, then drag everybody back to Violet's house for a sleepover. Practically all the women they knew in town—plus Aaron and Nick—were invited, so it would be a raucous time.

"We better hide this box before Rose sees it. She has eagle eyes." Lily hefted the big box on her hip. "Maybe I should hide this on a high shelf."

Lily called out in the showroom, "Can somebody help me put this box up?"

"I can," Nash said, walking over.

Lily stared daggers at him. "Anybody else? *Annnnybody* else want to help me lift this box up?"

A beat of silence dragged on in the showroom. Finally, a TV crew guy stepped forward. Gray put a hand on his chest and slowly shook his head.

Lily ran her tongue over her teeth.

"Ugh, fine. Here," she said, shoving the box at Nash. "Follow me."

Rose walked through the front door of Bloom a few seconds later, unaware of their dastardly plan for her bachelorette party.

"Phew, close call," Violet said, giggling with Mrs. Maroo. "Can you stay for the next segment? It would be great to get your reaction to Lily's designs."

"Look at my little Violet. I missed having you around town," Mrs. Maroo said, her hand coming to Violet's cheek.

After Jack had finished filming the Christmas movie in the English countryside, they'd hit the ground running to produce a pilot. Violet had enjoyed four glorious weeks off, doing nothing but reading, baking, and gardening in Jack's childhood home, but she was happy to be back in Bloom.

They would have a few weeks together before he'd return

to Vancouver to finish the final filming of *Beyond the Manor Walls*. She didn't know how he had enough energy to juggle it all, but they'd never been happier. They'd already started planning what six months, two years, three years might look like, but Violet tried to savor every moment.

Every moment of her wildest dreams come true.

Rose dusted the sleet off her coat and walked over to them with a shipping box.

"I have samples." She shook the box with a happy smile.

"Oh my gosh," Violet said, jumping. "Is it the overalls?"

"It is." Rose set the box down and pulled out the sample Violet and Lily had worked on with a local fashion designer. "Reggie said these can ship next week if you approve the final version."

This was the final test of the first Bloom-branded overalls, and Violet wanted to get it just right, making sure there was ample room for bending over, twisting, and lifting things. It also had to pass Lily and Rose's style check.

Violet hardly recognized her life now. They were already one month into a partnership with a gardening supply line where Violet and Lily had collaborated on chic, functional designs. These overalls would complement Rose's vision to set them up as a national brand.

"Do we have time for me to try these on?" Violet said to Jack as he chatted with a crew member.

Jack's eyes twinkled as he caught her gaze and bent down to kiss her. "Always time for you, my love."

She wiggled with excitement and ran to the supply closet.

She ditched her flirty floral skirt and kept on her Bloom t-shirt that was expertly tailored. Being in front of the camera didn't even bother her anymore, now that everything in her closet finally fit and she wasn't worried about fainting.

She pulled on the overalls, and the soft cotton fabric felt deliciously breathable against her skin.

She stepped into the hallway and looked at herself in the reflection of the flower cooler. The overalls hit her waist at precisely the right place. The pockets were nice and big, large enough to hold a tool or a pair of gloves. The wide-leg bottoms were comfortable and had just the right amount of room to move around in.

She danced out to show everyone, and Rose and Lily applauded with beaming faces.

"Oh my gosh, these are going to be an instant bestseller," Lily said, checking out the floral pattern she'd custom designed for it. It was a take on Bloom's logo featuring their three flowers, a rose, a lily, and a violet, woven together with ivy.

"I think it looks fucking amazing. Please please pleeeease approve it," Rose said with a pleading face at Violet.

Violet happily shouted, "Approved! Can you believe we'll have our own line of clothes and custom stuff in two months?"

"Yes," Lily said, stretching, "because I'm exhausted."

"We should start looking for your replacement soon. It will take a while." Rose leaned against the counter with a sad smile.

They'd promised their commitment-phobic, no-roots little sister she wouldn't need to stay past the one-year commitment of opening Bloom. But Violet had hoped she'd just forget about it and stay in Fairwick Falls forever.

"I don't know," Lily said, her hand still fiddling with

Violet's overalls, lost in thought. "Seems soon, don't you think?"

Rose's face was sad but resigned. "You said you'd give us a year. We only have six months left."

"We'd love if you stayed," Violet said, pouting. It wouldn't be the same without Lily's energy in the store every day.

"Maybe we can wait until January to talk about it?" Lily's brow furrowed. "I can't even *think* about interviewing people on top of our current workload."

"Speaking of which," Rose said, clapping her hands together, "our new part-time help starts next week. She's a *trip*. Kind of a ballbuster, and so obviously I love her."

"Praise be to Jack's handsome face and his ability to do any ad we need him to," Lily said, raising her hands.

"Love, you ready to get going again?" Jack called over from the side of the store with the crew.

A few minutes later, Jack introduced Mrs. Maroo as the episode guest as the cameras rolled.

"Now, Mrs. Maroo-Cannon," he said, turning to her, "you wanted something tropical, so it would feel like your recent honeymoon."

"Something to set the mood," she said, giggling. "We want to feel like we never left."

"But also, you wanted low maintenance," Violet piped in. "Because you're both busy business owners."

"And we'll be busy till the day we croak," Mrs. Maroo said, shrugging.

Oh my gosh, the network will eat this up.

Lily revealed the design sketches she and Violet had worked on together. Jack had even pitched in ideas when they'd hit a stumbling block on making the production budget work.

Mrs. Maroo's eyes filled, and she clasped her hands in front of her mouth. She was, for the first time Violet had ever known her, speechless.

"It's just...it's just exactly right," Mrs. Maroo-Cannon said through a choked voice. "Oh, I'm sorry," She fluttered her hands and wiped her eyes. "I know some people might just see a sunroom, but I'm just so proud of you girls. Your mom and dad would be so proud." She wrapped them both in a tight hug.

Violet felt emotion clutch her throat, and Lily discreetly wiped away a tear from the inside corner of her eye as she pulled away.

Violet felt tears on her cheeks and tried to shake them away. She had to get through this pilot and couldn't let anybody down. She felt a thumb come to her cheek as Jack brushed one away.

"Sausages." She whispered in a watery voice and smiled up at him.

Jack winked at her and turned to the camera. "Well, I *think* we have a winner," he said with a bright voice that had everyone chuckling and wiping their eyes.

Violet sniffed through a laugh. "Now, if someone will pass me a tissue, we can get going on these renovations."

"And cut!" Jack yelled. "That's it for today." The film crew immediately started disassembling camera equipment.

"Oh, shoot. I'm sorry. I can do it again," Mrs. Maroo said in a reedy, nervous voice. "I won't cry this time, I promise."

"It was absolute perfection." He leaned down, hugging the tiny woman. "Wayridge likes earnest."

Violet's heart clutched at how sweet he was, how much he'd become entangled in every part of her life in the last three months.

Lily walked Mrs. Maroo-Cannon to the door as Nash and Gray walked up with their bags.

"We gotta go, buddy," Gray said, throwing a hand on Jack's shoulder. "Flight's in a few hours."

"I'll see you in two days." Jack wrapped his arms around Violet.

It had already felt like they'd been apart a lifetime when he'd been away for a week, filming in Vancouver. Thankfully, they'd have four weeks together soon for the holidays. His part had been significantly cut down in the final season of *Beyond the Manor Walls* as they teed up the next spinoff series.

"And then it's just four weeks of us," Violet whispered as Nash and Gray walked toward the door. She pulled back and looked at him with mock seriousness. "Behave yourself. No punching people or being thrown in jail," she said with a smirk.

He slowly kissed her, his nose grazing her cheek. "I know a girl I can fake date if my reputation needs fixing afterward."

She let herself just nuzzle in for a moment, enjoying his scent. Remembering how he'd ravaged her that morning.

"Enjoy your last few nights of debauched drinking and carousing while I'm gone." He leaned down to whisper in her ear. "You sure you're okay to go to the doctor's appointment alone tomorrow?"

Violet nodded. She'd have her IUD removed to give her body plenty of time to adjust before they started trying. They weren't even engaged yet, but they'd already planned the timeline, and she wanted plenty of runway for practicing.

Phew. She shivered with excitement at the thought of *practicing.*

"It'll be nothing but sushi, tequila, and soft cheeses for the next 48 hours." She beamed up at him.

His eyes grew hungry as he nipped at her neck. "And then I'll be back, and we can keep checking things off the list." The slight growl in his voice had her needy already.

They'd gone through a third of her list by this point, but he kept surprising her with inventive things she should have added to it.

She captured his mouth as his hands dug into her hips, and she tried to memorize the feeling in her heart. The unending hopes she had for the future with Jack, with Bloom, with *herself.*

She pulled back and ran her hands over his chest. "I can't wait."

She couldn't wait. She couldn't wait for the future, for her forever, to *finally* get started.

THE END

Want *even more* of Violet and Jack? Or see how the Rose/Gray proposal went down?? Or get a sneak peek of Lily and Nash in their bonus prequel?

Sign up for Elise's (monthlyish) newsletter and get access to free bonus content!

MORE BY ELISE KENNEDY

***LOVE IN FAIRWICK Falls* Novels**
    Accidentally in Bloom (Rose & Gray)
    Wallflower in Bloom (Violet & Jack)
    Conveniently in Bloom (Lily & Nash)
    Unexpectedly Bookish (Pearl & Reed)
    Falling at the Barre (Olivia & Luca)
    Forever in Bloom (Allison & Wells)

~

***COZY NIGHTS in Vermont* Novellas**
    Fall Inn Love
    Falling in Vermont

~

***JINGLE BELL SPRINGS* Novellas**
    The Grump in Jingle Bell Springs - October 2026

~

***ONLY ONE COZY Bed* Novellas**
    Pumpkin Spice & Pour-overs
    Apple Cider & Subterfuge
    Hot Cocoa & Mistletoe
    Snowed In & Snuggle Weather

CONTENT WARNINGS

Off Page

Death of a parent due to heart attack (off the page), Death of a parent due to addiction (off the page).

On Page

Emotionally manipulative parent (on screen), Body image concerns (MMC) and body discomfort with clothes (Plus size FMC), Minor injury.

Breeding kink (MMC), Watching porn together, Oral and penetrative sex, Anal play and sex toy play.

About the Author

Elise Kennedy is an author of cozy, spicy, heartfelt small-town romances. She lives in the midwest with her (very) patient husband and two perfect pups.

Join Elise's private Facebook reader group to chat, vote on future books, and make general romantic merriment the small town romantics or her Instagram channel the small town romantics.